Rosie is an author of comic commercial fiction. She spent her university years writing pantomimes based on old classics (highlight: 'Harry Potter: The Musical') and went on to write short stories and features for a range of publications including: *Cosmopolitan*, *The Lady*, *Sunday People*, *Best* and *Reveal* magazines. She worked in television as a presenter on both live and pre-recorded shows in Bristol and London. She has written three novels and plans to write many more.

Rosie likes baked items, taking long walks by the river and speaking about herself in the third person. Her greatest ambition in life is to become Julia Roberts's best friend.

Also by Rosie Blake

How to Get a (Love) Life
How to Stuff Up Christmas

How to Find your (FIRST) HUSBAND

Rosie Blake

First published in paperback in Great Britain in 2016 by Corvus,
an imprint of Atlantic Books Ltd.

10 9 8 7 6 5 4 3 2 1

A CIP catalogue record for this book is available from the British Library.

Paperback ISBN: 978 1 78239 862 2
E-book ISBN: 978 1 78239 863 9

Printed and bound by CPI Group (UK) Ltd, Croydon, CR0 4YY

Corvus
An imprint of Atlantic Books Ltd
Ormond House
26–27 Boswell Street
London
WC1N 3JZ

www.corvus-books.co.uk

To Ben – the BEST (first and last) husband.

Prologue

Dorset

'Do you, Isobel Graves, take Andrew Parker to be your lawful wedded husband?'

This was it.

I looked across at him, sucked in all my breath. He was facing forward, wasn't looking at me. His hair was spiked up at the front. I liked it when it was spiked like that. I swallowed and looked back at the priest. 'I do.'

'And do you, Andrew Parker...'

'Andrew *James* Parker...'

'What?'

'James is my middle name.'

He was so proper! I grinned; I liked the name James.

'Oh sorry.' The priest fiddled with his collar. '...Um... and do you, Andrew *James* Parker, take Isobel...'

Then his eyes went wide so you could see all the whites round the middle bit and there was a pause as he panicked, looking at me for my middle name. I shook my head quickly, my hair snapping from side to side, and the priest continued with a sigh, '...Graves to be your lawfully wedded wife?'

'I do,' Andrew said in his most solemn voice. My heart skipped: pitter, patter.

'In sickness and in health?' the priest checked.

We both nodded a 'yes'.

'Good,' he commented.

Sniggers could be heard behind us. Then someone said 'ssh' and it went quiet again.

'To death you do part?'

We nodded again, slightly less enthusiastically. I could feel God looking at me from the clouds to see if I was for real.

The mood was serious. It was like everyone there was holding their breath in all at the same time.

'Do you have the ring?' the priest asked.

Lyndon walked forward and placed the ring in the priest's out-stretched hand, bowing and shuffling backwards to his place in the front row.

'Excellent,' the priest stated. 'So then...' He paused, sticking the ring quickly on my finger.

I sucked in all the air, waiting for the words, the words I had thought about for the last week, the words I had scribbled all over my diary. The words I knew would come.

'I now pronounce you man and wife. You may...'

There was an explosion of laughter, and the priest started stuttering the next bit, embarrassed. '...kiss the bride.'

There was general whooping and a lone 'Woooo!' was heard. Over the noise I could hear my own breaths buzzing in my brain.

Andrew Parker drew back my veil to reveal my flushed face (it was hot under there; Beth had told me it was when she got married but I hadn't believed her until now). And then he leaned right in, really close, right up to my face and he smelled of chewing gum and...That was it. All of a sudden. A kiss from Andrew James Parker that bashed the top of my lip.

My nostril felt wet. Someone had started playing 'Three Blind Mice' on a violin. People threw leaves at us for confetti. Andrew walked off. But I was happy, all warm inside my tummy. Sort of stunned as well as I didn't think it would feel like this. And now everyone was cheering us and smiling and Harry started shaking Andrew's hand and then Sammy and Lyndon decided to lift him up and carry him around and then all the girls were surrounding me because they wanted to know what the ring looked like and what the kiss had felt like. They were all unmarried, apart from Beth who got married last term, but then Chris left the school and she had only seen him once, in town, but he had been with his mum and she'd been too embarrassed so hadn't even waved, just pretended he wasn't there. I would never do that to Andrew.

I looked across at him – my husband. He had taken his shirt off and was wearing his school tie as a bandana. I looked down at the ring someone had made out of a yellow pipe cleaner and smiled.

Two weeks later, I wondered what had gone so wrong.

Yesterday Andrew Parker had been seen in the playground pushing Jenny Murray around on those big plastic barrels. I'd seen red and pushed Sammy Layton round on the barrels as he was always begging me to push him. Then Katie Sanderson saw us and told Andrew Parker that I was going out with Sammy Layton now and Andrew Parker came storming over to me, his bottom lip quivering, a hand swiping at the wave in his hair. Slowly he raised one hand and pointed straight at me.

'You, Isobel Graves, are no longer my wife and you won't be able to find a new husband, from this day forth till death you do part.'

Then there was a clap of thunder and, as the rain beat down and everyone rushed inside, I watched him turn on his heel and leave me. Water streamed down my face, my arms broke out into goosebumps.

My first husband walked out on me.

Chapter 1

Los Angeles

'Twenty per cent off all shellfish today. It's prawntast— Shit.'

'Stop dropping them, Iz.'

'I can't keep hold of them in these stupid claws.'

'Prawns don't have cla— Hello, sir, twenty per cent off all shellfish today. It's the *plaice* to be...They don't have claws, Iz, they have like pink arms or something.'

'Well, then what the bejeezus are these?' I stood up, waving various pink appendages at Mel's massive prawn face. I couldn't make out her eyes.

'They're the arm legs; it's like a whole limb thing going on. They are like the fish version of spiders or something.'

'AGGGGHH, I don't even care.' My voice was muffled inside the giant prawn costume and I felt more leaflets fall to the floor in my frustration.

'STOP DROPPING THEM, Iz.'

'Is it lunch yet?'

'Sweetheart, it's not even time for your "elevenses".' She

tried to do the quotation marks with her big fish claws, almost decapitating a coiffured passer-by. 'Oh hello, madam, it's twenty per cent off today on all shellfish. It's an eely, eely good deal.'

'What's with the fish puns?' I asked, adjusting my prawn head and smiling at a little girl in a sundress nearby who couldn't see my smile and ran screaming behind the legs of her father as the massive prawn focused in ON HER.

'I like to mix it up, Iz, leave the punter wanting more. I am like the most dynamic prawn since, shit, has a prawn ever done anything?'

'It's a prawn, Mel, I don't think prawns *do* anything.'

'Well that's lazy, they've got enough limbs for something. Hello, sir, care for twenty per cent off today? Thank Cod for us, eh!'

I exhaled loudly in my prawn head, my breath clogging the inside making me feel sweaty and boxed in and disgusting. The sun was dazzling in a way that only the LA sun could, some girl in hotpants and a tiny crop top just rollerbladed past, smirking at our sad little prawn party for two. The manager of the store, the most enormous man with five chins and a gut that rested over his thighs, was bound to come out at any moment and give us another lecture about the promotion we were running. And we still had about five hours of this hell to go.

'Where did Celine go?' Mel asked, turning in a slow circle so that her prawn tail whipped round and tripped up a boy dressed in dungarees too busy sucking his thumb and staring to move out of the way. He started crying and ran away to tell his mum. Mel obviously hadn't felt anything and was oblivious as we could barely see a metre in front of us through the little pink mesh panel over our eyes.

I tried to shrug, but the outfit was so heavy nothing moved. 'Dunno.'

'So typical of her. She's probably chatting up some sexy man and we are left doing all the work.'

'How come she's the mermaid anyway?' I asked. 'It's not right. Why are we never the hot character? Do you remember that job in the mall where we spent all day on our knees pretending to be dwarves and she was Snow White? She's not even white, she's orange.'

As if our talking had summoned her, Celine swanned over dressed in a long fishtail skirt, all green and turquoise chiffon frills, two stars placed precariously over her fake-tanned boobs. A man nearby wearing a baseball cap on backwards slammed himself into a rubbish bin he was gawping so hard.

'He-ll-o, ladies, celeb spot, I am pre-tt-y sure I just saw Amanda – *Gossip Girl* season two wearing a pink playsuit,' she said, fanning her face, framed with abundant gold curls, with a fan that looked like a seashell. She looked like she was on a beach in Hawaii, not outside a supermarket in downtown LA handing out leaflets to the general public.

Celeb spot?

There was silence.

'I must have er...missed that season,' said Mel from inside her prawn costume.

'We can't see out of these things anyway,' I grumbled, trying to fold my prawn arms but taking about six limbs with me. I dropped the remaining leaflets. 'Aaggghhhh! I hate this bloody job.'

'Stop dropping them, Iz.'

'Hey,' trilled Celine. 'It's not so bad y'all.'

'That's because you're not dressed as a piece of seafood with a ginormous prawn head,' I pointed out.

'Hey, you look totally cute,' she laughed.

I wanted to smack her mermaid face with all my arms and legs. I wobbled as I walked towards her. She would have looked afraid if she could move her face more than a centimetre, but her Botox-addled forehead was frozen. She backed away, fish tail swishing from side to side.

'Hey, babe, no need to be on such a downer. Mel is enjoying herself, aren't you, Mel?'

The other prawn turned. 'I am having a turbotlly AMAZING time.'

'God, I need a coffee,' I said pulling off my prawn head which made a different child run behind the legs of her mother, her long plait streaming behind her as she fled.

I leaned down, human head with a prawn body, the outfit limiting my movements, and started attempting to scoop up the dropped leaflets. My long brown hair fell around me and I tried to swipe it back with a claw.

Just how had my career plumbed these depths?

'Excuse me,' I said, depositing my massive prawn head on a spare chair. 'Do you mind if I put this here?' Amazing how a hollowed-out giant fish head could clear a table of people pronto.

Ordering a cappuccino, I sat down carefully, trapping my numerous appendages under my chair to avoid tripping people up. One guy smirked at me as I lost control of a leg. When done I placed both elbows back on the table, my reflection in the cafe glass window staring unsmiling back at me.

The waitress slid my drink across to me, her gaze fixed on one of my six arms.

'Thanks,' I muttered, tearing a sugar sachet open and sprinkling its contents over the chocolate-striped froth.

I'd been in LA for two years. I'd been doing jobs like this for most of that time. It was easy money in many ways: dress up, smile, be nice. I knew things could be worse, but it was so far removed from what I had hoped. I had big dreams, had arrived fresh from England with stories of LA and the glamorous world of television. I was going to be a TV presenter; with my experience reporting news items and real-life events, my adorable English accent and my buoyant enthusiasm, I was going to make it. I wasn't going to be handing out leaflets as a life-size prawn.

I took a sip, froth sticking to my lips, as Mel walked in, holding her prawn head under one arm. Her red hair was sticking to her forehead as she scanned the tables for me. I gave her a weak wave and she swiped at her fringe, grinned and came over, appendages wobbling, smirky guy rolling his eyes as if to say, 'Oh man alive, there are two of them.'

Looming over my table, she put her free hand on her hip. 'Is someone a sad-face shellfish?'

'Shut your face,' I said, mouth twitching, not wanting to meet her eye.

'Who's a sad shellfish?' she said in a baby voice. 'You are. You are.'

When I didn't respond, she shrugged. 'Do you want me to do the Prawn Dance? I've been working on it for a while. Okay, fine, since you left me five minutes ago but I think it's good.'

'No, I'm okay,' I said.

'Too late,' she said, breaking into a routine: prawn legs and arms waving about uselessly, out of time, culminating in the 'Prawn Body Pop' where she knocked over someone's empty glass on the table behind us.

'Sit down, woman,' I said, pushing out the chair and giggling.

'Sorry,' she called to the waitress as, scowling, she came to remove the glass and wipe at the table.

'Coffee, please, us fish get up a thirst,' she laughed, earning herself another scowl. 'So what's wrong, babe?'

'Er, I really hate it when you call me "babe" – we are so not "babe" type friends.'

'Okay, homie, I hear you,' she said in a solemn voice, raising her prawn arm.

I sighed, tapping my teaspoon on the edge of the cup. 'I'm being a dick,' I said. 'It's not like today is any worse, ignore me.'

'Ha, I love that you are being so English when you're depressed. "I'm being a dick,"' she parroted at me, her head lolling as she put on a dreadful low English accent. ''kay...' she said in her own voice again. 'So am totally thinking hot yoga – should I or should I not?'

I stopped her with a prawn claw and an annoyed expression. 'Hello, I didn't ACTUALLY mean ignore me. Shit, give me three minutes of self-pity time.'

'Oh sorry, sorry, right, well yes today is fine. I mean it's not fine in the sense that we perhaps didn't dream that we might one day be LA's finest talking Man Prawns, but we are used to this ritual humiliation, yes? Do you remember that New Year's Sexual Health Campaign – we could be dressed as worse, Iz.' She shivered with the memory. 'Ribbed for your pleasure. I genuinely thought I might never recover from that one. We HAD to drink through it.'

'Er, you spent the entire time asking men to rub lube on you and cackling in drunk hysteria.'

'Not my finest hour,' she admitted.

'Didn't you just think,' I started in a quiet voice, interrupted by the plonking down of Mel's coffee, 'didn't you just think we would have stopped all this by now? It was meant to be temporary money – you know, while you became a dancer and my show reel went out.'

Mel's mouth turned down and I felt guilty for making her mood plummet. Then she shrugged at me. 'I still kind of believe that will happen; we've just got to stick at it and have some faith.'

'I guess,' I said, draining the last of my coffee and then ducking as Celine swept past, tail flapping, head swivelling left to right as she scanned for us in the street outside.

'Oops,' Mel giggled.

'Do you ever wonder how long we will be d—?'

'I don't get how mermaids have sex,' mused Mel, cutting me off.

'Sorry?' I stopped mid-flow. Mel was clearly not focused on me and my problems.

She tilted her head to indicate outside. 'Just looking

at Celine there and I don't get it, physically, how can they manage it?'

'You know mermaids don't exist, Mel,' I confirmed.

'Well yeah, but if they did, I don't get how they would do it. Where is the access?'

'Access?

'You know, like...' She held up two claws...

'Yes, I can imagine.' I held up a hand, interrupting. 'Maybe merpeople make babies just by hugging?' I suggested.

'How awful.'

'Dreadful,' I agreed. 'Um...can we possibly, if it's not too much of a problem, talk about me again?' I asked.

Mel dragged her eyes back to my face. 'Yes sorry, sorry... just worried about the logistics.'

'Clearly.'

'Anyway, am totally focused...shoot!' she said, trying to click with her claw.

'Okay, so I was asking how long do you think we will have to be at all this and when do you think we will be doing what we rea— Actually, do you know what,' I said, throwing up my hands, 'I'm boring myself.' I sipped at my coffee and looked at Mel. 'So do you think there's a hole?'

'What, in your life?' Mel asked, forehead creasing.

'No, in the mermaid.'

Mel considered this, sipping slowly at her coffee, 'Honestly, Iz, I just don't know.'

Chapter 2

Four hours later, I'd showered and thrown on some cotton shorts and a vest top. My hair was scraped back off my face and, as I stared at my reflection in the mirror, I felt marginally more myself. Rubbing moisturiser into my skin, lightly tanned from some recent good weather, I breathed out slowly, feeling my shoulders drop. It had been a long day. Despite Mel trying to cheer me up by pretending to be 'Killer Prawn' – chasing Celine down the promenade growling at her and snapping her claws. Celine had started screaming, dodging Mel's diving limbs as her hair flowed behind her and her boobs bobbed up and down. She had lost one of her seashells and wouldn't speak to us for the rest of the afternoon, even when Mel apologised by bringing her a fork, called it a thinga-me-bob and sang to her from *The Little Mermaid*. The hours dragged by and I got hotter and more uncomfortable as the sun sat stubbornly overhead, its rays uninterrupted by any passing clouds.

Emerging downstairs, I snuggled on the sofa next to Stewie who had gallantly suggested he cook and had brought back a Chinese takeaway. Nibbling on a piece of cold prawn toast (rub it in, Stewie, why don't you?), I tried to show an interest in the movie he was watching (something about a robot who could love) but got bored and reached for a magazine. Flicking aimlessly through its pages I became more and more depressed that I didn't have a 'Bikini-Ready Body' – WHAT DOES THIS EVEN MEAN?, did not know '10 ways to impress my man' and didn't have enough of this season's yellow in my wardrobe. Flinging it to one side, I rested my head on Stewie's shoulder.

Without taking his eyes from the television, he whispered in a low voice, fish breath on my face, one hand creeping over my thigh, 'You know what I like, baby.'

I closed my eyes and sighed. *Really? Tonight? Now?*

'Mmm,' I mumbled, wrapping an arm around him, buying myself some time.

Squeezing him tightly, I hoped the robot on screen might distract him.

He shifted next to me. 'Come on, baby, it's been ages,' he said in his East Coast twang, his voice rising at the end.

I snatched my arm back. 'I just...' I didn't know what I just. I just *can't* was what I was thinking. I just was not in the mood. I just couldn't face it. I just...Stewie had been away for a while though, twelve days in fact (he had announced it when he had appeared on my doorstep that evening). I licked my lips, tried to gear myself up, prepare mentally. I could do this. It was fun, playful. He loved it.

His hand crept higher up my thigh and he turned,

snuffling at my neck like an excited piglet. I let him, lying on the sofa, trying to relax, trying to shake off the day. He tugged at my vest top, exposing one breast that he threw himself on with glee. I needed to do this, I needed to remind myself why Stewie was good for me. Recently I had been so mean to him and he hadn't really done anything wrong. It was my fault and no one deserved that.

So with a breath and both eyes closed I began, 'Goose, you big stuuuuuud.' I could feel Stewie's hand tense in anticipation, mouth frozen over my nipple, and pause briefly before continuing. 'Take me to bed or lo...' Stewie's hand was pawing at the elastic to my knickers now. I petered out and pushed it away.

He looked up at me. He had a dash of soy sauce in the corner of his mouth.

I exhaled slowly, tucking a piece of hair behind my ear. 'I can't, my heart's not in it,' I announced.

'But you always love that line,' Stewie said, wrinkling his nose and looking lost. 'You always do Meg Ryan's accent just perfect.'

'Perfectly.'

'That's what I said.'

'Can't we just have sex tonight rather than all this...?' I threw my arms wide. 'All this role-playing. I'm just not in the mood. I've spent today being a prawn, Stewie, A PRAWN. I have had enough play-acting.'

I pulled my top back up from around my waist.

Stewie drew away, folding his arms. His narrow shoulders and over-large head made him look like an angry letter 'i'. 'Fine, have it your way. Anyway, I am now not in the mood.'

You're not in the mood?

'Good, well we'll call it quits then,' I said, getting up off the sofa, readjusting my shorts and walking through to the kitchen trying to maintain some semblance of dignity.

I leaned against the counter noting Stewie's sulking face as he riffled through my magazines on the table next door, his bottom lip jutting out like I'd taken his train set away. Turning around and twisting the tap on, I pretended to do the washing up, circling the cloth over one plate furiously. Stewie had sat back on the sofa watching the wrestling, his mousy hair just visible. Another evening together stretched ahead. *Don't focus on the negatives, Iz. Why do you always have to be such a Thought Bitch? Think of Stewie's good qualities. The fact he is nice to you, asks about your career, shows an interest.* Butting against all this was my uncertainty. *How had it come to this? Was this really it?*

Before I moved to America, things had been going reasonably well back in the UK – I'd trained up on live channels selling vacuum cleaners and jewellery at 3 a.m. and had worked on the ITV West news and sports desks for a few months. But I wanted a big break and I'd been single and in need of an adventure. I'd descended on LA with wild hopes, hoping to find fame, fortune and a good-looking homeboy to sweep me off my feet. But all I'd really found was a tiny box of an apartment in a down-trodden part of town, a part-time relationship with Stewie and a 'temporary' job as a promotional girl whilst my show reel got ignored on the desks of various producers.

I could hear Stewie sighing next door, super subtly, and tried to remember what it was about him that I had first been attracted to. We'd met at a party in West Hollywood when I'd been showing off my best party trick (rapping the entire theme tune of *Prince of Bel Air*, then downing a sambuca shot using no hands). He had looked all dashing and suave standing by a marble column, the reflections from the outdoor pool making him shimmer in the light. He had brought me over a drink, told me he had flown in that night and was flying out again the next morning. I had been bowled over by the Sexy Pilot routine (he had been wearing a jacket with stripes on – very *Top Gun*) and I'd also had more than the one sambuca. Somehow I found myself crushed up against him in a spare room as he kissed my neck and told me I was beautiful.

Since then we had seen each other on and off for eight months. He flew internal flights for Cheapee, the budget airline in America, so no transatlantic freebies on the cards. He liked video games, wrestling and watching repeats of *Airport*. When he kissed me, he liked to hold my face between both hands and look at me. I found it quite unnerving. He never raised his voice or got angry with me, he didn't say mean things or hurt me. He was sweet: he would bring me freshly squeezed orange juice because he knew I loved it, and he would rub my feet if I said they hurt. Recently it was me who had been the one acting unpleasantly. I hated myself sometimes, when I caught myself in a moment of annoyance, felt guilt prickling: a small voice telling me he didn't deserve it, hadn't done anything to warrant my stroppy mood.

I swallowed. It was just me. Eight hours dressed as a prawn tends to depress a girl. I had to try not to blame others. Stewie was here, wasn't he? He meant well and he'd been so pleased to see me after twelve days.

Plastering a smile on my face, I appeared in the kitchen doorway. Clearing my throat, I looked at the sofa. 'Take me to bed or lose me for ever.'

The head twitched to the side.

I repeated the line and turned to walk up the stairs.

Stewie jumped enthusiastically off the sofa, calling in my wake, 'Show me the way home, honey.'

I closed my eyes and stepped into my bedroom.

Dear diary,

Andrew is my best friend out of all my friends at school and he said that we will always be friends for ever long. He said I could always go to his house for tea after school if I wanted to. I like playing with him on the Nintendo. We play *Duck Hunt* and he lets me shoot the laser gun from behind the sofa like we are in a cowboy film.

It is fun at Andrew's house as his mum makes us brownies and we have big glasses of cold milk. Andrew's dad isn't there at all because he lives in another house with a new wife. It is fun playing. Sometimes I get sad that I don't have another brother and sister but Andrew says it doesn't matter if you have friends.

I x

Chapter 3

Stewie left for an early flight and I woke late, stretching both legs out wide and wiggling my toes. Through the white muslin curtains of my bedroom I could make out more white: a cloudy day, some light straining to get in but mostly a nothing-weather day, overcast, not sunny, not rainy, not *doing* anything. I twisted round, plumped up a pillow and snuggled into it again. Sunday. Sleepy Day. No work required: just me and the apartment. Maybe I would bake something. Maybe I'd finally buy all the ingredients for a Black Forest Gateau: today could be that day.

I opened an eye. There was no point trying to snooze now as I'd made myself hungry. I needed to get up and forage. Rubbing my face, I opened up a few of the kitchen cupboards, perhaps hoping that some house elf had magically filled them with titbits and treats. There was very little in the flat of note so I improvised and ate an over-ripe banana slathered on a Confetti Cluster Pop Tart that had gone off a while ago.

Perched on the bar stool, I looked blankly at the calendar on the wall: a picture of a rabbit trying to kill itself with a cheese grater. The Bunny Suicides never failed to crack my mum up and I smiled as I thought of her back in England, banana sticking as I swallowed.

Glad to be on the last bite, I looked across at my laptop, abandoned by the sofa. Firing it up, I sat back, snuggled in the cushions, and waited for the page to load. Clicking on the email icon, I felt a little thrill at seeing four new emails, then depressed to note two of them were trying to sell me something and one wanted to help me attract women with my giant new penis, which was nice but not really necessary. Clicking on the one from Mum, I felt a rush of warmth as the email opened, her flushed face flashing across my mind as I read.

Hello darling,

I'm painting in the garden, it's completely glorious, the brooding hills beyond, the light on the sand, the water frantically lashing at the rocks. My painting is bloody awful but the scenery is just marvellous at the moment. Violent weather. I have bought a brilliant little thing for judging distance from a painting website in America but I think I'm holding it wrong. ANYWAY, how are you getting on with work? Have you had to do any more of those dreadful jobs? I am CERTAIN that someone will soon recognise your potential, darling, and you'll get a presenting job or five. We thought you were marvellous in that commercial for contact lenses. I definitely believed you were short-sighted.

So, darling, the main reason I'm writing is to say your father has managed to get himself on the television too! He'll be on the BBC News tomorrow night (Sunday) being interviewed about something terribly dull to do with vintage cars, but I wanted to let you know as I think he's really rather proud of himself. As am I. Tune in 9 p.m. our time, it will be towards the end, around those 'fun' features that are meant to cheer you up before the weather forecast comes on and we all want to kill ourselves.

Right, I must be off, this bloody awful picture won't paint itself, you know.

A thousand kisses from both of us, well mostly me as your father would NEVER be so OTT, so maybe a quick hug, only shoulders touching, from him.

Mum x x x x x x

I giggled and felt a lurch in my stomach for my parents and their warm farmhouse in Cornwall. Dad sitting down with the paper, the blue teapot with the chip in the spout and a buttered crumpet, quietly grumbling because Mum would have spent £800 on something techy that she couldn't work. Mum flying around the kitchen, striped apron on, probably covered in flour even if she wasn't using any, producing some gorgeous lopsided sponge cake with real strawberries inside and a tiny jug of single cream to be poured all over it. In the distance through the kitchen window a few stray surfers will be picking their way back over the sands of Polzeath beach.

So my gentle dad would be on the television doting over the latest vintage car he would have been working on. I hadn't seen this latest one; he always had something dismantled in the garage and would lovingly clean parts over newspaper on the outside bench after Mum banished him there. His half-moon glasses would be perched on the end of his nose, his tongue poked out in concentration, Brahms playing through the open living-room window. I suddenly felt very alone in the kitchen and reached for my mobile.

'You are cordially invited to English high tea at mine,' I tapped.

Mel, obsessed with my 'kooky' British accent and strange British rituals, replied almost immediately: 'I mean, you guys have finger sandwiches with only cucumber in. I am there. Will you wear the tiara again and pretend to be Kate Middleton?'

'It's a deal,' I texted back.

'Dex has to come too. We are currently having the sex!'

'Er...he is very welcome but please stop having the sex when here.'

'I can't promise that. He is so good at it!'

'Eurgh, you disgust me.'

Firing up the oven in my galley kitchen, so narrow you can get two people wedged into the middle of it if they cross paths at the same time, I started to rummage through the cupboard for baking equipment. Dusting off the plastic scales and reaching for the sieve, I already felt lighter. Flour, eggs, butter, milk. I decided to make lemon cupcakes in large muffin cases so the sponge would spill over the top of them. The recipe learned years ago during a break-up where I lived on lemon cake and Crackerbread. I tapped out the ingredients. Twisting round to turn on my iPod, I did a single, unashamed 'whoop' as Olly Murs pumped out. Stirring everything in together, my arm starting to ache with the effort, my head emptied and I felt calm.

'You wore it!' Mel exclaimed with glee a few hours later when I opened the door dressed in a pink tea dress and a tiara.

'BOW TO ME, MINION, BEFORE YOU ENTER,' I said, pointing to the dirt-streaked pavement outside the flat.

'Of course, so sorry, your majesty,' said Mel, plunging to one knee. 'Dex,' she hissed, tugging on his sleeve and dragging him down with her.

'Oh geez, ladies, if you are going to start like that I need to go and buy beer.'

'That is no way to talk to a PRINCESS,' I boomed. 'But actually I do have beer. For after.'

Dex struggled to his feet, rubbing the top of his stubbled head with a tanned hand.

I craned my neck to reach and give him a kiss. 'Hey, Dex.'

'Hey, your majesty.'

Mel was still staring at the ground, her eyes lowered in respect.

'You may rise, Miss Conboy.' I reached out a hand for her.

'I like your shoes, Kate,' she said, 'Now can I wear your tiara?'

Plonking it on her head, the glossy red hair dazzling in the daylight, I ushered them both inside and up to the flat which smelled satisfyingly of cake and fresh air, the breeze lifting the bottoms of the curtains as we sat at the small table in the living room.

Pouring Dex a cup of tea and laughing as Mel made 'oohing' noises over the cupcakes, I collapsed onto the armchair, threads worn loose on its arms which I picked at as we talked.

Above the tiny fake fireplace, my mantelpiece was littered with postcards, wedding invitations from friends in England who I hadn't seen for years who were marrying men I hadn't met, a small Rubik's Cube key ring, a dusty tea tin filled with pens and an empty blue ashtray. Dex was absent-mindedly casting his eye along it and then pulled out a postcard, worn at the edges, from behind an invite.

'Cute,' he commented, holding it up to me.

'It's one from my grandma in Cornwall,' I explained. Dex handed it to me and I traced a finger over the cottages in the postcard. The picture was of a tiny village in south west Cornwall and it made me ache for home. This attempt at an English high tea had not come at the best time. I always thought I would be living that chocolate-box dream and had regular fantasies about my life. It always involved some upstanding English gent and I thought wistfully back to my first husband, Andrew, the boy that had said 'I do' in the playground all those years ago. He'd left at the end of the term and we'd never had a formal divorce. Beth had hers and I had been witness to it. They signed a sheet of paper that confirmed it in case God had been watching, but I had never done the same and somehow Andrew had always stayed in my mind as the one that got away. The man I might have built my life with. The English husband I dreamed of when I thought about the future.

'I can't believe you are from there,' Mel said. She was always asking me to tell her more about England and the queen and whether it was really true that morris dancing was an actual thing that people did and whether I had ever killed a fox on a hunt, met 'Wills' or danced around a maypole draped in the St George's Cross whilst singing the national anthem. I closed my eyes as Dex and Mel giggled over the wedding invitation from 'Penelope Blythington-Smythe' and did their version of English accents that made them sound mostly like they were suffering from a dreadful throat illness.

'Will you be so kind as to kiss me, my love?'

'Kiss you!' screeched Mel, sounding like Dick Van Dyke in *Mary Poppins*. ''Ee, I don't think that is rather proper now.'

Smiling, I floated away from them to the usual scene in my head. Where I thought I'd be living now, aged twenty-nine, and who I would be living with. A small Victorian cottage, red bricks, tiled roof, porch in the front, roses trained around the side. Lovely white sash windows open, the glass reflecting a perfect English summer's day: twenty-one degrees, a couple of clouds in the sky, a light breeze, the BBQ waiting on the paved stone terrace to be fired up. A meandering path leading you past an apple tree, strawberry plants clustered around the roots so you could pick one or two and taste a sweet burst of flavour as you bit into the delicate flesh. The smell of lavender hitting you as you step up and push open the door into the house. This would be replaced with the smell of baking bread, the sound of something on vinyl tripping gently through the house as you move through into a hall, all wooden floorboards, a large gilt mirror above, freshly cut flowers in a pottery vase on the side.

You move through to the large farmhouse kitchen, enormous slate tiles on the floor, a scrubbed pine table, a dresser piled high with glasses, mugs and leaflets about a local farmers' market. A stable door leading to a small garden bursting with colour, the fields beyond, creeping ivy covering the fences, the lawn complete with cushioned swing set where you could sit and watch the sun sink below a line of trees on the horizon as your husband – cue Andrew – brings you a perfectly made G&T, with cubes of ice, a sprig of rosemary and a slice of lemon in a heavy-bottomed crystal tumbler.

Andrew's back from doing something heroic (doctor? vet?) and he appears again over the top of the stable door to smile at you on the swing set, the sunset giving your skin a golden glow so you look absurdly young and healthy. He is tall, broad-shouldered and has thick light-brown hair that will never recede because it is not in his genes. He has an open face that smiles at you indulgently. Maybe he offers you a chocolate on a little plate? He scoots next to you on the swing set and suddenly there is a big tartan rug there and you two cuddle together watching the day end in your perfect home. You hear the sound of a quiet, sleepy village and watch as a few birds overhead fly by.

'Iz, IZ...Earth to Iz, come back to us, Iz.'

I was roused from my daydream by Mel and Dex standing over me holding out a beer. Dex was now wearing the tiara.

'You were like totally zoned out. Where were you?' asked Dex his nose wrinkling, having never seen this trance before.

Mel, an old hand, had seen it plenty of times. 'England,' she said to him, cuffing me on the arm. 'She's got this thing with this guy from her past in her head in England. It's weird but she's weird.'

'Er and sitting right here,' I said.

'Come on, babe, you know you're a little wacko.'

'A guy in England,' Dex said, leaning forward as he sat down.

'Not just any guy,' I said to Dex. 'My husband,' I added in reverential tones.

'Hardly,' Mel scoffed.

I rolled my eyes at her.

'Jeez, there's no need to go abroad for your guys, we're all right here,' Dex said, arms flung wide.

Mel pushed his shoulder. 'You wouldn't leave the state, let alone the country.'

'Well it's lucky I don't have a wife living in foreign climes,' Dex said solemnly.

'Do you even have a passport, Dex?' I laughed. Dex was a proper homeboy; he had a real Southern drawl, Johnny Cash style, and wore cowboy boots. Actual cowboy boots that looked strangely cool on him.

'Yeah, but I only got it so I could be served alcohol in bars.'

'Dex still looked about twelve when he was twenty-one,' Mel explained.

I nodded as Dex nudged Mel. 'But the sexiest twelve-year-old ever, am I right? Am I right?'

'No, you are disgusting.'

'Oh.' Dex hung his head as I started giggling, watching as Mel launched herself across him, his face smothered in kisses and her flame-red hair.

Dex winked at me. 'Still got it,' he said, drawing Mel into the crook of his arm.

Mel settled there, her hand idly stroking his leg. Then she seemed to wake up, springing to her feet. 'Right, we're heading out on the town to shoot the breeze and down some shots. Get your gladdest gladrags on.'

Dex jumped up too, scooping her up into a bad waltz. 'It's going to be a gooooooood night,' he said, leaning her backwards and kissing her gently.

'Oh man, I am going to have to get good and drunk if you two are going to do that all night.'

And they did, so I did.

Dear diary,

Andrew and I climbed up the highest in the tree today and I was quite scared but I didn't say anything to him. I didn't walk out on the branch like he did, but I did hang upside down from the branch at the bottom of the tree and all my hair flew down and I looked funny. Andrew said I looked like a wombat who sleeps like that and I was worried I would fall off because I was laughing but I didn't.

I x

Chapter 4

Bleary-eyed and with an Unidentified Flesh Wound – a purpling bruise on my left thigh – to contend with, Sunday dawned way too bright. The curtains hadn't been closed and a strip of LA sunshine was cutting across my face forcing me to squint. I was facing the wrong way up, feet resting on my pillow, my face a dribbling wreck pressed against my grey sequinned throw. A sent text message told me that I had been up at 4.07 a.m.:

> To: STEWIE 'Karoaeek, lost in cassino. Sex now could do'

There was no way that I could now do sex. Sitting seemed an impossible dream right now.

When I got up, I felt tiny bumps where the sequins had pressed into my cheek. Glancing in the mirror at the marks it looked like a mini-tractor had been driving up and down my face in the night.

'Gahhhhhhhhhhhhh,' I called down the answerphone to Mel. It responded with an aggressive 'beep'.

Most of the day was spent moving gingerly through my house, cake crumbs still sprayed over the table from our high tea (and possible 4 a.m.) feast and the pot still had the remnants of yesterday's stone-cold English Breakfast in it. Stewie arrived mid-afternoon and let himself in after I threw the keys out of the window to him in the street.

'Can't. Dying,' I said as he pushed me up against the corridor wall before crawling back under my duvet on the sofa.

He moved past me to the kitchen, calling over his shoulder, 'I'm flying out late tonight so we will need to make love at some point,' which only made me pull the duvet round me tighter. He smelled of burned toast and strong aftershave.

'Great, looking forward to it.'

He was riffling through cupboards now, clattering about in search of food. I didn't know my cupboards could make that much noise: it was like he was ripping them out of the wall. *What was he like, the American Hulk? Is the Hulk always American?* RIP. BANG. *Gah.* 'God, you never have any food,' he shouted through.

Why did I invite him over?

He returned with a mug of coffee in the shape of a Dalmatian's head and a bag of pretzels. Moving my feet off the sofa, he sat down, opening the bag with a loud tear. Changing the channel to an American football game and ignoring my, 'But I was watching that' with a dismissive, 'It was animals falling off shelves' (I love those videos), he sat there spitting out pretzels and slurping on his coffee, like his tongue was too big for his mouth. I tried not to sit there hating him but as I watched another crumb land on my gorgeous cream shag pile carpet, I couldn't help but hope he might be killed by the next pretzel in a terrible and unlikely pretzel-related death. Realising that if he did start choking I might actually have to move, I dismissed this thought as quickly as it came and just willed for the ceiling to collapse only on him.

It was hours later, I was horizontal and Stewie had managed to sneak behind me and was doing the lovely tummy rubbing thing I liked. I stretched out like a cat, boobs thrust upwards so that Stewie was given his signal that Sofa Sex was a go-go and he had whipped off my tracksuit bottoms before I could say, 'Not on the pretzels.'

Zipping himself back up and smiling smugly over me, he sauntered through to the bathroom leaving me a sweaty heap under my duvet, hair stuck to my face and my tracksuit bottoms still looped round an ankle. The postcard was just within reach on the carpet and I picked it up, staring at the foreign scene, with me feeling like I was moving further and further away from that idyllic life.

This was it, I thought as I tucked a strand of hair behind my ear. *Deal with it, Stewie is here and you haven't met anyone else, you haven't even tried.* Groaning with those thoughts, I pushed myself up and headed to the bathroom to shower. As I dried myself off, I caught sight of the clock and realised that I would miss the news in England if I didn't turn on the TV now.

'It's on, it's on, I need to watch the laptop! Dad!' I panted, flying back to the living room, leaving wet footsteps and switching my laptop on. Clicking on the ITV West webpage, I tuned into the news being streamed. I'd missed the headlines as the story was something local from a chocolate factory in Somerset. Everyone was wearing blue shower caps and stirring giant vessels of dark chocolate around. Then it changed to the newsroom and the new feature.

'There he is,' I said, wiggling to an upright sitting position, the laptop wobbling on top of the cushion on my lap.

My dad was standing to the right, being interviewed off camera. His mild-mannered voice, short responses and slightly frightened look made me grin. The village green was perfectly, impeccably English – a triangle of lush grass surrounded by cottages, a pub one side and people meandering past in Barbour jackets.

My dad's overgrown eyebrows, streaked with grey, moved up and down as he spoke about the sky-blue convertible Coupé behind him, parked up on the side of the road.

'Oh doesn't he look good,' I said. He had combed his grey hair back from his face and taken off his glasses. The lines around his eyes creased when he was listening to the question. Villagers were watching the piece behind him and moving across the green looking at the car.

And then, suddenly, in the crowd behind him saw a face I instantly recognised. My jaw dropped open and I didn't take a breath. Stewie's voice melted into background noise as I frantically clicked the arrow to wind the frames back. No longer honing in on my dad's face, I scanned the crowd again, saw a back turned, a brown jacket made of some kind of tweed, dirty-blond hair, a profile. And then I paused as the man turned and I felt the room go completely still as I stared.

Stared at a face I hadn't seen in over twenty years, a face I'd thought about for over twenty years. The whole flat seemed to be waiting, my head was shouting thoughts, filling every crevice of my brain. I moved towards the screen so that the images started to blur. I rewound again, paused, forwarded, paused, rewound. I was certain. It was him.

I had found Andrew Parker.

Dear diary,

Dad came home early for my birthday party and Mum had made the house look all nice with lots of balloons that had big 9s written on them. One of them floated up to the ceiling without its string and is still there now but it is all floppy and bent. It looks sad and you can't read the '9' on it any more. We had party games and played pass the parcel and also sleeping lions which I am really bad at. I always lose, because I laugh when Dad comes over and calls me Munchkin and does a funny growling lion roar and it is so funny because Dad isn't normally like a lion.

The second-best game was the one where we all became statues and had to hold it still or be out and I made it to the last two again with Andrew and we had to dance and then freeze and he froze a second after me and I won and then he smiled a really massive smile that split his face in half and hugged me. It was the best birthday. I think he froze after me deliberately and that was why he smiled.

Also, there were party bags with fizzy cola bottles in and Andrew said it was the best party bag he had *ever* got and Mum danced to the 'Superman' song because she had wine in her hand. It was fun.

I x

Chapter 5

'Can you zip me up, Iz?' asked Mel stepping into her carrot costume. 'Let me just put my feet through the body bit. Jeez.'

'Oh god, Mel, I can't do this today,' I wailed, my outfit in a red pool on the ground beside me, hands frozen by my side.

Mel, one foot in her costume, one out, twisted round. 'Don't be silly. We're going to be peas in a pod on this one; lettuce not get depressed about it. We'll have the best time. You can't beet it! You'll see.'

I groaned, 'Not today with your puns, woman,' and walked over to her, helping her squeeze into the long orange outfit. Finding the zip I drew it up and then stood back. She was a carrot, the stalk waving around in the breeze above her head. A cut-out hole for her face. She was smiling, her white straight teeth sparkling in the sunshine.

'God, why are you always so bloody happy,' I grumbled.

The carrot shrugged. 'Dex thinks it's an illness. Pathological happiness.'

'I could do with that,' I said, wearily turning around to pick up my outfit for the day.

Nearby, a tinkly, high, annoying laugh carried on the wind. 'You joker.'

I turned and spotted Celine chatting to a guy with shoulder-length blond hair, a skateboard under one arm and a hat on backwards. She was wearing a really cute farm-girl-type outfit: fringed cowboy boots, Daisy Duke denim hot pants, gingham shirt tied in a knot over her bronzed flat stomach. My eyes narrowed as I kept watching them and placed two feet into the two holes at the bottom of my large, round bright-red tomato costume. Heaving it up and putting my hands through a sort of leotard thing inside it, I then had the dilemma of bending down again, the tomato squeezing disgustingly into rolls around my middle, as I scooped up the hat. I had to wear the green stalk bit on top of my head; it looped under my chin on elastic and bits of it flopped over my face shading my eyes.

My voice was croaky as I turned to a woman walking past me, handbag looped over one shoulder, set hair. 'Good morning, madam, there's a promotion today on Christie's Canned Vegetables...'

Working in a daze, I had plenty of time to mull over the previous night's sighting. I'd woken wondering whether it had really happened – whether in my hungover state, Stewie clambering over me, the heat of the flat, my recent thoughts about England and home, whether my poor addled imagination had just conjured him up in a pathetic attempt to cheer me up. Fabricated my hero. But I'd watched the piece again this morning and there he had been, clearer than

I remembered. He would look like that now. He still had the slight wave in his hair at the front.

It was that hair that I had last seen ducking into his mum's car after the Christmas term ended. I'd been walking out holding my collage of a winter scene made entirely of macaroni (pr-e-tty awesome) when he left. We hadn't really spoken since the day of the cursing and the rain and, as I watched him leave, I wished I'd said goodbye. He'd been an excellent bringer of myrrh in the nativity play earlier that week and I should have said something nice about the crown he'd made from tin foil. He never came back in the New Year and I always wondered what had happened to him. His neat pulled-up grey socks, straight nose and wavy hair. Where had he got to? Why had he left? And, most importantly, were we still married in the eyes of God? For weeks I wondered, looking out for him at school, as if he might appear at milk time, a stab as I realised he might never reappear.

Mel found some shade on a bench underneath an awning. We had pilfered one of the cans and were eating fresh peaches out of it as we tried to stop steaming up in our outfits. Juice dribbled down my chin as I sat perched on the edge of the bench, my massive tomato bottom not letting me lean too far back. Reaching a hand up, I moved my head down to wipe a line of sweat from my brow.

'God I am actually melting,' I announced.

Mel had her eyes closed and was leaning back, her circle of face tilted to the sun, her long green stalk flopped back like hair. She didn't appear to hear me.

'Hmm.'

'You alright?' I asked, concerned that I had been a bit too gloomy recently, that I needed to be a better friend to her. 'There's not,' I paused briefly before ploughing on, 'there's not BEAN something wrong? ApPEAse me.' I nudged her.

'That's the spirit, Iz,' she said, giggling and opening one eye to view me in my little tomato hat. 'Sorry, just...' She yawned as if to emphasise her next point. 'Late night,' she explained. 'Dex and I tried out this new move called "The Spider"; it's totally AMAZING.'

Oh noooooooo. I hated it when Mel did this, she couldn't resist. It was some kind of bizarre American thing that she felt the need to share EVERYTHING with her friends like we were permanently on some kind of X-rated Oprah sofa. Or maybe it was a Mel thing; I wasn't sure. It was certainly not a Me thing. I felt myself turning as red as my tomato outfit as she described in detail just what her and Dex decided to do together last night with a pot of yoghurt and a camera. I shivered even though the sun was still a quivering circle of flame high in the sky and there wasn't a whisper of a cloud, or a breeze.

'Just exhausted now: he is so energetic and sometimes I...'

I pictured Stewie just before leaving last night, pinging hopelessly at the back of the bra and then making me twizzle it around to my front so he could undo it. Then his routine breast/butt grab combo that went: left breast, squeeze, butt grab one hand, right breast squeeze, squeeze, butt grab both hands, clamber on top of me, pant a little, insert little Stewie. At no point would I ever suggest introducing yoghurt into the mix but, at the same time, I admired a little creativity.

'And you see then he wanted to add sugar, or something with texture you know, to make it more...'

Just block her out, Iz, there's a good girl. She will finish soon and you can return to other conversations about fully clothed people and...

'So then he licked it off there and I thought it was over but, oh god, he just...'

I thought back to my exes with a sinking realisation that I appeared to have been missing out all along. Adventurous sex had never really featured. Unless you call adventurous someone trying to finger me in the boat of the Bubbleworks at Chessington? After school there'd been Patrick who used to cry after every time, Al who used to high-five me and Will who had to look up 'foreplay' in the dictionary because he genuinely thought it was the name of a band. How had I attracted these sexual no-hopers? Was I always doomed to have a sex life this predictable? Was it me? Was I the one lacking in imagination?

Mel was still describing in graphic detail the complex manoeuvring of her bedroom romp last night so I fell into my daydream of choice. It was the same scene. It was the same man, the same house, the same life that I had built up over the years in pain-staking, loving detail.

He had brought me the second G&T and had started massaging my feet, rubbing his thumbs into the middle so that I purred like a contented kitten. The evening sun was sinking, leaving trails of pinks and purples and the shadows fell across his features giving him a broody tint. He started stroking the inside of my legs, slowly and tantalisingly edging upwards – his touch and the evening breeze causing my skin to break out into goosebumps. I was tugging on his bow tie that he wore loose on either side of his shirt collar; he was in black tie again, like James Bond after a successful assassination. He was leaning over me now, his fingers expertly lingering over the fabric of my knickers, tantalising and so close. I had unbuttoned the top buttons of his shirt, was running my hands over the smoothness of his ches...

'Earth to Iz, come in, Iz.'

'Hmm...what...WHAT?' I half-shouted, my floppy green hat falling right over my face. 'Gah.'

'You were having the fantasy again, weren't you?'

'I was not!' I felt myself grow as red as the outfit I was wearing, 'Well...maybe.'

'Was it the sex one?'

'Nooo...' I shifted, my worst lying voice see-through as anything.

'Was he wearing the tux again? Were you downstairs or upstairs in the cottage? Oh wait, were you on the swing set?'

'Er...'

Dammit.

Mel clutched her sides. 'Amazing. I love how English you are: even your sex daydreams are polite. Did he ask whether he could enter you?'

'Stop it!' I squealed, clapping my hands to the side of my face.

'Tell meeeeeee...' She clasped both her hands together in prayer, looking over at me expectantly.

Quietly chewing on the last of the peach, I said in a half-whisper, 'I saw him.'

Mel dropped her hands. 'I know, that is the whole point

of a sex dream. Unless you were blindfolded which, by the way, I highly recommend...'

'No, not in my dream,' I interrupted, placing the can on the bench by my side. 'Saw him, saw him in the flesh, for real, alive.'

My man, my fantasy Andrew Parker. I thought back to his shoulders, wide and reliable, his confident gaze as he passed the camera.

'I really saw him, Mel,' I repeated.

'Not in your head?' she checked.

I shook my head from side to side. 'No.'

Her eyes widened in surprise. 'Yeah, right, where did you see him? Here?'

I shook my head again, feeling the green stalk hat move with me. 'On the television, back home, I mean he was back home on the television. On the news.'

'He presents the news! Cool!'

'No. Not presenting, he was *on* the news...'

'He was a criminal on the news,' Mel interrupted.

'No, not a criminal – and thanks for that. No, he was just on the news. Behind my dad.'

'Your dad was on the news too?' Mel frowned.

'Yes, talking about a vintage car, but that's not the point, focus, I SAW him, he was right there, right in England.'

Mel turned her whole carrot body around to look at me. 'Well that's like completely mental.'

'I know,' I said.

'So what are you going to do? Track him down and make him marry you?' she laughed.

I didn't respond at first. 'No, no, I couldn't do that.'

'Er...no, you could not, weird English girl, because, well, there are many reasons – for example, it might not have been him, you...'

'It was him,' I interrupted.

'...don't know where he lives...'

'England.' I pouted.

'Well that narrows it right down.' She rolled her eyes. 'And, HA!' She pointed at me. 'He might already be married.'

'Hmm...he didn't look married.'

'What? How is that even possible? Do married men have like a weary stoop or something?'

'He is married to me so if he were married again, he would be a polygamist and I would know.'

'You mean a bigamist.'

'I mean what I mean,' I said cryptically (because I wasn't absolutely sure who was right).

I wasn't ready for Mel to shatter my illusions. I felt I would have known somehow if he was married (again) – that my brain would have given up thinking back to him and conjuring up that life with him if he had been taken off the market.

'So what are you planning, Iz? Just to appear and be like, "Hey, random man I haven't seen in two decades who I dream about, want to get hitched?"'

'No of course not,' I snapped, hot and bothered in my costume and feeling the truth of her words.

'Hey, lovely, it's not so bad, you need to focus on what is here and now. Maybe you'll get a break.'

'Maybe.' I sighed, feeling guilty. Recently I had been on such a downer, I wondered why Mel stuck around. 'Thanks for being such a supportive carrot,' I said, making her grin.

'It's my *pea*leasure.'

'You're a prat, you know that, don't you?'

She lowered her head, the long green tendrils of stalk flopping forward. 'Yeah. Hey,' she looked up at me quickly, 'aren't you seeing your agent later today?'

My stomach flipped as I remembered the email I'd received the previous week. He had things he wanted to talk about face to face and I was really hoping this was it – the big audition I had hoped for, maybe for one of the networks. 'It's probably nothing,' I tried to say but Mel was hushing me with a hand.

'Maybe this is it, Iz?' She grinned.

I felt my whole face lift. 'Maybe it is,' I said, hope bursting in my chest. 'Thanks, Mel.'

Celine sashayed over at that moment. She had found a bit of straw to chew on between her glossy plump lips

'Hellooooo, am I like the only one working here?'

Mel readjusted her carrot face and stood up. 'Keep your tiny hot pants on, Celine, we were just discussing strategy.'

'Yes,' I said, standing up and patting the front of my tomato costume. 'Let's courgette them,' I said putting on my most gung-ho voice.

'Sorry?'

'Courgette, you know, go, get 'em.'

'Oh right, leave the puns to me, babe.'

'Seriously, Mel, we are not babe-type girls.'

'I feel ya, sista.'

'Well please don't.'

The morning dragged by and the only highlight was when Mel decided to start a line dance as a carrot and made some people join in. I think someone put it on YouTube so at least I am on TV a little now.

Traipsing across town to my agent's office on a tree-lined avenue off Santa Monica Boulevard, I buzzed the intercom.

'The Starlight Agency.'

'Isobel for...Randy?' I said into it, feeling foolish for stuttering over his name. As I did, every time.

The buzz sounded with no response and I pushed through, pausing to check my face in the reflection of the next internal door, pushing my hair behind my ears and licking my lips. Right. Crossing all my fingers and toes in an imaginary way, I started up the first flight of stairs arriving outside the office two minutes before I was due to be there. *This could be exciting, Isobel,* I thought as I opened the door to the outer room and his receptionist, Demi. Maybe he had news...

Demi looked up from her desk. 'He's on a phone call, Annabel.' She had one of those Bluetooth headsets on which always makes me suspicious.

'Isobel,' I said, trying not to let the frustration show in my face. *Keep smiling, Iz. Today could be the start of big change for you...*

'Isobel,' she repeated as if it were a new word in her vocabulary. 'Take a couch.' She pointed to the corner where I went to sit on the hardest, slipperiest sofa, the red faux leather making it impossible to remain still.

I idly trawled through my phone as I waited, five minutes, ten minutes, fifteen. At twenty, I surreptitiously sent Mel a photo message of me pretending to hang myself with boredom. Demi stared at me as I panicked, coughed and slipped about some more.

'Ha!' I held my phone up as some kind of further explanation. *Stop this, Isobel. Behave.* I popped it back in my bag to end further temptation.

I waited for ten more minutes and realised I had now been waiting long enough to complete a game of Imperial Yahtzee, which is longer than anyone should wait for an appointment. By the time the door opened, I had practically forgotten why I was there. *Your CAREER, Iz. This man has your career in his manicured hands.* (Yes, once a week; last time we met, someone was doing them for him, hand propped on a little pouffe by his desk. It was like being interviewed by a camp Henry VIII.)

'Darling, darling, darling, darling, darling.' He said the last three leaning wide and going for a double air-kiss.

I puckered my lips belatedly, smacking at the air in return. 'Randy,' I said, tripping over the word as in England this is just NOT A NAME.

He drew me back with two arms, assessing me. 'You look great. Open brackets. Have you had work? Close brackets. FOLLOW, you gorgeous creature, follow.' Spinning on one foot he marched ahead into his office, his suit trousers obscenely tight, forcing me to stare.

I felt exhausted already.

His office was a confusing mix of Bond Villain meets kitsch. A lot of gold discs in frames on the wall, a lot of china cats and a globe glittering with jewelled patches in one corner. His enormous high-backed armchair looked out onto the Avenue, glowing people buzzing past, cars at a standstill, air filled with the occasional toot of horns, shouts and chatter.

'So you're here,' he said, throwing himself into his chair and pointing to the seat opposite. 'Shoot, baby girl,' he said, two arms up on the rests of his chair, unfathomably white teeth flashing in his tanned face.

'Well,' I said, sitting abruptly, tucking a piece of hair behind my ear. 'Well, when we spoke on the phone last week you said we needed to talk urgently. And, well, I wondered if there'd been any news, over at the networks; did they like the latest stuff on my show reel?'

'You are divine, do you know that? Business, business you are.' Then he tilted his head to one side and held up his hands, making a square with his fingers to frame me in. 'You would suit being a redhead, you know. I don't have many on the books; a fiery redhead.' He waved both hands as if drawing a rainbow. He did this. He did this every time I saw him and I knew it was my job to bring him back.

'So did they?' I asked, slowly lowering my head, as if to look at him over imaginary glasses. Very school ma'am.

The trick worked and he shot one arm out to click on the mouse, staring at the screen.

'They did not, my darling, full stop.'

Oh no, I hated it when he spelled out punctuation.

'Look, baby girl, I did call you and I did need to see you and I think you know why.' His finely plucked eyebrows raised as I scrabbled about for a reason.

'This, sweetheart, this,' he said pointing to me and him. 'Between us, it's not going anywhere, is it?'

Where was this headed? What was he saying? This didn't seem good, the networks hadn't called. Was he...? Was he...?

'Look, you are super-cute with your little British ways and I totally thought they'd fall over their shiny little asses to sign you up but, baby girl, it's been an age now and we've been pushing you all over town and no one is biting.'

Oh no, this was bad.

'Are you? Do you think...?' I felt my usual fight drain away. He was telling me, clear as day, that he was dropping me. That it was over. I was agent-less, which in LA meant that I wouldn't be able to get anywhere in TV.

'I mean, you're dreamy, you know? In that sort of royal way you have with your brown hair and your accent. Hello, I would DIE for it, but it's never happened, has it? So we need to part ways.' He mimed the last two words with both hands separating and a pseudo-sad expression on his face.

'I...' I didn't know what to say; this was the last thing I'd imagined. I mean, Randy was peculiar, and pretty irritating, but he was a great agent. He knew EVERYONE in LA and at the start I had been his cute English pet, attending parties, meeting executives from production companies. Now that I thought about it though, that had all been a while ago. When had I really last heard from him? Randy had started one of his anecdotes about a party he had been to in Beverly Hills the week before.

'...So I said to him I wouldn't make out with a man in upturned jeans unless he were Michael J. Fox and it was 1994.'

I tried to raise a smile as he came to a stop.

'Look, baby, my girl, let's not make this hashtag awkward,'

he said, moving round from his chair to give me a hug. 'Randy is here for you if things happen, but for now...'

He let the sentence linger and returned to his desk, fiddling at his computer to show that this meeting was over. I felt my throat thicken and, choking a goodbye, I picked up my bag and walked out of the office, past Demi, down the stairs and out into the hustle and crowd-filled street. Staring up at the pedestrian crossing opposite, watching it turn to DON'T WALK. Like my career I thought, letting a tear fall now. Not going anywhere. *What the hell was I going to do?*

Wearily inserting the key into my apartment door, picking up a stray crisp packet that had blown onto the step and noticing mould in the corners of the downstairs flat windows, my phone buzzed.

Mel: 'See you tomorrow, BABE.'

Stewie: 'I think I have an infected toe. The nail is a funny colour.'

I couldn't face speaking to anyone now. I needed to have a night on my own. Not bothering to reply to either, I spent the next few hours mindlessly browsing the Internet looking at videos of people doing crap hair tutorials, cats doing funny shit and beauty pageants gone wrong.

None of these raised a smile and I found myself staring around the room as if looking for answers on the walls. How had I ended up here? What if my life had been different? What if I'd never come to LA. What if...? My finger hovered uncertainly in the Google search bar and then before I could stop myself I had done it. I had typed 12 letters. Andrew Parker.

Pressing 'Enter' I held my breath as numerous websites appeared in a long list. Scrolling quickly down them it became clear that one Andrew Parker was a pretty big deal in the world of espionage. Clicking on an article announcing his appointment as Head of MI5 my hands became clammy. He was Actual James Bond. This was unbelievable. My mouth lifted for the first time that night as the page loaded. A spy. A man of mystery. A...perfect stranger. The man staring back at me bore no resemblance to the Andrew Parker I knew.

The search for the real Andrew Parker seemed to rouse me and I clicked on some travel websites and looked up the cost of flights to England. I had saved money doing the promotional jobs, thought maybe I would need it if and when I went back to trying to get work as a presenter. It sat in my bank like a permanent reminder that I was giving up on my dreams. I thought back to today, the work, the hideous meeting with Randy. Everything seemed to become clear in my mind. I knew what I had to do.

Walking through to my bedroom, I opened up my bedside table, rummaging through it for what I was looking for. I'd kept it all these years – couldn't bring myself to throw it away. It was nestled in an old plastic jewellery box. Pulling it out, I pushed it onto my finger. It slipped on. The yellow pipe cleaner, faded with time but still the reminder of that day. I stared at it from every angle, memories flooding through me.

Still wearing it, I moved back through to my laptop and, without another thought, entered my details, chose a seat by the window, a meal choice and then emailed my mum.

I picked up my phone and texted Mel.

'Can you tell Scott I'm not coming into work tomorrow. I'm going to England. Bye.'

Mel: 'WTF? Tomorrow? Don't do it, I'll be the tomato this time.'

Darling,

Just received your email. How completely wonderful. We'll pick you up from Bodmin station. I'll tell your father he is not to go to boules and start beating the red carpet for your arrival. Today we saw a dolphin so maybe he heard the news too and is getting excited. Can't WAIT to see you, my darling, do you need money for the flight?

Mum x

Chapter 6

I started packing that night for a flight the next day. It was sad really how little I'd accumulated in the last couple of years, so most of my belongings were coming with me. Mel had been texting me all night with comforting things like: 'England will be cold', 'Andrew will be a jerk' and my personal favourite, 'WHAT IF CELINE AND I HAVE TO BECOME BFFs?'

Snuggling down in my bed I felt certainty wash over me (and also White Musk because I had lit a scented candle). In the half-light I could see the outline of my suitcase, sunhat perched on top, handbag by its side. I set my alarm, closed my eyes, sank into the pillow and had a totally dreamless sleep.

When I woke, I felt pumped for the day ahead, blocking out the day before and trying to shake the hopeless feeling that had followed me around these past few weeks. This would be a fabulous adventure and I would answer those questions that had been bugging me all these years. Cramming the last items in and zipping up the suitcase, I cast my eye over my bedroom. The muslin curtains were tied back, a strip of blue sky seen over the flats beyond. A horn blasted and I knew this was it. Everything looked tidy. I'd left a pile of books and a framed photo of me and Mum and Dad outside a fish restaurant in Fowey by the bed. I turned down the duvet, plumped the pillows and took a last look around before turning off the light. Rolling my suitcase out and down the stairs to the street below I stepped into the waiting cab.

Dear diary,

In school it was funny because we all stood on big plastic barrels and made a line of us and tried to roll the barrels along, all rolling them at the same speed. If we fell down it was okay because it was on the grass so no one was hurt. I didn't fall down. To get balanced, we held hands and I held Jenny's hand and Andrew's hand and it was good because when Jenny let go I was safe because Andrew didn't.

I x

Chapter 7

Bodmin

My mother was wearing a mustard-yellow shawl over a knee-length navy-blue dress and Wellington boots and was waving at every train carriage, just in case it contained me. I couldn't help grinning and waving back, despite the fact that she was looking in a completely different direction. As we came to a stop, I attempted to manoeuvre my suitcase off the rack and out onto the platform. A guy who looked like a surfer (early twenties, dreadlocked hair, filthy tan) managed to do much of the hard work for me. I followed behind him, daintily carrying my handbag in two hands to my chest like it contained something precious like the map to Atlantis/ massive diamonds.

'Thanks,' I said to him as he hauled it up the steps, over the platform and down the other side where my mother had already started squealing and running towards us. He looked mildly alarmed before loping off with an ''t's okay,' at me.

She smelled like Mum – her floral scent, mixed with ginger and chocolate. She held me at arm's length and then frowned.

'You look tired,' she concluded.

'Mum, I've just travelled halfway across the world – of course I'm tired.'

'Hmm...I'll take this,' she said, seizing the handle of my suitcase and taking my handbag from me.

'Mum,' I laughed, 'I can carry something.'

'To the Mum-mobile,' she called over her shoulder.

'Seriously?' I said, following in her wake.

'Ooh I am EXCITED you're home!' She threw me a massive smile over her shoulder and I returned it.

Me too.

She'd re-painted the kitchen cupboards a gorgeous duck-egg blue and had put up blue and white gingham curtains in the window. The room smelled familiar – of rosemary, lemons and home. Local pottery, blue and cream striped, lined the dresser which was crammed with scrawled postcards, old photographs of relations I couldn't remember ever meeting, me as a child, a couple of small tacky plastic toys and a dusty silver tankard of my dad's from his rowing days. Leaflets of local events, old newspapers and scribbled messages on a lined notepad had been hastily piled up to the side. The telephone was balanced precariously on top of the pile and the wall calendar hanging next to it all suggested that my parents had a far wilder social life in the back and beyond of Cornwall than I had had in LA.

'It's so good to have you home, darling. Your father is out doing a coastal walk with Bob who lost his wife last year. But he is under strict instructions to be home by 4 o'clock. We're having cheese scones so I imagine he will be right on time.'

'And I'm home after almost two years,' I reminded her.

'True, true, darling, but the cheese scones will definitely still play a part. They have Gruyère in!'

True to his promise, my father appeared with five minutes to spare and gave me a long, warm hug and told me he'd missed me. Both these events were pretty High Emotion coming from my lovely gentle dad and seeing him there – in his faded corduroys smelling of salt and fresh air, it made tears sting the back of my throat and I coughed and looked away.

The cheese scones were so good we all had three and I sat, one hand on my stomach, marvelling at how my parents stayed slim. My limbs unfurled and my thoughts slowed down as I looked between both my parents. Mum then jumped up to show me a new infrared thermometer which had cost about a hundred pounds that she used to measure fudge and then my dad gave her a look and the air became fraught with an atmosphere, expectant. Both sets of eyes swivelled over to stare at me intently. I coughed and dabbed at a cheese scone crumb on my lip.

'So, darling,' my mother said, reaching out a hand, 'why this sudden appearance?'

'Oh, um...' I didn't feel like sharing my plan, realising I didn't really know how to phrase things just yet. It all seemed rather extreme and I didn't want the atmosphere to shift and for them to judge me. I didn't want to tell them yet about my agent dropping me, about LA, about me being an uber Bitch to Stewie. I wasn't ready yet to share all that stuff. 'I just missed home,' I said, biting into a fourth cheese scone and nearly groaning.

'Nothing to, nothing to tell us?' Mum said with an attempt at a nonchalant shrug.

'Um...not especially,' I said, wondering why Dad was avoiding my eyes.

'No news, no...little surprises,' she continued, leaning forward, her necklace dangling precariously close to her mug of tea. I could see all the whites round her eyes now.

'Nope!' I laughed.

Her shoulders lowered. 'So you're not pregnant?'

It was a moment before the words sunk in. 'Pregnant? No, why would I be...? Why would you...?'

She waved a hand. 'We would have supported you whatever, darling.'

'Well that is a comforting thought,' I said, 'but no, not pregnant and there is no big mystery.'

My dad reached for another scone. 'I told you, Jilly. Now who wants some Battenberg?'

Hours later, tucked under the eaves in my attic bedroom staring at the exposed beams in a white ceiling, I wondered whether I had been daft to come. Could I really start gallivanting across the country in search of him? How would this plan sound? 'Oh, parents, I came home to chase a man I saw in the background of the news item Dad did so that I can meet him, marry him and have all the babies.'

Then I thought of his face on the television and the sure knowledge that I had finally found him after all these years of wondering about him and I knew I was so close. I had to try, I had to look. What was the worst that could happen? I stretched up and turned off the lamp by my bed, plunging the room into darkness. Through the thin strip of curtain I could just make out an enormous bright moon in the sky, its reflection bouncing off the ocean below making the water sparkle with promise.

Chapter 8

Polzeath

'I am not speaking to you,' said Mel after I answered Mel's phone call.

'I think we both know that's a lie,' I said, smiling as I sat in the window seat of my parents' kitchen watching a seagull shit on top of our car.

'Look, this has already cost me a hundred dollars so I am really only ringing to say COME BACK, I MISS YOU, WHY DID YOU LEAVE MEEEEE!'

I held the phone away from my ear. 'MEL, STOP SHOUTING AT ME!' I shouted.

Dad ran into the kitchen, a startled look on his face, holding the bellows in one hand as if about to brain an intruder.

'Sorry, Dad,' I said covering the phone with my hand. 'Phone call.'

'Ah,' he said, stumbling out, relief palpable.

'Mel, are you still there?' I asked.

'Er...yes, ABANDONNER.'

'Okay, I am going to hang up now and we will Skype later, okay?'

'Not okay. I only have Celine to talk to and I swear if she tells me any more about her new superfood powder diet, I am going to cut off all her hair and wear it as a CLOAK.'

'Okay, well that seems psychotic, so maybe you need to go and find someone else to talk to.'

'I did find someone, I found you. And today we were superheroes. You would have liked this one. We wore catsuits and gave out doughnuts and all the fat people followed us around.'

'Er...massive sad face that I missed that,' I said, leaning my head back and watching the ocean shift from grey to dark navy as a cloud passed over it.

'Look, can you just make sure you do this quickly, find the Andrew dude, make him love you and then come back pronto. Deal?'

'You make it sound so easy,' I said, fiddling with a cushion with a smiling squirrel on it. *God, whose cushion was this? It was hideous.*

'Well get to it, woman, you don't sound like you are getting to it.'

'I totally am,' I said, wondering whether to have a crumpet or a teacake.

'Right, this phone call has officially made me re-mortgage my flat so...'

'You don't own your flat, Mel.'

'OH RUIN EVERYTHING,' she wailed.

'Right, unbalanced woman, I am going and will Skype my progress soon, or email, or communicate somehow with you for free, okay?'

'Okay, oh man, Celine is on the other line, she probably wants to tell me what I did wrong today. She is like Angry Barbie. I might kill her. Bye, babe.'

'I'm not a...'

She'd hung up.

Dad was in his faded armchair in the sitting room, a fire flickering in the grate as he read the newspaper through half-moon glasses, a half-empty cafetière on the table beside him.

'Where's Mum?' I asked, looking around the living room as if she might suddenly appear from inside the drink's cabinet: 'Ta da!'

'Communing with nature, I fear,' he said, pointing to the window where I could see into the bay beside our house and my mother in a swimming costume plunging into a rock pool surrounded by normal people wearing wetsuits.

'Crikey,' I said, shivering at the thought of the icy cold water, even in July. 'It's England. Is she aware?'

'Quite and perhaps not are your answers.'

I flopped onto the sofa opposite. Dad peered at me over his newspaper. 'Who were you shouting at in the kitchen?'

I batted the question away with a hand. 'Best friend.'

'Right.'

Getting out my Kindle, feet up on a worn leather pouffe, there was no need for further talk as we sat in perfect companionable silence, glancing at each other every now and again with contented smiles.

Twenty minutes later, Mum appeared in the doorway to trash the calm. Wrapped in a hot-pink towel, she rubbed at her wet hair.

'Darling, you're up. I was about to come into your bedroom and drag you out.'

'How was the water?'

'Bracing but brilliant,' she said, calling over her shoulder. 'I just need to blow dry my nipples back to normal.' I could see my dad's cheeks glowing red as we both pretended we hadn't heard.

Putting down the Kindle and picking up a notepad, I put my feet up on the worn pouffe and nestled into the hundreds of cushions. Doodling faces and stars, I started to form a plan in my mind. I had come all the way here and Mel was right, I had to find this dude. I would head to where they had filmed Dad and go from there. It looked like a small sort of place; he'd probably be easy to find. Not even a village, maybe, a hamlet. How many people live in an English hamlet? Twelve? Fourteen? It couldn't be many.

'So where did they film you for that car piece?' I asked, smoothing my hand over the sofa.

Dad looked up, eyes round, surprised by my sudden

interest perhaps. 'Oh, um, a little village near Exeter, I forget exactly where,' he said.

'Nice place?' I enquired.

He put down his newspaper. 'Nice enough. Good fish and chips in the pub,' he added with a nod.

'Always important,' I said and then, with a quick swallow, 'so I was thinking of going there. To the village, I mean, to um...see it for myself so if you could think really hard...'

'The car's been sold now, Iz, did your mother not tell you? You can't see it there.'

'No, no, not to see the car, just to, get a feel for the place, where history was made so to speak. Ha, ha,' I trailed away.

'Well we drove through a lot of places that day and...'

'Hmm...' I pondered his previous statement and then, sitting bolt upright, realised how I could find out.

'Coffee?' I asked, jumping up and making Dad twitch in his chair. Rushing back to the kitchen, hearing his befuddled 'Okay then', I pulled my laptop from its case, turned it on, sat at the table and started tapping out an email.

Hello people at ITV,

On a news programme for ITV West on 13th July of this year you ran a segment on the West's Best Vintage Cars (14 mins and 38 seconds in from start). You interviewed a man – Mr Graves – about his car in a village. I am trying to find out what village this was near Exeter, with a pub that does excellent fish and chips. Please could you advise?

Best wishes,

Isobel Graves

Then I put on the kettle, waited for the water to boil and pressed 'Refresh' seven times. No email back. Gah. IT'S OVER. MY SEARCH IS OVER. Ooh, ASOS sale.

Returning to the sitting room and handing Dad a coffee, I jumped as Mum bustled in after me, dressed in turquoise leggings and a large white cotton shirt, a neckscarf round her hair.

'Out we go, darling, you must come with me, I am in the mood to greet the day,' she said, planting a kiss on Dad's cheek and taking my hand.

I looked at my half finished coffee and laptop. 'Oh, I...'

'Come on, we're going to go and shout at the sea. You'll feel completely marvellous when you're done.'

'Well I feel pretty marvellous already really.'

Dad was sniggering into his paper.

'Nonsense. There is honestly nothing like it and you've come all this way.'

I threw my hands up in the air, relenting. 'Okay, okay, I'm coming. Am I dressed appropriately for shouting at the sea?'

She eyed up my old university tracksuit bottoms and pale-blue polo shirt. 'Perfectly.'

She strode out of the conservatory door, through the back garden and out into the field beyond. A startled sheep bleated furiously as she scampered away and Mum told me to face towards the ocean and assume the pose.

'Follow my lead, darling,' she called over one shoulder as she lifted both her hands in the air and exhaled slowly out.

Feeling ridiculous, I did the same.

'Right, now, after me we are going to take in a huge breath and scream loudly, "Good Morning, World." It's exhilarating. Ready?'

And, without waiting for a response, she began, 'GOOOOOOOOOD MOOOOORRRRNNIIING, WOOOOORRRL... Darling—' She stopped abruptly. 'You're not joining in. You need to join in.'

'Sorry, can we start again?'

We did the whole breathing out slowly thing and the arm lifting and I went to open my mouth as she screamed, 'GOOOOOOOOOOOD MOOOOORRRRRNNNN—' She looked over her shoulder. 'Come on.'

I scratched my elbow. 'Mum, I feel like a jerk.'

'Prat, darling, jerk is so American. You feel like a prat.' She turned back to face the ocean – a vast sheet of grey, squalls of white flashing intermittently over the surface, low, angry clouds in the distance threatening to spill their load all over north Cornwall. The morning sun quit trying to break through the bank hours ago and was probably off having a cuppa somewhere warm.

'And you won't if you join in. You'll love it.'

I looked out and said, 'Okay, I'm ready, Ma.'

'After three,' she directed. 'One, two, three – GOOOOD. MOOOORRRRNNIIING, WORRRRLLLD.'

I got to the 'wor' bit of world and then collapsed laughing. Scooping up the hoody at my feet, I went and kissed her on the cheek. 'I'm off for a walk, not sure this is quite up my street.'

'Well you tried that time, darling, that's all I can ask for,' she said, eyes closed, breathing in heavily. 'Just heaven,' she said to no one in particular.

I smiled and walked away, down a well-worn path that ran along the side of the house that led to a gate in a stone arch. Pushing it open and avoiding a verge of stinging nettles leaning over the path, I felt a little flutter inside at being home, at seeing my parents again, the wonderfully familiar landscape I conjured up whenever I thought of England. The stones under my feet soon gave way to tufts of yellowed grass and weeds and I tramped down to the path before heading across the top of Baby Bay.

It was mid-morning but hardly anyone was around. Across the beach I could make out a couple of figures: a woman gingerly picking her way over the rocks, a man in a Barbour throwing a ball at a dog which was doing excited spins in the shallows, water spraying up as he streaked off. A lone surfer was lying on his board a few waves out, waiting for a swell to pick him up. The air smelled of seaweed and seemed to fill my head. LA and my life there seemed a million miles away.

Picking my way down the path, I loped around the bay, paddling in the shallows and looking back at the house perched above the rocks. I headed back towards it.

Padding through to the kitchen, the sand still in between my toes, I flicked the kettle on. My mobile started ringing in my pocket and I frowned when I saw 'Stewie' on the screen.

'Hello,' I answered.

'Where are you? I'm at the flat,' he asked after a second's delay.

'Oh I'm not at the flat, I'm um, I'm in England,' I said.

'You're WHERE?' he squawked. I didn't know his voice could go that high. It made me start giggling and he sat on the other end in stony silence as I then apologised repeatedly.

'England,' I repeated as the kettle began to bubble in earnest.

Balls, had I really not told him I was leaving the country? I felt a fleeting moment of guilt picturing him staring at my empty doorstep, calling through the letterbox and then scratching his head and looking at his mobile phone.

'It's 3 a.m.,' he said.

'Well that's not actually true here,' I pointed out, feeling a bubble of laughter again. This was bad, poor Stewie.

'But I brought you a bagel, and where am I going to sleep?' he whined. I could hear the rustle of a bag in the background.

'Oh well, that was nice of you. Um...I'm sorry, I sort of forgot everything in the rush really. Can you stay at yours?' I said.

'I'll have to pay for a cab.'

'Yes that will have to happen,' I said, looking out of the window at the blurred line of the horizon.

'Did someone die? Has your mom died?' he asked.

'What? Er...no, why would you think that?'

'Well why else would you suddenly leave for England? Are you in actual England, England the country not like, New England?'

'No, well it was a rushed decision and I just wanted to

come home and, yes England, England.'

'Well, thanks for telling me,' he sniffed.

'Look, Stewie, this isn't ideal but maybe we need to talk,' I said, gripping the phone under my chin as I reached up to get the teabags.

'We are tal...Oh my god, are you breaking up with me from England at 3 a.m.?'

'Well it's not 3 a.m. here and the thing is, we really are different people and well...'

'This is ridiculous.'

'No, listen, I think you'll see this is the right thing for both of us, I mean, our hearts haven't really been in it recently have they and...'

'La, la, la, la not happening,' he chanted down the phone.

'Er...'

I reached for the kettle as he carried on chanting. I tried to get a word in. How the hell do you dump a man who blocks you out with 'Las'? Was he waking up my neighbours?

'Stewie, STEWIE!' I shouted.

Dad burst into the room, panting lightly, an empty mug raised in his hand, hair dishevelled.

I pointed at the phone, apologetically whispering 'Sorry'.

He sloped off again, hand on his chest.

'Stewie,' I breathed out slowly. 'Listen, I think you know things haven't been great between us recently. You like things and I like um...other things.' *Eloquent, Isobel, really eloquent.*

'But it were good,' he protested.

'It were not good, I mean, it wasn't good, well it wasn't bad, Stewie, it just wasn't *right*, you know?'

There was a long silence on the other end and I thought I had lost him in a tunnel or something. 'Stewie?'

'I'll give you some time to think about it,' he said.

'I don't need ti—'

'Then we'll talk.' And with that he hung up and I was left staring at my mobile.

Well that went well.

Dragging a chair over to the Aga in the kitchen, I curled myself into it, mug of tea warming both hands. My brain full of Stewie and our relationship. I wondered why it had taken me so long to say anything to him. Maybe it was being away from LA and my life there that allowed me to realise what was really important. I didn't miss any of it, well, I missed Mel and Dex, but I felt so hemmed in there in the miniscule box flat and the never-ending jobs to nowhere. It felt good to be here. I should have talked to Stewie months ago. We had never really got off the ground – seeing each other too sporadically – but Stewie had been nice to me and recently I had prickled at everything. It wasn't fair; he needed someone who would really appreciate him. I vowed to call him back, to sort things out.

I had come this way to make a change, to find Andrew Parker. I needed to do that now, make that a reality. It would surely help me to see him, to see what kind of life I might have had if I'd stayed in England. I pulled over the laptop and logged back onto my email muttering as I waited for it to load. 'Come on, come on, come on.' Hooray! A reply! Grinning, I pressed to open it and waited to see the information I needed.

Dear Ms Graves,

Thank you for your email. ITV West is pleased that you enjoyed the news programme on 13th July, but is sadly unable to assist you in this matter. We know there are plenty of villages near Exeter that do excellent fish and chips so we hope this is some consolation.

Yours sincerely,

Linda Raddick

Dear Ms Raddick,

It wasn't the fish and chips I needed – I am, in fact, desperately seeking someone. We were torn apart twenty years ago and I am searching for him now. He was in the village on the news item and I need to know where this village is so I can try to find him, find my way back to him.

Izzy

Dear Ms Graves,

Thank you for your interest in ITV West. I am afraid I have been unable to track down the name of this village and wish you all the best in your search.

Yours sincerely,

Linda Raddick

Look, Linda, woman to woman, I need the name of this village. I have flown from LA to find this man. LA is a long way to fly from and I need you to help me with this last part. You are holding the final piece in my jigsaw, Linda, it literally all rests on you. Please, Linda, have you ever known true love? Have you ever looked across at a man (or woman, Linda, we don't know each other!) and felt truly happy? Because I know I might be able to find that kind of love, that kind of breathless, crazy love if only you were able to find out where he was, which village they were in. Please, Linda, you are my last hope. If you care a jot for me (we're basically pen pals), you should act.

With many thanks,

Izzy x

Dear Ms Graves,

Fortunately, something has come to light. This particular news item was filmed in the village of Kenley. Thank you for your interest in the show! There is no need for further communication on this matter.

Linda Raddick

YES, LINDA, YES! I was punching the air over the laptop when her reply came through. Mum had arrived in the kitchen to whip up dinner and joined me in a dance that involved a lot of hip waggling and yodelling. Dad had peeked a head round the door and legged it back to the safety of his sitting room.

'Why are we yodelling, darling?' she panted.

I opened my mouth to reply and realised it was too soon to tell her. What if I didn't find him? What if she tried to dissuade me?

'It's twenty per cent off Monsoon this week.'

'Oh well, that is something to celebrate,' Mum said popping a bottle of Prosecco. 'To Monsoon,' she cried, 'and their fabulous jersey dresses in all colours.'

'Hear, hear,' I agreed, clinking glasses with her and feeling the sharp bubbly loveliness on my tongue. Hugging my secret close to myself, I felt warm all over.

Dinner was sea bream with a hollandaise sauce and Dad walked in tentatively, looking relieved not to have to yodel as he went to unload the dishwasher and lay the table. I was sitting cradling my head in my hands looking dreamily at the screen of my laptop thinking of Linda and Kenley.

Mum looked up from stirring something. 'Well, darlings, what is new with the world?'

'Nothing.'

'I finished the crossword,' said Dad.

'Fabulous. Finished it, finished it or cheated a little by making up an imaginary word in one of the lines to make everything fit?' she asked.

Dad opened a bottle of wine. 'The latter,' he said, hanging his head.

Mum came and kissed him on the cheek. 'One day, one day you will actually finish it.'

Dad sat down and poured the drinks. I closed my laptop and moved it to the window seat.

'And you, darling?' Mum asked, pouring the sauce over my fish, her chair squeaking on the tiled floor as she sat.

'Isobel was shouting at someone on the phone again,' Dad said, already munching.

'Tittle-tattle,' I said, trying to kick him in the shins and missing.

He smiled at me slowly, his bushy eyebrows wiggling in amusement.

'Who were you shouting at?' asked Mum.

'Stewie,' I sighed, my happy bubble bursting for a moment as I thought back to the phone call.

'And who is Stewie?' she asked, pointing her fork at me.

'Boyfriend. Well, ex-boyfriend. Well I don't know...'

How had I never told them about Stewie? Wouldn't I have told them about him if I had been really into him? I knew the answer to that and felt guilty; my parents waiting politely to eat their food, clearly not wanting me to feel worse. I needed to tell them about everything, try to get them to help me get my thoughts in order. *What was I doing scarpering around the place instead of just thinking things through...?*

'Iz,' my mum said in a very gentle voice. 'Don't worry about this Stewie.'

'Oh I'm not,' I said, smiling at her.

'Well that is a relief, darling – I'm not going to lie. I mean it is simply NOT a grown man's name, it is a baby food, so don't think more on it,' she said, patting my hand and taking her first mouthful. 'Oh I am an actual genius,' she announced, holding a finger to her lips. 'An actual genius.'

Chapter 9

Devon

It was a scorching day, bright with possibility, and I leaped out of my narrow single bed in my joie de vivre, forgetting the eaves above my head so I now had joie de buggery hell that hurt. Rubbing at the lump emerging, eyes watering, I thrust the curtains back. The sun light burst in and, as I opened the window, the sound of seagulls outside filled the room. The smell of Dad's famous fry-up wafted through my room and I cast about for an appropriate outfit to mark this important first day – the real start of this adventure. Today I would find answers, well Andrew Parker, and then, hopefully, answers.

The outfit I selected that seemed to best reflect this mood was a cut-off pair of denim dungarees over a coral vest top.

Slapping on some pink lip gloss and a flick of eyeliner, I was raring to go. Shovelling breakfast into my mouth as my mother moved round the kitchen humming along to Holst's 'The Planets' (Mars = terrifying), I felt a gnawing excitement in my belly. This must have been the feeling that Ranulph Fiennes had on exploring the Antarctica or that other man before he hiked up Everest. Although neither will have been as well dressed.

Backing Mum's comedy Smart car out of the drive (Dad: 'It's not a car it's a toy'), I received a double thumbs-up from her in the kitchen window. Bumping over the grassy driveway and reversing into the little lane, I waited as a teenage girl on a horse trotted by, plaits flying as she bounced past. Then I was off, window down, music blaring. Chris de Burgh had always been a favourite of my mother and now, as I listened to him singing about his 'Lady in Red', I realised with a soaring heart that by the end of the day I could be Andrew's 'Lady in Shit-hot Denim'.

What did I remember of Andrew Parker? I pictured a grinning boy, upside down in one of the school trees, celebrating a victory at conkers with a lap of the playground, sharing a Walkman on the pier, his laughing face on the day when we'd got Jenny and Lyndon stuck in a plastic barrel because we'd dared them to see if two people could fit at the same time (transpires that was a no), his pleasure over 'Zoom' ice lollies: 'It's like the banana bit zooms me to heaven.' We had spent so much time together and then, of course, we had got married. How had the little boy morphed from childhood? What would his interests be now? I remember his personality lifting a room/treehouse; he was someone everyone liked, easy, and I hoped I would be able to get to know him all over again. He had been the one to get away and now I was tracking him down again.

I pressed down on the gas and sailed along the A30, accelerating past dozens of caravans and cars loaded up with bicycles and surfboards going the other way. When I finally turned off the M5 into a little hamlet just south of Exeter, I was a little wearier. The adrenaline had worn off and Chris de Burgh had sung all his songs twice now. I had almost started wishing his lady could have worn another colour. I was in need of a coffee.

The village of Kenley seemed to emerge from a winding road of overgrown hedgerows crammed with blackberries, thistles and dotted dandelion heads. The black faded letters on the white sign stood on poles hidden by the long grass and there seemed to be honeysuckle cottages with neat low stone walls in every direction. Explosions of colour – fuchsias, of oranges and blues – were displayed in every border and one man was bent over plucking up weeds in his gloved hand. I moved past, to the centre of the village: a triangle with a white-chained loop around the edge, a couple of large oak trees providing some shade from the day. A pub sat along the length of one side of the common, signposted 'The Bell', a rambling thatched cottage with faded pink roses climbing up its walls. A small car park just off the road seemed empty and I pulled into a spot.

Opening the door and unravelling myself from the tiny vehicle, I was struck by the strength of the noon sun beating down on me. Reaching for my bag, I thought I should probably seize the day and set off for a walk around the green to find the spot Dad had spoken from. The Bell had been in the top left of the screen, so I moved across the triangle and over the common heading for a row of houses, all white paint, timber beams and large wooden doors. The air smelled of bonfire smoke and sunshine and I pictured the occupants of the village beyond all pottering around their squares of lawn, pruning and planting whilst drinking jugs of elderflower juice served on a tray with a picture of some chickens.

Turning my back to the houses, I looked at the pub and tried to align myself with where my dad had stood, looking to my right to see where Andrew might have been. A couple of stone steps led to a green painted door surrounded by a trellis of honeysuckle. A sign to one side announced the house was in fact the local post office and my heart skipped as I recognised it from the TV. I pictured Andrew walking up the stone steps, pushing the green door open. I rushed quickly over to it, heart skipping as I saw the 'Open' sign on the windowsill inside. Pushing open the door, I heard a bell and was struck by the smell of polish, paper and flowers. A small woman on a stool put down the book she was reading and stood up behind the counter.

'Hello,' I said, nodding at her.

'Hello, dear,' she said, waiting expectantly as I stepped inside the store. The room itself was tiny, lined with newspapers, magazines and a corkboard on which were pinned higgledy-piggeldy flash cards with handwritten adverts; cleaning services, gardening, babysitting and prams and other paraphernalia being sold for £30 ONO. There were a set of shelves in the middle with homemade marmalade, honey, rows of gorgeous-looking shortbreads and cookies. I picked up some local honey – Dad would love it – and moved over to the counter.

The woman tore off a brown paper bag from a pile of them and placed the honey inside. Her hands were skeletal, the veins popping out, bright blue. Her eyes were the same colour and she smiled as she tapped the amount into her till.

'That's two ninety-nine,' she said.

I handed her a fiver. She handed me the change. This was my cue to leave. I remained standing.

'Anything else I can get you?' she asked, clearly sensing I had something else in mind.

I wondered how I was going to gear up to it. Without thinking a great deal about it, I simply blurted out: 'I'm looking for a man.'

'Aren't we all, dear,' she replied.

I felt myself growing hot and laughed. 'No, not just, well you see, a specific man. I think he came here, to your shop, last Wednesday, 13 July around 14.27, I mean to be precise about it.'

'That does seem precise, yes,' she said, eyes crinkling kindly.

'Well he didn't stay long, but I thought perhaps you might remember him, that he might live round here.'

'Well what does he look like, my love, and then I might be able to help you?'

'He was tallish, with sort of curling blondy-brown hair and he had chinos on – or cords – I'm not sure and they were brownish and he had a red jumper on. I thought it made him look very dapper,' I trailed off as the woman stood looking at me.

'Well now,' she said, finger to one lip. Catalogue pose for thinking. 'Well,' she repeated.

I waited, practically falling over the counter in my enthusiasm, certain that she would know him and be able to point me in the right direction.

'Tallish, you say.'

'Hmm, hmm.' I nodded.

'Blond, with curls,' she added.

'Yes, well not blond, blond but dark blond and not so much curly as wavy, very matinee idol.'

'Matinee,' she repeated.

Another pause; her mouth moved into tight line that puckered her skin.

'I'm afraid he doesn't ring a bell, my love,' she said.

I felt like she'd reached across the counter with a pin and pushed it into my skin. I physically deflated in front of her, shoulders down, arms limp at my sides.

'Oh.'

I couldn't believe it, she couldn't remember him. Couldn't recall him at all. And he had definitely been in this very room, less than a week before. Nothing.

She looked up at me. 'I'm sorry, my love,' she said.

I went to apologise for wasting her time, went to glance at the clock over her head, work out the time it would take me to get home, and then saw it.

Black, in the corner of the room, screwed into the wall. A small black CCTV camera.

'Does that work?' I asked, pointing towards it.

She followed the line of my finger, not quite with me.

'Oh.' She took a reverential step backwards. 'My son made me put it in; I didn't want it but he'd read something in the papers and said I should get it for protection,' she explained.

'So do you keep the discs?' I asked.

'Only a few days' worth, but...' Realisation seemed to dawn and she stopped. 'When did you say he was in here?'

She called her son and told him he was to get over there right this minute from his workplace. I looked aghast at this and then realised he worked in The Bell as a chef. It took him all of about two minutes. He appeared, complete with chef's hat, huffing lightly, wondering why he had been summoned in such an urgent way.

'Darren, this young lady needs our assistance,' Maureen announced. Maureen had introduced herself while we were waiting. She lifted up one-third of the counter and ushered us both through.

I gave him an apologetic smile and a half-wave. 'Hello.' My voice sounded loud in the small space.

He looked at me, eyes narrowed; he had flour on one cheek.

I let his mother explain. He nodded and beckoned me over to a machine that looked not dissimilar to my DVD player.

'Right then...' Plucking a disc out, he slotted another in and pressed 'Play'. The date in digital numbers in the corner of the screen showed it was from yesterday, a grainy image of the empty shop inside. He took it out and tried again.

'Wednesday last week, we need Wednesday last week.' I inhaled sharply, making him jump. 'Sorry, sorry, just excited,' I sputtered, eyes wide as he reached for the next disc.

WEDNESDAY! The disc was Wednesday.

'It was 14.27 p.m. I said, er, give or take,' I added when Darren looked at me.

'Odd, isn't she?' Maureen said, smiling at him like I wasn't there. She'd found some giant glasses from somewhere and her blue eyes looked enormous behind the thick lenses.

Darren forwarded the disc, an hour, two, my eyes scanned the screen, people came in, sped up, grabbed things from shelves, moved forward, hands going everywhere, slapping money on the counter and looking like a Benny Hill sketch.

'Wait, stop, HALT!' I shouted when the first two failed. I believe HALT had the right amount of authority as Darren instantly reached to pause it.

'Rewind that bit,' I said, feeling my cheeks get hot (brought on no doubt by the use of 'Halt'). 'Um...please.'

The man emerged, backwards, turned to the counter, put the items back and left again.

'Play, play,' I urged.

The scene slowed down and in walked the man of my description, stooping a little in the doorway (tallish), the grey screen unable to show his hair colour or eye colour.

'That's him,' came the voice on my left. Maureen was peering through her glasses, nose tilted in the air as she followed his movements.

I turned to her. 'So do you recognise him?' I asked.

She shuffled towards the screen; Darren had frozen it in place so Andrew stood, hand held out, unseeing ahead. She narrowed her eyes, sucked in her breath and finally said, 'No.'

All the air whooshed out of my lungs and I dropped my head. 'Oh.'

'What's he buying?' she asked. 'That could be your clue, my love.'

I leaned forward. 'Newspaper, Yorkie, lottery ticket.'

'Yorkie's a chocolate bar for men,' she nodded reassuringly.

'But I know he's a man, it doesn't tell me anything.'

'Newspaper suggests he's the educated sort,' she continued.

So this manly, educated, tall man was Andrew – but how was I meant to find him?

Darren was quiet by my side, and then he put a hand on my shoulder, 'I think he was in the pub that day,' he said.

I spun around. 'Really?'

'I think so.' He nodded. 'He ate there, caused a fuss over a steak and kidney pie from what I remember.'

'Well I'm sure he would have had good reason,' I said, bristling in defence of him already.

'What are you saying about our pies?'

'Now, now, you two, don't lose focus,' Maureen said.

'Yes, sorry,' I said, keen not to lose my one lead. I looked at him. 'Do you think. Well, could we see if anyone remembers anything?' I asked.

'We'll go and see Paul.'

This event was deemed so important by Maureen that she insisted on locking up the post office and marching over to the pub with us. So we followed, like cygnets after the mama duck, as she led us over the green and into the back entrance of the pub. The kitchen windows were steamed up and there was a sound of metal clanging and water bubbling. An enormous man, ample rolls of flesh rippling down him, his chin sticking out like a small ping-pong ball jutting out of his bearded face, emerged from a cloud of steam. He was wearing a similar striped apron and had a perplexed expression on his face – no doubt due to the sudden invasion of his kitchen by two eager women and his chef.

'Paul, do you remember last week that gentleman who had a problem with the steak and kidney pie?'

Paul's eyes narrowed, perhaps assuming me to be from the Council of Pie Complaints board, and he was slow to respond. 'P'rhaps.' The one word was drawn out in a thick West Country accent.

'You do remember!' I jumped up and down like a child on Christmas morning.

'Right,' Darren said. 'Well this is...' He turned to me.

'Isobel Graves,' I dived in, adding my surname in case that would help give me more gravitas.

'Isobel Graves and she wants to track him down. I thought we might have his details around. Didn't he stay the night?'

Oh, I thought, head dropping a fraction, if he stayed the night he couldn't be local. I had been picturing him in the kitchen of one of the cottages that lined the green, puffing over an Aga as he put together his dinner for one, me bursting in, him startled (until he saw who it was), inviting me to stay, drawing across a gingham curtain, pouring a wine...This would not be possible if he had stayed the night.

'He did not, but he did write me an email. First one we had in over four months too.'

'An email!' I gushed like he had just unveiled some incredible new invention.

'Yar.'

I felt Maureen bristle with excitement beside me, muttering, 'Oh my,' under her breath.

'Could you, if it's not much trouble, could you show me?' I asked, pleading eyes trained on him.

Perhaps sensing the desperation, he sighed and walked through a door to a side room. 'Wai' there.'

I waited, grimacing at Darren and Maureen as the second hand on the kitchen clock dragged round, each tick loud, despite the bustle of the kitchen.

Paul emerged from the office holding a sheet of paper in his hand. 'Printed it, didn't I.'

I sucked in all my breath as Paul came round to show me it. He was sneering at the email, distaste hardening his features.

To whom it may concern,

I recently ate the 'Award-Winning' Steak and Kidney Pie in your establishment. It was advertised in the menu as containing the finest cuts of British beef but, as I pointed out to your barman, my cuts were mostly fatty gristle. I would like to know which prize you entered where...

'Pompous...'

I wasn't tuning into the mutterings around me. I was too busy looking at the bottom of the sheet, underneath where Andrew had signed off. At the email signature where it said in italics: 'Andrew Parker, teacher of Geography, Somerset House'.

Squee.

Got him.

Dear diary,

Mum dressed me us up as a pirate today and said that we were going to the beach to build a castle and also find treasure with our spades. It was fun because she invited friends from school too and I played with them all but I most liked playing with them in this order:

1. Andrew because he kept being a parrot and it made us all laugh and he gave me his chocolate gold.
2. Lyndon because he let me wear his eye patch.
3. Annie because she helped me make the moat really good.
4. Jenny

At the bottom is Jenny but she was still quite fun.

I x

Chapter 10

Helford

I was off to see Moregran. It had been nearly two years and aside from the regular postcards postmarked 'Helford', there had been no other contact. Moregran was so named because of me. On meeting a second 'Gran' in a two-week period, I had turned to Mum and asked, 'More Gran?' and the name had stuck. Moregran lived in a bungalow in a tiny road in Helford, a stream flowing past the bottom of her garden. She owned a shocking collection of garden ornaments so ugly that her neighbours had been forced to plant very tall hedges to block them out. There was the usual array of sleeping cats and frogs on lily pads, but one of my favourites was a large rat seeming to emerge out of the earth, his body cut off and his little rat hands pressed to the ground. He had featured in many a nightmare of 1993.

She was sitting, knitting furiously, by the window in the front room as I turned into the narrow driveway. The sound of the gravel made her look up and her face broke into the most melting smile. Switching the ignition off, I couldn't wait to get out and give her a massive hug. I had missed her – her easy humour, kind words and non-judgemental ways. Never once had she told me to do anything, scolded me if she felt I was in the wrong, she just seemed keen to hear all about the goings-on in my life. She also made the world's greatest oatmeal and raisin cookies and, as I walked up the path and she opened the door to me, the familiar smell fresh from the oven hit my nostrils.

'Moregran,' I said, giving her a hug. She was a little shorter than me and her bobbed grey hair smelled of rosewater and Earl Grey tea.

'I've put the kettle on,' she said as way of greeting, 'and I thought you might like to stretch your legs.'

'Perfect,' I said, not bothering to take off my jacket but following her through to the kitchen, glancing briefly into the living room.

Moregran had taken her interest in ornaments to another extreme in there and over the fireplace there was an entire collection of porcelain ducklings following their mother and a family of strangely blue glass owls on a sideboard.

'I'll pop it in flasks. You still like your tea sweet, don't you?' she asked, heaped spoonful hovering.

I nodded and watched her stir it in, closing up the flask and handing it to me.

'Cookies are in the silver foil,' she said, patting what I now saw was a bumbag around her waist.

'Where did you get that?' I asked, pointing at it and realising I hadn't seen one since 1988.

'The fanny pack?'

If I had sipped the tea, I would have spat it.

'The, er, bumbag.'

'The Internet, an American company. I needed something to keep my mincemeat cake in,' she said matter of factly.

'Who doesn't,' I agreed, following her out of the kitchen giggling.

'Get on,' she smiled, rolling her eyes.

We walked along the footpath at the back of her house and wound our way around the village, over the bridge, a sharp intake of breath on seeing the still blue of the Helford River beyond, boats idle in the water, their reflections quivering in the ripples. Turned a corner and dove into the wild crop of trees, skirted our way down past hedges filled with stinging nettles, sporadic clusters of tiny orange flowers and ivy that clambered over tree trunks, suffocating branches. A shady, winding path led down to a view over Frenchman's Creek. We both stopped to stare at it as Moregran summed it up, 'It never gets old, this view.'

Finding a bench in memory of 'Jack who loved to sit by the creek next to Mary' surrounded by long grass quivering in a light breeze, we sat side by side watching a kite floating on the breeze scanning the trees ahead, a man hauling a canoe to the edge of the muddy water and I felt a calm wash over me as I drank the sweet tea and smelled damp earth and garlic. Moregran hadn't fallen for my first explanation of my unexpected appearance in the West Country and was probing, ready to unearth the big secret. 'Yes, you missed us all but come on, Isobel, we know that isn't it. What's happened? Is everything alright?'

And rather than lay open all my problems, the feeling that things were going nowhere – the hopeless jobs, the lack of an agent, the fact my career was at a standstill – I found myself telling her about Andrew, about seeing him on the screen in front of me and feeling that I had to see what had happened to him, had to know.

'It felt like fate,' I added as an after-thought. 'I'd always wondered and then, bam, he was there in front of me and I realised I didn't want to always wonder any more. I have to try.'

I expected laughter, some light mocking perhaps. Now that I said it, it did sound so silly; absurd to go streaking over the planet on a whim because you always thought you'd live a certain way. Moregran was quiet for a moment, her flask at her side. 'I do understand,' she said, looking out at the sea. Then she shifted to look at me. 'I wish I'd been as brave.'

'What do you mean?'

'I'd always thought Patrick Thomas was a lovely man and he'd asked me to dance before the war and your grandfather and all of that time,' she said with a quick flick of her wrist. 'But after, when I was alone and just with your mother, he'd written to me. Asked whether I would see him. Me being a fool I didn't do anything about it, I was still so tied up in it all: your mum's dad dying and all the misery of life then. Then I heard he'd moved away. Scotland. And I never did anything. But I thought of him, I wondered.'

By the end of this outburst I could feel my eyes were wide in my head; I'd never heard anything about this Patrick or the idea that Moregran had ever lived her life with any regrets. So stupidly selfish of me, of course; she'd lived in Helford all her life, was widowed at twenty-three and raised Mum on her own. Of course she would have had men after her; she was a lovely, warm woman. I'd seen photographs of her when she was younger; she'd had the tiniest waist I'd ever seen and incredibly glossy hair that hung in waves.

I imagined Patrick writing her a letter, hoping to hear from her, wondering and worrying about her, this girl he'd asked to dance as a young man.

'I didn't know.'

'I never even told your mother, darling heart, so how could you?'

'Do you still wonder?' I asked her.

She smoothed her skirt down, a tiny hole from a moth ruining the line of the fabric. 'Yes sometimes, fleetingly. He had a wonderfully infectious laugh, gentle and slow, building like a train.'

'Do you know what happened to him?'

'No, no, it's a long time ago now, isn't it?'

We sat a while longer, watching for nothing and enjoying each other's company. Wrapping my cardigan around myself, I felt better for telling someone; it was typical of Moregran to be supportive.

'I think it's wonderful,' she said, getting slowly to her feet, one hand on her side. 'Will you let me know how you get on?'

'Of course.'

'Because even if he's not right and, darling, he probably isn't, you've tried, you've done something.'

I went to interrupt but realised she was right; this wasn't simply about finding Andrew. I knew that; it was more than that, it was making a change, following a new path. I needed to stage an intervention and this seemed like the first time in a long time that I wasn't just being swept along by my life. I was actively making decisions, odd ones at times perhaps, but still I was being proactive.

'You're right,' I said, standing up.

'Let's a have a pasty and shake on it,' she said, heading back and in the direction of the pub.

Seeing Moregran had given me the courage to tell Mum what I was really doing home and that I thought I had tracked Andrew down. She had been in the middle of practising 'Edelweiss' on her new electronic flute.

She paused, tapping the flute to her mouth. 'There was never a twenty per cent sale at Monsoon this week, was there?'

'What?'

'You seemed so happy the other day,' she pointed out. 'And I wondered then, but I just thought you were really, really into shopping now.'

'Oh,' I said, feeling a flood of guilt. 'No, I had picked up on a lead,' I said, sounding like I was a character in a detective novel. 'And you came in when I got the news. I'm sorry.'

'You lied,' she said, looking at me, pulling her green shawl about her.

I squirmed in front of her, looking at my toes. 'I did,' I confirmed.

'Oh well, no matter,' she trilled. 'The truth all sounds rather marvellous. You will of course need to look your absolute best then, darling. Hairdresser, tomorrow, you and me.'

Starting to practise once more, her eyes twinkled at me in delight.

Dear diary,

H'l stxhmf to write in code. That said 'I'm trying' but it is tiring as I forget the order of the letters in the alphabet sometimes but because I am going to be a spy like Pussy in *James Bond* I have to otzbshbd. That said practice. Obviously when I write in the real code I won't write down what word it is as that would be stupid and probably get me killed. I like spies because they kick boys down in the straw when they are mean and boys are stupid apart from Andrew who is my best friend today.

We have written things in code together and he says this is the special way we can talk. He tells me secrets like how he is sad sometimes that his dad doesn't live with them any more and I tell him about things too at home, about Mum sometimes making me embarrassed when she wears odd things to pick me up in, and he says we will always have our special way of talking.

I x

Chapter 11

'Is that a good temperature for you?' Tanya asked.

'Hmm, yes,' I mumbled, distracted by her rubbing at my head in a circular motion. God, I loved a head massage in a hairdresser and Tanya was amazing at them. She scratched behind my ears. *Oh, Tanya, come and live with me.* I had to bite my tongue and focus on the rank swirled ceiling tiles so as not to start moaning and thrashing about in the leather chair.

We were on a 'girls' day out', which basically involved: hairdresser, random loitering in jewellery shops and some kind of patisserie visit. Mum was currently trussed up in foils under a heater that emitted terrifying beeps, occasionally summoning one of the colourists to run from the back as if her hair might suddenly set on fire.

It had been a couple of days ago now that I had returned from Moregran's and sat Mum down to explain to her what I had really been doing in Cornwall. On hearing news of the email in the pub, she had moved into a whirlwind of activity.

'The Internet,' she explained, beckoning me into 'her office' (aka the attic), 'is basically magic.'

She fired up a state-of-the-art computer that rested under the wooden eaves, next to a photograph of Dad, her and I on the beach looking windswept and happy. 'I am totes on LinkedIn,' she said, tapping his name into the search engine. 'Everyone is; we'll easily find him now.'

'Totes, Mum?'

'It means totally,' she explained. 'But apparently it's the new way of saying it. I like it.'

'You totes do,' I said, grinning at her.

'Be careful or I shall totes not make you any food.'

'I apologise sincerely,' I said, hand on my heart, earning myself a smile and the certainty that lasagne would be mine.

'Okay,' she announced. 'No Andrew Parker from Somerset House on LinkedIn, but we should just Google him, darling. Google, Google images,' she cried, jabbing at the keys.

'Oh I've tried, I just saw lots of articles about the man who runs MI5,' I explained, feeling more than a little absurd.

'MI5 how wonderful. I would make an excellent spy, can winkle anything out of anyone, and no one would suspect. Your father never knows when I'm lying to him...'

'When do you lie to Dad?'

'Oh come on darling, we've been married a lifetime. I lie to him all the time. "Yes of course I've paid the TV licence, no I don't think Justin in the Surf Shop is more gorgeous than you, yes it's gluten-free..."'

'Right, well...'

'Oh look,' Mum's voice rose as she pointed to the screen, 'There're millions of photos, he's bound to be here. Was he the boy with the funny ears?' she said, throwing the comment over her shoulder.

'No, that was Lyndon, and I heard he got them pinned.'

'Oh shame, strange ears give a man character,' she said, scrolling down the page. 'Look, darling, look.'

There were so many photos of 'Andrew Parker'. Images after images were thrown up and I scanned them all. Google showed me: old Andrew in narrow square-framed glasses, Andrew in a pin-stripe suit and red tie, windswept Andrew posing in a manicured garden, Andrew with a scarf as a turban, a random woman with her tits out in an armchair, Andrew with a clarinet (I peered closer at this one as he was the first to fit within the appropriate age range), Black Andrew holding a cat in a tube carriage and, lastly, Andrew meeting Camilla Parker Bowles in a marquee and then Andrew in sunglasses with a rucksack.

It was between Clarinet Boy and Rucksack Man and with some trepidation, we clicked on Clarinet Boy's face. A tiny square popped up, a grainy image. 'Visit Page'. We discovered a few things: it was not a clarinet, it was an oboe. Andrew was really good at playing it and he lived in Utah. So I had just travelled all the way from America to discover Andrew Parker was in fact living in America. The CV was impressive and as I enlarged his face I felt my chest tighten. Andrew was not The Andrew.

Our attentions moved quickly to Andrew the Rucksack Carrier and we visited the page. It was a travel blog from a girl called Melody who was posting photos of her friends on a walking trip to the Alps. 'Chillin' with Andrew', she had typed beneath it and then written a post about how the sunset had been 'really pretty'. The blog was snippets from other trips, but no other photos of Andrew appeared.

I tilted my head to the side. 'That could be him,' I said, noting the wave in the front of his hair. Hadn't Andrew had a wave right there? Staring at his image, wondering what his eyes were like beneath those sunglasses, I was pretty sure it was him.

'Type in Somerset House,' I said, getting excited myself now.

Mum did just that and the images reduced and now we were staring at a tiny square, a headshot of a teacher at an ancient-looking independent day school in Devon. A Geography teacher. With a wave in his hair. This was Andrew Parker, Geography Teacher, Rucksack Carrier and First Husband.

Mum had, of course, shouted most of the story across the hairdressers to Tanya who had been gawping at my efforts to track Andrew down and was impressed, I think, with the mileage. 'Can't believe you flew from LA.'

'I know,' I said, seeing myself grow red in the mirror as she lifted two lengths of hair and cut.

'That's like America!'

'That it is,' I confirmed. 'Land of the Free,' I added for no discernible reason.

'So where is he now?' she said, looking around the hairdresser and almost making me hope he might be here getting his roots done. Actually, he wouldn't need his roots doing; he didn't go in for that kind of thing. Or did he? I wondered briefly whether he would be the type of man to go to the barbers or the hairdressers; would he tint his hair? Would he have a beard? I pictured him now all dirty blond and wild and decided he would be a barber man, a 'Give me a grade four all over' kind of guy. The no-nonsense sort. He likes his hair like he likes his life: uncomplicated.

'... and when they found her she had died. Isn't that beautiful?'

Tanya paused to stare at me in the mirror, her sculpted eyebrows raised, waiting for my response.

'Beautiful,' I nodded.

Who died? I thought, curiosity piqued. Why were we suddenly talking about death?

I eyed her hairdressing scissors suspiciously.

'They say elephants stand over their dead partner for days, so maybe they were like them, unable to live without each other. That could be you and this fella Andrew; elephants, or maybe not like elephants, like penguins or shit who only marry once.'

'I think that's swans,' I said. 'Penguins only stay monogamous in the mating season and then they choose another one next time round. They're basically bird slags,' I said, feeling bad when Tanya looked horrified.

'That's a tattoo I now regret,' she said, pulling up her T-shirt sleeve and showing me two penguins kissing. Oh.

After Tanya had worked her magic, I caught sight of myself in the long mirror. There I was: Isobel Graves, Intrepid Chaser of Husbands and owner of Fabulous New Swishy Hair. Tomorrow would be the day I headed to see Andrew. I vowed to head to Somerset House first thing. He couldn't possibly say no to this vision from a L'Oréal advert I thought, as I swung my locks from side to side, pouting at my reflection.

'Yes, you're very beautiful, darling, but let's get going, eh?' Mum called from behind me.

Mumbling something about, 'Just thought I had a bug in my hair,' I grabbed my bag and ran outside to join her.

Dear diary,

Today was the best day ever because Andrew and I went crabbing in the canoe lake and we raced all the crabs back. Well, first we put bacon on bits of string and we kept a bucket by the side. Mum said it was cruel if we didn't have a bucket for them with water in so she gave us one that normally has the mop in.

Andrew was the best at grabbing the crabs as I was a bit scared when they came out of the water and dangled around snapping their spare claw as the other claw was on the bacon. He put them straight into the bucket and some were so big it was brilliant. When I looked into the bucket they were all crawling over each other and Andrew carried it and tipped the bucket over so that the crabs had to race back to the lake and it was so funny watching them move sideways; quick little steps all in different directions and the small one nearly beat everyone but I think he got confused and Andrew had to help him find his way home which Mum said was really nice of him and showed what a kind boy he was. Andrew is always smiling and I think he is kind too.

I x

Chapter 12

Expecting to see empty buildings – as per a school on holiday in July – I was surprised when I appeared at the gates of Somerset House campus to see groups of teenage children wearing orange baseball caps and carrying orange rucksacks wandering about the place. Notices pinned to some of the blocks of classrooms told me that there was a visiting language school in residence.

Three boys – one gangly, one pimply and one with the start of the world's most pathetic moustache – approached me, a questioning look in their eyes and a square of map in their hands. They said stuff in a foreign language and I froze, nodding at them when they finished. They repeated other words, now with gestures, and I found myself doing a Gaelic shrug and rootled around in my head. I plumped for, 'Me no understandee,' which I was fairly confident was Crap English rather than words in a foreign tongue. As they looked at one another I took the opportunity to leg it, speedily walking away, head down so the other orange baseball caps kept their distance.

Moving past classroom blocks, I could make out the main school building in the distance. A large Gothic house surrounded by impeccably neat flowerbeds and a small working fountain in the centre of a circular gravel driveway. To my right, the cricket pitch, mown in stripes, waited for players. At the far end of the pitch a line of trees obscured the view beyond and emerging from them was a figure in a flapping coat holding a stick.

Yapping and growling filled the air as three labradors spun and circled the stick, racing to compete for it after it had been thrown. One dog, chocolate-covered, its tongue lolling out as it neared me, seemed oblivious to the stick.

'Koalemos!' hollered the figure, the low, booming voice causing me to jump.

The chocolate lab raced over to me, not heeding the figure, jumping up playfully and making me laugh.

'Down, Koalemos, down,' the woman had started briskly walking to me. 'I'm so sorry,' she said in an impossibly low voice. 'Koalemos is completely thick and half-deaf with it.'

'It's fine, I don't mind,' I said, tickling Koalemos's ears so he closed his eyes in pleasure. 'He's gorgeous. And his name is um...very impressive.'

'Gorgeous but completely stupid, like so many men I know,' the woman added. 'And he is named after the God of Foolishness, so completely apt.'

'Oh, how very...' I tailed off, not sure what it was.

The woman looked at me with narrowed eyes, her short auburn hair severely chopped beneath her jawline.

'Are you working at the language school?' she asked.

'Oh no, I'm...' I paused, realising I didn't know this woman at all. 'I'm sort of looking for someone.'

'Someone who?' She had such an authoritative tone and was wearing a tweed cloak (a cloak, who wears cloaks apart from Sherlock Holmes and vampires?) that I found myself responding honestly. 'Andrew,' I said quickly, 'Andrew Parker, he's a teacher here.'

'Well I know that, I hired the man,' she said, turning to call, 'BAUCIS, PHILEMON' so that the other two dogs perked up their ears and bounded over. 'I'm Joan Henderson, the headmistress here,' she said. I went to curtsy and then remembered that was just for the queen, although this woman had that kind of royal presence. 'He's one of the few who live on-site; one of the cottages that back onto the river...' she said, pointing to the line of trees.

My heart soared with the announcement. A cottage, backing onto a river. It sent a shiver down my back and arms as I thought of my fantasy, played out so many times I could picture the cottage already. Was I picturing the very cottage he lived in? Would it have roses trained around the windows? Would it have a swing seat in the garden? Honey-stone walls?

'He's not there, of course, volunteers every summer holiday; you probably just missed him.'

The last part of her sentence disrupted my thoughts of the cottage, its walls crumbling, roses crushed as I heard her say he was not there.

'Where is he then?' I asked, hoping it would be somewhere close by. I really had to get the car back before dinner: Dad was doing the pub quiz around the headland in Port Isaac.

'Malaysia,' was the reply.

'Malaysia, as in, abroad,' I repeated, stunned and momentarily hoping that Malaysia was a small village in Somerset.

'Indeed, the country,' she said, in the same voice that she spoke to Koalemos.

'Oh,' I muttered, feeling ridiculously like I might have a little cry.

Malaysia. I had just travelled half the globe to discover Andrew Parker wasn't even in the country. After all my efforts I had been thwarted. Standing in the grounds of his school, feeling so close to him, it seemed absurd that he was really not there.

'Tioman Island, to be precise, he did a wonderful assembly on it to the Year 10...'

'Tioman,' I repeated. It sounded foreign and exotic and bloody miles away. What was I going to do? Was this really over? My hopes lifted a fraction as I took in the tweed cloak. Maybe this woman was mad? Maybe she knew nothing?

'It was lovely, all the pupils started clapping when he showed them a photo of a baby turtle in his hand. It cheered us all right up after that dreadful episode of *Life* – did you see it? Where those birds ripped them to shreds. Brutal animals, birds. Brutal.'

'Aren't they,' I said, wanting her to finish, convinced now this bird-hating, cloak-wearing wizard woman might have it all wrong. 'I might...leave him a note then,' I said. He would be at home, I thought, he hadn't gone anywhere, I could still find him.

'Well of course, if you like,' she said, leashing her dogs.

Koalemos started licking the leather.

'Um where exactly is his house again? I forget,' I added breezily.

'It's the one on the end of the three cottages over there.' She waved in the direction of some trees, and I could just make out a chimney.

'Thank you for the help,' I whispered, moving away, my body feeling heavier with each step.

'Well he's an excellent teacher, I'm always happy to help an excellent teacher,' she said.

'That's nice,' I said, trying to take some consolation from the fact Andrew was an excellent teacher. My beloved had achieved excellence in his area of work: that was good, nice.

Heading towards the chimney, I threw up a little prayer to the sky. Come on, be in, I said to myself. Be in and let the She-Sherlock be wrong.

Nearing the rows of cottages, it was clear Andrew Parker's house was not going to be the cottage from my fantasy. Shaded by a row of enormous beech trees, the cottages all looked crooked, the white-washed walls bumpy, there were tiles missing from the roof, weeds littering the beds in the front. A peeling label on a small metal box screwed into the wall confirmed that 'A. Parker' lived in the one at the end. I touched his name, feeling strange to see it written in bold. A circular for a local garden centre was bursting out of the slot. I pushed it back in gently, feeling the weight of other letters resisting. Maybe he just didn't collect his mail. It didn't mean he definitely wasn't in. And, yes, the lights were off, but maybe he was saving electricity as he was such an eco-warrior. And there wouldn't be smoke from the chimney; it was July not bloomin' Christmas.

Taking a breath I pushed open the faded wooden gate, cream paint flaking off its surface, the hinges orangey-brown and resistant. The front door was tiny and had been painted red about a million years ago. Breathing out slowly, I curled my hand into a fist and knocked. No answer. My palms became damp as I looked for a doorbell, a knocker. Nothing. I rapped harder and called 'Hellooo' in a voice that sounded like my mother. The silence crept all around me and with the last of my energy I moved down the path and towards the garden. Perhaps he was on the loo, perhaps he had temporarily popped out to the shops, perhaps...

The garden was narrow and neglected. Clusters of stinging nettles sprouted from the disintegrating wooden fence, a path led to a tumbledown shed containing a rusting lawnmower, a garden fork and a dirty mountain bike. So many clues I felt like Miss Marple herself (although younger and edgier) as I tried to piece Andrew together. A man who loathed gardening because he was too busy cycling to places. A grubby white plastic chair, tipped and resting in the long grass, was no swing seat. Thin slivers of the stream at the end could be made out in between the trees and bushes. I looked back at the house from this angle. Net curtains obscured the view of the rooms at the back and frosted glass in a back door ensured all I could make out were dark shadows of a possible coat rack. A dusty windowpane littered with dead insects and remnants of cobwebs put me off peeking in. The house was clearly uninhabited. Andrew was in Malaysia.

It had been a pointless search, a reckless, expensive waste of time and I couldn't believe I had to return home with the news. Then it would be back to LA and normal life would resume. Tears of disappointment threatened and I blinked. It wasn't just the disappointment of not finding him here, it was everything the search for him had represented. I had finally started to pursue the life I had always imagined and I didn't want to just give up now. As I crossed the border back into Cornwall, my mood seemed as immoveable as the clouds over Bodmin Moor. I had failed and made a fool of myself.

'Darling, you can't keep moping about looking like you are about to throw yourself into the sea, it is very off-putting.'

Dressed in a hoody and pyjama bottoms, my new fabulous hair falling lank and unloved, I spooned dry cereal into my mouth. 'I just need a small grieving period. I will try to be depressed out of sight of you from now on.'

'That would be more favourable, but I'd rather you weren't depressed at all, darling. What is there to be depressed about?' she asked, catching a leak in the ceiling with a saucepan, rain battering the windows behind her, trees bent under the wind.

I raised an eyebrow.

'This is just a teensy shower, it will pass,' she said watching Dad stooped, shielding his face with his mac as he made his way into the house.

'God,' he said as he opened the doorway, shrugging off his coat and putting a hand up to his wet patch of hair.

'It is disgusting out there,' he announced.

'See,' I munched, pointing my spoon at Dad, 'we might as well all spend the day curled up in front of the fire watching movies that make us cry.'

'Not me,' said Mum, balancing a bowl on the Aga to catch the latest drip, 'I will be seizing the day. I will be walking, my darlings, with my new MP3 player that is also a pedometer so clever it knows when I stop to tie my shoes.'

A roll of thunder blocked out my response.

Dad was putting on toast and rubbing his hands together. 'Gorgeous summer we're having,' he muttered to himself.

Rain bounced off the windowsill outside, sliding in blurred sheets down the glass so the sea beyond just looked like a dripping grey watercolour.

Mum sat with her hands round a mug staring at me. 'You've given up,' she deduced.

I fiddled with the placemat.

'You can't give up,' she said.

'I have to,' I sighed, explaining for the tenth time about my hopeless search.

Dad joined us, slapping honey on his toast and causing Mum to growl at him. He bit into it. 'Staying for a bit longer then or returning to LA?' he asked.

Mum placed a flat palm down on the table and in her dangerous voice said, 'She will not be returning to LA.'

'Well not this second,' I started.

'Not until you have found him,' she cut in. 'You wanted an adventure, now this is just that.'

'Mum...he's in Malaysia. The country. I checked and it is still next door to Thailand aka MILES away.'

Mum waved a hand. 'A trifle. You need a holiday and we haven't given you a proper Christmas present in years.'

'Er, that is not true. You have sent me a necklace, boxsets, that cashmere cardigan and I treasure the photo of Polzeath you got printed on that T-shirt with your faces interposed over it.'

Dad shivered. 'Bad year.'

'Well we haven't been on a family holiday of sorts...'

'Sending me somewhere alone doesn't qualify,' I pointed out.

'I'm serious, Isobel, we think you should go,' she said, spelling it out. 'You need to do something drastic, you need a break from it all. We really want you to go.'

I looked at Dad who nodded at me. 'We do. We've been... well...we thought you needed some time to think about things and know more about what you want...' He tugged at his collar looking at Mum, who picked up his thread.

'This isn't all about Andrew is it, darling? This is about you and you need to do this. So,' she said with a decisive clap, 'it's settled.'

So it seemed I was off to Malaysia.

Moregran,

Sitting at the airport about to get on a flight to Singapore! I tracked down Andrew; he's a teacher at a school in Somerset, but he goes to Malaysia for his summer to volunteer. Eco-warrior alert, I bet he has an amazing bouffant beard and can fish using just a spear! So I am going to go and find him. Wish me luck! I am posting this from the airport. They are doing a deal in duty-free now where I can buy my bodyweight in Toblerone for about 10p, so have to run...

Love you,

Isobel x x

Chapter 13

Singapore

Why do they make you walk through First Class when you board a flight? Is this for the satisfaction of those in First Class – we shall throw you some mere mortals to sniff at – to really make the extra money seem worth it or perhaps a complicated plot by the airlines to bring about class warfare? Either way, there is nothing more galling than seeing someone lying prostrate, plump little pillow under their head, blanket made from cashmere/spun GOLD, sipping at a nightcap of pink champagne as you bustle through to the back of the plane, the section reserved for the unlucky thousand, who are about to spend ten hours squashed up against each other, swapping their germs across the pungent air and praying for the flight to end.

''Scuse me, 'scuse me, sorry, can I just...?' I was sweating by the time I was sat in my upright seat, belt fixed, sweets crushed next to the sick bag in the pouch in front of me. Kindle in my lap, despair in my heart, I looked about. Children were standing on seats, a baby was already crying, a large lady opposite had found peanuts from about her person and was religiously loading them into her mouth one by one. Frazzled air hostesses with stick-on smiles skirted their way down the aisle and around passengers. I waited for the pilot's voice. I always wanted confident, experienced professional. He sounded nasal but bored, like he had done this before, so I relaxed and looked out at the wing on the runway, trying to block out the crush.

The moment we were in the air, turbulence seemed to hit and the cabin was filled with chatter, children squealing and that baby who might be going for some kind of Crying World Record. There was one guy, however, who seemed totally nonplussed by the flying experience. He was across the way from me, one long leg stretched out into the aisle, one eye open to move it for the trolley. Headphones on and what looked suspiciously like Disney's *Frozen* playing out on the screen in front of him. I surreptitiously stared at his profile from behind my book. He had dark hair the colour of an espresso coffee, tanned cheeks, a spattering of stubble and thick eyelashes that seemed to fringe his blue eyes so that they seemed almost turquoise.

'You know I can see you,' he said, his eyes ahead, still on *Frozen*.

I froze myself, unsure if he was talking to me or not. Surely n...

'I'm talking to you,' he said, turning his head to the left, tilting one headphone away from his ear and looking at me.

'Oh, I...' I shifted in my seat, my knees bumping the magazine pouch in front, no room to manoeuvre. I noticed the picture of the woman being sick into a bag.

'Wondering how a strapping man like me can take pleasure from an in-flight cartoon, eh?' He smiled.

'I...' I spluttered.

He put up a hand. 'It's okay, I am happy to be judged. Please feel free to continue.' He readjusted his headphone and went back to staring.

'No, I...'

He couldn't hear me. He was tapping one finger on his thigh in time to the song the main lady was singing. I wasn't judging him, I thought silently. I was just bored and looking around the plane and I didn't mind that he watches cartoons. It's fine, each to their own; live and let live. I have never been one to cast aspersions. I turned my head to look at him again, mouth half-open, ready with my spiel, but he was having none of it. I sat there, tried to read, words swimming in front of me. He was very cheeky to assume all that about me. I was the innocent party here, how dare he project his insecurities onto me? It was outrageous. I was a warm person who has been brought up well. Ooh, my mother would have a word with him over this. She would defend me to the hilt.

I could feel myself getting hotter with every thought so I took the inflight manual out of the pouch and wafted it in front of my face to cool down. Eyes flicked to the right again. Why would he think that?

Before I could think, I had reached across the aisle and had tapped him on his one long, outstretched leg. His eyes opened so that the sharp blue was now entirely encircled by white. He took off both headphones.

'Can I help you?'

'Well I wanted to say, that, well I wasn't judging, you know, you, because of...' What had I begun? *Iz, what are you blathering about?* 'You know,' I jerked my head at his screen, 'it's a free country! I was just looking around at the... scenery.' I came to a stop.

He followed my gaze around the carriage, a smug half-smile playing on his lips. A dribbling teenage girl slept soundly, a toddler was pushing polo mints into his mother's handbag while she slept. The baby was still crying.

'Ah, well thank you for clearing that up,' he said, returning to the headphones and the screen.

I sat back in my seat stiffly, Kindle forgotten. Then I leaned over again and prodded him. I didn't give him time to react. 'Look, sorry, I just think I need this cleared up: I was just looking about the plane being entirely non-judgmental. I am a very laid-back person.' I smiled and could feel my face all taut. Laidback and chilled, that's me!

He raised one eyebrow at me and spoke slowly, 'Okey-doke.' Headphones back on.

For the next hour I sat there, pretending to read but really trying to focus on looking super-free and easy. If I glanced around I was careful to keep my expression neutral. Ha! That would show him.

The air hostess appeared at his side, giggling as she handed him a Coke and miniature bottle of rum. *Oh I am the King of the Aeroplane, All the Airhostesses Love Me*, I thought, making a face.

'You know I can see you in the reflection of my screen,' he said, tipping the Coke into a plastic glass.

'Well that's nice,' I sniffed.

'You were gurning,' he pointed out.

'Well the character in my book is annoying,' I explained, holding up my Kindle and then trying to turn it the right way up before he noticed.

I could see his eyes watching me in the screen and, sticking on headphones, I decided to immerse myself in a movie too. Something serious and sensible, an adult's movie. A drama.

Oh man. Two hours later, all other passengers forgotten, I was a total wreck. Snot and tears merged on my face hopelessly as I tried not to cry aloud. Why had I picked this movie? This destroyer of all good emotions? Oh I felt drained and useless. The credits rolled and I couldn't stop thinking back to the main character and all that she'd gone through, and for what?

A tissue was proffered in the aisle by a hand and I took it, dragged back to the aeroplane and Mr Smug sitting in front of me. I could tell he was looking at my leaky red eyes and I dabbed hopelessly, wishing I had my compact mirror which was nestled somewhere above my head in the locker.

'Thanks,' I muttered, not wanting to seem ungrateful for the tissue.

'Not to worry – *Frozen* gets me every time,' he said, a solemn look on his face.

'I wasn't watc...oh a joke. Ha,' I said in a deadpan voice, still back in the drama on screen.

Coiled, waiting for more, I was surprised to see his head loll to the side and his eyes flutter close. The air hostess moved past, looking at him, blushing when I caught her eye.

'Anything from the trolley?' she asked.

Shaking my head I turned the screen off, took off my headphones and tried to sleep too.

Waiting for our plane to refuel in Dubai airport, I had managed to escape the man's amused smirk and hurtle out into the airy concourse and the lines of shops. Sitting eating a frozen yoghurt, bits of strawberry and crushed nuts stuck to my lips, I sighed. It felt slightly bizarre travelling alone, bizarre but freeing. LA had been so crammed, dirty and busy, so completely different to my gentle Cornish upbringing: the fields, the space, the people private and unobtrusive. I stretched out my legs, licking my lips slowly over the spoon. Man, frozen yoghurt was delicious.

The man from the airport was waiting at the gate, one eye looking at me over the tattered pages of his thriller. He gave me a warm smile and, perhaps it was memory of the yoghurt, I grinned right back. It lasted a second before I lost myself in my Kindle once more and then moved through to the second flight of the day, one step closer to finding Andrew Parker.

Groggy and dry-mouthed, I moved through Passport Control at Singapore airport in a fug. My skin felt patchy and dry and my teeth seemed to be coated in sugar and aeroplane hideousness. I wanted a shower, a bath, some kind of water anyway and a change of clothes. As I waited for my suitcase, smiling weakly at a child who was sitting on it, cross-legged, being chased by his mother round the edge, I thought of the next few days and the plan that I had come up with. I only had one night in Singapore and then tomorrow I would be off to the tiny drop in the South China Sea that was Tioman Island where I would find my love! This thought made my face stretch into a grin and I tugged my suitcase off the carousel as it came my way, standing it upright and tipping it forward before wheeling away.

Before I could make it too far, a hand shot out and I yelped, turning quickly, my hair snapping around with me.

'Gah, wha.'

'Sorry, sorry,' he panted. It was the man from the aeroplane.

I narrowed my eyes in suspicion, holding my handbag to my chest as if to provide some kind of protection.

'I didn't want you to be wandering the streets of Singapore without knowing my name,' he said, going for a charming smile which sort of worked as his dark hair stuck up in places as if he had just woken up, his shirt crumpled, hints of chest hair peeking through the top. He stuck out a hand. 'Zeb, nice to meet you.'

I took his hand. 'Zeb,' I repeated slowly.

He started laughing. 'Mum had a thing for *The Magic Roundabout* and it sort of stuck.' He dragged a hand through his hair.

'Well nice to meet you,' I said, clamping my mouth closed halfway through speaking, unsure of my breath at this point. I really needed to splash my face and clean my teeth.

He seemed to be waiting for more and I hastily gushed my own name at him. 'Isobel, my mum, well it's just Isobel.'

'Great. Well I might see you round.'

'Yep.' I nodded once, pursing my lips.

'Look, I'm heading to the Marine Bay Sands Hotel tonight if you're free – it's pretty awesome, actually, if you were at a loose end.'

I looked down and fiddled with the in-flight label on my suitcase, tearing it off so that the elastic band pinged back and bit me on the finger.

'Ow, oh I'm um...'

Why was he inviting me out? He was waiting, all expectant with those turquoise eyes.

'I'm not sure. I'm seeing, seeing about some things.'

'Sounds important.' He nodded solemnly.

Was he taking the piss? *It's your fault if he was, Isobel Graves. You should have said seeing FRIENDS, Iz, FRIENDS not things, he would have thought you had mates, now he knows you are a saddo. A saddo loser with no friends just hanging out in Singapore for no good reason.*

I hated it when the voice in my head got really judgy.

'Yes, well best get on,' I said, taking off with my trolley in the first direction to hand and then having to make an embarrassing loop back to the taxi queue behind him. What was it about this man that turned me into a complete idiot?

I thought he was laughing into his hand as I passed. Tilting my chin up, I walked on, trying not to look at him. Maybe it had been a cough.

Chapter 14

Leaning back in the air-conditioned taxi, I felt the smooth leather on my bare legs and breathed a sigh of relief. Citing the name of the hotel I'd booked, we moved away from the rank and along the manicured roads around Singapore. The buildings along the edge of the harbour soared upwards, practically lost in the folds of the clouds that had descended like a fog over the city as we sped across the flyover. The radio seemed to be running through a list of nineties disco classics and I was impressed by the taxi driver's ability to recollect most of the words to Step's '5,6,7,8'. I nodded along, our eyes briefly meeting in mutual appreciation in the driving mirror.

Pulling up outside one of the saddest buildings I'd ever seen, my heart sank on reading the peeling painted sign: 'Hotel'. The 'o' and 't' were so badly faded it simply read 'Hel' which, from my vantage point, didn't seem far off. Tipping the taxi driver after he'd put his back out unloading my suitcase from the boot, I felt a wash of warm air encircle me. Rolling my belongings up a little ramp, I noticed with some relief a small bar area to the left of Reception. There were unoccupied faded velvet stools and low scattered tables waiting for paying guests. Me! I checked in quickly, trying not to take in too many details from the narrow lilac room, a tiny window covered in bars making it look exactly like a cell. Heading back downstairs to the bar, I headed over and ordered a Singapore Sling, earning myself a barely perceptible eye-roll from the waiter.

Moving across to a booth by the window, I got out my guide, purchased at the last moment at the airport, and looked at Malaysia; focusing on the tiny spot that was Tioman Island off its eastern coast. Tomorrow I would be flying there, tomorrow I would truly start the search for Andrew Parker. I momentarily wondered what he might think of me sitting alone in the bar of a Singapore hotel, having spent my life savings on a trip spanning the globe to find him. But then I remembered the sunny boy he had been, the tree-climbing adventurer who would only admire my spirit and intrepid nature. The Singapore Sling arrived and I took a deep gulp, the cherry brandy and gin warming my insides. This was an evening to explore a new location and drink to the old life I was leaving behind and the new life I was embracing. The trouble was, there was no one to share it with and after my second Singapore Sling I found myself wandering back to the hotel reception and booking a taxi to the Marine Bay Sands Hotel.

The taxi was completely dwarfed by the first of the three towers. I craned my neck to try to see the top, a large deck that looked like a ship resting on top of three columns. It was an extraordinary building and, as I tumbled through its revolving doors, I tried not to gape at the huge chandeliers dripping from the ceiling, the polished marble-clad space, airy and inviting. A queue of people being stamped and welcomed stood to my right and I automatically joined the back, assuming it would lead me to a bar and to people.

A guy in front of me, wobbly and smiling, raised his trilby hat at me.

'Hey,' I responded, nodding to an unheard beat and then looking back around the lobby.

'Barney.' He thrust his hand out and I took it. 'You heading up to the top?' he asked.

'Isobel...oh, um, yeah, I think so,' I said, trying to look like I knew what I was up to. 'What's um...what's up there?'

'Pumping nightclub, one of three, are you a Marine Sands Virgin?' he asked, pursing his mouth in shock.

'Yup,' I said, noting his accent. 'And you're English,' I said.

'Manchester. But I work out here. You?'

'LA, well Cornwall, well, sort of,' I babbled, realising I didn't need to make things so complicated.

'You work here?'

'No I'm um...'

'Hand,' said the bouncer, holding a stamp threateningly.

'Sorry,' I gushed quickly, producing a hand.

'I'm going to find someone,' I announced as Barney walked into a lift to our left.

'Cool,' he said, readjusting his hat in the mirrored walls of the lift.

Tottering into the lift after him, I felt a thrill of excitement. As we climbed fifty-six floors, my head felt tight and as I stepped out onto the top floor, my ears popped. We had emerged on a terrace crammed with people. The balmy air of a Singapore evening meant that there was no need for a cardigan or a jumper and I gasped at the night sky resplendent above me; stars and clouds reflected off the buildings across the still water of the harbour below.

'Swwweeeet,' said Barney, grinning at me.

The top deck was bursting with gorgeous people with tinkly laughs drinking cocktails and bottled beers. The men had open-necked shirts, the women coloured dresses and everyone had a tan. I felt relieved to be wearing my orange shift dress, flung into my suitcase in a last-moment panic all the way back in LA, and tried to stand up straight and ooze confidence. I pictured my mum urging me on with some kind of crazy mantra: 'Feel the earth wanting to help you. Feel the celebrity in you wash through you and out of you and around you and...'

'I'll get us past security, Isobel, into the VIP bit okay? Back soon,' Barney interrupted, waving back at me as he marched through the crowds with a purposeful stride.

Barney did just that and I found myself ushered through to a large, low table outside. A white leather sofa was emptied of people and we sunk into it sharing a bottle of champagne. Deciding Barney might be my new best friend, I over-shared why I was there and he sat, mouth half-open, as I explained what I was doing in Malaysia.

'That dude is going to be one amazed bloke,' he said, toasting me with a flute. 'You are my hero, Isobel, you're like the personification of carpe diem.'

'Yes I am,' I agreed happily, glad my plan had so impressed him.

'You're a warrior in the Love War,' he went on, 'a soldier of the heart.' He stood up and pumped his chest before turning back to me, his trilby cocked. 'I'll be back soon, warrior.'

'Er, okay,' I said, getting up to follow him and then loitering as I lost his hat in amongst the crowds of beautiful folk.

Smiling nervously at strangers, I felt someone watching me and spun round to scan the enormous length of balcony above. I couldn't make anyone out, well, there were a group of gorgeous women all wearing feathered white dresses like a gaggle of skinny swans and a photographer snapping at them as they posed but no one looking at me. *Paranoid*, I chimed in my head. Then realised, as a man nearby flinched, I might have said it out loud too.

'Stalking me, eh?' came a low chuckle. I whipped around to see Zeb from the aeroplane standing in front of me. In this tight space he seemed even taller than I remembered. He was wearing a black shirt tucked into black trousers, almost blending into the night apart from his startling blue eyes.

'What are you doing here?' I asked, only just noticing the enormous camera round his neck as I finished.

'Well that *is* a greeting, oh mysterious aeroplane buddy.' He smirked and raised his camera towards me. 'I'm working.' So he had been the man taking pictures of the swan women.

'Working.'

'Yes I am, taking photos of guests at some VIP's party.' He jerked a thumb over his shoulder. 'I think he calls himself T Dog for real, for actual real,' he said, making a face.

'So you're a photographer,' I said.

'And you're clearly exceptionally bright,' he laughed, holding his camera out. 'What gave it away?'

'Fine, fine, you're hilarious,' I said, rolling my eyes.

'Look I'm sorry, I'll be nice. I'm actually glad you're here. I needed someone to talk to me about Disney classics and... I'm also completely mental about timing. I mean what time is it now and when should we have slept? Are we meant to be jetlagged because I feel fine?'

'You are the one with the Disney fetish and I feel fine too but I think it's morning in England so that is not surprising.'

'We need breakfast then. I could kill someone for a croissant.'

My eyes widened in surprise.

'Sorry, bad turn of phrase when meeting a stranger – I am not some psycho who stabs people for porridge and things.'

'Well, that's a relief.'

'Unless I was starving and they were the last person alive and it was either them or me eating breakfast things.'

'That's understandable,' I agreed, believing myself to be entirely capable of wrestling another human being to the floor if it meant I could eat more of that frozen yoghurt.

'How long are you staying in Singapore for?' Zeb asked.

'Only a night, I'm going to Tioman Island tomorrow to um...see about some things.' Carefully avoiding sharing my journey with more than one stranger, I internally high-fived myself for skirting the question. Next stop: *Newsnight*.

'You definitely do like to see about things.'

'Yes well...'

'Tioman's meant to be pretty stunning,' mused Zeb. 'Maybe it'll...'

My phone started ringing, cutting off whatever he was about to say. 'Mel' lit up the screen and I frowned at her name. 'Sorry, I just need to take this,' I explained, turning my back on Zeb to answer the call. Mel hadn't phoned since Cornwall, maybe something was wrong.

'All okay, lovely?' I asked.

There was nothing on the other end, no cheery hello or screech of greeting. We spoke to each other every day at home so it had been strange not swapping more news in the last week or so. 'Mel?' I said. The silence continued. 'Mel, are you ignoring me?' I asked, wondering when she would speak.

Then something in the background confused me. 'Ahhhhooooh.'

'Mel? All okay? Are you there? I can't...'

'YES, YES, NO...'

I held the phone out in front of me. That voice had sounded a lot lower than Mel.

'Ahhhoooooh.'

Oh god. As the noise was joined with another 'NO, NO, YES, YESSSSS', my mouth fell open and I blinked quickly. Was I hearing what I thought I was hearing?

'Mel!' I squealed and a few of the VIP guests glanced my way. 'Mel!' I hissed.

'Ahhhhhoooh that's it, right, yes, that's...'

I couldn't find the red Cancel button quicker, pressing it three, four times to be sure it was off, that it was over. That this NIGHTMARE would end.

Zeb was still standing in front of me, camera in both hands which were slowly lowered. Had he taken a photo of me?

'What was that all about?' he asked, his face serious, mouth in a thin line, forehead creased in worry.

I felt a warmth spread through me that he cared, that he seemed to be concerned. Then I realised I had to answer him. 'It was my best friend, she, um, wrong number, wasn't, um...'

Singapore really is a hot city. I flapped my hand in front of my face. 'A drink, I think perhaps I could do with a drink and well...'

Zeb had tilted his head to one side and was looking at me, a question on his lips.

Before he could ask it, however, Barney had bustled over with two beer bottles coated with droplets. 'I bring drinks, Goddess Nicola, DRINKS!' he announced. I looked at him, assuming the beers in his hand were not his first.

Gratefully accepting one of the bottles, I turned to introduce Zeb but he had disappeared into the crowds; all I could make out were the distant flashes of his camera. I felt a brief stab of disappointment and was then distracted by Barney wanting to clink bottles.

Seizing me by my free arm, he practically dragged me across the dance floor. 'Isobel, you have to check out the pool! It's AMAZING, it spills over the edge.'

About to ask more, we emerged on the other side of the bumping bodies and I felt my breath leave me. Ahead was a long infinity pool stretching across the length of the rooftop, lights in the walls casting blue shimmering trails in the water. Black-tied people were sitting around tables and stools, drinking. Beyond the pool, the Singapore buildings winked in the darkness, some office lights still left on; squares of yellow light dotted about the city.

'It's amazing!' I gasped.

'Totally,' said Barney. 'We basically HAVE to skinny-dip drunk tonight; it is like THE LAW in a place like this.'

I giggled nervously and sipped at my beer. 'Er...'

Barney was waving at someone on the terrace above him. It was one of the girls dressed like a swan. Now he was beckoning her. He turned to me, seized my arm again and shook it. 'I think this might turn into the best night ever.' You couldn't help but be swept up in his excitement and I found myself agreeing that 'strawpedoing' my beer was an amazing idea. Then we ordered more.

A few hours later and I was standing on a table swaying to the music, champagne in one hand, a straw in the other, a feather headdress lopsided over one eye, lipstick EVERYWHERE. I had lost my shoes, and Barney, hours ago but on the plus side I had made lots of new friends. Mostly because Barney had told them all about why I had come to Singapore and I'd been grilled about Andrew and I might have embellished somewhat and added some details. Two twins, with the shiniest brown hair I had ever seen in real life, over from Hong Kong for the weekend were desperate to confirm more.

'So when you last saw him as a child he really promised that you would be together for eternity?'

'Er, yes!' I said, bouncing on the smooth leather of the curved booth we were drinking in. 'He said he couldn't imagine life without me.'

Both twins tipped their heads to the side and 'ahhed'.

Were they twins, I suddenly panicked? Was I so drunk I was seeing double? Where was Barney?

'Barney,' I called. A flash went off on my right. 'Zeb!' I announced, grinning at him and tottering towards him. Zeb was holding something up in his hand.

'My shoooooes!' I launched myself at him. I felt ear and beard.

'I would have brought them over earlier if I knew you were that keen on them.'

'Thank you,' I mumbled, having found myself on the ground putting one of them on. I looked up at him, seeing a leg in front of me.

'Your leg,' I pointed out.

'Literally nothing gets past you.'

I frowned as I realised now that I had my shoes on, I might not be able to gracefully get myself back up into my booth in an elegant, lady-like sort of way. So I stayed on the floor.

'Er, you okay down there, mad woman?'

'Hmm.' I looked up. Zeb's head was MILES away. He was very tall.

'Do you need help?' he asked, holding out one hand.

Then, before I could take it, I found myself being wrenched up under both arms and swept back into my seat.

'Barney!' I shouted in glee. 'You're back and I have shoes.'

'Hooray,' Barney cheered. 'More champagne for good news!'

'Hooray.'

Dear diary,

It was my first-ever trip to the skate park today and there were sooooo many people there all going in big circles on rollerskates. Some went really fast but I had to hold onto the side a lot and Mum helped me by holding onto my jumper on the back and only letting go when she was sure and would only grab me again when I wobbled. She only forgot once when she was calling to Lyndon's mum about a book club they were having and then she said sorry because she felt bad that I had fallen down. It didn't hurt very much but later she put one of the Disney plasters on and I chose Tigger because he is my favourite character. Andrew said it was brilliant as now that I rollerskate, we can meet together sometimes as he goes skateboarding there and we can play.

I x

Chapter 15

I woke to heat. Having failed to close the curtains of my hotel room, I felt the smog of Singapore seeping between the cracks of the windows. I lay there, momentarily shell-shocked as, hungover and jet-lagged, I tried to remember what I was doing today. Something important. Lurching bolt upright, the room spinning in all its lilac horrificness, I remembered Tioman, and the flight that was booked – the daily flight, the only flight. Leaving in less than two hours.

Pressing '0' on the phone in the room repeatedly and staring at the receiver as I realised it wasn't connected, I padded out onto the landing in my skimpy pyjama shorts and vest top, one arm wrapped protectively across my chest.

'Taxi,' I croaked as I finally made it to reception, the full horror of my appearance clear in the large mirror hanging above the hooks for keys. Eyeliner tracks dribbling down my cheeks, deep-pink lipstick smudged on the side of my mouth, hair like a wild, angry bird, 'Taxi, airport, ten minutes,' I said, shuffling away as if I were fifty years older.

Clawing up my belongings and splashing under my armpits, I would have to shower when I got there. I limped out of the hotel, wincing as the heat started cooking me, bringing me out in a sweat so that the taxi driver must have assumed I had run from somewhere far, far away.

Sunhat on my head, massive sunglasses shielding the worst of it, I sunk down into the leather trying to keep my eyes closed so that my stomach would stop churning. I would feel better after food. Gah, food. Don't think about food. I just needed to get on the plane and get there and sleep and drink water.

Rolling my suitcase into the departure lounge, I jostled with hundreds of other travellers. The whole concourse smelled of chip fat and hot dogs and I was overwhelmed with cravings for salt, meat, bread. Barging my way to the front of McDonald's, with no shame at all, I ordered a meal, happy to discover that you could 'Go Large' anywhere in the world and took a bite of my hamburger, pickle, mustard and ketchup meeting in a magical explosion on my tongue. I moved, unseeing, to Check-in, making 'nommy' noises as I stuffed my face.

'You are a delight,' came a familiar voice.

How could this be? Was I in a dream?

'Zeb,' I said, wiping fruitlessly at my mouth.

'You missed a bit,' he said, pointing to my cheek.

Gah.

'Thanks,' I smiled weakly, my streaked napkin making little progress. 'Why are you here?'

Why is he here? How is this possible? Did he follow me?

'I'm going to Tioman,' he said. holding up his camera.

'But...how...'

'Well I was looking to photograph some animals for *National Geographic* and it seems sort of ideal, and then last night when you were showing me pictures of it on your phone from the Internet I reckoned I had to see it for myself.'

'Oh,' I said, not sure I was allowed to point and say LIAR, you are FOLLOWING ME, YOU ESPRESSO-HAIRED STALKER. I narrowed my eyes instead. What pictures on my phone? I hadn't shown him any...I checked my phone. There were loads of pictures of an island, a long pier, white sand, a selfie with, I peered closer, a man in a trilby. 'Barney,' I croaked. I scrolled through them faster, gah, champagne, beer, selfies with a girl dressed like an anorexic swan, Barney, more beer, argh, loads of swan girls, Zeb and me; it looked dark, outside, our faces were joined together, grinning unashamedly into the lens. Gah. I dropped the phone on the airport floor and the back came off, spinning to a standstill as I dived down to collect it.

When I got up, Zeb had gone, but I knew this was the only flight; there was no real escape. I slid my passport over to a shiny-faced woman with blue eye shadow and finished the last of my chips.

Waddling into Gate 38 loaded down with snacks after an impulsive airport buying spree, I stared in slack-jawed horror through the floor-to-ceiling windows.

'We're flying in that?' I said to nobody, stuttering over the sentence as I took in the tin-box plane, the tiny wheels, the little wings. Where was the jet? Where was the steel with reinforced steel holding everything in place? This plane was basically made of Lego.

Before I could protest, I was following the rest of the passengers out into a bus and over the tarmac towards the plane. It seemed smaller the closer we got, if that was possible. Zeb was nose-deep in a book, one hand holding a leather strap from the ceiling, and I was pleased that at least he hadn't seen my little freak-out.

Getting out of the bus and gulping, I followed a pair of legs all the way to the stairs and then up them, to the door at the back, well the only door of the plane. A polished, tanned hostess greeted me with a toothy smile, her teal uniform impeccable. I wanted to grab her by the collar and scream, 'HAVE YOU SEEN THIS PLANE, IT'S SO SMALL! SURELY THIS IS A JOKE?' But I just returned her smile – it was hard not to it was so massive and toothy – and moved on through, finding my seat towards the back and shifting myself in, staying next to the aisle, glad not to be near the wing to see it was as long as me.

Zeb leaned over to me and grinned on his way past. 'Have a good flight.'

'Seriously, why are you coming?' I blurted in a rush, not sure what possessed me.

'You asked me to, Iz,' he said, laughing.

'I did?'

'Yes, remember? In the taxi on the—'

'What taxi?' I asked, brow crinkled, cutting him off.

'The taxi back to your hotel, oh...' he said, seeing my face. 'You have no memory of it,' he said, a hand clapped over his mouth. 'Wow, what a wasted chivalrous gesture.'

'You dropped me back there,' I said, memory dawning. 'You dropped me there and then went on to your hotel,' I said, recalling him leaving the night before. A large woman was standing rolling her eyes behind him, gesturing to the overhead locker.

'I thought someone should.' He shrugged and moved through to the front of the plane, leaving me gaping after him, wondering why I hadn't said thank you.

Zeb had dropped me back to my hotel. I felt hot and fidgety in my seat. I was in his debt; pieces of the evening were returning. I had clearly been worse for wear. I should get up and say thank you but I was worried that a) it would be horribly embarrassing and b) me crossing the aisle might tip the weight balance out of whack on this tin and we would all plummet into the ocean. So I remained seated, thighs stuck to my chair, looking at the back of his head. One tanned hand on the arm rest, full of a drink that no one else on the flight appeared to have been offered. Now the air hostess was whispering so close to him I thought she might fall into his lap. I snapped the pencil I was holding. Oh, damn, I was never going to finish this Sudoku anyway. I had just filled in my third '7' in a square. HOW DO THESE WORK?

What had he meant I'd asked him to come? Er, hello, unlikely; I was on a mission to find my future husband and wouldn't have invited another man along for the ride. Unless I was paying him to photograph the happy reunion? Now he was tearing into a hot baguette. What was his power over the air hostess? How was he finding food? I hadn't been offered tap water. The meat from earlier was rolling about and I needed something to settle my stomach.

Closing my eyes, I focused on imagining water and I drifted off, suddenly back around the infinity pool of the Marine Bay Sands Hotel. I was dancing on a sun lounger, champagne glass in hand, a pair of twins snaking and twisting in the shallows of the pool, Barney passed out on another lounger. Someone was steering me gently out of the bar area. I sung to him in the lift and did a dance which I had been working on with the twins. He said it was lovely and that if I kept practising, maybe I would be a professional one day. I had nodded and then slumped on him, offering him my hair to smell. But that was just a dream I thought as I jolted away on the plane, examining Zeb's profile as he grinned up at the air hostess. Wow, he just winked at her. I crumpled up the Sudoku, my knuckles white as I squeezed the paper. Then I lost all other thoughts as, circling the island, I glanced out of the window at what appeared to be a tiny strip of tarmac no bigger than a driveway. And a massive forest at the end of it. So no more worries about my life as it was clearly about to come to a dramatic end anyway.

Chapter 16

Tioman Island

We survived! We survived! We didn't fly into the forest despite the fact the runway appeared to be designed by someone who thought the island was a model village! Hooray to the genius pilot! Now that we had actually landed on the ground and I had got over the urge to high-five the entire plane of people, 'Hey, buddy we're alive; looking good, lady, we made it; hey, you, we're here, our persons intact!' I had to stop to take in the extraordinary scenery.

The plane taxied over the tarmac, moving in a slow, bumpy semi-circle before coming to a stop. Towering over the runway, the lush greens of the forest rose up majestically. The sky above was a striking bright blue, punctuated by thin wisps of cloud that failed to provide any kind of cover from the pulsing heat. The fog and grey of Singapore had long been left behind. As we stepped down the stairs and onto the tarmac, the ground seemed to sizzle and the air smelled like salt, soil and coconut oil.

This was the scene of my reunion, I thought with a thrill. This was where I would meet my childhood sweetheart. I couldn't think of a more appropriate place for us to reunite. The tropical location seemed to exude sex and mystery and 'MONKEY!' I squealed. 'MONKEY!' There was a monkey, plain as day, sitting on the other side of the airstrip. He was looking at me, one finger in his nose. I spun around to tell someone and caught the amused expression of Zeb who, being Zeb, would probably not be excited by a monkey at an airport in the slightest. Too cool for mammals. When I looked back, the monkey had gone. Wondering briefly whether I was more hungover than I first thought, I trooped over to collect my suitcase from the dusty floor of the arrivals lounge, which was essentially an open-aired wooden shack on concrete stilts.

Moving through to have my passport checked and meet the allotted bus that would take me to the hotel I'd booked, I could see Zeb walking off down the dirt road in front, beaten-up leather bag slung over his back, a straw cowboy hat on his head like he was auditioning to be a model in the Next summer catalogue. I sniffed, curious as to where he was walking to and maybe a tiny bit disappointed he hadn't said goodbye. Silly Iz, he's annoying and too edgy for his own good, you don't need him to notice you. Ooh, MONKEY! He was back!

An hour or so later, with one rather ineffectual fan simply whirring hot air back towards me, I had unpacked my things in the world's cutest wooden beach hut. The walls were made of deep-brown panels with carved-out holes for windows. These were covered in a criss-crossed wooden frame so that the light that filtered through left a dappled pattern on the crisp white sheets. The hut itself was simplicity personified. I was like Mother Earth. A simple shower, sink and loo had been tacked on almost as an after-thought and there was a single bed and a tiny wooden wardrobe for my things. A sand-spattered terrace wound itself around the whole hut and, as I opened the door, I was greeted with a stretch of white sand and the turquoise blue of the sea beyond. Hello, awesome Instagram photos. I was basically on my dream honeymoon destination. I just needed a groom.

Turning to the bed I inspected the tools I had acquired to hunt down said groom. A pen and small black leather notepad for noting things rested on the top of the duvet next to a camera with a lens that could zoom an excellent length, overly complicated binoculars (fruits of one of Mum's online technology sprees during her bird-watching phase), a basic map of the island with hotels identified, photocopies of Internet Andrew and another from my old school, a line-up of the class of 1989 with Andrew's face circled in red pen. Target identified. I had everything I needed to make this mission a success. I mean, this finding an old friend a success.

I sighed and lowered myself onto the bed. Maybe I had taken things a little far? It suddenly seemed rather impossible and now I was all alone on a tropical island (well me and the monkeys, really), I missed Mel and Mum; they'd give me the confidence I needed to do this, they'd make me feel anything was possible.

Grabbing my iPad, I headed off to the hotel reception to seek Wi-Fi. I would Skype home and explain the latest from here and Mum would give me some of her hearty advice. Trying to do the maths in my head, I decided we were about nine hours ahead of the UK and nine hours behind LA. I reckoned it would be about 7.30 a.m., but that was okay in Mum World as she liked to 'seize the day', normally through song.

Settling on a low wicker sofa, I propped up the iPad on a cushion and then texted Mum to tell her to turn on her Skype. The number dialled and the photo I had uploaded of her laughing at Pentire Point as the wind whipped the hair across her face made me smile in anticipation. Yay to mums making you feel better. The dialling came to an end and I frowned and leaned over to re-dial. Then there was a muffled sound and my mum's voice – her thick, plummy English accent – wafted around me. 'Hello, hello, is it on? Is it? I think it's Isobel, she texted, hello—'

'Mum,' I called, only able to see the kitchen at a slant; the Aga dotted with pans, a tea towel draped over the rung, the window seat, tattered terrifying squirrel cushion resting on its side. Everything had a warm-yellow glow to it and my stomach lurched. I wanted to be drinking tea around the scrubbed pine table, laughing as Mum concocted something suitably weird in her new juice maker.

'Mum,' I repeated, 'move in front of the camera.'

'I can hear her voice. Darling, darling, we are ONLINE. We are HERE FOR YOU,' she shouted.

'Yes, I know, I just said...' Mum walked past the camera at that moment. 'Hold it, Mum, turn around, here, here, closer, closer. Stop. Can you see me?'

In the camera Mum had wheeled around and was staring at the ceiling like my voice was coming from Oz. Then she looked again at the screen and jumped. 'Darling, why didn't you say?'

I grinned and did a double thumbs-up at her. 'Big progress on Skype, kudos.'

Mum pulled her hands together like she was praying and bowed. 'Skype shall not defeat me.'

'Where's Dad?' I asked.

'In bed, of course, waiting for me to bring him up his customary Earl Grey tea. It's like a slave labour camp around here, darling. I am rushed off my feet waiting on him. I have calluses, darling, calluses.' She lifted one foot off the floor and tried to point the sole at the computer screen.

'I get it, Ma,' I said, shielding my eyes behind one hand. 'Thank you for that graphic insight into your domestic bliss.'

Mum sat down and was now gazing at me intently. 'Darling, you look thin, are you eating properly? Where are you now? Have you seen him yet?'

'Mum, I've been gone less than seventy-two hours. I am eating my body weight in cheap hamburgers mostly, and I'm in the Barracuda Hotel on Tioman Island which you have to Google as it is completely amazing and, no, I have yet to see him.'

'Barracuda Hotel, darling, that sounds rather dangerous. STAY OUT OF THE WATER.'

'I'm assuming it is sort of cute and quirky rather than a warning.'

'Well, hotel names aside, darling, I think the whole thing is all wonderfully romantic,' she sighed, sitting back in her chair. 'He'll be more than lucky to have you and he'd be a fool to turn you down.'

I could feel my confidence restored as she spoke.

'I bought this completely fabulous thing for recording things. Wait, I must show you, and you must tell me if you want one too. It's a Dictaphone disguised as a pen! So handy, I am not sure how it works yet but I am super-excited to find out.' Her voice grew weaker as she left the camera to rummage for the mystery object and, returning, hair somewhat askew, to hold it up for me to see.

'What would I record?' I shouted at her departing back.

She returned, puffing. 'Wonderful, isn't it,' she said, holding up what looked like a biro. 'And only £199, which your father thought was rather decadent but your father thinks sending mail first class is pushing the boat out so what does he know?'

'That's great, so er... what are you going to record?'

'Oh ideas, stuff. I might record your father at dinner and see if he gets mad.'

'I'm sure he will.'

'Yes it will be hilarious. I'll try and work out how to send you the recording.'

'Well, Mum, you certainly know how to live so I shall be off, back on my mission.'

Mum looked into the camera. 'Oh good luck.' She smiled at me. 'I saw a seal yesterday, a slippery little head in the water so I waved at him and told him to swim over to you and give you a kiss.'

'That sounds terrifying,' I said, laughing now. 'Please don't set any more sea life onto me.'

'Oh, darling, he was too busy basking about on the rocks here to listen anyway.'

'Well that's a relief.'

'Now, you go get him,' she said, leaning forward to send me a puckered kiss.

'Love you, Mum,' I said, going to press the 'Off' button, and then I was left with my faint reflection in the screen of the iPad and a smile on my face.

I would go and get him, I thought as I rested my head back on the sofa, the strands of wicker creating tiny pressed lines into my thighs. I looked up through the palm trees and the sea beyond. But first I should probably have a swim.

Floating effortlessly in the sea like a starfish, I wasn't sure I could have felt calmer. Raising my arm and spreading my fingers, my skin glistened with a hundred beads of water. The whole world was a deep turquoise, the horizon barely there, my surroundings all sea and sky. There were a few people a hundred yards out, snorkels on and heads down, roaming along the line of coral. Every now and again one of them would wave the other over to look at something. Fishing boats pootled past in the distance and the odd bird dipped into my field of vision. The heat was incredible; I was practically dry by the time I had reached my towel and as I went to reach for my Kindle I paused, outstretched hand frozen.

Further along the beach, on the terrace of one of the huts, a man lazed in a hammock. Wearing board shorts and aviator sunglasses, he seemed to be asleep, one foot resting on the boards. He had curling light hair, caramel skin and full lips. He had the body of an athlete or a tennis player's body, all lean. I lifted up my sunglasses, squinting as I tried to get a better look at him. It couldn't be? On my first day here? But then it was a relatively small island. It wasn't COMPLETELY impossible that it was him.

Kindle forgotten, I got up as if in a daze and found myself starting to walk over to him. Grinding to a halt in the sand, my head yelled, *'Take a prop, Iz.'* I would need a reason to head his way. Beyond his hut was a beach bar and I turned back around, pulling out my purse from my bag. *A drink! I needed a drink. I was parched.* With a smile I grabbed my sarong, knotted it quickly, raked a quick hand through my hair and set off.

Shoulders back, Iz, just in case he is watching you. I licked my lips, feeling a buzzing in my stomach as I headed closer towards him. My palms slipped over the leather of my purse. The nearer I got, the more distinct he became. His hair was definitely lighter than it had been on the television, but that was only natural out here. And he seemed to look tallish but he was lying down so it was hard to tell that too. His stomach was flat and he had excellent taste in swimwear, so all of that was how I imagined it to be.

I tried to walk in a straight line and keep my eyes ahead but kept falling in sand divots, stumbling like I had only just learned to walk, mouth dry. As I passed him, I couldn't help turning my whole head in his direction and staring. He was asleep, mouth slightly ajar, a bottle of beer empty on a table beside him. Was it him? I tried to picture the 1989 schoolboy, the man from the television and this Hammock Dude.

In the shade of the bar, clutching my lemonade, I waited for my heart to settle down. From my vantage point on the high stool wedged deep into the sand, I could simply see his right foot. It was tanned, quite narrow, had the right number of toes, but really gave me no other clues to his identity. I suppose his name in some kind of elaborate italic foot tattoo was probably a hope too far. And would I really want to be married to a man who feels the urge to tattoo his own name into lower appendages? An anklet might have worked, perhaps? A simple chain with the letter 'A' dangling as a single charm. But then again, did men wear anklets? Did anyone really wear anklets? Should anyone wear anklets? I went back to my lemonade and then yawned. The travelling had made me sleepy and all that swimming/starfishing in the water had really tired me out.

As I wandered back over to my towel, I knew Andrew wouldn't wake. I paused. Should I walk over to his hut and say hello? See if it was him close up? Pretend to want to borrow sugar/a coconut? My foot wavered over the hot sand and then I changed my mind.

Dear diary,

Yesterday Moregran fell down the stairs and hit her head and it was scary because I found her and had to ring the ambulance. Mum dropped me off to Andrew's house when she went to the hospital to be with Moregran and Andrew was really good at sitting with me. We played *Legend of Zelda* and he let me have double the goes because he knew I was thinking about Moregran and when I cried a bit he just went and got me a custard cream because he knew they were my favourites.

We didn't talk much but he held my hand when I cried and I felt a lot better.

I x

Chapter 17

Sleeping Andrew had returned inside his hut a while ago. I had read thirty-six per cent on the Kindle and was starting to feel woozy. Surely he would return soon? I needed to keep a close eye, but I also needed the loo. Scrabbling up, I raced to my hut, desperate to keep this visit quick. Peeing with the door open, splashing water over my hands, I smoothed my hair, adjusted my white and yellow striped bikini and seized my biggest sunglasses, grabbing the binoculars Mum had given me before I left: 'They have exceptional light transmission.'

His hut door was still shut when I emerged, panting, back on the sand. Heading over to a row of peddle boats I rented one for an hour, setting off at a slow crawl, binoculars on the seat beside me. I'd be working out and keeping a keen eye open. Ten minutes later and the peddle boat was becoming an effort. It had looked less hard work than the reality. My thighs were burning as I pushed and turned the pedals, making slow progress. Swimmers were everywhere, searching the coral and lounging on lilos. There was laughter and shouting from a volleyball pitch set up further down the beach. Startled birds launched themselves into the sky at the noise. Starting to feel woozy again, I closed my eyes, pedalling now almost at a standstill. Then a shout and my eyes snapped open as the boat started rocking and I was covered in spray.

'What the hell?' I jabbered, a hand shooting out to steady myself as a man emerged from the water, straddling the front of the boat.

'Permission to come aboard,' Zeb roared, laughing at my expression.

'Permission not granted.' I scowled, wiping at my face and starting to pedal again.

The extra weight wasn't helping and Zeb was now balanced on either side of the front of the boat grinning down at me.

'What are you doing, Crazy Lady?' he asked, looking at my binoculars and then back at me. 'And I like your sunglasses.'

Narrowing my eyes, I put my nose in my air. 'I was getting some fresh air, some peace and ALONE time.'

'And the binoculars? What are they for?'

'Bird watching,' I said, picking them up and training them on the sky. Bloody birds had all gone, I put them down again.

Zeb was now standing on one foot, about to move into the body of the boat. 'What are you doing?'

He froze in mid-air. 'Sitting down?' he said hopefully. 'You look like you could do with some manpower.'

'I don't think so,' I said, pushing furiously at the pedals.

The boat wobbled violently and Zeb grabbed at the front.

'Well you leave me little choice but to throw myself into the water and drown.'

'Don't be ridiculous.'

'I'm not; your rejection would cut me so deep I would not have the energy to paddle my little legs.'

I rolled my eyes. 'Okay, fine.' I gave up, raising both hands in surrender. 'SIT, sit and be silent.'

Zipping his lips, Zeb crept over into the spare seat and, sticking his thumb at me, started a complicated mime about pedalling.

Feeling a bubble of unwanted laughter rise in my throat, I focused on pushing one foot after the other. We made speedy progress as we coursed back across the sea, churning the water up in our path and feeling the breeze on our skin.

Nervous I might have missed Andrew leaving his hut, I lifted the binoculars to my eyes, scanning the beach and then resting on the hut. There was movement in the window, a shadow! I might have made a small, excited noise.

Zeb had stopped pedalling and when I lowered the binoculars I realised he was looking at me.

'Soooo,' he said, indicating the binoculars. 'Explain.'

'Explain what?'

'Explain what you're looking at.'

'Nothing,' I said, panicking.

'Rubbish.'

His blue eyes were trained on me. I licked my lips. Could I really tell him? No, I couldn't tell him, I would sound crazy. He would laugh.

'Oi, woman, I am here to help. Stop worrying and let me aid your secret mission. Why the focus on that hut?' He pointed. 'Why the binoculars? What are we scoping out, 008?'

I took another sideways look at him. Something about his expression prompted me to clear my throat and start to explain.

'I'm looking for a man,' I admitted in a half-whisper, unable to look him in the eye. A pause. I sneaked a quick sideways glance. His expression hadn't changed. He wasn't pointing and laughing...yet.

'A specific one, I assume?'

'Yes, a specific one.'

'A famous one?'

I shook my head quickly. 'No.'

'An ex-boyfriend?'

I went to shake my head and did a sort of half shake and nod.

'Oh no,' Zeb said, putting his head in his hands. He looked at me, one eye through the gap in his fingers. 'Are you an actual stalker? Are you going to be on the front of the *Daily Mail* in a week's time?'

I went to punch him on the arm, just stopping myself as I remembered I didn't know this guy, not really, and that might be a bit over-familiar. And might confirm his fears I was a violent stalker.

I breathed out, trying my hardest to look the least mad I could look.

'We were best friends when we were really young and then we had one of those weddings in the playground, you know the type?'

'Ahhhh.' He lowered both hands. 'Yes I do, Penelope Smith, you little beauty,' he said to the sky.

I couldn't help a giggle. 'Well I always wondered what happened to him. Wanted to see him. We had been close and well...'

As I said it all aloud, I realised how deranged it sounded. How could I explain to him that it was an instinct in my gut, something I had dreamed about for years? I felt certain about it in my core. I should be here, I should be finding Andrew Parker.

'So that's why you came all the way out here for this man. All this way. From England.'

'Er...' I faltered, not sure whether to correct him.

I found myself saying it anyway. 'LA actually,' I corrected. 'LA, to England to Malaysia,' I finished, feeling strangely proud of myself.

'Well,' Zeb paused, his brow furrowed. It was strange seeing him so serious; he nearly always seemed to be on the edge of a joke, eyes sparkling with some fresh amusement. 'Well that is pretty extreme,' he concluded.

As he was finishing his sentence, it finally happened: the hut door opened and a figure appeared. I scrabbled to raise the binoculars again as the man, my man, walked out of the doorway onto the terrace. Andrew was dressed in combat shorts now, still bare-chested. He put his hands on the balcony in front of him and seemed to be breathing in the fresh air. I inhaled with him, smelling plants, orange and promise.

Zeb prodded me in my side. 'Is that him?' he whispered as if he might hear us from where we bobbed on the waves.

I nodded, quickly adjusting my binoculars to focus in on him.

He was taller than I thought but just as gorgeous. Now that he wasn't wearing aviators, I really wanted to get a close-up of his face. Well I would, I supposed as I twisted the dials, the hut and him blurring in and out. How the hell does Mum work these things? I had to get over there, I had to do this. I automatically started to pedal towards shore.

'Come o...' My sentence fell away as I noticed movement behind Andrew. A woman appeared, framed in the doorway, a woman in a tiny T-shirt and little bikini bottoms, hair mussed up. A woman. Oh no. I sank lower in the peddle boat as if I could disappear into the seat.

'Who's that?' Zeb pointed.

I practically launched myself onto him, pushing his hand down. 'Don't, they'll see.'

The two figures on the terrace turned in our direction to stare out at the sea.

I froze half-bent over Zeb as if we were playing musical statues. My brain raced with questions. Maybe she was his sister? Or the room maid or, argh, DON'T PUT YOUR ARM AROUND HIM, ROOM MAID, DON'T DO...

'She looks nice,' Zeb said, his voice wobbling as if he were about to giggle. Then he caught my expression. 'Oh I'm sorry, this is bad.'

'It IS bad,' I insisted as Andrew put an arm over her shoulders.

'But you don't actually know that's him, do you?'

'Well, I, it's hard to tell from this distance, he looks familiar,' I said, my voice wavering with uncertainty.

'Look, Iz, it's probably not him, is it? I mean, when was the last time you actually saw him?' Zeb's voice sounded serious and the look he gave me made me feel like he'd reached over and dropped pebbles in my stomach. I gulped, concerned that I would break down here on the peddle boat.

'A while ago but...' I faded away, not really sure any more and feeling silly and exposed.

'Hey,' he said, reaching across to me and stopping just before we connected. 'If you really want to know, why don't you just ask at Reception? See if it's him.'

'I can't just...' I trailed off, realising he was right. *Why couldn't I do that?*

'Wouldn't that be a bit...weird?' I asked, biting my lip.

'Weird asking whether he is staying in a hut or weird going to stake out his place with binoculars for a second day running. Hmm, weird, weird, weird...' he repeated, one finger on his lips.

'Fine, you make your point,' I said. 'And I wasn't "staking out his place", I just...Well, you know nothing.' *What are you five years old, Iz? Way to defeat someone with your powerful argument. Not.*

We paddled in silence for a while and I almost forgot why I was there as the heat of the day and the views out to sea and around the island made my head spin. Zeb had slung an arm over the side of the boat and was looking relaxed and at ease. Up ahead a tiny island covered in thick green trees sprouted out of the water like an enormous piece of broccoli.

'The snorkelling is great round there,' Zeb pointed.

'How do you already know that?'

'I'm an early bird,' he shrugged. 'Went out this morning. It was amazing. We could go later?' he suggested.

'Oh I'm too busy,' I said quickly, not sure I wanted to

spend more time with Zeb. Something about him made me feel silly, as if I had three legs and no sensible thoughts at all. We were close to shore now.

He was wearing the binoculars around his neck and raised them once in a while to peer through.

'What are you looking for?' I asked him as he trained them on my face, forcing me to hold a hand up as a shield.

'Not sure, I think I've done something funny, you are basically a pink blur.'

'Nice,' I said peddling faster.

'A really pretty pink blur,' he corrected, making me look in the opposite direction, tongue too big for my mouth.

'Hey,' I said, glancing over at the hut and holding out a hand for the binoculars. 'He's moved,' I explained, panic rising in my voice.

Zeb handed them over and I focused in on the shoreline, moving the binoculars over various sunbathing bodies, kids splashing in the shallows, to the Mystery Man. Got him. My body relaxed and without thinking I muttered, 'I don't remember his eyes being shaped like that.'

'Funny eyes, eh?' Zeb chuckled.

I lowered the binoculars. 'Not funny, just different,' I explained, looking through the lens once more. 'But maybe eye shape changes with age. It's possible, isn't it?' I asked.

'Like noses. Noses keep growing forever.'

I touched my nose in alarm and looked at him. 'Is that really true? How big is my nose going to be?'

Zeb looked at me solemnly. 'Who's to say, Isobel, who is to say?'

Chapter 18

Traipsing into the hotel reception, I felt my pulse drumming through my body. My hands were slippery as I clutched the handles of my bag. I felt nauseous, ready to turn and run... *LOOK RELAXED* my brain shouted, which only made me perspire more. Taking a long, slow breath I focused on the receptionist with the kindest eyes and headed their way. He was young and wearing a jaunty Hawaiian shirt buttoned to the neck. Leaning over the counter and looking up shyly through my eyelashes, I asked him in a half-whisper, 'Could I, do you, could I check the name of a guest staying with you?'

He frowned at my question and clicked on his computer. 'Name?' he asked.

My stomach gurgled and I put a hand over it, giggling with nervous relief. 'Andrew. Andrew Parker,' I whispered.

He stared at the computer, his kind eyes scanning back and forward. I could hear the tick of the eight clocks behind him, all telling the time around the world and felt like the ticks were growing louder with every passing second. TICK, TICK, YOUR TIME HAS COME, ISOBEL. THIS IS IT.

The kind eyes looked back at me and with another frown the receptionist said, 'No booking.'

'Sorry?'

'No booking. Would you like to book?'

'No, no, you see I am booked. So you have no one of that name here?'

He shook his head. 'No, ma'am.'

'Oh I'm not a ma'am.'

'Yes, ma'am.'

'Well,' I swallowed, my throat scratchy. 'Thank you for checking, thank you,' I repeated, stumbling backwards.

He wasn't here, it wasn't him and there was no one of that name at all.

And then, as if to confirm it, the man from that hut appeared in Reception and walked straight past me to the drinks machine. The girl followed too, running up the short flight of stairs. 'Mark,' she called, 'will you get me a lemonade?'

'Sure, darl,' he called back in an Australian accent.

Mark. Australian Mark.

Not Andrew Parker.

I felt like someone had plonked me right back at Square One.

Walking aimlessly around the complex, feet dragging along the ground, I found myself sitting on one side of a see-saw in the children's play area. It was silly to feel this low; I should have known it wasn't him immediately. He had seemed too tall, his hair too blond.

I couldn't just sit back and wait for him to magically appear. I had to muster the energy to search for him. I could start with the other hotels and B&Bs; perhaps I would get lucky early on? I hadn't booked my return flight yet but my funds were already worryingly low and this mission couldn't last forever.

I would have to go back sometime; I needed to find a new agent, update my show reel, focus more on what I wanted from my career. Randy hadn't been right, I knew that. I needed to find someone who wanted to help me present programmes I was really interested in. This could be a restorative break. I was seeking change, I knew that really; I hadn't liked to admit that this change seemed to be so tied up with finding Andrew, but he seemed important. I had always wondered what my life might have been like if we had stayed in touch. Perhaps I would have more success in my career with someone like Andrew supporting me, cheering me on? I needed answers and he seemed to be holding a whole handful of them and he was somewhere, somewhere close and I would find him.

Digging into the woodchips with a toe, I smiled at the memory of our school playground, sharing the see-saw with Andrew who would bounce with his feet, soar into the air, his bottom leaving the seat, his hair flying up so he looked like he'd been electrocuted, and then his laugh as I did the same. The rush of the wind, the simple pleasure of playing made me suddenly wish that someone else was sitting opposite.

My phone rang out in the silence. I pulled it out, eyebrows lifting as I read the name on the screen. Stewie. 'Hello,' I said, my voice on the wrong side of gloomy.

'Was it my clothes?' he started without a greeting.

'What?'

'My clothes, was it my clothes; my ex hated the way I dressed, said I was colour blind, was it that?'

'What do you mean, Stewie?' I asked, my brow crinkling.

'Were they the reason you broke up with me?' he asked, his voice rising. 'Was it my clothes?'

Oh. Christ. I took a breath, not really feeling I had the mental energy to deal with this conversation right now and hoping on hope I might suddenly walk through a tunnel.

'I'm not that shallow, Stewie,' I said.

'So you didn't like them,' he crowed triumphantly.

'What? No, your clothes were fine.'

'Is it because I'm receding? I have spoken to friends and there are transplants for that. I'm considering my options. They can do amazing things with hair from your anu—'

'It wasn't your hair, clothes or anything like that, Stewie, god, give me some credit.'

I smiled briefly at a mother as she arrived in the park, two children in tow, heading straight for the swings.

'Well I have made a list of things so I'll read to you from it and you stop me when I get to it.' He started reciting things before I could interrupt. 'Was it the long absences? Was I too unimaginative in the bedroom? Was it my love of wrestling? Was it because I kept clipping my nails in bed even after you asked me specifically not to do that...?'

Eugh yes, that was gross I thought as I tuned out for

a while. This couldn't continue though. I hadn't realised Stewie had such low self-esteem. 'Stewie,' I called.

'... was it because I refused to sleep on the window side of the bedroom because that side wasn't my normal side? Was I a bad listener? Was my crush on Jessica Alba overwhelming? Was it because I couldn't cook? Was it—?'

'Stewie,' I repeated, making the mother look up in alarm at me. *Why was I always shouting at Stewie down the phone?*

'... because...'

'Stewie, stop this, don't be absurd. It wasn't any one thing; it was just not right, it was...'

'But that doesn't make any sense,' he whined.

'Look.' I breathed out slowly, my toe burrowing further into the wood chips. 'We were just not quite right; it didn't feel like we'd found our soulmate, did it?'

'Soulmates?' he repeated uncertainly.

'Yes, you know, when two people are totally immersed in each other, when they're completely excited about seeing each other, when that other person brings out the absolute best in them and they just can't imagine the world without them in it and it hurts, hurts to be apart...' I realised I'd raised my voice again and was now breathing heavily into the phone, carried away by my soliloquy.

'Oh.'

'Exactly,' I said quietly. 'So, do you see?'

There was a pause and I pictured Stewie puckering his mouth in thought. 'So it WASN'T my clothes?' he confirmed.

Dear diary,

Andrew and I are getting married tomorrow. Everyone at school has been talking about it this week. I am really excited and Andrew says it will be good because we always hang out together and are best friends already. Dad always said marriage was a sign that you wanted to spend the rest of your life with someone and I know Andrew and I will always be together so I think it is a good idea.

I x

Chapter 19

Two hotels and five B&Bs later and I was none the wiser. There'd been a very exciting moment in the second of the hotels when the receptionist had misheard and phoned Mr Marker's room to summon him to meet his beau. Mr Marker had been pushing eighty and had proceeded to invite me back to his room for some brandy. I'd politely declined.

The whole debacle was proving utterly hopeless and I'd found myself alone in a beach bar, bottle in hand, watching the sun sink on another day. Even a Skype call from my mum had failed to rally the spirits, despite the fact that she had spent much of it dancing around the kitchen convincing me that she was channelling good energy my way. She'd sprained her ankle towards the end and Dad had been summoned to ice it and prop it up on the terrifying squirrel cushion.

The waitress, a middle-aged woman wearing a lime green dress and the most enormous earrings, brought me over another beer.

'Best view on the island,' she commented, hands on her hips, her gaze on the wide expanse of sky streaked with a hundred shades of orange.

'It's lovely,' I nodded.

'Romantic,' she cackled, her earrings wobbling as she laughed. 'Boyfriend?' She pointed to the empty chair next door to me and for a moment I was alarmed that she thought I had an imaginary man.

'Just me,' I said in a voice that I hoped didn't sound too bitter.

'Shame.'

'Tell me about it,' I laughed, bringing the beer to my lips. 'Actually,' I said, lowering the bottle and looking at her. Should I? Would it be another dead-end?

She raised one eyebrow.

'I'm, um, sort of looking for someone. He's here on the island somewhere. English. Andrew, Andrew Parker?' I paused after his name, hoping to see a glimmer of recognition in her brown eyes, a quick nod of her head which would set her earrings off again. I got no such thing.

'No, no Andrew,' she said, patting me on the shoulder.

It was then that a couple walked past the table, joining a small crowd of people who had gathered at the mouth of the stream that ran down the side of the bar. A little girl was pointing over the bank into the water and I watched her face light up with excitement, tugging on the hem of her mother's skirt.

'What's all that about?' I asked, burying the disappointment of another dud.

'Every evening people come to see the monitor lizards

swim there,' she said, a nonchalant shrug of her shoulders.

'Monitor lizards?' I repeated, lifting up my feet automatically; I'd never been overly keen on reptiles.

'Take a look, they don't hurt,' she said, smiling at me.

Taking my beer I walked over to the edge of the group peering down into the stream, the water a muddy reflection of plants and trees. Then a sudden movement in the shallows and a smooth, slimy-looking head appeared with beady eyes and a stubby snout for a nose. Its stumpy legs paddled furiously in the water, its snake-like body one big muscle. Another head emerged and I could feel my mouth hang open at the unfamiliar sight. They were elegantly repulsive and I felt a small hint of alarm whenever one of their heads disappeared from view. The buzz of my mobile phone made me squeak and some of the onlookers spun round to look at me.

'Sorry,' I whispered, reaching to press 'Answer'.

'Mel,' I whispered, backing away, 'I have just seen the biggest f'ing lizard ever.'

'Is that a euphemism?'

'What? No, I have actually just seen a massive lizard. They're huge, Mel, like dinosaurs.'

'Nice,' Mel said. 'Will you take photos?'

'Maybe, it was enormous.'

Mel started giggling on the other end. 'Wow, Iz, I haven't heard you this enamoured in a while.'

Sitting back down at my circular table, I grinned down the phone at her. 'Maybe it's my future. I could be Queen of the Lizards.'

'Well we're not there yet. Or are we? How's the hunt going?'

'Waste of time,' I grunted.

'Oh dear. Now look, I can't be long because frankly phoning you makes working for a living a bit pointless but I wanted you to check your emails as I'm sending you some info about a new TV job over here. I think you'll be perfect; honestly, it's just the kind of thing you are looking for.'

'Trying to get me home, eh?' I said, feeling a lurch for Mel and her silly face.

'Maybe. Right, I really do have to go, Dex has been acting we-i-rd recently and he has SUMMONED me to dinner. Shit, do you think he's going to break up with me?'

'Er, no, you two are completely brilliant together and he loves you.'

'He does, doesn't he, and who wouldn't, I am great!'

'And modest,' I added.

'Yeah, yeah, gotta go, love you, Lizard Girl.'

There was a commotion as I was signing off and I turned to look at what was going on, fully expecting to see a lizard or some kind of reptile taking off, a crowd of people snapping in its wake. It was the waitress, though, making a determined line for my table.

'Andrew,' she said, streaking towards me, a vison in bright green. 'He know Andrew,' she said pulling over what I could only guess was her teenage son, the smattering of an early beard sprouting on his chin.

I felt a little flicker in my stomach as the boy was pushed in front of me, his mother panting behind him. Was this it? Hope drove me to ask him in a careful voice, 'Andrew Parker, you have met him?'

The boy nodded quickly.'I say, he and friend like Arsenal.

They come here to watch game.' He pointed over his shoulder to a television screwed into the corner of the wall behind him.

'Really,' I said, breaking into a smile, not yet ready to believe it. Had I found him? Was this it?

'Where is he? Do you know?'

Chapter 20

Loading up my rucksack with just the essentials (bottle of water, towel, insect repellent, map, sun cream, binoculars, pressed powder, eyeliner, lip salve, bikini, photo of Internet Andrew Parker, lucky charm in shape of a troll doll on a key ring), I tied my hair back in a ponytail, did a last check of my appearance in the mirror and left the hut behind. I would be trekking across the centre of the island to the East Coast, through the forest and was supposed to follow the telegraph poles if I didn't want to get lost/eaten by something wild and creepy. The journey would take me between two and a half and three hours. Andrew was staying on the other side of the island, the waitress – Nor – and her son Haziq had been certain of it. He had been over there for a week or so and had come in to watch some sport in their bar. Juara beach was my destination. It sounded ideal.

It had seemed romantic, a trek across the island, me appearing like Model Student on a Geography Field Trip.

Andrew impressed: tick. But by the entrance to the forest, a half mile up from the hotel resort, I was already sweating and had drunk half of my bottled water. The sun seemed to be an unrelenting ball of lava overhead and there was not a cloud around. From the incline I was standing on to my left I could see the stretch of tempting ocean reaching for miles, children playing in the shallows, others lying on towels on the beach. I could go back and arrange a 4x4 across the island, but I wasn't sure how to find one and whether I'd have to wait another day. I dived into the forest before I could change my mind, focusing on the reason for doing this. Andrew.

Ducking under stray branches and hearing the buzz of the jungle, I flinched as something shot out from a nearby bush. The light was speckled and everything had a greenish tinge to it. The air smelled of damp earth and throbbed with the hum of a thousand insects. The island guide did mention that Tioman was home to giant rhinoceros beetles (excellent!), but others had clearly walked this path; the trail was flattened and eleven kilometres wasn't that far. I'd done a half marathon in LA the year before, so throw in a little incline, some pit stops to drink water and check the map and I could surely make it by lunch.

The path wound higher, narrowing and twisting, and the backs of my calves were burning with the effort. My plimsolls weren't the best at gripping things so it was hard-going on the sloped earth. Flat-leaved plants nibbled on by insects crowded along the edges of the path as tree roots snaked across the track leaving bumps and knots to trip over. I patted fruitlessly at my forehead for the twentieth time and kept my eyes focused on where I was going. Just up ahead, bold as you like, in the centre of the path was one small monkey, hunched over examining something in his little monkey paws.

He looked up at me through miniature lashes, his round eyes curious as I approached him. Smiling, pathetically pleased for the company, I went to look in my bag for something to offer him. Lip salve wasn't probably the thing. Rummaging deeper and making encouraging 'cooing' noises so he wouldn't scuttle away, I paused, alert, as a hissing noise to my right grew louder. Spinning in the direction of the noise, I could feel my heart jumping in my chest. A nearby bush shook violently and three more monkeys bounded out of it. Then I heard the whoosh and disturbance of more foliage, and two more swung off low branches. That was a lot of monkeys. And they weren't looking cute any more; they had their mouths open, teeth on full display and were hissing at me, shrieks coming from the backs of their throats so that I backed off, hands held high. They continued to spit, little round eyes cold and menacing. They were a family of Devil Monkeys. Even the original monkey had strutted across to stand behind his buddies and seemed to be smirking at me as if to say, 'Ha, fool woman, I coaxed you in with my little paws and my coy little look from my cute tiny eyes and you FELL for it. I am a GENIUS monkey, moo ha ha.'

How was I going to get round this British Bulldog line-up of monkeys? They were still hissing and one of them had circled around and seemed to be coming in from the rear like he was Commando-trained. Any moment I expected another to roll in, knife in his teeth, to seal my fate. There was only one thing for it; animals knew when humans were afraid, so I couldn't act afraid. It was dog logic but I assumed it might work for monkeys, too, so I did what any self-respecting woman on her own would do; I straightened both my arms in the air, opened my mouth wide, screamed and ran forward shouting, 'CHAAARGGGGGGEEE!'

Monkeys scattered EVERYWHERE before me. I ran on, dipping and diving and keeping up the screaming just in case they were after me and might swing on tendrils to block me, then I realised I had screamed my way off the beaten path and the flattened foliage and I was in the middle of a buzzing forest, crawling with life, and was alone. I lowered my arms and then, someway off to my right, heard a splash.

Do I walk towards the noise or away from the noise? What could be big enough to make a splash? Shark! No, no sea. I'm in jungle, Isobel, think. Crocodile? No, the guide did not have anything about them. They did have information about the monitor lizards. Giant ones. I could picture one now, a slithering, juddering long lizard frantically walking on four crooked legs splashing about in a bog of slime. I turned to search for the path in the opposite direction, but then another hiss not far from me got me screaming again and yelling, 'Charge!' Running away from the hissing, I stumbled past bushes and trees straight into a clearing, hands still high, mouth still open and then heard another cry, a deep shout of fear and a naked man standing on a rock holding his heart and panting.

'What the fuck?' he said, bent double.

Breathing heavily, I lowered my arms, mouth still hanging open.

Zeb turned towards me. 'Iz, what ARE you doing? You basically just gave me a heart attack.'

With absolutely no attempt to cover himself up, Zeb admonished me. I averted my eyes, feeling my whole body get hotter and hotter, like a light was shining straight on to me. 'I, the monkey, I didn't—' I got a hold of myself as he slipped into the pool next to his rock.

Losing sight of his buttocks helped give me a little more confidence. 'What do you mean, what am I doing? What are you doing out here, splashing about?'

'It's called swimming, Iz, people do it as a leisure activity.'

'Well I know what you were doing but obviously it was quite a shock to see, you know, what you were wearing to do it in.' I rolled my shoulders, trying to keep my voice steady.

Zeb raised an eyebrow. 'If it hadn't escaped your notice, I thought I was alone and having a lovely uninterrupted swim in my birthday suit. It's hugely refreshing. You should try it.'

I bristled. 'Well I can't, I am trekking,' I said with my nose in the air.

'Suit yourself, Edmund Hillary.'

Clutching my side, I paused for breath. The whole monkey chase had worked me into more of a dripping mess. Slowing my breathing, I took in the scenery. It was the most incredible copse. Rocks burst out of the earth and disappeared up into the trees, a small waterfall tumbling through them to the pool below throwing up white froth as it smacked the surface. The pool itself was olive green, the ripples made by Zeb the only things disrupting the surface. It looked incredibly relaxing and I was well aware of the beads of sweat on my hairline, in between my clothes, trickling down my spine. The bottle of water had long gone and I gulped, tempted to whip off my T-shirt and dive in.

But then I looked at Zeb's face, peaceful as he paddled around the place, and I felt a shot of resentment fire through me. I looked at him with his 'I am so at-one-with-the-island' face and his 'I'm so laid-back,-me,-I-don't-need-clothes' and knew I couldn't. As enticing as it would be to place a toe into the cool, deep water, I couldn't join him in there.

'I need to get on,' I said sniffily, like I was justifying things to myself.

Zeb continued to breaststroke about the place, dipping his head back and then standing up to flick it back like he was some kind of merman in a porno.

'Come on, Iz, I won't look, you have to get in here, it's just brilliant.' He flicked water towards me and then roared with laughter.

'Stop it, I have to get across the island,' I said in a tight voice I didn't recognise as my own. Why was I being like this? I needed to calm down; he didn't mean anything by it and, anyway, I had just run screaming into his private pool party – what did I expect? Turning, I didn't see the tangled roots of a nearby tree and found myself lurching forward to land in the soil, amongst the leaves, pebbles and debris.

'Ow,' I squealed.

'You okay?' Zeb called.

The pain made me more abrupt than I'd meant. 'I'm bloody fine thanks, bloody fine.'

Feeling hot tears of humiliation sting the back of my eyes, I blinked once and went to get up, body aching. I could feel mud sticking to the side of my face and I was fairly certain I had twigs and leaves stuck in my hair. Zeb was looking at me with real concern on his face, clearly uncertain whether to risk emerging from the pool and over in my direction where he might have his head snapped off. Or worse.

'Get in, you'll feel so much better. I am turning away so you can get changed,' he called.

I brushed leaves and soil off my clothes, damp with sweat and suncream.

'I don't need t...'

'If you do, I will even escort you to the other side of the island. I've worked out a way from here. Iz?'

'Gah. Okay, okay, I give up, I'm coming, look away then,' I said, waving one arm at him and dumping my bag on the floor.

Hopping quickly into my bikini and leaving my clothes in a pile, I stepped gingerly into the water, gasping at the sudden change in temperature. My ankles stung as I kept walking over the flat ledge of rock and then stepped into the pool itself. Water flooded over my legs and quickly around my stomach which had already developed a tan, deeper against the white of the bikini. Plunging my head back, I felt instant relief as the sharp cold washed around me. Running my hands through my hair, I waded towards the middle of the pool. Standing up and flicking back my hair, the water up to my hips, I realised Zeb was still looking towards the rocks away from me.

'You can turn around now,' I said, feeling a little foolish.

He did and there was a moment where I thought I could see something cross his face. A look I couldn't place and then it was gone in a whisper as he smiled at me. 'Told you.'

'Yes, yes, well done,' I said, swimming away from him towards the waterfall, remembering briefly that Zeb was completely naked and in the same pool as me. If the water hadn't been so cold, I might have turned red.

Clutching a couple of rocks and hauling myself up onto them, I closed my eyes as the water from the waterfall smacked over my head and shoulders. It was an incredible feeling; gentle thumping on my back as it struck me and soothed. Gasping in pleasure, I pictured myself in one of those exotic shampoo adverts and wondered whether there was a better experience in the world than this.

Moving away from the waterfall, I flung my arms wide and looked up towards the canopy of trees. The sun was still above us, finding the cracks and gaps between the leaves and making the pool sparkle and shimmer in those spots. Zeb had looked across at me and was now choking back a laugh, half-turning away from me.

I frowned. 'What's so funny?'

Zeb had his back to me. 'You might want to adjust your attire.'

I looked down, feeling my eyebrows knit together, and then froze in horror as I was greeted with one rather large lone white breast.

'Oh,' I breathed, hauling my bikini top back from where it had slipped sideways.

'I knew that waterfall was good for something,' Zeb said, his back shaking, the muscles in his back rippling as he giggled to himself.

'Ha, ha, very funny,' I said, embarrassed.

I stomped out of the pool and over to my clothes, wanting to get away from this clearing and Zeb's mocking laughter.

'Don't worry, we all do things that make us feel like a bit of a tit sometim—' He stopped mid-sentence and slapped a hand over his mouth, not before letting out a bark of laughter. 'Sorry, slip of the tongue,' he choked.

Stepping into my shorts and pulling my vest top over my head, I fumbled to put my shoes back on.

'Hey, don't ignore me, Iz, I would get out and apologise properly but I'm naked and I'm not sure you would appreciate that.'

'It's fine,' I said in a voice much higher than my own. 'I'm glad I amuse you.'

'Oh come on, Iz, I'm kidding, wait for me to come with you, we can walk tog—'

'No, I need to get on,' I said, tying my hair back in a tight ponytail and feeling droplets of water drip down my spine. Picking up my bag and avoiding his eyes completely, I left the way I had arrived, determined to find the nearest telegraph pole and the path to the beach.

'Have it your own way. Up there, take a right on the path,' he called.

As I left the clearing and started walking again, I felt a pang of regret for snapping at him. I was pretty sure I should have seen the funny side and I'd behaved a little like a petulant child. But he had the ability to push my buttons no end. He would be swimming about down there, laughing at me again. He wouldn't care. Delighted at finding the path, I turned right and headed towards Juara, cursing myself for thinking of Zeb's bottom when I got bored.

Chapter 21

Emerging at the edge of the forest, I blinked and realised with an overwhelming sense of wonder that I had done it. I had trekked, navigated. I was an explorer. IN YOUR FACE, Gold D of E instructor, now who doesn't have the mental fortitude for hard work? Ha! I could climb mountains, swim oceans... Mostly, though, I was in desperate need of food and water. I seemed to have burst out of the forest at one end of a large strip of beach that curved inland as if it were an enormous sandy smile. A floating man-made raft lay a hundred yards offshore and the sea was completely still, protected from the rocks and forest from the wind.

Snorkellers paddled about and a couple walked hand in hand along the shoreline just ahead of me. The beach was littered with overturned rowing boats, fraying straw ropes attached to their helms, a spattering of sand along the bottoms where the paint had worn away completely. I found a path that wound its way behind the beach and through a pop-up street of wooden huts and cafes and then noticed a small shop with an ancient chest freezer plugged into a socket outside, a buzzing emanating from a generator screwed into the wall above it. An empty stool and a dustpan and brush were stowed next to it.

Pushing open the door, warm air circled, a tilted single fan, trying to cool down the shop floor. I opened the fridge door and felt an overwhelming temptation to climb inside, sit on the bottom rack and stay there. Instead I grabbed a bottle of water and a Diet Coke and went to pay, realising as I caught my face in the mirror behind the counter, that I wasn't looking my most elegant. My hair had dried into waves, my face was red from the efforts of the afternoon and I had large rings under both arms. However, I had just crossed an entire ISLAND and taking the crumpled photocopy of Andrew's face from the Internet I slid it across the counter to the man serving me. No time to waste. I was totally seizing this day.

'Excuse me, but do you recognise him?'

The man, middle-aged, patted at a mop of dark-brown hair flecked with grey, then took the picture from me. Lifting a pair of glasses from next to the till and hovering them over the image, he squinted at it.

'Don't think so, no,' he said, looking back at me. 'Is it important?' he asked as my shoulders slumped and that familiar wash of impossibility flooded over me.

'Someone thought perhaps they'd seen him on this side of the island.'

'Not in here but you never know: Juara beach is long and there are lots of men here,' he said with a slightly seedy wink.

My heart lifted a little, although many men still sounded like a lot and Andrew was definitely becoming the needle in the haystack. Thanking him, I pushed out of his shop. Twisting the bottle of water and drinking half of it just outside the doorway, I felt a sliver of possibility. There was something in the air: hope, I thought. Or maybe grilled fish. Either way, I had come this far and I had to search this beach and try to get back to the hotel tonight. Wiping my mouth with the back of my hand, I walked right along the path.

Three beach bars and a restaurant later and I was sitting miserably on a sun lounger staring at the lapping sea in front of me and trying to coax myself into happier thoughts. This was useless. I lay back, shielding the sun from my face with one hand and closed my eyes. Andrew's Internet picture fluttered out of my hand onto the beach. A voice from nearby started talking and I felt a light spray of sand across my arm as someone walked over to me, their shadow blocking the sun from my face. I squinted up at the silhouette.

'You dropped this,' the silhouette said, bending to retrieve the piece of paper from the sand.

The silhouette was a woman about my age, wearing a floppy sunhat and a baby-pink bikini top.

'Hey, that's Andy,' she said, the surprise lifting her voice at the end.

I opened the other eye as the words filtered into my consciousness. Then I sat up so abruptly that she jumped back.

'Sorry, sorry,' I spluttered, lifting myself right off the lounger now. 'What did you just say?'

'Your picture.' She gestured with her hand. 'It's Andy.'

'Andy. Do you know him?' I asked, feeling all my breath suspended in my body as I waited for her response.

Her eyes narrowed a little and she put one hand on her hip. 'Why?' she challenged. 'Has he done something?'

I supposed the photo did look a little foreboding; I had seen many stills like this on *America's Most Wanted*.

'No, no, he hasn't,' I assured her. 'I just know him, well, I've been looking for him. Is he here?' I said, looking around and behind me in case Andrew suddenly walked over, a voiceover saying, 'ISOBEL – THIS IS YOUR LIFE!'

He wasn't walking over, no one was, and the girl nervously licked her lips. She had a nose ring which glinted in the sunlight as she asked her next question. 'Well, who are you and then maybe I can tell you where he is,' she said slowly. *Man, what was she like? The Gate Keeper of Andrew?*

I tried to keep the resentment out of my voice. 'I'm just an old friend,' I said, tempted to add, 'AND HIS WIFE' but figuring that might scare her a little and anyway, as his wife, perhaps she might have expected me to have a better handle on where he was.

'Where did you meet him?'

God, what was this? Twenty questions? Why didn't she just shine a light in my eye?

'Southsea,' I responded, certain she had no idea where that was.

'Occupation?'

'Teacher.' I smiled. *Ha, ha, I am passing your stupid test, Lady Face!*

'Country of origin?'

WHO SPEAKS LIKE THAT?

'England,' I sighed, trying to look weary and not rattled.

Her forehead creased as her brain ticked over and then light appeared in her eyes. She clearly had the Killer Question. I got nervous, felt my palms dampen; I mean, I didn't know a lot. He liked milk but maybe that was Child Andrew, for all I knew he was now lactose intolerant. Oh jeez, would this woman bar me?

'What's his surname?' she asked.

I paused, mostly to mess with her, before slowly leaning forward. 'Parker.' I finished with a triumphant, largely smug, smile.

Satisfied that I had passed her investigation – if there had been a chair and an overhead lamp she would have sat me in it. She asked me to follow her. She was now walking two paces in front of me along the dirt track. Her long strawberry-blonde hair swung side to side as she moved. She had a tiny waist and a dis proportionally large bottom straining in tight denim shorts. Her legs were stubbornly pale and she had a light spattering of sand on her feet that were encased in flip-flops. It was like following Strawberry-Blonde Beyoncé. She looked back at me over her left shoulder.

'He might not be there today,' she warned.

'Okay.'

I wasn't sure where 'there' was and she didn't seem to be giving up additional information, so I contented myself with this. It was also not 'okay' – I had crossed the island for him, nay THE GLOBE, and to not see him now, after all of these efforts, seemed absurd.

She pointed with one finger to a sign painted on a rock on our right. ''s here.'

Words spelled in Malay were written on top of an enormous picture of a turtle painted in purples and blues. There was an arrow below the turtle pointing down the path in the direction we were walking.

Did Andrew live here then? Did he have a drink regularly somewhere that this girl knew about? I pictured him holed up in his favourite bar, atop a stool, telling an amusing anecdote from his day as the bar owner smiled and dried a glass with a tea towel. Or perhaps he would be sitting outside a small house on a chair, feet up on the balcony, writing in a travel diary and looking out across the blue sea beyond.

I could feel my palms becoming clammy as the minutes passed and we diverted off the main path on to a dusty, narrow footpath made up of rutted sand and pebbles. Sporadic weeds trailed lifelessly under our feet and bicycle tracks could clearly be made out in the sand. Perhaps we weren't going to find Andrew at all, I panicked. I looked at the large bottom sashaying in front of me, so confident; perhaps she had sized up the competition and was taking me to a far-off cave to confront me in some kind of Creepy Psycho Girl show-down and then brain me with a large shell? I was being so trusting trooping after her and I didn't know anything about her.

'So…' I said, swallowing, 'how do you know Andrew?'

She didn't look back at me. 'We've spent some time together…on the island.'

She made it sound very *The Beach* – at any moment I was expecting to stumble upon a commune of free-thinking Westerners, breaking out of their consumerist lives in the West, probably naked and covered in dolphin tattoos.

‘So only just recently,’ I confirmed, assuming it might rile her a bit to point out that, unlike me who had known Andrew for YEARS, she had in fact known him for days. Ha, ha.

‘It feels like we’ve known each other for ever.’

Ah. Touché.

I started scuffing my feet along the ground, and when she asked me things, I repeated her questions silently to myself miming them at her back with a mocking expression on my face. It made me feel marginally better.

The track had widened again and we were now at the other end of the beach. On the right, the jungle climbed beyond us, the sumptuous greens of the trees merging with each other. As we rounded the next bend, the beach opened up in front of us, stark white in the light, and I saw some areas, no bigger than boxing rings, netted off in the corner, a jumble of plastic boxes and water butts to the side. There were six or so huts just beyond them and a semi-circle of people gathered round something on the shoreline.

Strawberry Blonde Girl breathed out as she said, ‘He *is* here,’ and when she turned she had a dreamy expression on her face and a sparkle in her eyes that only emphasised her perfect English Rose complexion. Still, I hadn’t time to fester on the image as her words sunk in.

He was here.

As in here.

Here.

Now.

I had travelled across half the world, I had taken two long-haul flights, one tiny rickety flight, a bus, a car, some taxis, and I’d even scoured the jungle on foot for him. And he was here. I could feel my heart drumming a beat in my chest, as if, at any second, it could burst right out of there and judder about on the sand crying, 'He is here, he is here, he is here.'

I swallowed, licked my lips, attempted to de-tangle my hair with my fingers, pinched my cheeks like I'd seen girls do in period dramas and then I asked, 'Can you...?' My voice came out as a strangled whisper. 'Can you point him out to me?'

Strawberry Blonde Girl smirked at me and pointed in the direction of the group on the shoreline. 'Well, obviously, he's right there,' she said.

I took a step forward, scanning the group.

Strawberry Blonde Girl put a hand on my arm. 'You do know him?' she said, her voice lower, laden with suspicion now.

'Oh yes, it's just, my eyes, the light, I was momentarily blinded by the sun.' Shaking her off, I walked towards the group, eyes flicking back and forth, a blur of shorts, T-shirts, white teeth, dark hair, blonde hair, bikinis, towels. Most of them were centred around one man – my throat stopped working – he had sandy hair, slight curls, wide bare shoulders, and he was kneeling in the shallows. They were all staring at his lap. It was quite bizarre actually. Some of them were making cooing noises at it.

I took another step forward, drawn to the scene, unable to look anywhere else. His head was still bent over his lap and, as I moved closer, I realised it was a tiny turtle in his arms, its minuscule shell and short, stumpy legs sitting in his hands as he stroked it with one thumb.

As I drew nearer, mesmerised, he looked up at me, mid-stroke, and smiled, one eyebrow fractionally raised as if he had a question. I stared straight at him holding the baby turtle and grinned. 'Andrew,' I said, 'Andrew Parker.'

And then his smile faded and his eyebrows knitted together. He handed the turtle to one of the group and stood up, arms crossed in front of him.

'Er. Sorry, do I know you?'

I could practically feel Strawberry Blonde's triumph from behind me.

Chapter 22

Andrew had taken me off to a hut with a tiny fridge on the terrace and two deckchairs that were so low you spent most of the time fighting gravity. Sitting became quite a stressful experience and, clutching my pineapple juice in a rather warm glass, I found myself toppling backwards and spilling some down my top in the first minute.

'Here you go,' he said, almost about to dab my chest with a filthy cloth and then handing it to me at the last moment.

'Thanks,' I mumbled, hoping he might pass my red cheeks off as an onset of spontaneous sunburn.

He sat forward in his deckchair, legs bent and sipped at his juice. He looked to his left, rubbed his leg and then fiddled with the lip of his glass, picking away at some imaginary spot until I was forced to start talking.

'So, Andrew,' I said in my poshest voice. 'It has taken me a while to find you,' I admitted with a small bark of laughter. Very scary.

'Yes,' he commented, back to picking at the glass again, 'So you were...looking for me,' he checked. 'Liz said you had a photo of me.'

'Well, I...'

Realising it would sound somewhat eccentric slash STALKER SCARY to admit I had, in fact, travelled the globe in search of him – a man who on first sight had not recognised me – I tried to think of another reason that I was on an obscure beach on Tioman Island, in the middle of the South China Sea off the coast of Malaysia. So I played the search down, not wanting to alarm him and ruin our reunion.

'Well, I was on the island on holiday and I heard you were here, this side, and I thought, I'll print off a photo and go and look for him.'

He scratched his head. That news had clearly thrown him, so I thought it was better not to add anything more. He need never know.

'Oh right, so you were on holiday,' he repeated.

'Yes, I was just having a bit of "Me" time,' I smiled, encouraged that he seemed to look more relaxed, was drinking, eyes weren't too wide, breathing patterns were normal.

'Oh right.'

I pursed my lips, did a smile without teeth and nodded a few times. Right, so, what to do now? Down on the beach less than a hundred yards away Strawberry Blonde Girl, aka Liz, was glancing back at us through slanted eyes. She was currently tending to a sick turtle and looked like Turtle Nurse, all long, wavy hair and concern. Andrew half-raised a hand at her and I instantly said, 'Liz seems nice,' in a voice that suggested I thought she was anything but.

Fortunately, Andrew didn't appear to notice and just nodded once and sipped his drink. 'Yeah she's cool.'

This wasn't going very well; this was not the warm, gushy reunion I had envisaged. I imagined me saying his name, his light-brown eyes opening in surprise, a hundred memories flashing across his face as he drank me in, in the flesh, there, with him, after all these years. I had imagined him smiling widely, opening his arms so that I could run (slo-mo) into them and we could embrace like we should never have been torn apart, like he should never have left me. Then, slowly, we would drop into the sand, probably holding hands, to swap news, gush at each other, laugh over long-forgotten memories sparked by seeing each other again, reminisce over old names and faces. Maybe the recreation of our secret handshake?

Not this. This awkward silence with Andrew avoiding my eyes and stilted conversation as we tried to find common ground. I hadn't even told him my name yet. I'd assumed it would have instantly tripped off his tongue.

'So how long have you been out here?' I asked, trying not to stare too much at his bare chest. It was practically hairless, amazing. I wonder if he waxed? Lucky colouring, I mused. FOCUS, ISOBEL. HE IS TALKING.

'Just over a week, you know,' he said, leaning forward, his eyes intent on me. 'You do look really familiar.'

Not really hearing the last part, I jumped on his sentence. 'Yes, you're a Geography teacher,' I announced.

'Er yes, I am,' he said, brow wrinkling. 'How did you know?'

And, without thinking, I said, 'Your headmistress told me!'

'You know Joan?' he asked.

'Jo…Mrs Henderson, um, well not exactly but I was, um, sort of at your school and I bumped into her with her dogs Koalemos, and, you know, well they were sweet things – and well, she…' I trailed off as Andrew had lost a lot of colour in his cheeks. 'Nice woman,' I mumbled. Then I looked up, coming to a decision. 'Have you got anything to go with this?' I asked, indicating the glass.

'I think so,' he said slowly. 'Let me go and look.' And he practically dived into the hut in search of spirits as I fretted and wrung my hands and spoke to myself, which was just what I was doing when his head popped back around the door. 'Gin or vodka?'

I stopped muttering and turned to him. 'Vodka,' I said in a voice that made me sound like I had trailed a desert and this was the first prospect of a drink on the horizon.

He returned, downing half of his drink and asked, 'So you were at my school?'

'Yes,' I laughed, reciting what I had just rehearsed in my head. 'I was there researching English schools for a new TV show I might present. They like real English places in LA and well I have visited loads and…'

'Which ones?'

'Oh, too many to mention,' I waved a hand, swallowing. 'Look, Liz has stood up!' I said loudly.

'Er so she has.'

Drinks full again, blessed ice found, I tried to be more relaxed. Andrew had found a T-shirt from somewhere which

I think also helped me to focus. He had obviously had a little talking-to himself too, as we both clashed on our next question,

'So, how can I help?'

'So, Andrew, you must be wondering why I am here.'

Then we laughed, short, quickly. Liz looked up from the beach again at us. I raised my glass at her. Childish.

How can I help? His last sentence tore through me: how could he help? Why was I here? What did he think? Should I just come out with it?

I half-opened my mouth to explain and then shut it again. I couldn't just tell him. He didn't appear to really be able to place us yet, needed more time to remember all the times we had spent together in our childhood. And it would sound a bit odd to just come out and say it. So I swirled my glass around, hearing the ice knock against the side whilst I played for time.

'Do you remember those big plastic barrels in the playground?' I asked, thinking back to some of my sunnier memories. Lining up as a human chain, clinging to each other as we giggled and rolled and fell down.

Andrew laughed easily. 'Yeah,' he grinned, one hand pushing through his hair. 'I got Lyndon to push me in one down that slope in the back, you know, round by the tennis court...'

'I don't remember that,' I said, encouraged that he was back in our old haunt. We had married only a few yards from the slope.

'Do you remember the arcade? Pushing 2p coins into those machines for hours, buying candy floss with our winnings?'

Andrew had grown watchful, nodding slowly as I continued. 'Do you remember us at your house, your mum giving us the cake bowl to share...?'

'Isobel?' he whispered suddenly.

'What?' I asked, heart in my mouth, muffling my speech.

He looked up and down at me. 'Oh my god, you're Isobel, Issy,' he said slowly. Then his face changed, understanding seeming to filter across his features as his face finally broke into an easy smile. 'As in Issy round the corner. We used to go to the canoe lake and the pier and stuff. Oh my, woah,' he said looking me up and down like he still expected me to be the nine-year-old in pigtails and a chequered school skirt.

'Yes, yes exactly,' I said, voice climbing higher, the ice clinking in my glass.

'God, I haven't thought about Southsea in years. I loved it there,' Andrew mused, eyes far away for a moment as if he were back on that pier watching the water move gently below us. 'We had a lot of fun: at the roller-skate park, the Pyramid's Centre —'

'The wave machine there,' I said grinning and enjoying a flashback of both of us in the Pyramids Swimming Centre leaping over waves made by the machine.

'Exactly.'

Andrew sat back. 'I missed that place so much. I missed you all.'

'We missed you...' I said, voice quieter now, thick with emotion. 'And how's your mum?' I said, picturing his mum bustling about their house, vacuum in one hand, drink in the other. 'She was always so lovely to me.'

'Mum,' he repeated. 'Yeah, Mum's alright, she re-married a couple of years ago actually.'

'Oh, right.' I remembered his dad, and Andrew telling me he wanted to run away and find him one day. I bit back the next question, not wanting to get too heavy; he had only just recognised me after all.

I had so many more questions for him. Where did he end up? Did he miss me more than the rest? Had he ever wondered what had happened to me? I shifted in my chair again, desperate to know more, feeling triumphant that I had found him.

He leaned forward then, staring at me. 'You look so different.'

I patted at my hair self-consciously. *Was that a good thing? A bad thing?*

'Do you remember the crabs?' Crabs? He was mentioning crabs. I panicked, bizarrely racing through various STIs in my mind before I got his gist.

'That day at the canoe lake where we raced them,' he said, suddenly laughing. His laugh sounded like joyful bells trilling a tune.

Then the memory caught me, beside the lake, capturing crabs on bacon, placing them in a bucket and then, 'I remember,' I said excitedly, leaning forward to joining in. 'You raced them back to the lake and there was a tiny one that nearly lost his way and you had to steer him back around.'

'Did I?' he said, a half-smile and a slightly faraway expression on his face. 'I don't recall the details, just that we had a whole bucket of the things.'

My heart soared and I downed the rest of my drink feeling full of hope. This is what it will be like. Reminiscing about the good old days. Our precious childhoods seen through the warm sepia shade of the past. Me in pigtails and tie-dye skirts (mahoosive hippy phase), him in plaid shirts and three-quarter length shorts (Backstreet Boys phase), laughing and enjoying spending sunshiny days hanging out together. The sure knowledge that the world would continue to be okay if we could just stay like that, remain in those moments where life had been so simple.

Disrupting our momentary bubble of bonding was Liz, who had sidled over, no doubt drawn by the pull of our shared mirth. She was looking at us both. 'And what are you two giggling about?' she asked in a voice that suggested she really did not want to know.

'Crabs,' I said with delight and then cackled as she grimaced.

'Hey, Liz, have you seen the latest little guy? He hatched this morning…' Andrew said, then turned back to me. 'Isobel, I can't believe it is actually you. It's been for ever,' he said, his face breaking into the warmest smile so I could see the boy beneath.

I felt triumph course through my veins. 'I'll get more vodka,' I said, lurching to my feet and heading into the hut.

Bustling into the hut I was momentarily blinded by the sudden darkness, scraps of grubby cloth on a piece of drooping string acting as makeshift curtains. I reached a hand out to open one and, as I pulled it back, it revealed a half-naked man below it. WHAT WAS WITH TODAY? I jumped back, drawing my hand up to my chest like I had just put it on the hob and squeaked.

The half-naked man opened one eye and didn't raise his head from the pillow. 'Andy,' he called. 'Andy, I'm dreaming about hot girls again.'

'Oh, I'm sorry I... Vodka, well, the thing is, I...'

'ANDY!' he yelled, half-mumbled by pillow as he was still yet to lift his head. 'The hot girl is babbling at me.'

Andrew appeared in the doorway looking at us both. 'Oh, Isobel, I didn't warn you, Duncan here is sleeping off last night.'

'Was,' Duncan mumbled, his mouth drooping on to the pillow.

'Well, I was just telling Duncan I was here to find a drink and...'

'Hot girl, hush, Andy, hush her...'

'There's no need to hush me.'

'Andy, husssssh her,' he groaned, putting his free hand over this one exposed ear. 'Hot Girl, ssshhh.'

I bristled, secretly a teeny bit pleased he thought I was attractive, but still thinking he was being rude. I put on my most hoity-toity voice and turned away. 'I will get a drink and be gone.'

'Sorry, Isobel, it was a late one last night,' Andrew said, giving me an embarrassed smile.

'Not at all,' I grinned back at him, delighted he cared.

Duncan chose that moment to lurch upwards into a sitting position so we all took a step backwards. A wave of rum and stale breath struck me as he stretched up and breathed out deeply. Like a lion on safari, his long, wavy blond hair was scruffy as a mane. His bare chest was finely defined and I couldn't not look. It wasn't so much a six pack as a ten pack.

He had a scratchy-looking beard and rings under his eyes and did I mention a TEN PACK?

Duncan noticed my gaze and smirked at me, slapping his stomach with one hand. 'The ladies love it,' he said, licking his bottom lip.

'Oh no, I was looking at, looking at...your...duvet cover. I think my dad has one similar and...' I trailed away, realising I had basically been busted and should probably quit.

Andrew handed me a drink and walked back out to the terrace. 'Hey, Isobel, there's something I want to show you.'

'Great,' I said, throwing back more of my drink, a little dribbling down my chin. I wiped it away quickly. 'Well, great to meet you, Duncan.' I nodded, going to leave.

Duncan lay back down on his side. 'Bye, Hot Girl,' he said, closing his eyes once more.

I stepped out onto the sand in front of the hut. The sand was scorching under my bare feet and I hopped quickly after Andrew as he moved towards the shoreline, a beer in one hand. It was the first time I could really look him up and down. He was a little shorter than I had thought he'd be; his shoulders were wide, spattered with freckles and he had good, clear skin. His hair was messy and wavy at the front and I smiled as I remembered Andrew the Boy's frustration at having hair that curled when he had always wanted to grow his hair into straight curtains like his idol Nick Carter.

He stepped into the sea up to his ankles and turned to beckon me across, pointing to the area to our right and the netted-off squares.

'We're waiting for the babies to hatch, then we look out for them in those early days and make sure they get back to the sea unharmed. It is amazing how many blighters are out to get them,' he explained. He had a kind voice, like a weatherman trying to soften the blow.

'Oh.' My heart lifted. 'Good, well, the thing is I had heard...' I cleared my throat. 'Someone had mentioned, on the other side of the island, that, well, you might need some help,' I said, my eyes scanning the beach and Liz looking more and more like Ariel by the second. 'And I have always loved marine life and I thought, well I wondered if you would be able to make use of me and well...' I trailed away hoping this wasn't the end of my journey, that this might be the start of something.

'Well if you did want to help, you could stick around and...'

'Yes.' I leapt on his words before he could finish. 'I would love that.'

I pictured my things in the hotel on the other side of the island. 'Do you have a number for a taxi?'

The taxi (of sorts) arrived within half an hour, a mud-streaked 4x4 and a taxi driver, Ahmad, who had a permanent smile plastered to his face and a monobrow. It was a baffling mixture and made him look permanently like he might laugh at you and then punch you in the face. I slid myself in behind the driver's seat on to the back seats, foam tufts sticking out of the leather and a seatbelt I would soon find out was a pretty vital part of the experience.

Diving off the track and into the jungle to venture up the road into Tekek, the village in the centre of the island, Ahmad decided to shout over his shoulder as he began a magic trick that involved a small coin and a lot of hand movements. Too nervous to really focus on what he was doing, I clung to the bar above the window as we trundled over tree roots and through narrow, shady gaps, the engine straining as we ascended, something heavy sliding to the back of the boot.

We arrived on the other side of the island and back at my hotel in less than half an hour and I asked Ahmad to wait as I went to check out. Wheeling my suitcase out and thanking Ahmad as he took it from me and threw it effortlessly into the boot, I clambered back in.

'Where you from?'

'England,' I said, now sitting in the front with him.

'Ahhh, London.' He nodded.

'Sort of.'

We moved back onto the jungle road and the 4x4 shook as we gently made our way up and back down the other side waiting for the turquoise blue of the sea in Juara to peek hopefully through the canopy of leaves in front of us. Ahmad had repeated his trick involving the coin and I had 'oohed' appropriately, despite seeing him put it in his other hand for the duration of the trick.

'Very impressive,' I shouted over the engine and he glowed, monobrow wiggling in pleasure.

Andrew was back on the beach and I wheeled and heaved my way over to the hut. Duncan, slick with water from a recent swim, stared at my suitcase.

'Oh, um I...'

Why was I bringing all my belongings? I definitely looked like I was planning to move in indefinitely.

'I was going to book a room somewhere later today,' I said, gesturing back to the track.

'Okey dokey,' Duncan said, lugging my suitcase inside the hut. 'Later, Hot Girl,' he called over his shoulder, flexing his muscles as he hauled the case up the stairs.

I spent the afternoon being introduced to the project. There were various tanks and nesting places for the turtles. There were information boards about the process and phrases like 'pipping' that I had explained to me. Andrew was a tentative tour guide but, just as he was pointing out one thing, Liz would bustle over with a question about something, always turtle-related, and he would be whisked away, replaced by Duncan who spent a lot of time flashing me white teeth and pointing to things I couldn't see in the distance so that he could lean over me.

It was going to be a balmy evening and we had started drinking beers on the beach in some low-slung deckchairs. The hazy blue sky was streaked with ribbons of cloud and red strips of light from the setting sun. The pier stuck out into the cove, a dark silhouette, and fishing boats returned to moor up in the calm water. Juara seemed less frantic, a real bohemian paradise, and the scent of smoke from a nearby fire and the sound of distant birds settled me in the moment. Peeking shyly across at Andrew, I smiled and raised a bottle to my lips.

How was I going to get him to love me? How was I going to go about this? First plan, I thought, feeling the bubbles spark on my tongue, was to make a good impression.

Second step was to make myself indispensable. I would become Queen of this Turtle Project.

Having not eaten much all day, I found the beer racing to my head pretty quickly and soon I was snuggled down in the chair woozily laughing at the chatter all around me. Andrew was sitting next to me now and I had made some good attempts to haul him back to the nineties and our childhood experiences.

'Do you remember seeing me on your last day?' I asked, picturing his face as he disappeared into his mother's car. 'I'd wanted to tell you how good you'd been in the nativity play.'

'You were always nice like that,' he said simply, his face taking on a dreamy look as he time-travelled. 'I did miss you; I missed the school, missed the pier and all the stuff we'd done.'

I nodded as he spoke. With every new memory, I felt one teensy step closer to him and was feeling more and more sure that coming here had been the right thing. My life in LA seemed a million miles away. Liz had left an hour ago, a scowl and a backwards glance in my direction. Andrew had been talking to me about the island's rock formations. *Ha, ha, I win, Liz. Check me out listening about rocks!*

Andrew had got up to replenish our drinks and we had continued to talk about the island and the years in between. It had been a few hours and about six beers later when I felt bold enough to make my move. Leaning towards him I trailed a hand in the sand. 'Need to check into a hotel,' I mumbled half-heartedly. *Invite me to stay, invite me to stay, invite me to stay.* I looked at him, unblinking.

Andrew returned the look, eyes slightly crossing as he clinked beers with me. 'You can stay here tonight,' he slurred.

Bingo.

Chapter 23

Waking up to the smell of dust and aftershave, a thinning rag barely able to hold back the early morning light, I wondered briefly where I was. My feet were poking out into thin air and the pillow was lumpy and unfamiliar. Then, as I turned my head and looked down to see Andrew sleeping on a camping mat, wrapped in jumpers and towels, I smiled sleepily.

Yay!

My mobile trilled on the floor beside the bed and I cast an eye briefly over the display. 'MEL'. I couldn't resist answering it, I also had to or the buzzing might wake up Andrew and it was all too perfect right now. I wanted to just stay and stare at him like we were in a film but decided not to because a) that might freak him out, and some people might not like to be woken in that way and b) it would be worth answering just to tell her where I was; she wouldn't BELIEVE it.

'I don't BELIEVE it,' she said when I explained. 'Seriously?'

'Yes,' I whispered, padding out onto the terrace and closing the door behind me, desperate to not wake anyone up. I paced in front of the hut, grimacing at last night's dying fire and the empty beer cans and bottles casually littered around the place. 'He is asleep in the hut like five yards away from me.'

'How long is a yard? I have always pretended to know but I don't actually have a clue. Is he close or far away?' she asked.

'Close, really close, it's like a metre or something,' I said, realising I didn't really know how long it was either.

'So he is like five metres away from you?' she confirmed.

'Yeah, about ten feet,' I said.

'Feet?'

'Look, he's close, really close, that is what we need to focus on.'

'Agreed. So he is right there?' she squeaked and I heard her clapping her hands.

I smiled. 'Exactly, so I have to keep my voice down.'

This didn't appear to stop Mel. 'Isobel Graves, did you SLEEP with him?'

'Noooo,' I giggled, interrupting her. Mel was whistling. 'Hey, I didn't.' I lowered my voice again. 'I didn't, I just slept in the same space as him.'

'Well, that's a new way of putting it. Oh jeez, Iz, I love this, you trek halfway round the globe, actually FIND this guy and then end up...' She stopped to mimic my English accent, 'sleeping in the same space.'

'I suppose,' I said, suddenly not wanting the attention. 'How is it going with you and Dex?'

There was silence on the end of the phone and I frowned.

'Mel, you okay?'

She sighed. 'Well we had a bit of a fight,' she said. 'Asshole.'

'What? You guys never really fight, what happened?'

'He did something stupid,' she said, getting quiet.

Oh no, Dex. Dex, you cock, I fumed to myself. I didn't see it coming, the lying, cheating... My fist gripped the phone so tightly my knuckles turned white.

'I'll kill him,' I said.

'What?'

'I'll kill him,' I repeated slowly. 'The lying cheat of a monkey scumba—'

'He didn't cheat on me, Iz,' she interrupted.

'Oh.' I felt relieved immediately. I knew it. Dex would never do that. I wouldn't have to kill him. I sat on the sand, chilled and scratchy on my legs. 'So what did he do?'

'Oh I don't want to talk about it, actually, I don't want to think about it.'

Shit, this was serious.

'Mel, what is it?'

A pause and then Mel's voice sounded quieter, more hopeless. 'He asked me to bloody marry him, didn't he.'

'The NO-GOOD SCUM OF A...what?' I stopped. 'Wait, rewind, he asked you to what him?'

'Marry him,' she grumbled. 'So annoying, everything was going so well, Iz.'

'Well, yes, that's the thing about marriage, Mel, it's meant to celebrate that fact; it's like the Ultimate Sign things are going well.'

'No, you don't get it, look at my mom,' she said, sounding tearful.

'What do you mean, Mel?'

Mel never talked about her mum; in the past she had always brushed conversations off about it, frozen up. When I'd teased her about marrying Dex once, she hadn't spoken to me for the rest of the day, wouldn't budge on opening up about it. I knew there had always been this problem in her head but she'd never really shared it with me, it was the one area we didn't go.

'She always said they were so happy before they were married and that it...' And then Mel did what Mel NEVER does; her voice broke and she started to cry. '...it totally changed things for her, she changed, she became so miserable...and she always regretted it. And I...love him, Dex...and I don't want to...' She had moved into sniffy singular words now so it was really hard to make out and I strained my whole body to hear her.

'Hey,' I soothed. 'Hey, Mel, it's okay.' I wished I was over with her in LA now, sitting on her red corner sofa and able to put an arm around her. Mel didn't do crying.

'Dex is a great guy,' I said.

'So why did he do this to me?' she wailed. 'Why couldn't he just have left things how they were? He knows what I think about it all and we were really happy. And we have great s...e...ex...' She started crying in earnest now which was really hard to tackle when you're eight thousand miles away. 'Only last week he taught me how to hold onto my orgasm for longer than...'

'Okay, Mel. Okay, do you remember we talked about this? STILL gross.'

'But now no one will ever make me do that and I'll be

with a man who only knows the missionary position and who doesn't bring me Top Ramen Noodles when I'm sick and who doesn't wear the duvet like a Superman cape just because I find it funnnnnnny...'

'You're not going to break up with Dex,' I reassured her. 'That would be ridiculous and I won't allow it.' The phone was quiet now, just the odd sniff coming down the line.

Panicking and with few options before me, I did the only thing I knew might have a hope in hell of cheering her up. 'Oh I'm the King of the Swingers yeah, the jungle...'

Her sniffing slowed and she asked me in a sad little voice, 'Iz, what are you doing?'

'Singing our song. Is it cheering you up yet? You love this song. "Oh I wanna be a man man cub and stroll right into town and be just like the other cubs I'm ti..."'

'It will only cheer me up if you do all the actions. ALL of them,' she insisted, interrupting my wobbly attempt to sing.

'But you can't see me,' I said.

'But I'll know,' she replied simply.

'I might wake the others and...'

She whimpered again and that was enough for me.

Running away from the hut over the sand, I broke out into, 'Oh oobeee doo I wanna be like you oo oo...' Swinging my arms like a monkey and shaking my hair around wildly, I giggled as I sang and danced and lifted the mobile every now and again to my lips to do the chorus. 'Do oo oo, you see it's true oo oo...'

'The other one, the other one,' she sniffed, a giggle filtering through her voice.

'What? The double-whammy? I hate that one.'

'You would do it if you were here.'

'It's too early, Mel.'

'Pleasssssssse.'

'Okay, for you.' I smiled.

'Whoop.'

Shaking both hands out in front of me, knees bent, I started to hum down the phone. 'A whumba whoppa whumba whoppa...'

She was really laughing now.

'Whumba whoppa whumba whoppa in the jungle, the mighty jungle...'

Mel was joining in down the other end of the line and I put the mobile on speaker so I could really shake it up. Dropping to my knees, hair swinging wildly as we did it in my flat in LA, I carried on. 'The lion sleeps tonight.' I could hear Mel's loud 'Awoooooo' as back-up and grinned, getting louder as I called, 'A whumba whoppa whumba whoppa.'

I was so loud I hadn't heard the person creep up behind me, only stopping as his long shadow appeared in the sand beside me.

Closing my eyes, I prayed it wasn't Andrew. Mel was still doing 'Awoooooo' noises down the phone and they were reverberating in the silence. 'Awoooo, awoooo.'

'What are you doing?' Zeb asked, bleary-eyed, a tuft of hair sticking straight up at the back.

My mouth dropped open and I froze, pelvis thrust out, both arms flung out to my side, hair all over my face so I had to blow it out of the way.

I slowly lowered my arms, 'Oh I...Mel, I've got to go,' I said, speaking into the phone.

'Thanks, Iz. Love you.'

'Love you too,' I said, speaking slowly into the phone and looking at Zeb in the most dignified way I could manage. 'Hello,' I said, flicking my hair behind my shoulder. 'How are you?'

'You are proper weird,' he laughed, taking a quick photo of me.

'Hey, don't do that,' I said, shielding my face like I was some A-Lister stumbling drunkenly out of a club.

'I couldn't resist,' he shrugged. 'I wanted to record this moment. So...what was it?'

'What was what?' I asked, nose in the air.

'Sun dance? Welcoming in the new harvest? Summoning the Beach Witches? The dance, Iz.'

'It was designed to cheer someone up,' I said.

'Someone?' He raised an eyebrow.

'None of your business,' I said, feeling foolish for being caught on the hop. Literally.

Zeb raised his hands. 'You are a woman of mystery and I wouldn't want to ruin that. Please continue to dance away.'

'What are you doing here anyway?' I asked, my surprise making me sound abrupt. I slanted my eyes in suspicion. 'Are you following me?'

'God no, I would never follow anyone around an island to spend time with them.'

I felt my face go red and my eyes darted desperately over to the door of the hut, picturing Andrew listening to our exchange.

‘Shhh,’ I said, dragging Zeb down the beach in the other direction. He had caught the sun since being here; his arm was a deep brown in this light.

He looked back over his shoulder. ‘Oh my god, is he here? Did you actually find him?’ he asked in a voice that, if I wasn’t mistaken, sounded almost impressed. ‘Up to this point I genuinely thought he was a figment of your imagination.’

‘What?’

‘An imaginary friend, Isobel. The fact he exists makes me less concerned about your mental well-being.’ Then he looked at me, all wild hair and big eyes. ‘*Less* concerned: the jury is still out with how well you are.’

I hit him on the upper arm. ‘Ow,’ he said, rubbing the spot I had struck. Then he smiled at me. ‘I can add anger-management problems to your symptoms.’

I couldn’t help a half-smile. ‘I do not have anger-management problems; you have being nice, easy to get along with human being problems.’

‘I’m not sure that’s a thing,’ he said.

‘It’s a thing.’

‘That’s what a mentally unwell person would say,’ he sighed.

Looking over my shoulder for movement, for Andrew stirring, I repeated my question. ‘Seriously, what are you doing here?’

‘Juara’s meant to be the best beach on the island and I like the vibe here. I want to stick around for a bit.’

‘Vibe?’ I repeated, raising one eyebrow (unsuccessfully, sort of waggling both).

'Yeah, it seems chilled and there are some incredible places to take photos. Also,' he added, 'someone should probably look out for you. Alone and mad. Not a good combo.'

'I'm not mad,' I insisted, smoothing my hair down to help convince him.

'Alone and strangely eccentric. It still requires someone to keep a watchful eye.'

'It's a free country,' I sniffed, secretly a bit touched he had said it.

Dear diary,

Boys are so stupid. I had a big fight with Andrew today because he ignored me at school in lunch. I don't know what I have done but Lyndon said that he was embarrassed about being married. Then, in English when Jenny said something about me, he laughed even though I don't think Jenny was being nice. I hate Jenny and Andrew.

I x

Chapter 24

I wanted to take it back, twenty-four hours later when Zeb found me kneeled in a tank, dirty cloth in one hand, Marigold gloves on, a bucket of slop next door to me as I was hastily rubbing at slime and turtle poo from one of the tanks.

He started snapping me as, hair tied in a knot, slime smeared on a cheek, I scrubbed. Raising the cloth, I glared at him. 'Don't get any closer. I warn you, I will slime you.'

'What are you doing, woman?'

'Cleaning,' I said, not willing to admit that I had been left in this tank for a good hour. We were meant to be working on rotation, but Andrew had missed his slot. I wanted to believe he was really busy, but the orange Frisbee that had been sitting on the terrace of the hut that morning had gone, as had Duncan. Still, no doubt he would make up for it later, and I had been living for free these past couple of nights so I really had no right to complain. And turtle poo was not as bad as other poo. I had seen worse.

Zeb had sat cross-legged in the sand, bored of snapping angry shots of me covered in slime. 'Want to go and explore stuff?' he asked, sounding like an excited eight-year-old.

'Well I shouldn't really,' I said, indicating a new patch of slime.

'You do have a lot of shit to clear up,' he commented, bending and looking into the tank. 'Wow, that is quite a fragrance.'

I laughed and carried on attacking the same spot. 'It's Odour de Turtle Crap.'

There was a beat and then I felt the air shift as Zeb bundled himself into the tank.

'Okay, I will assist,' he said, seizing another cloth from the next-door tank and hauling my bucket away. 'This needs new water for a start,' he announced, heading off to the tap on the side of the hut next door.

Sitting back on my haunches I watched him leave, feeling a swell of thanks for the man.

We worked away in the small metal tank, watching the walls turn back to their normal colour, the bucket becoming gradually less disgusting. The heat was unbearable and we had been sweating through our clothes, beads meeting on my hairline as I circled the cloth furiously back and forward. Zeb had started humming 'It's a Hard Knock Life' from *Annie*.

'Your commitment to children's movies is impressive,' I said, as he launched into a *Prison Break* style rendition of 'Hi, Ho, Hi, Ho, it's off to Work we Go' from *Snow White and the Seven Dwarfs*.

'Thank you. What we really need is someone playing a mournful mouth organ outside our tank. Bloody hell, it is so hot I might melt right here.'

'Swim?' I suggested.

'Definitely.'

Racing down to the beach, we threw shorts and T-shirts down in a heap and splashed into the shallows to sink on to the sand half submerged, shoulders bare and the sun pelting us from on high. It felt blissful and, as I dunked my head below the water and blocked the sounds out, I felt the satisfying ache of a job well done.

'Incredible, isn't it?' Zeb said, floating on his back, hands locked behind his head. 'Home feels like a million miles away; I feel like I could travel forever.'

'Me, too,' I said, realising as I said it that my fantasy, the cottage in England, seemed to have faded over the last few days as I explored new places and saw such different things. I felt like recently my world had expanded and I wanted to carry on seeing more places, visiting new haunts.

Stepping back into our clothes and heading back up the beach feeling noticeably cleaner and more relaxed, I noticed the long blond hair before hearing Duncan shout, 'Oi, Hot Girl, get over here now.' He was standing by our abandoned tank.

Feeling strangely awkward, I indicated in Duncan's direction. 'Um, that's me,' I said quietly.

'Get hereeeeee,' Duncan called, beckoning me.

'Is that him?' Zeb asked, looking over at Duncan. *Was that a glimmer of curiosity in his voice?*

'No, his friend. Well, I suppose I'd better go,' I mumbled, feeling a wave of something wash over me. He had been so kind and I was being so ungrateful.

Zeb was drying his hair off with his T-shirt. I should

spend some more time with him. We were having fun. Before I could say anything though, he stopped patting his hair. 'Thank god, it was basically slave labour and you were about to make me do MORE,' he announced, instantly making me feel a little better. I giggled and reached to flick off a bit of mud still on his face, pausing and blushing as I realised what I was doing so automatically. 'Sorry.'

He gave me an easy smile and turned to walk away. 'It's been a disgusting pleasure. I'll see you round, Isobel.'

'Thanks for your help,' I called after him.

His hand twitched as he walked away. I think he heard.

Chapter 25

I was given five minutes to get ready after Duncan told me he had borrowed a boat for the day to take us around the island. Annoyingly, Liz appeared to have snuck an invite from somewhere too so I had to put up with her glowering at me from behind her bright-yellow Ray Bans for most of the trip. Duncan appeared to have found some sun cream from somewhere and stepped onto the boat looking like a model in a baby oil advert; he glistened under the sunshine. When he caught me staring, he held up one arm like a strong man, kissed his biceps and asked me if I was enjoying 'the gun show'. Flustered, I looked anywhere but at him and found myself locking eyes with Andrew who gave me a shy half-smile that made my insides melt a little. Yay, I secretly thought, I am on a boat on an exotic island with my husband. The sea is turquoise, the air is calm and sweetly scented, and the sun is caressing us. Perfect, perfect, perfect.

Chugging out from the pier on Juara beach, the boat hugged the coastline as the waves grew a little bigger beyond the protection of the bay. The island was edged with a sliver of sand, rocks jutting out at every angle. The forest towered beyond and on the other side of the boat the sea stretched for miles, the horizon a hazy line in the distance. Zeb would have loved this scene. I could imagine him snapping away furiously.

Closing my eyes and enjoying the warmth overhead, we bounced over the waves, surf thrown up on either side of the boat, a hint of diesel in the air every time we revved the engine. Birds circled the forest and Duncan spent a lot of time pointing to them, muscles flexed, then smirking back at me. Liz was sitting primly, life jacket zipped up to her throat, pale freckled legs neatly tucked under her like she was one of the first-class passengers on the *Titanic*. She was speaking quietly to Andrew, something to do with stratospheric clouds and he was being sweet and encouraging her, avidly nodding as she formed some shapes with her hands. I think she was trying to explain rain or something.

The boat slowed up just off the shore of a gorgeous pale stretch of sand and Duncan dropped the anchor and switched the engine off. We idled in the water, all just staring at the tropical paradise that had opened up in front of us. The boat bobbed, sending ripples out over the water. We were sitting over quivering purple shadows of coral and yellow patches of sand. The water rolled gently onto the shore less than fifty feet away and the beach was deserted, trees leaning gracefully over the sand casting long shadows.

Duncan did a low whistle and leaned towards me. 'Amazing, isn't it?'

I nodded wordlessly. He was absolutely right.

Feeling excited, I reached for a snorkel set I had stored under my seat and whipped off my T-shirt.

Andrew's face darted away and I felt a warmth flood into my cheeks, wondering if I had embarrassed him. To hide my humiliation, I asked in my heartiest voice, 'Who's coming in?' and Duncan picked up a snorkel, too.

Flippers on, I lowered myself into the water, dropping at the last moment under the waves. Kicking myself back up and out, I gasped at the sudden change in temperature but, paddling quickly, soon warmed up. Adjusting my snorkel and mask, I dipped my head under the water and almost opened my mouth at the sight.

Immersed in an underwater world that was crystal clear beneath me, all noises were muted and the colours seemed heightened because of it. About ten feet below, a fat, sponge-like coral, pocked orange, sat on the sea bed, fish darting quickly out and back in from under it, checking for danger, snatching moments when they could. A longer fish, shimmering silver, moved below me at a leisurely pace and I watched his trail. The water quivering with tiny bubbles. Shafts of sunlight cut through the water making every fish brighter and bolder. It was mesmerising and I forgot about where I was, about Andrew and the island and LA and work and I just swam gently, trying not to disturb, trying to simply observe and let everything unfold naturally beneath me.

I passed over clumps of waving coral, fish packed tightly together, parting and meeting as if they were one. A small beige stingray rose out of the sand, turquoise spots on his back just visible. Then, as if I had conjured him, I saw the slow-moving swim of the most enormous turtle just ahead. I paddled over to him as he swam only ten feet beneath me, utterly oblivious – his shell made up of intricate patterns in brown and green on its uneven surface and his head tiny in comparison. He moved, unhurried, in a steady line and my mind suddenly flitted to Moregran back by the creek in Helford, making steady progress as she put together our tea. The pace leisurely. Lifting my head out of the water, I waved the others over, knowing they'd want to see him, too.

Duncan appeared first and was about to speak. I spat my snorkel out and raised my finger to my mouth, pointing quickly to where the turtle was slowly moving away. Duncan put his head in the water and then Liz and Andrew were there, all of us paddling at the same pace of the turtle, moving above him like we didn't have anywhere else to be in the world. And we didn't.

Sitting back on the boat an hour later, I couldn't keep the grin from my face.

'He was beautiful, don't you think?'

Andrew was still cleaning his mask and didn't react. Liz was watching him do it.

Duncan looked at me. 'He?'

I frowned. 'He seemed like a he, was he not a "he"?' I asked, turning as I did so towards Andrew, who was removing something from deep in his ear.

'Water in it,' he explained, slapping at his head.

'Look, Isobel, she was a she, she had curves,' Duncan said, moving both hands in the air.

I cringed. 'Nooo – don't be pervy about turtles.'

'Woman, I can be pervy about anything,' he promised.

'I believe she was a female, too, actually,' Andrew said seriously, leaning forward, both palms up, clearly keen to explain things. I put on my most-interested face and rested my chin in my hand as he began.

'I couldn't see the cloaca, the hole on its tail, but certainly the tail seemed narrower than most. In a male I would have expected it to be thicker and longer.'

'Thicker and longer, eh?' I felt heat creep up through my neck. *You naughty man.*

He didn't return the smile. 'Also, the fore claws were not very long, again indicating we were dealing with a female turtle.'

'But he was really big,' I argued through my eyelashes, loving this serious side to Andrew. Teacher Andrew.

'Well, actually, female turtles are bigger than their male counterparts. It's a common mistake,' he chuckled to himself.

'Oh, I see,' I said, smiling, and adding a quick chuckle too. We were SO BONDING.

'It is hard to tell really as an amateur, so you are forgiven for mistaking its sex.'

'Right,' I said, narrowing my eyes to do my most intelligent face.

I noticed Liz sitting next door to me, her head tilted as she earnestly nodded at him, too.

I prayed for a sudden freak gust of wind, a cry, a lame 'Man Overboard' shout from me. Moo ha ha.

'...ISOBEL...'

'What?'

'Seawater blocking your ears, too?' Duncan asked. 'I

asked if you wanted to learn how to drive this thing,' he called from next to the engine.

'Oh, oh sure,' I said, shifting along my seat and sitting with Duncan. *Yeah, driving would make me look cool.* I looked back over my shoulder at Andrew, who was staring at my arse. Yay!

Duncan helped me start the engine, which mostly involved me pulling on a cord and him leaning over me, his chest on my back, arms looped around me as he showed me how to steer. I was relieved when we had moored up, thrown the anchor down and swum into shore.

As we stepped onto the beach, I heard Andrew's voice, a hand raised to his face. 'I think I've got a fly in my eye,' he said, blinking and looking round. Liz was still swimming in; she was like the slowest swimmer in the world, had a lazy left arm that made her swim the breaststroke funny. *Ha, ha, weird breaststrokey Liz,* I could call her. I ran to his aid.

'Here, let me,' I offered, leaning over to help him, my face inches from his, one hand on his cheek as I searched his eye.

He was looking upwards, rolling his eye back and forward. It was actually making me feel a little queasy and I forgot to enjoy the smooth sensation of his face in my hand, our tantalising closeness.

'Er, nothing there,' I announced, not really sure. 'Must have flown out again.'

'Oh,' he said, still blinking.

'Sunbathing time,' Duncan announced with a loud hand clap just behind us. We snapped apart.

Liz had finally arrived, panting lightly. 'I was planning on wandering up to the crest over there to take a photograph,' she said, one hand moving to rest lightly on Andrew's forearm. 'Want to come?'

Andrew was still blinking and looking up at intervals. 'Okay.'

Should I offer to go, too? Would that just make me seem desperate?

They started moving away. Liz had a smudge of eyeliner on her cheek and I went to tell her, but her hand was still on his arm so I didn't. *Weird breastrokey, smudgey Liz*, I thought, as they wandered off together.

'You and me, hottie,' chuckled Duncan as I rolled out my towel next to him.

'Indeed,' I mumbled distractedly. Up ahead, Andrew and Liz were strolling side by side, her hand hanging loosely in the gap between them both, itching perhaps for his to cross the distance and hold hers. Her hair seemed to glow in the sunlight. His broad shoulders and height made her seem fragile in comparison. *I should have gone with them.*

Duncan was smoothing down his towel.

'What is that?' I asked, pointing to a pocket of fabric dangling from the side of it.

'It's a towel which has pockets for things.'

'Like sun cream?' I asked.

'Yes sun cream,' Duncan smiled as he surreptitiously pushed a runaway condom back into it.

I rolled my eyes. 'You really shouldn't keep those near direct sunlight,' I said before thinking.

'Those?' He smirked at me, playing it dumb.

'You know, the...thingies,' I said, pointing to the pocket and feeling like a twelve-year-old. 'The...' *Say condom, Iz, for heaven's sake, you are a grown woman! You have a degree! You can drive.* '... The rubber.' *RUBBER? Who are you, Iz, your dad?*

'Rubber,' Duncan sniggered predictably.

'Condom,' I whispered. 'They don't work after they've been in the sun or something. I read about it in...' *On a blog when I was Googling one of Mel's new sex moves?* 'The newspaper,' I coughed importantly.

'Well thank you for the warning,' Duncan said seriously, tipping about twelve condoms out of the pocket and into his hand.

I looked away. 'Gosh, I might get sunburned,' I said, feeling my cheeks flame.

Duncan patted his walnut-brown oil-covered chest. 'No chance of that.'

He lay back down and I had to admit that he looked good, his rippled torso turning an even deeper brown. I hugged my knees to my chest and looked away from him.

Up ahead, Liz and Andrew were out of sight, probably wrapped up against the bark of a nearby tree, or carving their initials into it.

Relief washed over me when they returned a few moments later and we ate crisps and baguettes stuffed with ham and read books in a line, apart from Duncan who was asleep using *Fifty Shades* as a shade. Scooting next to Andrew, I pointed to what he was reading, a thick book, a muscled man with a sword on the front.

'Good?' I asked.

He swivelled one eye to me. 'Yes.' His mouth was in a thin line, not following the sentence up with anything more. I assumed Liz was smirking at me from her towel.

'Great,' I said, realising that I didn't know what else to say. We hadn't really explored a wide range of topics as yet, were more comfortable going over memories from when we were young.

'I like books,' I said, cringing as the line spilled out before I could stop it.

'Okay.'

'Yes. Always have.'

Andrew looked at me and nodded once.

'Books.' I repeated and added a chuckle at the end, as if suddenly remembering a funny book. I felt sticky and hot. 'I'm going to snorkel again.' I pointed at the sea as if he was unclear as to where I would be.

'Good idea,' he said, returning to the page.

That hadn't gone as well as I might have liked.

Scooping up my mask, I headed over to the shoreline. Paddling out, I wondered what else I could do to try to accelerate our relationship. I had found him, after all, so it must have been fate and, although perhaps we didn't seem to have completely fallen back into our familiar ways, the fact that I was here meant something. I just needed to try harder.

As I ducked my head beneath the water, all thoughts drained away once more and I became completely absorbed in my underwater world. Emerging from the water, legs aching, skin wrinkling, I realised I had been in there a while. The towels were lying empty and crumpled, the boys playing Frisbee down the other end of the strip of beach. Liz was watching them, looking all wistful and fragile in her bikini as she sat on a thick, low branch of a tree looking out over the ocean. Her skin was pale and seemed to glow in the late afternoon light. She had somehow found a lace fan from somewhere and was quietly fluttering it in front of her face like she was now starring in a Jane Austen drama. I removed a piece of seaweed out of my hair, my face patchy and red from where the snorkel mask had pressed into my skin, and went to join the others.

'Hey, Iz,' Andrew said, the Frisbee whistling across the gap between us. I stepped and caught it in my hands. 'We used to do this on the beach at Southsea.'

Grinning, I returned it, gently sloping down to land neatly in his hands. 'I remember.'

Yay! This wasn't so hard after all.

Dear diary,

I haven't spoken to Andrew for days and I miss him. Today in Maths he pushed a note over to my desk, but I screwed it up and didn't even read it. Then I threw it in the bin at the end of the lesson, but it was annoying as later that day I wanted to get it again and read what it said. The cleaners had emptied it though so all that was there was an empty plastic bag and I would never read what it had said.

I x

Chapter 26

Collapsing next to the fire, I sank my toes into the sand. It was still warm from the day and tickled the skin between them. Andrew was prodding at the twigs and logs in the fire, making it glow orange, the odd spark making a bid for freedom as it crackled away in front of us, throwing long shadows beyond. The air smelled smoky and intense and the whole scene brought back memories of my childhood toasting marshmallows on sticks on Halloween, watching the marshmallows become gooey and runny and then tipping back my head to guide them in.

'What are you smiling about?' he asked, his voice low, his eyes on me.

I blushed and told him.

He nodded. 'We did the same. Do you remember the school used to run a fireworks night every year? We ate three toffee apples and you helped me make a guy for the fire. I remember watching him bob over our heads before being thrown on the flames and I started to cry. I was so embarrassed and you just held my hand.'

'Traumatised, much?' I laughed, putting an arm around him before I could stop to think about it. That memory struck me then, too – so many moments in our childhood when we had been close like that.

Andrew didn't flinch, but instead gave me a big smile, his teeth sparkling in the half-light of the fire. 'Isn't this perfect?'

I nodded wordlessly. Perfect. He was so right. I couldn't believe my luck. I had started out on the other side of the world – a stranger, a girl on a crazy mission to meet this man before me. On a whim and an old memory. I was so glad I had taken the leap. LA, my rubbish jobs, Randy, Stewie, they all seemed a million miles away as I breathed in the woody scent of the fire, listened to the low hum of hundreds of insects, stared up at the sky spattered with stars, felt the warm breeze on my bare arms.

'Perfect,' I whispered.

It must have been hours later, and eight bottles of beer, that I felt a woozy pull on my arms, a quick walk across the sand, an arm guiding me carefully back, my head resting on a pillow. Someone saying goodnight, fingers brushing mine, and then sleep.

You FOUND him – how completely wonderful, darling. What is he like? Did he remember you? You must pass on hellos to his mother. Is she well? And what are you doing out there? Have you seen lots of marvellous things? I am so glad you are travelling and seeing the world. You MUST keep writing to us. Your father is sending love, well he would if he were here but he is actually out with Bob doing something to do with sheep's wool. All very strange but I think best not to ask too many questions. Let them retain their air of mystery.

Tell me everything, everything, and many kisses,

Mum x x x x x x x x x

Chapter 27

I think it's going really well. I woke up next to him again this morning, this time on the camping mat on the floor. I held my breath as I looked at him lying there, inches away, not daring to disturb the moment. Feeling a little woozy with the sun and the beer from the day before, I lay back. Someone had put one of the cushions under my head as a makeshift pillow. I was still wearing all my clothes, my shorts twisted, my knickers needing to be adjusted. The floor felt horribly hard underneath me but I wasn't ready yet to start the day. My stomach growled at me and I rested one hand on it. That was when he woke up and turned sideways to take me in. His eyes widened a fraction. This close I could see the flecks in his irises, his pupils dilated.

'Oh.' He sat up.

'Morning.' I grinned, then worried I looked a crazy mess; he seemed more alarmed than I'd expected. 'I was just getting up,' I said, grabbing the bed next door and getting to my feet.

Moving across the room and out, I leaned on the balcony, breathing in slowly, never bored of the view. The small fire on the beach had long since burned out, a sad wisp of smoke snaking upwards towards another gorgeous blue sky. It was early, and the whole forest seemed to be steaming behind us, a low mist covering the top trees so it seemed like the whole island was tinged with magic.

The village was slowly waking: a distant cough, a rumble of bicycle tyres, someone sweeping a wooden floor, back and forth, rhythmic. The air smelled of oranges and I grinned at the thought of another day ahead in this paradise. I was going to make it a day to remember. I turned back to the hut, smiling to myself as I planned what I would do. We would spend hours together, reminiscing, experiencing the island, squinting at each other through the sun, splashing in the waves and then I would come back here, offer to cook him dinner, see where the night would take us...

Eating banana pancakes for breakfast under the awning of a nearby cafe half an hour later, anything seemed possible. Andrew looked refreshed and gorgeous. His hair was still wet from the shower and he was dressed in a cream T-shirt and navy shorts. We'd been swapping gossip about pupils we'd both known twenty years ago for a while now. Andrew had not been aware that 'Big, Fat Josie' had totally lost the weight and had been on *Take Me Out* last year. Nor was he aware that 'Pirate Jimmy' had lost the patch and had had corrective surgery in his teens and now worked as a buyer for Topman. We laughed over old teachers yes, that had been our Mrs Thompson in the *Daily Mail* holding her world record-breaking rabbit. With his feet up on the seat next door to me, I had to resist the urge to reach over and fondle his toes. They were all tanned and sandy and they wiggled when he laughed. I was mesmerised by them. The short blond curls that led up his calf. My hand wavered.

Andrew had scraped all the bananas to one side and called the waiter over to remind him that he hated them too ripe. I tried to smile at the waiter, but he had already moved away.

'Well I'm sure he'll remember next time,' I said, trying to make light of it.

'How hard is it?' Andrew said, rolling his eyes.

I swallowed back a reply, feeling a momentary pang of relief when Duncan joined us, bleary-eyed and in need of a shave. He was drinking something bright green that he promised us was a 'miracle cure'.

We spent the day out on the boat again, dipping in and out of hidden coves, exploring more reefs, swimming through shoals of fish and sunbathing on patches of sand, relishing the warmth of the day as we lay prostrate on the sand, letting the water wash over our feet. I insisted on making dinner. The boys had been great at letting me crash at theirs and adding extra to their meals, so this was my chance to pay them back. Liz was coming over, too, but even this news hadn't dampened my mood. I bought coconut cream, chillis, rice, and chicken and was going to make a Thai curry. A lovely dinner, candlelight softening my features, a small nod of thanks as the compliments descended, maybe a toast to the chef, the certainty that I had fully ingratiated myself into the group, Andrew's eyes on me as I spooned him a second helping...

Humming to myself, I collected up the pots and pans I

could find. The boys had gone out to fetch beers from a shop on the other side of the beach and had no doubt got waylaid if they'd opened any. I stared at the contraption in front of me, a makeshift gas hob that Andrew had shown me how to use. Leaning over me he had wielded an extra-long match and held my arm as he instructed me how to turn it on. It hadn't looked too complicated, but all I had really taken in was the fact that he smelled of lemon and the sea. I had closed my eyes; the image of the cottage in England wafting into view as I pictured us there, by our Aga, in the future.

Fiddling with the dial, I started to get the ingredients together, chopping up chicken to fry and thinly slicing the chilli pieces – removing the seeds with the point of the knife. Stepping out onto the balcony for a moment, I smiled to myself. The evening was mild and the sky was a haze of blues and purples. The odd boat interrupted the calm in the distance as the sun sank lower in the sky. This was my favourite time of day I thought, breathing in the evening air which smelled of jasmine with a hint of something else...onions? I frowned a fraction, sniffing exaggeratedly. Shrugging, I moved back inside.

Reaching for the matchbox by the side of the oven, I felt a flood of pride. My ingredients were neatly chopped and ready to go, the chillies cut to perfection, the pile of mange tout crisp and inviting, the chicken cubed as if by an expert. It was going to be a fantastic dinner. The boys would fill their bellies, shout for more and we would sit around the small table in the hut laughing, sated and happy. Liz would begrudgingly raise a glass and toast me because my Thai curry would be THAT good she would be compelled. But then she would remember she had to be somewhere all of a sudden and would rush off. Maybe Duncan would go and help her, leaving me and Andrew alone, the candles rasping their last gasps, the hut plunged into darkness as we giggled and fumbled to light them again...

Bending down to light the oven, I drew the match slowly along the box. There was a brief scratchy sound, an almost imperceptible background hiss and then, before I really knew it, a quiet poof and suddenly flames.

Big flames.

I shot backwards, alarmed at the sudden appearance of orange. I needed to reach the dial and turn them down, but I was nervous at getting so close. In my haste I had knocked the kitchen roll over and, as if in slow motion, I watched it roll across the counter, nearer, coming to rest next to the oven and then, as my eyes widened and I started to squeal, the kitchen roll started to burn. Strong smells filled the air, the flames leapt higher and, panicking, I ran out onto the balcony flapping my hands and calling for help. It came out quietly in a strangled voice I didn't really recognise as my own.

'Fire, curry,' I jabbered, flapping some more, the night air silent in response. Even the sun had sunk, not interested in helping. The empty beach stretched before me, the sand a ghostly pale blue, the ocean a dark smudge of nothing. The lights from other huts and cafes were further along the beach, feeling impossibly far away.

I looked back at the open door of the hut, a glow now emanating from the smeared window to the side, pale smoke escaping from the cracks and door. I tried to remember what

I had learned about fire safety. Vague memories of a visit from the fire service at my last workplace told me I needed a fire blanket or an extinguisher, or water, but then something warned me gas was different and this was a gas fire. What was it about a gas fire? Which one was bad? One of them was definitely bad. Argh. I had to make a decision quickly, I thought, looking once more at the lights in the distance. Too far. I would have to face this myself.

I stepped back into the hut, scared now as I saw the tea towel I had put near the oven had caught. The flames were impossibly high, licking the top of the hut. Seeing the towels nearby, I took a breath and bundled them into my arms, edging closer to the flames and throwing them quickly at the fire.

The tea towel stopped smoking and the towels seemed to have some effect, but the flames on the other side of the counter had reached the thin net curtains and they were now alight. Squeaking, I looked around for more things to throw at them. My heart was drilling like a rabbit on speed and I was sweating from the heat and the panic and the fear. There were voices in the distance and I became vaguely aware that I might not be alone. Emerging into the balcony I shouted again for help and then watched, as if it were happening elsewhere, as Duncan and Andrew piled past me, rounded eyes huge in their faces and moved through into the hut, swearing and waving hands in front of their faces to clear the smoke. I started to cough, hand over my mouth and cried, 'It was gas,' so they could remember their fire safety, too.

We started throwing things out of the hut onto the sand: the bedding, the rolled-up camping mat, clothes. We stamped on towels and trapped the fire with them. I felt my hands, blistered and hot, and then when we had put it out we emerged coughing and hacking on the shadowy sand. My eyes stung as the smoke billowed out in clouds around the windows, door and roof, leaking out into the inky sky above. We stood side by side on the sand staring at the hut.

Duncan turned to me. 'So what's for dinner?' And that's when I started to cry.

Two hours later, we were eating pizza out of a cardboard box, sitting in deckchairs wrapped in rugs that smelled of smoke and drinking Coca-Cola. Andrew was quiet. Duncan found the whole thing vaguely amusing and took great delight in dubbing me 'Girl On Fire' and singing the chorus of the Alicia Keys' song at random moments. I found myself avoiding Andrew's gaze as he sighed wearily and looked out on to the horizon, the noise heavy and depressing.

Sifting sand through my fingers, my hair still smelling of smoke, I pictured my mum all the way back in England, and wanted to be there, have her give me a hug and tell me it wasn't a complete disaster. People had bounced back from these kind of set-backs before and at least no one had been hurt.

'At least no one was hurt,' I said in a soft voice.

Andrew looked at me, unable or unwilling to nod a response.

Duncan gave me a sad half-smile. 'Tell that to Nemo here.' He lifted a soft toy shaped as a clown fish with one singed eye and waved it at me. I sniffed, and started to cry again. Duncan scooted over and threw an arm around me. 'It was a joke, Iz, a joke, it's okay. Nemo made it, it's all good.'

'I'm just so sorry about Nemo,' I pointed out. 'And the hut and the fact we were all having such a lovely time and... And...' I trailed off, hiccoughing through the words.

Duncan had started to slowly circle my back, making 'sssh' noises repeatedly. The rub got slower and slower and I was aware his fingers seemed to be grazing around the side of my body. I shifted, whispering my thanks and then turned to Andrew.

'It's not a big deal; we'll let it die down and you guys can sleep in my hut tonight. That's good news isn't it, mate?' asked Duncan, slapping Andrew on the back and making him wince.

That was when Liz appeared in this fresh cloud of pale yellows and pinks. Her skirt wafted around her ankles as if she was in a Fairy Liquid advert, her hair was in ringlets like she'd just stepped from the salon. There was no smudge on her face, no smoke-filled hair around her ears, no sooty smears on her legs and arms. I looked like I'd just stepped out of an audition for a role as an eighteenth-century chimney sweep.

She raised both hands slowly to her face and covered her mouth. Her subtly kohl-lined eyes widened in horror and then she looked at the hut, hands still over her mouth, and back to us. Andrew held her gaze as she lowered her hands and whispered in the most wounded voice, 'What happened?'

Andrew flinched, twitching his head in my direction and then looking at the sand.

Duncan was the first to answer. 'Iz was showing us how well she can cook.'

Dear diary,

I can't believe it but Jenny and Andrew are married now, even though I never broke up with Andrew and Annie said that wasn't allowed because you can't marry two people at once unless you live in America. She said that Jenny said that I should never have married him as she wanted to marry him all the time and now he has married her I don't want to look at him because Jenny is rubbish and so Andrew must be rubbish too, even though I thought we were friends. Mum said I shouldn't worry about not being married any more as she was quite surprised when I said I was. She said, 'Gosh that was sudden' and then she made me promise her I wouldn't get married again unless we both went shopping for a dress first.

I x

Chapter 28

Liz offered me her spare bed and I couldn't think of any good reason not to take it. At least Andrew was with Duncan and not her, I thought, annoyingly pleased to be tucked up in such a fragrant hut.

'I normally light a scented candle but I think tonight...' She trailed off, looking at me as if at any moment I might make something spontaneously combust.

Putting on an eye mask, removing her nose ring and inserting ear plugs, she got into her bed and turned her back to me, bidding me a slightly louder 'Goodnight' than she perhaps meant. An end to a conversation that had never really started.

I curled up in a sad little ball, as small as I could make myself, disappearing into my T-shirt and wrapping the thin duvet that smelled of the hotel laundry tightly around my shoulders. Despite three showers, I still felt smoke cloying in my nostrils. Closing my eyes, I tried not to focus on the fire and what I had done. Andrew's face swum into my vision, though, his horror as we had lobbed all his T-shirts out onto the sand, the charred towels and pans, the sooty remnants of his wash bag. Blinking quickly, not wanting to cry, I reminded myself it would all seem better in the morning. I listened then to Liz's breathing in the darkness. Slow and steady and normal. And then I tried to sleep.

Walking along the sand the next morning, the weather overcast and miserable, banks of cloud lapping over other clouds, promising peaks of blue sky too few and far between, I shivered. Nearing the hut, I noticed Andrew already up, scrubbing down the wood wearing yellow Marigolds alongside a short man wearing a stripy apron who was directing operations – the owner of the hut. Duncan was sitting in a deckchair on the sand, pretending to clean pans but actually sleeping. And then, as if my eyes had conjured him, I felt my shoulders lighten as Zeb appeared, carrying a bin liner and giving me a toothy grin when he caught my eye.

'Hey, Iz, I heard what happened, you okay?' he asked, making my eyes well up.

Forcing a smile, I said, 'Of course, what are you doing here?'

'I came to see how you were, and er...saw this. Thought I'd help.'

'Oh well, that's nice, what can I do?' I avoided Andrew's eyes as I asked it. He was brushing backwards and forwards with his cloth; tiny, furious movements, the muscles in his shoulders tense, the knuckles of his hand squeezing the cloth tightly.

‘Actually, it’s pretty much done,’ Zeb shrugged, depositing a bin liner and wiping his forehead. ‘It looked a lot worse than it was, you know,’ he added.

Andrew gave us both a sideways glance, a ‘Tsk’ escaping from his mouth.

‘So why did you come?’ I asked, desperate to change the subject and lighten the mood. Andrew’s glowers seemed to invade every pore of my body.

‘I wondered if you wanted to trek north of here later. I’ve found this incredible pool in the forest. I think you’ll love it.’

‘Oh.’ I was distracted by Andrew again, scowling at the wood he was scrubbing. ‘Oh that’s nice but I suppose I should stay and um...’ I indicated the hut. ‘You know, help here,’ I said, licking my lips and looking at the sand.

Zeb shrugged. ‘Fine by me, I’ll be off then,’ he said and before I could change my mind he had shaken the man in the stripy apron’s hand, waved at Andrew and was on his way, camera bag over his shoulder, not looking back.

‘Well,’ I said forcing cheer into my voice and picking up a cloth, ‘that was nice of him, wasn’t it?’

Andrew gave me a tight smile, lips stretched tight.

Duncan was stretched out in his chair. His eyes lit on me as he woke. Then, smiling, he held up a pan he should have been cleaning. ‘Morning, Iz,’ and then he pretended to make the pan talk in a squeaky voice, ‘Don’t hurt me, lady, that’s the lady who made me hurt...’ Chuckling at his hilarious joke he scooped up a tea towel, singed at the corner, and put on another voice. ‘Why did you try and kill us, lady? What did we ever do to youoooooo...?’

'Duncan, that's not funny,' Liz's prim voice came from behind me.

'But...' Duncan continued in the tea towel voice, 'but that lady made me burn...why she make me burn, why?'

I stepped towards Duncan, keen to see the funny side now that it really did look like no real damage had been done. 'No,' Duncan squealed, holding the tea towel up as a shield, 'don't come closer, lady, I don't want to hurt no more.'

'Okay, you can stop now,' I said, knowing Duncan was only trying to lighten the mood. 'Ha, ha.'

'But, Isobel,' he said, grabbing a spoon that had completely melted at the top, 'I will never live again as a spoon, you have killed me, killed meeeeeeeee.'

I grabbed the spoon and hit him with it, feeling gloomy again when I turned to see Liz talking in a quiet voice to Andrew.

Duncan put a hand on my shoulder. 'It's fine, Iz,' he laughed. 'Honestly.'

'Thanks,' I smiled.

'Well, apart from spooney here who really will never spoon anything ever again.'

Pushing him, I took a breath and walked over to Andrew who was sitting on the step of the hut looking morosely at the grubby cloth in his hand. I should face this: I knew he was angry with me. When we were children he could get like this. I had a flash of memory: he'd once ignored me for a week after I'd teased him about loving Kylie.

'Hey,' I said quietly.

He didn't acknowledge me and I felt a brief flicker of annoyance that he was making me feel so bad. But it had been his hut, it had been a shock and all his stuff might have been ruined. Reaching out and grabbing his hand, my desperation making me bolder than I would normally be, I said, 'Andrew, I am truly sorry, about the hut. Truly.'

He looked at me, a hint of red colouring his cheeks and clashing with his sandy-coloured hair. 'It's okay, Isobel, no real harm done,' he said and then added in a stiff voice, 'it's okay.'

'Thank you,' I gushed, 'thank you, it means a lot.' And then I added, 'I won't do it again.'

He started, his eyes widening. 'What?'

'Nothing, I mean I won't, you know, do anything silly,' I said, trying to avoid adding, 'I will try not to burn all your possessions again.' I didn't want to remind him of what he had just lived through.

'I know,' he said weakly.

'Come on, Andrew,' Liz said over to the right. 'Breakfast,' she called.

'We're going to get pancakes,' he said, not inviting me.

'Good.' I felt my eyes well again. *Jeez, Iz, pull yourself together*. 'I'll help out here and see you later.'

''kay.'

Watching them move off together, Duncan in their wake (the mention of pancakes and he was anyone's), made me long for Mel, or my mum, or someone who would make me feel less hopeless. It had all been going so well, and then one silly mistake.

The man in the stripy apron locked up the hut, one eye on me as if he had heard I was the resident arsonist.

Turning towards the sea, leaving the hut behind me, I took my phone from my pocket and dialled home, keen to offload to someone who might not loathe me right now.

Dad answered after a few rings, a nervy 'hello, 9846' as he did so.

'Dad,' I said, feeling bad for instantly asking, 'is Mum there?'

'No.'

'Ah.'

I would have to go for it. 'How are you, Dad?'

'The same, the same.'

Well he was making this easy.

'Good.'

'What is new with you, Isobel?'

'Oh...Stuff.'

'Interesting stuff?'

'I've been out on a boat and I've seen a turtle,' I said, feeling like that day seemed an eternity ago. Had that laughing girl really been me?

I continued to walk along the sand, the clouds still unmoving above me, past the turtle nets to the end of the beach, listening to my dad trying to coax me out of myself.

'Well that does sound interesting but, knowing you, I don't think you were ringing your mother to tell her that. Is it a woman thing or can I try to help?' He coughed. This would not have been an easy question for him to ask and my heart softened.

'Not a woman thing as such I was sort of ringing because...' And then I felt my voice wobble. 'Because...' I coughed to clear it. 'The thing is, I sort of made a mistake cooking the dinner.'

Hello, world's biggest understatement. I imagined my dad, all concerned, sitting at the table in the kitchen, a crumpled newspaper abandoned, his crumpet half-eaten and I just couldn't find the words. He would only worry.

'Well that doesn't sound too bad, my love, your mother often makes mistakes cooking dinner. The other evening we had parsley sauce with no parsley in it. It was most peculiar.'

'Well,' I swallowed, 'that has made me feel better.'

'What did you do? It couldn't have been as bad as all that?'

'I...' I pictured my father's forehead wrinkling in concern, his hands greasy from working on one of his cars, his brown eyes kind. 'I burned it,' I said in a quiet voice, 'burned it all.'

A lone tear wobbled down my cheek and I swiped at it. 'I ruined it all.'

'Isobel, it's okay, these things happen, it doesn't sound all that serious.'

'No.' I gulped back further explanation. 'I'm just being silly, I suppose. How is Mum?'

'Probably on a hilltop screaming at the wind or having coffee with a friend. The two aren't necessarily mutually exclusive.'

'Will you tell her I called? But not to worry.'

'Of course, you take care and, Isobel, are you sure there isn't anything else?'

I thought of Andrew, forlorn and smeared in ash on the beach last night. I thought of Liz's triumphant smirk as she took in the devastation, of all the charred utensils lying about on the sand this morning, useless. I thought of all my plans to prove to Andrew that I could be good for him, for him to see me as someone capable and reliable. I thought of the thousands of miles I'd travelled in search of him and the start of perhaps a new chapter for me. Taking a breath, I swallowed, looking out over the vast expanse of ocean in front of me.

'No, Dad, that was it, I just wanted things to be perfect.'

'Well perfect can be overrated, my love. Sometimes I love things with a few dents and bangs. More interesting.'

I felt a slow smile lift my cheeks. 'Thanks, Dad.'

'Speak again soon.'

He started to bluster, as he always did at the end of phone calls, and I laughed softly, a glow in my stomach, and told him I loved him.

Wading into the sea, letting the surf wash against my calves, I followed the trail of a boat moving steadily around the coast. To my right, a jumble of rocks emerged from the water, pushed up against the bank. I walked towards them, throwing up droplets in the shallows. Sitting on one of the flatter rocks, the stone warm, heating my bare legs, I looked back over to the other end of the beach, perhaps imagining the sad little gathering of people in the cafe now bemoaning the loss of the hut and my arrival.

From this distance it was hard to tell whether the tiny pin people in the cafe were crying, but in my mind it became so. I called Mel four times but it just went straight to answerphone every time and I didn't want to snivel through a message. Wallowing in self-pity, I scrolled through my phone, once more hovering over various names and then realising with a sigh that I was on my own for this one.

I had to go back there and brazen it out. If I was serious about winning Andrew back, I couldn't let this setback be the end of things. Pushing my shoulders back and lifting my chin, I felt a bit of strength restored. What I needed to do was ask the universe for help – I knew if Mum was here that would be her advice.

Standing up slowly on the rock, smooth under my feet, swirling with greys and browns from a bygone age, I stared at the horizon in the distance and then at the sky above and, summoning my mum's confidence, called in a loud, clear voice, 'You can do this, Isobel Graves, you are a strong, fantastic wo... Oh crap.' Laughing at myself and feeling refreshed, I hopped off the stone onto the darkened sand, feeling it spill over my toes. I would never be that girl.

Tossing my hair behind me and pocketing my mobile phone, I started to walk back towards the hut to begin again. A sliver of sun was pushing the clouds apart, broken up now by larger patches of cerulean blue. I might not be able to chant without feeling like a fool, but I could go back and face the music alone.

Then, as if someone up there had engineered it, my phone started buzzing. Without thinking, I pressed 'Call', only realising at the last moment that 'Stewie' had been the name on the screen. I was so not in the right place for this now, I thought as I cringed and pulled the phone to my ear.

'Hey,' I said, the one word filled with guilt. I should have rung him back before now; I should have done lots of things before now.

'I won't be long, Isobel,' he said, which just made me feel worse. 'I know you haven't called to give me some space.'

Wow, Stewie was giving me way more credit than I deserved.

'Oh I'm sorry, Stewie, I—'

'And I have been thinking,' he said, his accent pronounced as if he were reading from a cue card. I let him go on. 'You were never as into me as I was into you, Isobel...'

I held my breath, not wanting him to say it but not wanting to interrupt him.

'And I knew that really, but I just kept trying.'

Oh wow, Isobel Graves, you really are an uber bitch. I gripped the phone, suddenly desperate to say something to make him feel better.

'You're really kind, Stewie, and you have always been nice to me and I am so sorry about how I behaved in the end,' I said, needing to apologise.

He let me, sighing once down the phone.

'You are going to find someone who will be much nicer to you than I was, and I am really sorry that we didn't work out.'

'Well maybe once you've had some time to think about things...' His voice was tinged with fresh hope.

'I think it's best not,' I said quietly, feeling dreadful for the thousandth time in the last twenty-four hours.

'Okay,' he said. 'Look, this is costing me a lot of money. So I better...'

He trailed away and I quickly jumped in.

'I'll call you another time, Stewie, okay, when I'm back in LA, check you're okay, not that you won't be...' I quickly reassured him. *Wow, Isobel, could you sound more arrogant? Oh you will be terrible because I dumped you, poor man...*

'Okay. That'd be good.'

'Great, well, you take care of yourself,' I babbled, wanting to cram my apology into that sentence. He had never been a mean person, had never deserted me when I was mooching around LA despairing at the state of my life.

'You too.'

I felt lighter when I'd hung up, a little guilt-ridden still, but that had to be expected. That hadn't been so awful and it must have taken Stewie quite a lot of effort to make the call. I would phone him when I was back; I wanted to. As I looked down the beach, I realised I could be home sooner than I thought. Taking a huge breath, I started over the sand, rehearsing what I would say, trying to take a leaf out of Stewie's book and be brave.

Man, what was today? Burn-a-Hut-Break-Up-With-Your-Boyfriend-Day – on to the next Big Apology. Not sure I would log this in the diary as one of my Top Ten Fave Days.

I returned to find Duncan lying prostrate on the sand, wearing a pair of the most obscene budgie smugglers I had ever had the misfortune of laying eyes on.

'The horizontal fluorescent stripes accentuate my massive knob,' he called out, his eyes still closed.

Liz had found a broom from somewhere and was sweeping the last of the splintered wood, ash and other paraphernalia onto the sand, finding time to stare at me intermittently between brushstrokes.

'Where's Andrew?'

'Sorting a hotel room; he doesn't want to stay in the hut,' mumbled Duncan.

I felt my toes curl and a rush of blood warm my cheeks.

Andrew was having to traipse around searching for a HOME because of me.

Duncan patted the sand by his side with one flat hand and, then, when I didn't respond, repeated the action whining, 'Izzz, get over here or I'll set your hair on fire.'

'That is not funny, Duncan,' the prim voice of Liz admonished him from the balcony.

Without looking at her, he called, 'It is a little bit funny.'

I tried to disguise a tiny laugh in my hand and moved to sit down on the sand.

Duncan opened one eye. 'Sexy top,' he commented.

'Thanks,' I replied, wondering whether that was why I had been summoned.

'Right, you moping loser,' he began. 'Stop hanging your little head and looking like a puppy that's been kicked.'

'I don't look like a puppy.'

'Okay, fine, one of those abused kittens in the RSPCA ads.'

'I don—'

'Shh, Isobel, let me finish. So you nearly burned the hut down. Stuff happens. No one's hurt and we got our things out so it's all good. Well, apart from for that guy that owns the hut, but let's hope that he has insurance.'

'But...'

Duncan held up a hand and I fell silent.

'Andrew is getting a room up the road and, as long as you promise never to cook us a lovely meal again, things will turn out peachy. Just peachy. End of lecture.'

I didn't really know immediately what to say to that; sifting sand through my hand, I felt grateful for the pep talk.

‘Thank you.’ My voice was low and quiet.

Duncan opened up an eye again. ‘Good, I’m glad you’re over it. I’ve been lying here thinking of different ways you could make it up to me.‘

‘You’re disgusting,’ I sighed. ‘And it wasn’t even your hut.’

‘But I have been through an emotional trauma, and probably do need tending to.’

I got up to leave while he was still talking and, as I walked away, heard him carry on regardless. ‘So if you could just let me nuzzle a bit, I might feel comforted...’

Focusing on the long, faint shadow I was making, sporadic weeds pushing their way through the sand as I walked towards the hut and Liz, I licked my lips and mentally prepared. Liz had sourced a small silk handkerchief for her hair and continued to sweep as I approached, sighing at intervals like she was auditioning for a part in *Les Mis*.

‘I’m really sorry about the hut, Liz, and thanks for, er, helping clear it up and for last night, the bed and that. Can I help?’

She looked at me with large round eyes. ‘I’m nearly finished; you lie down.’

I bristled at the suggestion that I would just want to lounge about and, seeing an abandoned dustpan and brush, grabbed at it and started forming little piles, mostly of sand, to make Liz realise that I too could play the martyr, I too could get my hands dirty. I clambered over the wood, sweeping dangerously close to her perfectly painted toenails. She stepped over me and went inside.

Andrew rounded the corner just at that moment and spotted me kneeling on the hard wood floor, dust on my knees (not a great deal in my dustpan) and a smudge on my forearms.

'Thanks, Isobel,' he said.

I couldn't resist peeking up through my lashes at him and whispering, 'Not at all,' in my most I-have-been-sweeping-so-much-all-morning-and-I-am-so-weary voice.

Liz appeared in the doorway, hands on hips, and I stood up quickly before she could say anything, stretched and asked, 'Did you find somewhere?'

I could feel Liz's annoyance wafting over me in waves as I tried to focus on what Andrew was saying.

'...Up the track next to the yellow house.'

'That's great.'

He walked off to join Duncan and I quickly carried on brushing in case he turned around to look back at me.

Liz's pale legs walked past me, leaving her dusty, dainty footprints behind.

Pondering my next move, relishing the memory of the look Andrew had given me, I swept absent-mindedly. Perhaps it had been a small step towards forgiveness and I hadn't completely ruined things after all? His quiet thanks suggested I hadn't completely blown it. What I needed to do now was to demonstrate to him the type of caring, reliable person I could be. I needed something to nurture, something to care for. No more fancy dinners, trying to impress him that way – something safe, something simple. Something to show I could look after things.

Perhaps I could secretly injure him and then win brownie points by nursing him effectively? Good bits: he would see my caring, committed nursing side. Bad points: I would have to injure him beforehand. Perhaps I could put something in his path that he would trip on? I shook my head, trying to clear my thoughts. This was a problem that I could solve. I suppose I could injure something and care for it in front of him. I looked over at Liz and Duncan, at their limbs, then stopped myself. *Note to self, Isobel: stop being a psycho.*

Focus, focus. Okay, okay, I could injure an animal, like a mouse or a bird or a stingray or something. Then nurse it back to life.

'We're going to move all our things and then grab some juice. Coming?' Duncan called.

I stood up, knees clicking, one hand on my lower back. 'Definitely.'

As Andrew walked ahead of me, backpack slung over one shoulder, I couldn't help a slow smile. I could do this, I could win him over. There's nothing like a good plan.

I had tried to be caring ALL DAY and it was getting really tiring. I had asked after everyone's health, had shown deep concern when Duncan had sneezed, throwing myself across the table to place a nursely palm on his forehead to see if he had a fever (he did not) and had even cared for a little insect that had been trotting across our table, ensuring its safety by cupping my hand around the path it was taking to protect it from danger. Andrew hadn't noticed any of these things.

I then decided to show my caring nature on the beach by defending the benefits of the sand fly even after two had bitten me on the legs. I had been especially careful when snorkelling to avoid harming coral and had given the others a lecture on the importance of not damaging the environment. Andrew had just carried on playing Frisbee. I had even 'oohed' and 'aahed' when Liz stubbed her toe on a big shell (ha, ha, the shell got Liz, Stubby-Toed Liz).

Caring and nurturing just wasn't cutting it, I thought when back in the hotel room after my shower.

I needed a new plan, a new persona; I needed Andrew to appreciate a different side to me.

How about fun-loving? Everyone loves a party girl, a girl who is at the centre of things, a girl who seems to have no cares, who wears hot pants and doesn't worry about cellulite, has a tattoo, drinks and dances and drags everyone along with her. Glamorous, sexy with one of those laughs that just makes you want to laugh, too. I started to do the laugh; it was lower and louder than my normal laugh and I adjusted the volume till I thought I'd got it just so...

'Are you laughing at yourself?'

I appeared to have my hands outstretched, and lowered them delicately to my side as I turned to Andrew.

Oh maaaaaan.

'There was a funny...funny-looking...moth,' I finished lamely, pointing to a corner of the room.

'Let's see.'

'Oh, he, he isn't around any more. He left. Moth stuff,' I shrugged. *Moth stuff?*

'That's a shame.'

He actually looked sad and I now wished there *was* a funny-looking moth around to buck him up a bit. Then I also remembered my new plan, my new persona. I was Party Girl. That happy-go-lucky girl with a great laugh. I felt relieved I'd had time to practice and I did a little mini version. Andrew didn't look like he wanted to laugh too, but I assumed he was just not over the moth disappointment.

'Soooooooo,' I said, clapping my hands. 'What brings you to my abode?' *Abode?* I realised with a panic that this might be how Party Girl speaks.

'Duncan and I were going to go to the bar for a drink and wondered if you wanted to come?'

He looked sort of blushy and endearing and, as he asked, my heart did a little leap.

'I totes would, Batman.' I clicked a finger at him.

Okay, Party Girl needs to not be a dick I told myself. Moving on from the clicking and calling him Batman, I asked, 'Is there a theme?'

'Theme?'

'Well it sounds like a night out, so we probably need a theme.'

Everyone knows that the best nights out involve fancy dress and as Party Girl I felt it was my duty to make sure this night out was the best night out ever.

'Theme?' said Duncan wandering into the room. 'We should absolutely have a theme. Tarts and other tarts?'

'That's not a legitimate theme, Duncan,' I said in a voice that was definitely not Party Girl's. I quickly corrected myself by doing the new laugh. Both boys took a step back.

'How about...?' Then I realised I didn't have a theme. I should have planned this. I started to panic. Was I already utterly useless at being Party Girl? 'HATS!' I shouted desperately. 'We should totally get...hats.'

'Er...Okay, I suppose,' said Duncan, 'if it will make you happy.'

'It would.'

'I don't have a hat,' said Andrew.

Duncan slapped him on the back. 'I'll sort you one, mate.'

'Great!'

Chapter 29

There was a wooden terrace outside the bar with long tables and benches running down the length of it. Colourful flowers floated in bowls and fairy lights were strung along the balustrade throwing light on to the sand below. A sliver of a moon meant that the sea from here was just a dark patch of inky blue and you couldn't tell where it ended and the sky began.

The bar smelled of coconut, warm bodies and perfume. I was perspiring a little under my chosen hat: a straw cowboy hat that had seen better days. Party Girl was, of course, wearing a strappy dress and a push-up bra. She was also wearing a necklace of plastic flowers that she always took on holiday and never had the guts to wear. It shouted: 'I am Fun' (or 'I grew up in Hawaii'). Either way, people would totally want to hang out with her.

Duncan was wearing a baseball cap that said, 'I DO IT DOGGY' above a picture of a dog and Andrew was wearing a large hot-pink sombrero.

‘Gosh, that’s very...’ I trailed off realising that Party Girl should love the look. ‘Bold.’

‘It’s Duncan’s,’ he explained.

‘I have a hat for every occasion.’ Duncan winked at me.

‘You certainly do.’

We sipped at our drinks and looked around the bar. There were a few couples scattered about, two guys playing pool and a gaggle of what looked like gap year students who were giving each other henna tattoos. I was pretty sure stripy apron owner of the hut was in residence, too, chatting to another middle-aged man, and I lifted my drink at him sheepishly when he caught my eye. I was almost relieved when I saw Liz arrive. She had clearly got the hat message, too, and was wearing a black floppy sun hat and looked like a strawberry-blonde version of Audrey Hepburn.

Andrew scooted up to make room on the bench for her and I offered to fetch another round of drinks. Returning with shots (standard fare for Party Girl) and a jug of vodka orange, I grinned round at the hatted clan. This was surely going to be a memorable night. Theme, check, drinks, check, good times, rolling.

We’d been drinking and chatting and it was all going fine. We’d played pool. I’d joined up with Andrew and cheered in a very loud way on potting both the black and the white simultaneously. Then Andrew explained the rules through gritted teeth. We had lost: no fair.

Now we were back at the table and talking again. This wasn’t quite the crazy go-getting evening I had envisaged. Andrew had just stifled a yawn. Everyone knows what a Party Girl should do to liven up an evening, I thought, smiling to myself. She should start a sing-along, one of those spontaneous ones where strangers join in and everyone ends up linking arms and making best friends. I felt confident having seen it in plenty of movies and cleared my throat. Looking over at Duncan, I started to croon.

'Hey, Duncan, do you remember...?'

I needed a good link in, a line that would make it natural that I begin a sing-along. I racked my brains.

Duncan was still looking at me so I needed to think quicker.

'Do you remember...that ...thing...that...?'

I was flailing now. They were all watching me. I readjusted my hat to buy some time.

'Do you remember...? Or, no, no, wait...' I got excited. Everybody loved the Backstreet Boys! Andrew had loved them when he was younger. I'll go for one of theirs. 'I think...we should get up,' I said slowly. 'Everyone get up, sing it.' I nodded my head twice to an imaginary beat. 'Everybody get up.'

Three faces looked at me. Liz had arched one of her eyebrows.

I persisted. 'Come on, everyone, get up, sing it, 1, 2, 3, 4.'

Shit, wait, this was so not a song from the Backstreet Boys, I was singing 5ive. Oh god, I'm not sure anyone liked 5ive. Maybe I could brazen it out.

'Are you singing 5ive?' asked Duncan.

'What? No, I'm...I was...'

'1, 2, 3, 4, 5ive will make you get down, yeah,' Duncan started singing.

Oh my god, this was it, it was a sing-along, a spontaneous sing-along. This was totally happening.

‘Bring it, bring it on, bring it on, bring it…on.’ I realised halfway through the sentence that I perhaps was not as down with these lyrics as I had initially thought. Duncan was smiling and I looked at Andrew in his big pink hat to see if he was joining in, too. He wasn’t, but that was probably because we hadn’t yet got to the chorus.

‘Everybody get up, sing it, 5, 6, 7, 8.’ I smiled encouragingly at Duncan for him to join me again, but we clashed over the next sentence.

‘5ive will make you get down, yeah.’

‘Bring it, bring it on, bring it on, bring it.’ I had definitely brought it a lot. If it needed to have been brought, I had brought it. I could not think of another line and started to mumble various numbers interspersed with the word ‘everybody’ in the hope that Duncan might have a finer grasp of 5ive’s backlist. He did not and petered out, offering to go and get more beers. I nodded, concerned that the evening was not going Party Girl’s way.

Liz and Andrew were now quietly talking and they were holding up their hands, seeing who had the biggest hand or something. It was a weird little game that gave me a feeling like a stone was sitting in the middle of my stomach. *How could I turn this around?*

Duncan returned, snaking round various chairs to get back, clutching four bottles of beer in one hand and I did a ‘Whoop, whoop!’ and started calling ‘strawpedoe’, reckoning that I needed to oil the wheels somewhat and get everyone more in the mood.

‘I’ll fetch the straws,’ I sang, leaping from my chair and practically knocking my cowboy hat off in my enthusiasm.

‘There’s really no need…’ Liz called from the table.

I rolled my eyes like any Party Girl would and headed to the bar, seizing a handful of straws and giving a massive grin to the barman.

It was a few hours later and the straws had gone down a treat; we’d been joined by the gap year henna group who were Canadian and were now teaching us their national anthem. At the moment I had definitely got the first line nailed and then turned to trusty mumbling for the rest. I’d lost my hat, but no matter. Andrew seemed to be the happiest I’d seen him in a while (well since I’d almost burned his house down) and I really thought he was seeing a new side to me tonight.

Still, there was nothing like an impromptu boat race to really double-check and I herded everyone into two lines, wondering why people kept putting tables and chairs in my way when I wanted to walk places.

‘Hip bruise.’ I lifted my top to show Andrew.

He hiccoughed.

Throwing an arm over my shoulders, I was blasted by the warm, beery breath of Duncan who was now wearing his cap backwards and appeared to have lost his shirt.

‘‘ello.’

‘Shirt.’ I pointed because I was really in a say-what-I-see mood.

He jiggled his pectoral muscles at me, which was both fascinating and a bit creepy.

Sitting on the floor of the bar in two lines, the Canadian students and a couple of German guys who’d swelled our numbers, we downed drinks in a race to win. There was back-slapping and laughter and dancing and sand and laughter and more songs and I also made best friends with someone in Canada. And there was Andrew, in the midst of it all; he was there. I found him in the darkest corners. I raised toasts to him and I admired his hat. I felt awash with good feelings and was so pleased I had travelled this far. I had really done it: I was trying to reach for the life I had always wanted. And hello, CV: I rock at boat races.

Hic.

Dear diary,

I miss Andrew so much. I haven't seen him at all since term ended and Mum says his mum has moved away so they can be nearer Andrew's dad. School is not the same and when I go to all the places we played it is not as fun any more. When we went on the trees he would always make me climb higher and I was so proud when I looked down. When we went to the pier we would sit and listen to my Walkman and Andrew made me a tape with brilliant songs on it so that we could listen to that. It isn't as fun now and the songs make me miss him more. I feel so sad now that he went away before we could be friends again, it was only a silly argument and Jenny said he always told her how much he missed me too

I x

Chapter 30

The hammock is the world's greatest ever invention. Paracetamol, you might cry, the steam engine, others would say. They would be wrong. The hammock is the world's greatest-ever invention.

I was suspended, encased in netting, drifting off to sleep shaded by the branches of the trees above me. If I reached out my left arm I could pick up my water bottle, raise it to my lips and drink from its watery goodness. A light breeze washed over me like a whisper on the air and for a few seconds I didn't want to throw up the contents of my stomach any more.

Five minutes ago, I had opened one of my eyes, the eyelashes sticking with last night's mascara, to see Duncan crawling across the sand for an early morning swim. I wasn't sure he made it. Andrew was yet to appear and I allowed myself a momentary sigh as I pieced together the night before. I kept my eyes shut this time, realising I wasn't ready for that movement again.

These are my memories: drinking beer through straws, something about Canada, something about boats or hats, Liz is a douche.

There had been a moment with Andrew, definitely a moment. We'd been sitting on the floor, cross-legged, waiting for our turn in a boat race that was fast turning into farce because no one had full drinks, the comforting presence of Andrew behind me, warm when I leaned back to talk to him. I remember his touch on my arm, his hair tickling my face as he said something over the din to me. I remember feeling my stomach plummet as I looked over my shoulder at him. Then there had been something else, at the end of the night...All this thinking was hurting my head. I had to dredge it up; it felt like the important piece of a puzzle. The one in the jigsaw that you need to make that sucker work.

To my right I heard a rustle and then the snap of a camera. I called, 'Andrew, is that you?' I admired my new throaty Radio 1 DJ voice. There was silence and I realised I was forced to open up another eye.

'How are you feeling?' I croaked, shielding my eyes with one hand and looking over in the direction of the noise.

Zeb had one knee planted in the sand, one foot behind him, his face obscured by the camera. It went off again.

Sitting up, the hammock rocking dangerously as I turned to him, I felt a surge of sickness which put off the moment at which I was planning to shout at him.

'Good morning, princess, you look very relaxed.'

Groaning, I lay back down. 'I was, oh harbinger of doom.'

He scooted next to me to sit in the sand, his bare legs in cut-off denim shorts, a strip of white flesh across both feet that looked like he was still wearing flip-flops. 'Dying?' he asked cheerfully.

'Bleurgh.'

'So dying.'

'Gahhhhh.'

'I was wondering if you wanted to walk round to something.'

'What kind of something?' I whispered, taking another sip from my water bottle.

'It's a surprise.'

'I can't deal with surprises today.'

'Can you deal with anything today?'

'Ha ha.' I trained an eye on him, he looked so horribly perky, his blue eyes fringed with dark lashes. I hadn't noticed the navy flecks in them before.

'Okay, fine, you win. It's a cave.'

'Cave?'

'It's brilliant, will you come?'

'My mother always told me not to go to dark caves with strange men.'

'Very sensible woman.'

He started whistling 'Club Tropicana'.

'No,' I said, pointing a finger to my lips.

The whistling stopped.

'I'll buy you an ice cream...'

I shifted in my hammock. It rocked left and right.

'I'll buy you Ibuprofen.'

I couldn't help smiling. 'Oh god. Okay, okay, I'm coming.'

'Good.'

Holding my head, I sat up again. I gingerly twisted and placed my feet on the soft sand below. I took Zeb's hand and wobbled upright, one hand automatically on my stomach.

'Where's the ice cream?' I whispered.

'Right this way, your majesty.' And he bent on one knee again, a palm outstretched, his head bowed.

'Very good.' I sniffed, walking past him, my nose in the air.

Walking up a winding path, loose pebbles forming a slippery layer over the dry earth, I wondered why I had agreed to come. Zeb was a few metres ahead, his white cotton shirt billowing behind him, his dark hair curling a little at the back. The heels of his feet were dusty and this thought made my stomach grumble again. I swigged at my water calling, 'How much further?' in as hopeful a voice as I could muster.

Zeb looked back over his shoulder at me, his white teeth flashing in his brown face. 'Not much further and it's downhill most of the way from here on.'

I nodded and kept my eyes on the ground, one foot in front of the other, feeling my calves burn like I was in a step class in a sauna. In a hot country. Like Hell. I could feel beads of sweat forming on my hairline and swiped the back of my hand to get rid of them. This cave better be made of diamonds. Or ice.

The path narrowed even further and I dodged round brambles protruding from the edge; there were marks in the sand that looked worryingly snake-like and little holes that disappeared into snake tunnels. These thoughts helped me quicken my pace and I was soon practically treading on Zeb's heels as we rounded a corner.

To the right, deep-green clouds of trees climbed above us, disappearing into a thin layer of mist at the top. Ahead of us, the path led down, twisting, disappearing and returning again. To our left, the turquoise-blue ocean shimmered in the heat and I imagined sinking beneath the water and feeling refreshed. I licked my lips feeling sand granules fill my mouth as if the air was filled with dust. The sun blazed on to my bare shoulders and the backs of my legs.

Winding our way further down the path, I could hear the occasional rustle of an animal in the bushes alongside us and, as the ground levelled out, the trees seemed bent over by the heat, their branches creating dark-brown shadows on the path.

'This is it,' said Zeb, pointing to the left where a rough track could just be made out, broken bracken trodden into the ground, twigs forming a channel through the undergrowth.

My nose wrinkled as he started down it, a large rustle to my left making me squeak and race after him. *Great*, I thought, *a path to who knows where*. How was I fooling myself that I was some intrepid explorer? Shouldn't I have a compass, a map or a backpack with supplies? How long would we be walking through the jungle for? Would I ever return to my friends? I pictured the hammock back at Juara beach, an iced tea perspiring slightly on a small table beside it, next to a book I had been reading.

Stumbling into the sunlight, I felt sand flick the back of my calves and realised I was on a thin stretch of beach, totally isolated and in its own bay. The water lapped gently, brown leaves turning over in the surf as it rolled in. Zeb had waded out, the bottom of his shorts dark blue from the water and was clambering over a cluster of rocks to the right, his camera bag slung over his shoulder, a towel round his neck like a scarf. He turned back to me. 'This is it,' he repeated, his smile so wide I couldn't help grin back.

Taking off my shoes, I walked down to meet him, gasping in delight as I moved over to the rocks. Placing a hand on the warm stone, I hauled myself up and stayed crouched pretty low to grope my way around. As I turned the corner, the sun disappeared, the air cooled and the noise of the water seemed heightened; slapping on to rocks and washing into shore.

The rocks flattened out and Zeb was standing on a shelf gazing into the cave. Inside, where the light couldn't reach, there was a strip of sand and then a border of rocks in which a deep-green circle of seawater formed a pool. The stone walls curved up and over our heads streaked in greys and disappearing into shadow at the back. In the ceiling there was a jagged hole in the rock and the sun had forced its way through slicing the air and showing up dancing particles and creating a circle of the brightest green on the water of the pool below. It was beautiful.

Zeb had removed his camera and was taking shots at different angles as I hopped down on to the wet sand. Feeling it squelch in between my toes and around my ankles, I laughed open-mouthed, hangover entirely forgotten, desperate to just take everything in.

Getting into the pool had been a shock and a relief, the stones underneath smoothed away over time. Propping myself up on my elbows, I looked out of the cave at the ocean. The blue of the sea seemed all the brighter, framed as it was in the dark, rough walls of the cave and I paddled my feet behind me and gazed at it, feeling my whole body unwind and relax. I had stumbled into paradise and my life in LA, the hut, the hangover, the guilt and the stress all melted away as I listened to the roll of the waves and felt the breeze on my face.

Zeb swum into the circle and was now framed in his own spotlight. His skin looked mahogany brown in the darkness of the cave and I gulped a little as he stood up, droplets clinging to his dark chest hair, a line running from his bellybutton to beneath the water. I found myself staring, remembering seeing him under the waterfall all those days ago and then felt heat in my cheeks as I looked away.

'I thought I would cover up this time,' he said, waggling an eyebrow at me. *Did his bark of laughter seem a fraction forced, too?*

I splashed him lightly and turned back around. 'Lucky me.' I laughed, swallowing the words, surprised by the higher pitch in my voice, my head starting to swim a bit, a woozy dream-like feeling wafting over me.

We stayed there mostly in silence, sitting and watching the odd passing bird or boat dip in and out of view, watching clouds skitter across our path, momentarily plunging the whole cave into darkness, the pool a glinting black shadow for a second.

'This is incredible,' I said, sitting on the side of the pool, now, my calves lost to the greenish water.

'We should film a clip here for the blog,' Zeb said, looking at me with a question on his lips.

'Blog?' I furrowed my brows.

'It's where I've been uploading all the photos. It's a travel blog I set up a year or so ago. I let it fester a bit but it's now fully back up and running, but it could do with some other content.'

'What were you thinking?' I asked, feeling an old feeling, a buzz of excitement at the thought of a project.

'Well, I think people would want to know places like this exist; you could talk to camera about it. You look sort of perfect there.' He paused to cough and, for a brief second, I thought he might be nervous, but then he continued, his voice the same, assured. 'Talk about what we've felt, how it seems, no more than two minutes. Can you?'

I felt warmth in my cheeks at the question. I knew I could really but I wanted to get it right, to talk about the intimate feeling of the place, the pool.

'Let me have a think and then I'll be ready.' I smiled, feeling my stomach hum with excitement. I missed presenting to camera, trying to communicate to people in this way.

'I'll set up,' Zeb said, hauling his camera bag over and rummaging through it. He removed a mini tripod and went about finding a place to set it up, lowering his eye to the viewfinder and framing me.

I had thought of the things I could say and was feeling ready, flicking my hair back and licking my lips. Nerves fired through me, mini and exhilarating, and we had a go testing the sound and making sure I knew what I was going to say.

It took a couple of times – I felt rusty, my tongue too big for my mouth – and Zeb handed me a bottle of water. On the third attempt I felt myself loosening up properly, jumbled thoughts straightened out and I was able to speak to camera.

Zeb looked at me at the end of the take and gave me a big thumbs-up as he turned the camera off.

'Fantastic.'

I lowered myself back in the water, biting my lip, pleased it had gone well. I stayed in the pool for a while, not really wanting to leave the sanctuary of this place. The heavy silence, the echoey sounds of our voices, conspiratorial laughter all a comfort.

Zeb offered me a hand as we left and I took it, allowing myself to be pulled back up and out, leaving the darkness and the mystery of the cave behind me.

Walking back, we barely spoke, swapping brief smiles. I felt as if my body had unfurled, everything was calmer and my movements were fluid and unhurried. The day had moved in a leisurely meander and as I looked across at Zeb, I wanted to reach across the gap between us and hold his hand, tell him how amazing it had all been.

Up ahead, the path was blocked by a man, his chest smooth and rippled as he bent and stretched, as if warming up for a run. I could make out blond hair, in waves, and realised it was Duncan. He stood up, attempting nonchalance as we approached.

'Hey, Isobel.'

'Hey,' I said, wondering why I found myself blushing, checking the gap between Zeb and me.

'Alright, mate,' Duncan said, nodding in his direction. The aviators were on and he was wearing teeny white shorts and nothing else.

'Hey,' Zeb said, taking a step closer to me.

I felt my breath suspended in my chest.

'Iz.' Duncan grinned, taking my hand. 'You have to see this, I've built a man out of beer cans. Entirely. He's as tall as me.'

He ran off, expecting me to follow.

'Oh well, I'd better...' I indicated with my thumb.

'Of course,' Zeb said, smiling, his lips stretched tight over his teeth. He didn't look at me.

I felt strange as I said a strangled goodbye, feeling like I had lost something.

'I'll see you soon,' I said, keeping my voice light.

'IZ, GET HERE NOW OR I'LL KICK HIM DOWN...' Duncan yelled.

'Coming!' I called back over my shoulder, then turned to give Zeb a small smile. 'I've got to um...thanks for...'

Zeb gave me a wave, a brief one hand up. 'It was great,' he said, and then he melted away before I could respond, taking the day's memories with him.

Chapter 31

Five hours later, I was sitting out on the terrace having just had a shower, my wet hair tied back, my bare feet resting on an upturned crate like the World's Worst Pouffe. My white cotton dress highlighted the tan I'd developed and my baby-pink nail varnish glimmered when I moved. Dusk was one of my favourite times of day, the whole sky taking on a ghostly lilac sheen, the horizon shimmering as a deep-orange sun sank behind a bank of cloud. I smelled Duncan's aftershave before I turned around to greet him. My mouth stopped when I saw it wasn't him at all. Andrew pulled up the chair beside me.

'It's you,' I said, pointing at him too in case he was unclear who I meant.

'Hello.'

'Good day?' I ventured, realising I had hardly seen him.

He coughed. Was he embarrassed?

'Bed for most of it. Hangover.' He left the word in the air

and I nodded. 'How about you? I haven't seen you.'

He'd noticed, I thought. That must be a good sign. I mentally mini high-fived myself, this was definitely progress.

I tried to sound super-cool and nonchalant, glad my voice was still a little husky. 'I've been around.'

'Oh.'

The silence dragged on, filled with the intermittent call of a bird somewhere overhead.

'Actually, I went to this amazing place...' I started and then pulled up short, suddenly not wanting to share it, and then frowning as that thought struck.

Fortunately, Andrew chose that moment to get up and offer me a drink and I raised an eyebrow at him.

'Hair of the dog?'

'I've never understood that phrase.'

He left the terrace with a baffled expression on his face and returned, handing me a bottle of beer. My stomach rumbled a protest, but I drowned it out with a determined first sip.

'Thanks. So...'

'So.'

I raised my bottle at him and looked back out to the horizon.

'I love this time of da—' I was cut off by the sound of a large smack, hand on flesh, and turned with a startled expression to Andrew.

'Mozzie.' He shrugged.

'So...' I wondered why I couldn't find anything to say. I usually found lots to say, but my tongue felt too big for my mouth and my mind seemed empty of thoughts. Well, apart from the thought that I couldn't find anything to say and then my brain started racing through things that it might mention: unicycles, circuses, domestic animals, stock prices, the perils of liquid eyeliner. *Stop, brain, stop this madness*. Andrew was looking at me, a question half formed on his lips.

'Where are the others?' I asked as if we were part of a group like in *Friends*. 'Where's Duncan?' I corrected (not really caring where Liz was unless it was 'kidnapped by pirates, gone for ever').

'Duncan,' Andrew repeated thoughtfully, blowing into his beer bottle so it emitted a hollow-sounding note.

I tried to copy it but made a raspberry and then coughed to disguise the fact.

'Actually, Isobel, I did want to talk to you about something.'

I didn't dare look up at him. Was this the moment, the moment I had travelled halfway across the world for? Was he about to spill his feelings for me? I squeezed the beer bottle so hard I suddenly worried it would smash in my hand, which I thought would really ruin the mood because he'd have to clear up my blood and stuff.

'Do you?' I squeaked, the husky, mysterious voice long gone.

I held in my breath, questions zipping across my brain. How much had we really got in common? Did I know him well enough to really know? I had all these childhood memories and we were great when talking about the past but did I really know this adult version?

'Isobel...' Andrew said, leaning forward, looking in my face.

'Yes...' I swallowed. Was this it?

'Well, you see, someone likes you and I think you know it already and I'm wondering if you like him, too?'

My brow wrinkled as I realised Andrew was talking about himself in the third person. I gamely tried to play along. 'I'm glad *someone* likes me. What might that *someone* do?' I looked up at him through my eyelashes in what I hoped was a coquettish way, but he was picking at his big toenail and didn't catch it.

'Well I think someone would be keen for something to happen.'

I turned in my chair, leaning forward, my elbows resting on my knees. I wanted Andrew to look into my eyes, and also my boobs looked great in this position.

'I would really like that.'

I couldn't believe this was actually happening. Last night had actually been a success. Last night had been a triumph and it was obviously Party Girl he'd been most attracted to. I have to say I was surprised; although my memories were patchy, I couldn't remember Andrew paying me too much attention. In fact, I got a sudden image of him cupping Liz's cheek in his hand. She was wearing his big pink sombrero and looking at him with mushy eyes. I shook my head, forcibly removing the image; that couldn't possibly be right if Andrew was now declaring his love for me.

I scraped my chair forward a few inches as Andrew sat up and clapped his hands together.

'Great, I'll tell him.'

'You do that,' I laughed, leaning forward a fraction in case he wanted to kiss me.

He stood up and almost whacked me with his thigh.

'He'll be chuffed,' he said, moving forward and putting both hands on the balcony. He was wearing a dark-brown leather bracelet and I stared at it, confused.

'He will be,' I repeated, realising Andrew might not actually be talking in the third person. 'Duncan,' I whispered.

He turned around. 'He's a great guy.'

I stood up quickly. 'Andrew, sorry I...I think you misunderstood. I don't...'

'MATE!' came a yell from behind me, making me leap.

'Duncan,' Andrew slowed down the name, looking meaningfully at me.

'What's up, you two?' Duncan flung himself into the chair I'd been sitting in.

'Nothing!' I sing-songed at the same time as Andrew replied, 'Your ears must have been burning.'

'Well I still feel like I ate a badger and need food so who's in?'

At the mention of food my tummy did a delighted rumble. *You've neglected me today* it seemed to say.

'I think I'm just going to have an early night,' I said doing a stretchy yawn as if to make my point abundantly clear. 'You two should go.' I mumbled a goodnight and rushed down the steps of the terrace landing on the cooling sand and waving a goodbye over my shoulder. Blinking, I walked away replaying that last scene with Andrew in my head. *How did he not realise? What was I doing with myself?* Then there was today: a snapshot popped up of me in the cave clutching my side over something Zeb had said. I'd had the feeling we had done something special when we'd filmed that vlog. I hadn't felt like that in years – that thrill in front of the camera, working with someone else to bounce ideas off; it had given me such a buzz.

As I got ready for bed, I realised today had taught me one thing: I needed to get a grip on my career again, get my old confidence back. I could present – I just needed to be fired up by something; I needed to want to tell the viewers all about it. I couldn't hide here for ever.

The sheets were cool and made me suck in my breath as I slid between them. Faces of Andrew, Zeb and Duncan seemed to roll into my mind, overlap, roll out again. Was I getting anywhere? Did I have my answers? I huffed in the dark, throwing off the duvet in frustration. As I lay on my bed that night, hot and bothered on top of the sheets, I stared at the fan making its pointlessly slow circulation and realised it might be time to go home and stop all this.

Next morning I woke feeling a renewed sense of purpose. I just needed a new action plan. And then, as if the universe had heard me, I opened an email from Mel that simply contained a photo attachment of an aeroplane ticket to Tioman Island, landing in two days' time. I couldn't believe it. I stared at the screen for ten minutes straight. Mel was coming here, my Mel. The thought revived me. I couldn't believe I'd been considering throwing in the towel. What I needed, of course, what I'd been missing, was a wing woman – and there was none finer than Mel Conboy. She'd sort me out.

Chapter 32

The tiny plane skirted the island and I could make out the dots of windows, imagining Mel's face as she looked down on the island: a lump of lush greens fringed with a strip of white sand and the bright-turquoise shallows out to the deeper blue of the sea. I smiled to myself, stomach drumming with excitement; I couldn't believe she was really going to be here.

The plane started making its descent and I tried not to focus too much on the shortest runway in the world and wait for the bump, bump of the tyres trundling along the surface, the engine coming to an idling stop, the noise and clatter of baggage handlers racing out to unload suitcases. The plane had taxied to a halt and I looked out through the canopy of the arrivals lounge (I like to call it that but it was really more of an arrivals shack) and saw three men in orange caps wheeling a small silver ladder over to the door of the plane, the first of the passengers blinking in the sunlight, putting on sunglasses, glancing down the tarmac as the air sizzled with petrol and heat.

Then there she was, her red hair under a straw hat. Her hot-pink skinny jeans, a white vest top and a pair of enormous sunglasses making her leap out of the crowd. She looked like she was from LA. I started waving at her frantically from the shade of the lounge, grinning as she caught my eye and waved back, dropping her handbag and whooping so that other passengers turned to look at her.

She had managed to convince a fellow passenger (male, average build, tattoo of an anchor on his arm) to roll her suitcase along with his and then spent three minutes swapping cards with the hopeful victim. I rolled my eyes to myself, tapping one foot and miming at a watch when she turned around to run at me.

'Youoooooo!' she squealed. She held me at arm's length. 'You look so brown, and *hellooooo*,' she said, slapping my bottom. 'Someone's lost weight.'

'It's my new diet of rice, with rice,' I said, laughing and pulling her in for a hug.

'I need to get me some of that,' she said into my hair.

'Right!' She clapped her hands together. 'Where's the nearest bar?'

She looked good. Confident, fun and the Mel I had left in LA. Was there a hint of something in her eyes? A sadness behind the smiles? There had to be a reason for her flying to the middle of nowhere to see me; it couldn't just be my extraordinarily cool personality. I am not that good.

'Wait there,' I instructed, ducking into a small, dusty supermarket on the road. She looked completely out of place standing alone on a patch of churned-up dry mud marked with track tyres and an old faded Coke sign. 'I won't be long,' I called.

Moving towards the large fridge in the corner, I passed a woman sweeping sand and dirt in the aisle, nodding at her. Her eyes crinkled into a hundred folds as she smiled at me. Opening the door, I pulled out four bottles of beer, cold to the touch, peeling price tags on the necks and went to pay.

Returning outside with my small plastic bag, I pointed down the road to a small track off to the left. 'Let's go and sit on the beach,' I suggested.

'You have the beer, woman, so wherever you go I will follow.'

We wheeled the suitcase down the road, one hand each on the handle and then turned left, bumping it down a grassy, wide path to the beach at the end. Dumping the suitcase under a palm tree weighted down with orange coconuts, I pointed to a couple of loungers.

Lying back on the loungers, the beers impressively opened on the wooden lounger frame, I finally asked her, 'So...?'

Mel closed her eyes. 'Can we just lie here a little longer?'

I sipped at my beer, swivelling my legs round so that I was sitting looking at her.

'Out with it, woman.'

She sighed and played with a loose strand of hair, twisting it and untwisting it as she took a breath. I couldn't make out her expression behind the uber glasses. She bit one side of her lip. 'I just wanted to see you. And I needed a holiday,' she tacked on.

'No. Sorry. Not good enough.'

Mel slanted her eyes. 'Could you sound a little more grateful?'

'I am grateful,' I laughed, nudging her with my beer bottle. 'But I also know you and this has "Mel Running Away From a Crisis" written all over it.'

'Maybe,' she sniffed.

'What did Dex say?' I asked.

'Um...' She circled a finger on the mattress of the lounger.

I gasped. 'You didn't tell him.'

She carried on circling.

'Did you really not tell him?'

'I left a note.'

'What?'

'Yeah, I think I spelled the island wrong on it, too. I'm lammmmmme,' she said.

'Yes, you are a bit lame,' I agreed, patting her knee.

'I just needed to get out of there, since the whole pr... proposal.' She stumbled over the word. 'It freaked me out, you know. Things were going so well with Dex. He was great.'

'Is great.' I chipped in.

'Is great, but then he goes and does that and we will become one of those couples who become all about the "wedding" and start all our conversations with information about venues and flower suppliers. Why he can't have a puppy as a ring bearer and why doves are out, too.'

'Oh no, I love a good dove at a wedding,' I say, earning myself a slap on the arm.

'I just know it will consume us. You know what we're like, Iz, we love a massive row; we would argue over every detail and kill each other before the big day. And for what?'

'A lifetime of commitment?' I supplied, earning myself a second slap.

'We are committed already, Iz.'

'I know.'

'So why do we need to load ourselves up with that pressure? Why did he have to go and change things?'

'Because he loves you,' I stated.

'Oi, you're not helping, Iz,' she said.

'But it's true. He just wants to do what lots of men before him have done and show the whole world he loves you.'

'The whole world knew – or rather the world I cared about. I've seen it before, Iz, normal, nice girls in good relationships screaming at their mother-in-law about what favours they want, shouting that it will be a cathedral veil or nothing. Then falling out with their fiancé because their mother said something derogatory about one of the bridesmaids...'

'Hey, who said something derogatory about me?'

Mel laughed and raised one eyebrow. 'Bridesmaid, eh?'

'Er hello, yes, chief...' I grinned. 'Anyway, I thought there wasn't going to be a wedding.'

Mel fell silent at that, pushing her beer bottle into the sand.

'Come on, Mel,' I said, my voice softer. 'What's this really all about? I know you hate talking about it, but you can tell me.'

Nothing. Which was not 'Shut up, Iz'. I continued, taking a breath. 'It's about your mum. How you think you might turn into her, isn't it? But, Mel, you won't,' I pleaded, wanting to get the next part out quickly so she could hear it. 'You and Dex are tough as anything. You're a team; he's your best friend and he's not going to suddenly flip and change into a different person, he's not going to walk out on you. And you won't take him for granted, you will work at it. If anything, you've probably learned more from your mum about how to make it work than anyone.'

I let these thoughts hang in the air and we finished our beers, swatting half-heartedly at the insects that hovered round us. People were wandering back along the beach and some teenage boys were still snorkelling on the reef, dipping down out of sight, and then calling to each other.

'Thanks,' she said quietly. 'Thanks, Iz, I knew you'd help.' She sounded unusually quiet for Mel. My heart reached out to my gorgeous friend.

'Come on, let's head back,' I said, standing up and offering her a hand.

We trundled back to the road to take a taxi back across the middle of the island to Juara beach. A grinning man in a dirty 4x4 drew up on the road with a screech of brakes, skidding on the stones. As we plunged off the road onto the uneven track through the forest, the air became cooler. I wound the window down further and closed my eyes, letting the breeze wash around me. Bumping over potholes and dried-out old tyre marks, we made the descent.

'Wow, this is awesome,' said Mel, peering out of her side at the knotted trees packed tightly together, the miniscule glimpses of the darkening sky through a canopy of green.

I smiled without opening my eyes. 'Very.'

Chapter 33

Yawning over my coffee, I'd directed Mel to our usual cafe a couple of doors down from our hotel. She had been faffing around drying her fringe and I had learned in LA that Mel worked on Mel Time. She appeared in the door of the cafe in a blue polka-dot bikini, white sarong loosely tied around her waist and her impressive boobs quivering when she sat. Her lips were pink and glossy and there was a light smattering of freckles on her arms. Andrew dropped his spoon. Duncan missed his mouth with his banana. For a flash, I wondered whether this had been the best idea. Then dismissed it almost as instantly; Mel was fantastic, my best buddy, and this was going to be brilliant.

I introduced her to the table. Liz looked up, raised an eyebrow. 'American,' she trilled.

Mel said, 'Sure thing,' in the most American accent I had ever heard her do.

Liz smiled tightly and returned to filling in a crossword in her special crossword book as Andrew kindly supplied her with some of the answers.

'I didn't know you were into crosswords,' I commented, buttering my toast and smiling at him.

'Cryptic,' he said.

I nudged him with my foot and giggled, 'I know, very.'

'No, cryptic crosswords,' he said, pointing to the book. 'They're so much more demanding.' I leaned forward and nodded seriously. 'Oh. Absolutely.'

Mel was watching me, one eyebrow raised and I sat back and crossed my arms over my chest, feeling suddenly self-conscious.

'So, Mel,' Duncan said. 'What are your plans for the day?' he asked in a new gung-ho voice I'd never heard before. I prickled a little, feeling a pang of envy; hadn't I been the one who had proved so interesting to Duncan only yesterday? Then I smacked my own head with a fist (imaginary). This was Mel and I was being ridiculous.

'Iz and I'll be catching up,' Mel said, smiling at him. She always had an open face.

'Yep, catching up,' I confirmed, hoping that maybe Andrew would look up and ask more.

He didn't and we finished our breakfasts. Mel begged me to show her the beach.

'See you guys later,' I said, taking a last, lingering look over my shoulder.

Only Duncan waved.

Leaving our belongings in a pile on the beach, we swam out to the square platform a hundred yards out. I stepped up onto it using the railing. Dangling our legs over the side, we rested back on our hands looking across to the beach laid out before us: pastel-coloured houses, tiny colourful fishing boats moored up on the sand, people sitting in the sunshine, palm trees leaning over the white sand casting long shadows.

'It is just paradise,' she announced. 'Actual paradise.'

'Brilliant, isn't it.'

Just then a stingray slowly wandered lazily underneath the platform, its flat body sloping elegantly by, its outline clearly defined against the cloudy blue of the seabed.

'Did you know stingrays can grow up to six and a half feet?'

'How the hell do you know that?' I asked, flicking sea-water at her legs.

'Came across all sorts of sealife facts when we did that fish job.'

'Oh god, don't remind me,' I said, putting my head in my hands. 'I know I am going to have to go back and be a prawn some time but please let me have a few more weeks of freedom...'

Mel started laughing. 'Iz, you need to get back to the presenting, send your show reel out again. You need to try it again.'

I bristled with the knowledge that she was right. It had always been such a sure-fire thing in my mind. When I was younger I'd been so geared up for it all. I had spent hours in my room with Mum's camcorder that she'd bought – 'They're all the rage, darling, and we can spend time setting up comedy scenarios: your father falling off the roof and so on. to try and get on *You've Been Framed.* It will make its money back' – filming news items, interviewing the men in my posters (thank you, Jason Donovan for sharing your thoughts about your time on *Neighbour*s and also for your thoughts on pollution). I had practised chatting as naturally as I could as all the best presenters did.

Later, I'd done work experience on the sports desk at ITV West, made a million cups of tea and buttered up the weatherman there who'd let me have a go with his clicky thing that changed the screen. I'd been an assistant on a shopping channel three times a week, doing the live links to camera and learning about the products. Then I'd started doing freelance shifts on local news items, going out with the cameramen to film a variety of clips. I'd loved the buzz and thrill of it all, standing in front of the camera reporting the news back, uncovering touching or amusing stories to share with the viewers. I'd dreamed of filming my own show one day. *What had happened to that girl so full of confidence that she could get there?*

Mel's words swum before me; I knew she was right. I needed to get a new agent because, frankly, I needed an agent who didn't spell out punctuation. Randy had never really got me, had never really understood the kind of presenter I wanted to be. I didn't want razzmatazz or lights, I just loved communicating my own excitement about something. I needed to throw myself into looking for someone who wanted to help me achieve that. Out here with the sun beating down on my shoulders, the water crystal clear and inviting and a cloudless sky, I felt anything might be possible.

'Actually, I have made a vlog this week, for a friend's travel website.' I felt heat rise to my cheeks and didn't know why.

Mel nudged me. 'Tell me more.'

'It was great, actually,' I said, my voice building in strength as I thought back to the cave. 'We were in this incredible place and I just wanted to share everything I was seeing and feeling and it just came back, that thing I used to love about presenting.'

Mel was looking at me, her jaw a little slack. Perhaps it had been a while since she had seen me this fired up about anything.

I quickly changed the subject. 'How about you, Mel?' I said. 'What are you going to do about Dex?'

Mel circled her foot in the water and didn't say anything.

'Hey.' I nudged her. 'You know it will be okay, don't you? You're not your mum, for a start.'

Mel glanced at me. 'I know that.'

'Well then.'

She continued to circle her foot. 'Oh, Iz, I don't know. I think he's brilliant you know? I've never doubted us. But he knew how I felt about things and he still went ahead.'

'Did he explain?'

She sighed aloud. 'I suppose I didn't give him a lot of opportunity to really talk much,' she said, looking at me, a guilty expression creeping across her face.

'You just ranted?'

'Yeah,' she admitted with a nod.

'And then left.'

'Yep.'

'Mel Conboy,' I announced, 'you are hopeless.'

'I know.'

'What are you going to do?'

'I don't know, I just needed time to think, stop being such a cow to him, too.'

'We've all been there,' I said, thinking sadly of Stewie. I hoped wherever he was he wasn't loathing me. It had been generous of him to call.

We were interrupted by Duncan and Andrew swimming out to us, sneaking a peek at each other in between the crawl then hauling themselves up on to the platform without using the ladder. Duncan lay flat on his back as Andrew leaned over to catch his breath.

'Well done,' I laughed at them both. 'Who won?'

'Me,' they chorused.

'What are you guys up to this afternoon?' I asked, throwing the question behind me to Andrew, aware that Mel had gone very quiet on me, mulling over our chat.

'They say the turtles might be hatching later so I definitely want to be around for that.'

'What does that mean?'

'It's when the babies are born and we help them back to the ocean, move things out of their way and stuff. It's going to be cool.'

'Count me out, mate, I have drinks to drink,' came Duncan.

Andrew looked at him, his face falling a fraction.

My heart reached out for him. 'That does sound great, I'd love to come.' I felt my face get hot. 'I mean, if you wanted the company,' I added.

'Yeah, cool.'

Whoop, mental skippy dance, yay.

'I'd love to see that, cute baby turtles! Hell, of course,' said Mel. 'Hey, boys, did you know a turtle's shell has like fifty bones in it.'

Duncan sat up, eyes wide: 'Really?' Andrew leaned forward. 'No way!'

'Yeah and they don't have vocal chords but can still make noise.'

'Woah,' they chorused.

Oh maaaaaaaaaaaaaan.

A few hours later, I found myself standing in a semi-circle on the sand with a load of other volunteers. The baby turtles had been 'pipping' over the last few days which was Turtle Speak for Breaking Out of Their Eggs and a man with a goatee was telling me something gross about it absorbing its umbilical yolk or some such to prepare for its epic journey to the sea. I really started to wonder why we didn't just carry them there. The turtles were tiny, fragile and scared.

They emerged in zig-zagged lines, tumbling into divots on the sand, scrambling back up the other side, making painful progess towards the sea that seemed to roll in threateningly. How would they make it past the insurmountable waves? The whole process seemed incredibly daunting and we found ourselves crouching down, nudging at any that were off track, smoothing out the path for others as they broke out.

Zeb was crouched low, taking photos of the turtles, fiddling with the lens as they moved past, their shells and legs a fraction of the size they would grow to be. His face, obscured by the camera, seemed entirely focused on capturing their journey and I marvelled at the way he threw himself down on to his front to ensure the best shot. When he looked up a few seconds later, he noticed me watching him. A lopsided smile and an unreadable expression on his face made me flush. I thought back to yesterday's trip to the cave, him behind his camera, him alone in the spotlight of green. I blinked, looking back at the small turtles stumbling pathetically over the sand as they made their way to the sea, and then looked sideways at Andrew, his hair sticking up, his face enthralled.

When the last of the turtles had made it, I turned to him, making a mental note to make more effort. I needed to really bond with him.

'So that was nice,' I said. *Ooh nice, Isobel, really push the boat out with your enthusiasm.*

'Yes.'

'Yup, yup, yup.' I wasn't sure where that had come from. I took my sunglasses off and rubbed at the lenses. 'They were so tiny,' I said.

'Very,' he agreed.

'Yup, yup...' *ISOBEL.* I closed my eyes briefly.

Mel had sidled up behind us both and had been listening, then, as the silence dragged on, she rolled her eyes. 'Iz, shall we wander?' she asked in a loud voice, her eyes wide.

Mel dragged me off by one hand.

'But I...'

She marched me away down the beach. 'I thought I would save you from further small talk pain. I'm not used to seeing you like that. You're so... "Oh how delightful it's a turtle." So English.'

'That's me, Mel, I am English, remember?'

'No, you are not being you, you. Silly, mischievous, a bit naughty,' she said.

I blushed wondering if she was right. *Was I not acting like myself?*

'I don't want to scare him,' I shrugged.

'So you really want him, he's The One?' she checked, an eyebrow up like I had to persuade her.

'Mel, have you not been listening to me for the past few years? You know I do,' I explained. 'It's the man, the life, I always dreamed of.'

Mel linked arms with me. 'That doesn't mean it's right. You have to go with your gut, Iz,' she said.

'I am,' I said in as certain a voice as I could muster. *Why did she doubt this?*

'Fine, so let's run though things,' Mel said. 'What kind of methods have you been using so far?'

We'd walked up to the other end of the beach and had discovered the wooden swing creaking gently in the breeze. The plank of wood was big enough for us both and as we sat on it the branch gave and the soles of our feet touched the sand.

I fiddled with the fraying blue rope and pondered Mel's question. 'The usual,' I concluded.

Mel ticked them off on her hand. 'Have you got him drunk? Have you reminisced about the old days? Have you tried to make him jealous? Have you scared off other competition? Have you flirted with him?'

'Yes, yes, yes, sort of, of course,' I replied.

'How did the flirting go?'

'Well...until I almost burned his house down.'

'Pfft, a minor detail and one we shouldn't dwell on,' she dismissed with a hand.

'Have you told him?' She twisted a little on the swing.

'What exactly?'

'That you looooove him.' She giggled.

'Sort of, well, I think it's obvious.'

'Earth to Isobel, hello, Andrew is a man. Obvious messages, things being spelled out to them, they understand. Subtle nuances, for example, looks, meaningful pauses, number of kisses on text messages, they do not understand.'

'You can't pigeonhole all of them like that; Andrew's not simple.'

'But, Iz, you've come all this way, you've just got to totally go for it.'

'But I said I don't want to scare him away. And, anyway, I don't love him.'

'Looovveeee him,' she corrected.

'I can't know that I love him yet. I just think I need to be with him. I think we'd be good together.'

I think of us in England sitting on the terrace of our little cottage reading books, a jug of half-finished Pimms in front of us, Andrew reading aloud a favourite quote to me. That's what I wanted – didn't I? For a second I imagined myself on another plane, heading to somewhere gorgeous, new. I blinked as the image faded.

'Well I'm here to help, if you truly, really want Andrew, we'll get you Andrew,' she said, slapping her thigh and making the swing wobble with the effort.

Bouncing onto her feet, the seat bobbing up as she left it, she spun around her arms wide.

'We couldn't have a better setting so let's draw up the battle lines and get to work.'

The Plan

- Engineer a scenario where Isobel can be alone with Andrew.
- Try to ensure some kind of lovely sunset/ other pretty view.
- Ensure that Andrew is in an excellent mood.
- Look devastatingly beautiful but like you have not tried at all.
- Try to get good background music if possible.
- Ensure plan remains a secret.
- Don't burn anything down.

We celebrated the plan with some sunbathing and swam around the edge of the beach sharing the snorkel and chasing silvery shoals of fish through patches of swaying coral. Back on the beach and breathless, Mel came up with various ideas for a location.

'How about sky-diving?'

'How about it?'

'Well Andrew could be strapped on your back – no escape there.'

I frowned. 'I wasn't planning on tying him up to get him alone.'

Mel had already started giggling on 'tying him up'. 'Okay, well you at least need to get him on his own, and then see where that sexual tension leads to. There is sexual tension, isn't there, Iz?'

I thought back to Andrew, wondering why I paused as I answered. 'Oh, oh yes.' Was there? Did I feel a frisson when he came close? Did I melt when he looked at me? YES, I shouted to myself, of course I did. Blinking, another face flashed up, laughing eyes...

'Well, let's get back and get going,' Mel said getting to her feet. 'I for one need a shower. I feel like the Little Mermaid I have been so at one with the ocean today.'

Dear diary,

Jenny's parents are getting a divorce and I asked Mum what happens on a divorce and she told me that it is breaking up the marriage. I told her that Andrew and I were divorced but Jenny's parents signed papers and I didn't sign anything so maybe God still thinks we're married.

I don't really mind if we are because I like being married to Andrew. I still miss him and when I go to the tree by the canoe lake I climb up to our branch and hang from it thinking of the day when I giggled so much because he said I was a wombat. I wonder where Andrew is now. I think I will always wonder.

I x

Chapter 34

There was a beach barbecue that night and Mel and I spent a while choosing my outfit. We plumped for a floral playsuit and matched it with a long gold necklace and beaded flip-flops. Brushing on some bronzer, I gave myself a confidence-boosting smile in the mirror.

'You can do it, girl,' I said.

'Yeah you can,' agreed Mel, emerging at that moment from the bathroom.

'Ah.'

She started laughing. 'I am not judging you,' she said, holding up both hands. 'Come on, lady, let's hit the town.'

'It's not so much a town, Mel, as a...'

'Oh you know what I mean. Let's stop talking to ourselves in mirrors and get this party started, et cetera, et cetera.'

Linking arms, we made our way down the track momentarily regretting not bringing a torch and having to whip out our mobile phones to guide the way. An ominous rustling from a spiky-looking bush made Mel swear and I was pretty relieved to get to the main track and the string of lights looped outside the wooden houses. As we neared the beach, the air was thick with the smell of smoke and the throb of music and talking. Making our way across the sand, I scanned the groups and saw Duncan and Andrew biting into burgers through a screen of cloudy smoke. Liz was there, too, I noted, and appeared to have found the only deckchair on the island. She was nibbling at some kind of vegetarian kebab.

I went to get two hot dogs and Liz grimaced at me as I returned. 'You should be careful, Isobel, as I was telling the boys' – she said 'the boys' in such a way that made me want to fling both sausages at her – 'you really can't know about that meat.'

'Thanksfortheadvhice,' I said between mouthfuls, giving her a breaded grin and handing the other hot dog to Mel.

'Oh, Iz, honey, you eat like such a lady,' Mel said in a mock-English accent.

'It's a skill.' I nodded, wiping a dot of ketchup from my mouth.

'Well isn't it a glorious evening,' said Mel, stretching out her legs and pushing her toes into the sand. 'Does anyone want to go for a walk?' she asked, making wide eyes at me.

I frowned. 'Er...'

What was Mel up to? She was waggling both eyebrows at me now so I had clearly missed something. I decided to play along.

'Yes a walk sounds good,' I said.

'Yes, a not-quite-midnight stroll. Boys? Would either of you like to join?'

'I wil—'

Duncan was cut off by Mel's hand. 'Oh I love this song. Andrew,' she said turning on him, 'walk?'

'Er...' Andrew looked wistfully over at the BBQ and then back to Mel. 'Okay, I could walk.'

'Excellent.' Mel clapped her hands like a delighted twelve-year-old. She went to stand and then bent down, clutching her ankle. 'Oh no,' she whispered, looking at me. 'My ankle, Iz, it's gone again.'

I felt my forehead wrinkle with confusion. 'Has it?'

'Oh, yes. Do you remember earlier with my ankle...'

Duncan leapt to her rescue, propping up her calf and asking where it hurt. Andrew asked whether he could get anything for her.

'Oh no, I'll be fine after a while, I wouldn't want to ruin the fun. Iz, Andrew you must still walk without me, please.'

Aaaaaaaaah. I see.

Andrew started to speak. 'We'll stay and make sure...'

She grabbed his forearm. 'I would hate to ruin things, do go.'

This was all ridiculously dramatic and I realised Andrew would probably be able to see right through it. I scuffed my toe on the ground. 'It's fine, Mel, we should stay.'

Duncan piped up. 'No, you guys go, we'll see to Mel.'

Liz chimed in, 'Well I wouldn't mind a little stroll...'

Mel turned towards her. 'But we've only just met, Liz, I so want to get to know you better,' she said in her most sincere voice, normally reserved for feigning illness at some of our worst promo jobs.

'Oh well...that's lovely,' finished Liz, a weak smile on her thin lips.

Mel patted her hand. 'I want to know all about you.'

'Well, shall we?' asked Andrew, turning to me. 'I feel like stretching my legs,' he said.

'Great,' I said in a half-whisper, my stomach giving a small flip. Mel had engineered me some alone time, the first item on The Plan. It had been so easy. It was up to me to do the rest. *Think of the plan, Iz, act cool, make sure he's in an excellent mood and so on. And breathe.* I felt my breaths coming shallow and fast and slowed them down.

He walked off out of the glow of the BBQ and into the blue shadows of the beach, the moon casting a wide strip on the sea, making the water seem like it was lit from below.

I almost tripped racing to catch up.

'Cooool,' Mel sung, no doubt directed at me. I turned back and Liz had followed Andrew with her eyes while Duncan was bending over, still intent on examining Mel's ankle. And was that a familiar face on the other side of the bonfire? I squinted for a moment but a curl of smoke drifted over the BBQ obscuring shapes.

Andrew had walked to the shoreline and was skimming stones along the surface of the water. This had always been one of the Top Three Things I'd wanted to learn to do:

1) Skim stones so they bounce a few times on the surface of the water.
2) Start a fashion trend, for example, neon tights.
3) Peel an apple in only one go.

I selected a stone and moved next to him, admiring his wide shoulders in the blue shirt he was wearing. I watched him throw the next one. The muscles in his back were pronounced as he drew his arm back, his shirt rolled up to the elbow, his gaze intent. He released the stone and it smacked the top of the water, skittering along four, five times before disappearing beneath the surface.

'Very good,' I said as if I were about to grade him.

He drew himself up a little taller and I felt pleased I had said something.

I copied the action – bent elbow, arm back, eyes steady – and released the stone. It landed with a distinct 'plop' which seemed to echo in the space between us, maximising my very public failure.

I couldn't expect to nail it on the first go. Laughing in what I hoped was a light and carefree way, I selected another stone and tried again.

'Plop'.

Andrew coughed.

I stared out at the sea, grappling now for my next move.

'Do you remember when we used to sit on the side of the pier in Southsea with my Walkman?' I said, looking out wistfully at the waves.

Andrew nodded quickly. 'Yeah you had one that was yellow and black and I thought it was the coolest thing I'd ever seen.'

'We must have looked cute,' I laughed.

'I used to love the pier: the 2p machines and those ones where you grabbed the toys with the claw...'

'Oh my god, remember when it broke once and we had...'

'99 goes...' We both chorused the last bit together, looking embarrassed as we did it.

I tried to break the mood. 'We left with armfuls of the things.'

'I loved Southsea.'

'Me too,' I smiled, enjoying sharing in the warmth of our golden childhood. It really had been golden: fun days out, the freedom to explore the town, the sea on our doorstep. No wonder I always had fond memories of it.

'So is that why you love Geography?' I asked, trying to steer things back to the here and now. This could surely work as a good opener for more conversation.

'Maybe. Hey, do you remember Jenny from school? You know she teaches at the school now!'

'I didn't,' I said, voice flat as I realised we were back on the safe ground of our shared childhood.

Did he feel it, too? Did he realise we had so little in common now? Or was I forcing things?

Wanting to cut off further thoughts, I turned to him desperately, my hair whipping round my shoulders. 'Have you ever been sky-diving?' I asked.

Oh, Isobel. Slow clap yourself, Isobel, slow clap yourself.

Andrew, however, lit up at this suggestion and we spent the rest of the walk talking about it. Returning to the campfire, it seemed that Liz had left, her deckchair now occupied by Ahmad who appeared to be in the middle of some kind of magic trick. Mel tried to ask me how the walk had gone by some intricate hand gestures and I gave her a small thumbs-up.

Andrew seemed fired up; kneeling on the sand he waited for the trick to end. The moment it was over, he announced, 'Isobel has just had the *best* idea.'

Duncan looked at him and Mel surreptitiously raised her glass to me. I glowed with the compliment, feeling like a light had been switched on in my stomach.

'We're going to go sky-diving,' Andrew said.

As we talked more, I noticed Zeb on the other side of the fire in amongst a group of locals. He was taking photos and laughing, taller than all of them, with the boldest laugh. I smiled as the distinctive noise hit me from this distance. When I turned back to the group Mel was watching me. She raised her glass, her expression lost in the smoke and the dark. I looked back at Andrew and Duncan still talking about the sky-dive and tried to concentrate.

Isobel,

Thank you for your lovely emails, it all sounds very special. I am sitting over the creek imagining myself with you there now. Turtles and the turquoise sea, so delicious (and a few degrees warmer, obviously). And you have actually found who you were searching for, what a gift! I hope you have had plenty of time to discover each other again. A blessing to have a second chance at something. Don't fool yourself though, remember you have grown up and are a wonderful woman with the whole world at your feet. Don't get stuck in a past.

With all my love darling,

Moregran x x

Chapter 35

We met at the end of the track and I climbed up into the back of the 4x4, sucking in my breath at the warm leather of the seats. Ahmad gave me the same toothless grin from the driving mirror as Duncan joined him in the front. Mel dived to do a shoelace at the last moment and I found myself sitting next to Andrew, who was in the middle of the back seat.

We set off, snaking our way through the back of the tiny village, past rubbish bins festering in wire baskets, hopeful flies picking at their contents, past a water tap that dripped, making a puddle in the mud beneath it. Looking out at the sky I saw plump clouds, edged with grey, cutting a course through the trees at the top. The air was muggy and smelled of dirt and the coming rain. As we moved into the shade of the trees, the world shifted through a dark-green filter. As we navigated up a steep track, one hand gripping the handle above the open window, I was grateful for the air that spilt inside. I allowed my thigh to bump up against Andrew's. The blond hairs on his leg seemed to administer a small shock every time I struck flesh.

'So you dive out of planes,' said Ahmad, laughing manically after the sentence.

My stomach plummeted as we dipped into a pothole and I felt my palm become sweaty on the handle.

'Yes,' I croaked, realising that this was true. *What had I been thinking?*

Duncan broke the atmosphere with a loud whoop and joined in the driver's laughter. Andrew cracked his knuckles and grinned. Only Mel seemed quieter, her green eyes large in the wing mirror, her face a little paler than normal.

'No Liz?' I asked, trying not to sound too delighted.

'Nope, she'd need a doctor's certificate from home,' Duncan explained.

'Why? What's wrong with her?' Guilt coursed through me. What hideous condition stopped Liz being there?

'She dislocated her shoulder a few months ago,' Andrew explained in a quiet voice.

'Oh, too bad,' I said, relieved it was nothing worse.

'Yeah it really is,' Andrew agreed.

And seeing him looking genuinely upset made me bristle. Typical Liz getting sympathy with her wonky shoulder.

We were ushered into a room next to the arrivals lounge of the tiny airport. The room was stifling, the heat trapped by netted curtains and small windows. A fan sat hopelessly circulating in the corner and the humidity seemed to make my nerves worse. There was no getting out of this. We were handed faded dark-blue jumpsuits and large plastic goggles, the type I'd worn in Science when doing Biology GCSE. There was one changing room in the corner and I moved across to it.

'No, no,' said the instructor, who was more beard than face. He waggled a finger at me. 'No, no,' he repeated, now looking at my bare legs. I crossed one foot over the other self-consciously.

'Tape the shoes,' he said, circling two of his fingers.

'Sorry?'

'Your shoes, not good, you tape them,' he said, getting on one knee next to me, a large roll of gaffer tape in his hands.

The gold beads on my flip-flops winked in the overhead light. 'Oh.'

'What did you think you should wear?' Andrew laughed, tightening the shoelace on his trainer.

'I hadn't thought,' I said, having to wobble on one foot as the instructor started rolling the tape around the middle of my foot and then up my calf, cutting it off with a snip of scissors and an impatient beckoning of the other foot. When he finished, I looked absurd: beautiful flip-flops now attached to me with a large wad of tape. When I had finished putting on the jumpsuit and the massive clear goggles, I had definitely not achieved 'Look devastat ingly beautiful'.

Waddling out with my flip-flopped feet, I took in the tin-box plane that would be taking us up into the air and dropping us out onto the beach. Gulping, I rearranged my goggles.

'You know you don't have to wear them now?' said Duncan, his propped on the top of his head.

'Oh,' I said, pushing them up into my hair and hearing a quiet sucking noise as they detached from my skin.

'Ooh, they've left a mark,' he laughed, his mouth puckered.

I tried to swagger off and play it cool, but I tripped a bit in the taped-up shoes.

After receiving the briefest safety instructions from The Beard, I wasn't ready. And, fine, I had spent most of it picking at the gaffer tape on my calf (bright side: at least it would be very thorough hair removal) and staring at Andrew's ass, but I thought he might repeat the important parts. Andrew's jumpsuit was on the small side and it had ridden up a bit. I then found myself being herded back out into the glaring sunshine, over the tarmac to the plane.

I turned to Mel. 'What was that bit about the cord?' I asked her frantically.

She rolled her eyes at me. 'It's fine, we're jumping with an instructor,' she said. My heart sank a little as I hissed at her, 'But I thought I was meant to be strapped to Andrew?'

Sadly my hiss was a little louder than I intended and Duncan gave me a sharp look.

'Who's being strapped to what now?' he asked, throwing his head back.

There was no turning back I thought as I wrenched myself into the plane and was told to scoot to the back and wait there. Sitting on the dusty floor, the scratched glass windows showing me the forest of trees and a flash of white sky overhead, I looked over at Mel who was, at least, looking pale again.

The Beard came and sat down behind me, linking us together with what seemed like a complicated range of rucksack attachments that joined in the most intimate of places. I could feel his beard tickle me when he leaned in to shout, 'Hold on!'

This was not going to be the romantic experience I had planned. He smelled of curry and damp.

Before I could work out how to sidle over and talk to Andrew with The Beard strapped to me, we were taxiing in a loop, slowly at first and then the engine revved and the whole floor vibrated with the noise and feel and I couldn't think or see anything then except my own thoughts whirling about what we were about to do. Nothing about Andrew, the plan, The Beard, nothing except my pulsing body, sweaty palms and dry throat.

This was it, we were up, we were off. And, suddenly, I was watching Mei sitting at the edge of the door. Her instructor (an absurdly young, good-looking guy with a dazzling smile) was strapped to her back. She gave me a wavering thumbs-up, took a breath and then was gone, her scream heard seconds later as she dropped. Oh god.

We shuffled up to the open doorway, the island laid out below us, the ring of cloud clinging to the trees, the gorgeous green forest that stretched before us laced with white beaches and turquoise shallows. It looked surreal, like I could step out, a giant on the top of it all. Small. And yet the minuscule orange squares were the hotels and bars. People weren't even dots. I heard The Beard urging me forward and gulped as I heard him countdown.

Pushing us off after '1' we seemed to tumble jerkily, the air stinging my cheeks and pushing my goggles into my skin. My cheeks wobbled as we fell so quickly, spinning manically towards earth. The land came up to meet us, the sea, then sky, then trees and sand merging into a wash of colours and then there was a huge wrench at my waist and thighs and our parachute was up and we were sitting in the sky, bobbing gently down to earth, facing the right way up, able to look across the blue sea to the neighbouring islands rising like humped creatures out of the water, the coast of Malaysia in the distance.

We descended effortlessly, aiming for a marked-out area on the big beach. The pink cones met us all too quickly and I found myself running for a few steps on the sand before tumbling into a pile of parachute and beard, laughing, breathless and exhilarated.

The Beard removed himself and I stood up on shaky legs, allowing myself to be engulfed by hands and arms. Andrew, Duncan and Mel spilled over towards me and we threw ourselves at each other, dancing around in a tight circle cheering and whooping and high. Andrew leaned back, the sun emerging from a bank of cloud at that moment to light his face, his light-brown eyes sparkling with the excitement of what we had just done. He slapped me on the back and grinned, showing both sets of teeth. I couldn't help but smile back. This was amazing.

It was thoughts of the drop that filled my head for the journey back, and the rest of the afternoon as we swam and read and played bat and ball. I kept myself to myself a bit, not yet ready to return to normality, still running through the jump. The slow ascent, my thumping heart, the feel of the wind as I swept down, the patches of land below my dangling feet before I leaped. These images seemed to return to me more vividly than in the moment itself, like I had stored them up at the time to be examined. It had felt liberating and brilliant and like nothing I had ever done before and I was so glad I had come out here, had taken a chance. There was so much I wanted to see and do and I had never been more glad to have left my tiny box flat, Stewie and LA behind. I felt like I was really living, really experiencing things.

I made a mental note to get Zeb to film the reaction; maybe we could come and film a piece for the company? I felt excitement building in my stomach. We could capture the feel of the jump, tell others how it went: the dread, the sweaty fear and then the incredible feel of whistling through the air, everything a patchwork of jumbled colour and your pulse in your ears thudding through your head and body. I wanted others to hear this, see it and take a chance.

Darling,

Sky-diving really? How dangerous and thrilling! I am, as the youth say, 'Well jell.' Your father says he's glad your parachute opened, which is nice if a bit of an understatement.

We're eating fish pie with scallops in so living the dream too!

Ma

Chapter 36

To celebrate the successful sky-dive, we arranged a meal at the restaurant back on the other side of the island. It supposedly did the only decent cocktails on Tioman. Actually it was apparently the only place that knew what a cocktail was (vodka and coke didn't count, we explained to the barman in our regular haunt).

Remembering Andrew's face that morning, his grin, his touch on my back, I was feeling pretty confident that tonight could be the night and Andrew was finally falling for me. Pouting at myself in the square of mirror to make Mel laugh, I dashed on some bronzer, lined my eyes with kohl pencil and rubbed in some lip salve to complete the look. Borrowing Mel's yellow maxi dress, I clipped my hair half up and gave her a twirl, gratified to hear her whistle at me.

'Thanks, friend,' I grinned.

Mel was wearing a strapless purple top and white cropped

trousers, her hair twisted into a bun, enormous silver earrings on display.

'You look great,' I said, passing her the lip salve.

'Nanks,' she said through half-closed lips as she applied it.

The boys picked us up, Andrew in chinos and a light-pink shirt, neatly ironed and Duncan in three-quarter-length shorts and his top on.

Squeezing into the 4x4 for the second time that day, we were appraised by Ahmad who declared us 'beautiful women' as we set off down the track once more, pools of orange light on either side of the road until we plunged into the darkness of the forest and the bumpy crossing, the headlights dipping erratically as we trundled over tree roots and stones.

Stepping out of the 4x4, I took a couple of wobbly steps forward, relieved to be back on hard ground.

'You look pretty,' said Andrew. 'I like that dress.'

Glad to be standing in the shadows, I felt my face burn with the compliment.

'Let's get this night started,' whooped Duncan, who had already managed to undo three of the buttons on his shirt, a nipple very nearly exposed. Linking arms with Mel and me, he steered us towards the entrance to the restaurant, walking up the polished wooden staircase and around a terrace that skirted the building.

The hub of chatter and a live pianist could be heard as we approached, the genteel clink of cutlery and the sizzle from the kitchen making me smile in anticipation. The large restaurant was cool, the unmistakable feeling of air conditioning circulating. Floor-to-ceiling windows at one end overlooked the beach, the sea a dark strip punctuated by buoy lights bobbing in the water.

A waiter ambled over to us, his face one big smile and his body suggesting he could do with a few more meals in the restaurant. He pulled out my chair and handed me my napkin with a flourish. Lighting one of the candles that had gone out, he passed round menus and left us to it. I smoothed my hands over the creamy tablecloth, scanning my eyes down the menu, my taste buds tingling at the variety on offer.

'Burger,' said Duncan, closing his menu after a couple of seconds.

'Same,' said Mel following suit.

'Me too,' agreed Andrew. 'But,' he stopped the waiter with a hand, 'can you please tell the chef I like my meat done medium, no pink at all. I really hate it when they're overdone though, so just so a knife can slice through it easily, but no blood.'

Duncan rolled his eyes and Mel made a noise into her napkin. I had been looking at Andrew with an open mouth as he spoke.

'How...precise.' I smiled and then realised Andrew had turned towards me and was waiting for me to order. I scanned the pages quickly, the slightly blurred coloured photographs making my mouth water. Plump prawns on a bed of flat noodles, meat crammed with juices, an entire page dedicated to pizzas.

'Mushroom pizza,' I decided.

'You won't want pudding after that,' said Duncan.

I frowned at him, 'Why not?'

'Because you won't have mushroom left, gettit?' His shirt was now entirely open and his stomach quivered as he laughed at his own joke. To my dismay, Mel joined in. Looking up at Andrew, he rolled his eyes at me and I felt that we were connected on this at least. Suddenly finding my napkin hugely interesting, I looked back down. *Was this the spark Mel had asked me about? I think I'd felt it then.*

Our food arrived and we threw ourselves enthusiastically into the process of eating. No one spoke for a good twenty minutes as we devoured what was on our plates. It was so fantastic to eat something other than rice for an evening; the fayre on Juara was delicious but not varied. As we munched, a live band started up in the corner and the restaurant was filled with the sounds of some nineties power ballads as they moved through the tables, stopping to serenade various people.

With inevitable speed, they headed straight to our table. They were playing 'Saving All my Love for You' by Whitney Houston which sounded stilted, but sort of wonderful in their thick Malaysian accents. I chewed slowly on my pizza as Mel clapped along beside them. It seemed like a movie and at any moment I was expecting the boys to offer their hands to us so we could start slow-dancing in between the tables, the crowd breaking into spontaneous applause, someone taking a video on their phone and posting it on social media entitled 'Luved-up Couple' to hundreds of 'Likes'. Instead, the boys ate their burgers, flicking their eyes sporadically at the musicians as if to check they were definitely still standing there.

One mushroom pizza later, overflowing with cheese, and a load of cocktails down, we made unsteady progress out of the restaurant to meet Ahmad. My stomach gurgled as I got in and I placed one hand on it as if to quieten it.

'Nightcap at ours?' said Duncan and I looked at Andrew, hair mussed up, eyes sparkling in the half-light of the 4x4 and nodded slowly.

'Definitely,' said Mel, tugging at the top of her strapless top and giggling.

Duncan helped her into the vehicle, one hand on her elbow, and I frowned a little at the gesture, picturing Dex back in LA, heartbroken and wondering when his girlfriend would be returning.

It was a humid evening but even sitting next to the window, air rushing past me, I started to feel clammy. My thighs stuck together and my hair was plastered to my forehead as I tried to create some distance between myself and Andrew. It was difficult as Ahmad was navigating potholes in his customary way, mostly leaping over them and I was thrust up against him repeatedly, watching as if from a distance as I thought I saw him smile and return the pressure.

My stomach gurgled again and I started to feel a loosening in my stomach. *Oh no.* Crossing one leg over another I cringed as another jolt made my stomach feel like it was filled with bouncy balls. *Get me back to the hotel, get me back to the hotel.* I sent my prayer out silently, focusing on taking one breath at a time, in, out and again. Mel was laughing as Duncan threw a joke back over his shoulder from the front seat, the noise reaching me as if I was underwater, their voices indistinct.

'So hot,' I whispered.

Andrew leaned towards me, a hand on my thigh. 'What's that?'

'Oh,' I said, a hand flying up to my mouth trying to force down the belch that I was sure was coming. *Oh no, please.*

We were back and had stopped and the hotel sign wavered in front of me as I put a hand up on to the warm metal of the car door.

'You okay, Iz?' asked Mel, reaching a hand out to me.

'Yeah,' I squeaked, clenching every part of my body, my stomach now swirling like a wave machine. 'Tired,' I gasped.

'Oh I thought we could join these guys on the beach?'

'Yeah do come, Isobel,' said Andrew, one arm over my shoulder.

My stomach lurched and I felt something rise in my throat. *Seriously, Isobel, this is the moment you are going to pick to throw up? Really?*

I couldn't return his sentence, vaguely aware of someone greeting us from across the road. Liz ambled over, resplendent in a short pink dress – the lace pattern on one of the panels blurring in front of my eyes. My stomach clenched, a cramp removing my ability to see anything.

Trying not to stagger away, I called over my shoulder, 'Brilliant evening, thank you, lovely dinner, see you back in the room in a bit, Mel,' and then half-walked, half-jogged into the door of the hotel, straight up to our room, poking the key uselessly in the lock before falling through the door into the bathroom to hug the basin of the loo and throw up a load of mushrooms. As I groaned, I just imagined Duncan's smirk if he'd been here – the contents of my stomach now having more room.

Not trusting myself to move, I reached up to the sink, attempting to splash my face with cold water from the tap, alarmed to hear the door to our room open and my name being called out.

Mel stood in the doorway, the yellow hallway light shining behind her, her face full of concern as she took in the scene. 'Oh you poor love.'

'You didn't need to come back,' I said, embarrassed to be found on the cold tiles of our shared bathroom but not having the energy to get up from there.

'Don't be silly, I thought something was wrong.'

I felt like someone was reaching a hand into my stomach and squeezing all my internal organs in turn. Whimpering, I turned away from her. 'I'm dissssgusssting.'

'Yes you are, but that's okay. I'm not here to mock you. That's for tomorrow.'

When I was finished and she had flushed the loo, she gently lifted me to my feet, guided me back to my bed, propped up my pillows and fetched me a glass of water and a bowl from the kitchen 'just in case'. Patting at my head with a damp flannel, I felt like I could be back home being nursed by my own mum.

'You're brilliant,' I said in a half-whisper, eyes closing and starting to feel like the worst might be over.

'You'd do it for me.'

I was too exhausted to make a joke and tried to sit still, force my body to forget. I spent an uncomfortable few hours drifting into a half-sleep and out again. Mel had changed into a T-shirt and shorts, her hair hastily tied in a bun and her face free of make-up. Sitting cross-legged on the bed, she looked about twelve years old and we had long conversations about the stupid jobs we'd done, our first meeting in LA when she had spent the entire day getting me to ask her in my finest English accent whether she would like a cup of tea. About inviting me round to her tiny box of a flat where Dex and her had taught me poker and introduced me to flaming sambucas and then, of course, making me sleep on their sofa bed.

Even through the net curtains, the moon cast a blue sheen over the room and, opening one eye, I made out Mel, a silhouette, her sitting on a chair looking out of the window, her bare feet perched on the windowsill as she spoke quietly into a phone.

'...I miss you, will you call me?'

She looked embarrassed when she turned to see the quizzical expression on my face. 'Dex?' I asked.

She nodded. 'It keeps going to answerphone.' She tried to sound nonchalant, but I knew it was clearly hurting her.

'He'll come round,' I said.

'God, Iz,' she said, putting her head in her hands. 'What if I've really messed things up?'

'You can't, Mel, you guys are meant to be together.'

She walked over to her bed, pulling the thin white sheet up to her chin. 'We are, aren't we,' she agreed, turning towards the wall so I couldn't see her face. 'Now get some sleep, sickie,' she said, trying to sound upbeat. Her voice broke in the middle.

They really were meant to be together. I thought of them both then, finishing each other's sentences, her ruffling his hair affectionately as he made a bad joke, the thoughtful way he would make room for her on the sofa without looking at her, bring her coffee the way she liked it, buy her favourite magazines because he'd thought of her. They had always been great together, didn't bitch or put each other down. I loved hanging out with them, well, apart from when they did the eskimo rubs and talked about a new sex toy. They laughed together about the same things and had so much in common. A thought flickered across my mind. *Did Andrew and I share the same things? Did we laugh in the same moment?* Woozily I tried to think of a time we had really connected in that way but perhaps I was too tired or too weary from being ill to focus properly and I went to sleep with nothing but a blank.

Chapter 37

Andrew was sat in the shade of the cafe, the sea behind him steely grey from the storm that was still threatening. Huge clouds bloated with the promise of an almighty downpour clung to the island. The beach was practically deserted, everyone no doubt hiding from the inevitable. He was stirring sugar into a second coffee and I moved towards him gingerly, an unconscious hand on my stomach, still feeling weak after the night before.

He half stood up as I approached and then sat back down quickly continuing to stir.

'Where's everyone?' I asked.

'Left. I waited. Well, you know, Mel said you weren't well last night and I was...'

Was he babbling?

'Thank you, that's really sweet,' I said, dragging over a chair so that it left dusty smears on the wooden floorboards.

I ordered coffee and some toast, refusing my usual waffles, and Andrew didn't embarrass me any more by talking about my sudden illness, my wan skin probably explanation enough.

The waitress brought over my coffee and toast and in that moment there was a low, long rumble that rolled across the sky and fat droplets of rain made dark divots in the sand beneath the terrace, dotting the whole beach with them in seconds. A couple took shelter under the awning of the cafe and they were joined by a man, dark hair already wet, a familiar-looking bag slung over his shoulder.

'Zeb,' I called out without really thinking. He turned and squinted into the doorway of the cafe, his face brightening as he caught my half wave. I pushed a strand of hair behind my ear self-consciously and, for a brief second, wished I looked a little better.

It seemed he almost needed to duck as he entered the cafe, bending down to greet me with a kiss on my cheek and holding out a hand across the table.

'Oh, Andrew, Zeb this is...'

'We've met, Iz,' Zeb said, grinning at me gently.

I felt a blush creep up my neck when I realised he had helped clear out the hut after the fire.

Zeb pulled out a spare chair beside me. I looked at him, grateful that he hadn't pointed it out.

'You helped after the fire,' Andrew said.

Fortunately much of the sentence was drowned out, competing with the rain drumming in an uneven rhythm on the tin roof above us. 'Were you going somewhere?'

Zeb signalled to his bag. 'I was heading over to the pier

to take some shots of this weather. It's kind of brilliant, isn't it?'

Beyond the pier a long, grey cloud brooded, edged with bright white light over a blue sky. It was an extraordinary sight.

'Brilliant,' I agreed.

'You should come and film another piece about it with me,' he suggested.

I turned to Andrew to fill him in. 'Zeb's a photographer, he's taking some shots for a blog about the island. They're fantastic, you should see them.'

'Photographer, as a job?' asked Andrew, his nose wrinkling a fraction.

'Yup,' said Zeb laughing. 'I'm going to be an astronaut when I grow up but, for now, this will definitely do.'

'So you spend a lot of time on Instagram?' Andrew chuckled.

'Er...not exactly,' said Zeb, raking a hand through his hair. 'So, Andrew, what do you do?' Zeb asked, a smile on his face I hadn't seen before, like it was plastered on. I shifted in my seat, regretting calling him over.

'I teach Geography,' Andrew said, lifting his chin.

'Cool,' replied Zeb in a voice that I think meant he thought it was anything but.

Feeling defensive, I jumped in. 'Andrew's headmistress thinks he's wonderful,' I gushed.

'Does she?'

'Did she say that?' beamed Andrew.

'She did,' I said, sipping at my coffee and praying Mel might burst in here and ease the atmosphere.

'So what are you doing today?' asked Zeb, turning to me, his eyes seeming to trap me in our own private bubble. 'Have you got time to film ano—'

'We're going to go out on the boat,' said Andrew, his hand suddenly on my forearm. I looked down at it, the freckles and veins unfamiliar. I felt like shrugging it off. *Why didn't I feel more pleased?*

'Yes, we're...' I coughed. 'Well I hadn't...but that sounds great,' I said, pulling myself together and smiling at Andrew. This WAS great: we were going out on the boat and he had his hand on my arm. This was exactly what I wanted.

Zeb stood up abruptly, towering over me in the small cafe. 'Well I wouldn't want to hold you up.'

'I'd love to film another tim—'

'Nice to meet you,' Zeb said, not catching Andrew's eye.

'Have a good....'

He turned and left before I could finish my sentence, stepping out into the deluge, rain instantly flattening his hair. He didn't look back. I felt my stomach grumble again. It must be the sickness still left over from last night. I watched Zeb disappear out of sight and then dragged my eyes back to Andrew.

'Right,' I said with phoney gusto. 'So...'

The storm had passed and the sand had soon started to dry out. The air felt fresher and cooler and the clouds had left leaving a blank expanse of gorgeous blue. I'd told Mel what Andrew had offered and she sent me off with a slap on my ass and a lecture about the list (play it cool, make sure he's in an excellent mood, be beautiful et cetera) so I was pretty buoyed up by the time I was back on the beach meeting him. He arrived carrying a bucket, a bait box and two rods and we loaded up the boat.

'Alright, me hearty,' I said to him in my best pirate voice but he must not have heard as he didn't respond. I dropped my pirate salute before he could see.

Dragging the tiny turquoise boat across the sand, its faded wood littered with splinters, I started to feel woozy again. Everything seemed to take more effort than normal and my stomach felt empty and vulnerable. As it bobbed in the shallows of the water, I put out a hand to steady myself, the cloudy yellow patchwork of sand around my ankles wobbling and then I was in and sitting on the hard plank in the middle, a dribble of water down the middle of the base, staining the wood a darker blue. The boat tipped as Andrew stepped in, too, nudging me up so that we were sat side by side, legs touching. He coughed as if he too recognised how intimate this felt, us out on the high seas together. My stomach stirred again.

Andrew tugged on the engine cord, placing a loop around his ankle and with a juddery putter the boat started up on the third attempt, slowly moving off out into the deeper sea, a trail of white foam in our wake, water coursing out in waves from the channel we had made. The sun was directly overhead, blazing and insistent, and I was glad to have my hat on, holding it with one hand when we got some speed up. Andrew tried to shout above the noise of the engine but his attempts proved pretty futile and we both spent the journey bouncing gently on the wood as we headed out and around the headland.

Ambling to a stop, the boat gently rocking on the surface, Andrew pointed to a basket in the corner of the boat. Loading us up with bait, he handed me a spool of twine, a loaded hook dangling ready to be dropped into the water. With a gentle plop I threw it down and felt the hook sink deeper into the navy-blue water below.

'What do I do when something bites?' I asked nervously.

'Haul it up and I'll deal with it,' he said, smiling at me. In the bright sunshine he seemed to dazzle, his skin lighter than mine, his sandy hair flecked with blonds and browns, his parting red from recent sunburn. I couldn't believe we were finally alone, together, doing something – hello – incredibly romantic. *Oh sure, I would love to fish with you in the middle of the South China Sea alone in a tiny boat where we have to be pressed up against each other.*

I realised this was my opportunity to seal the deal, so to speak. Here was an opportunity for me to dazzle him with my witty repertoire and excellent personality. My time to shine. I opened my mouth to speak, wavering as I realised I couldn't think of anything to say.

'Did you get something?' he asked, seeing my mouth half-open like I was Finding Frickin' Nemo.

'Oh yes, I thought I felt a...tug, but no, I think it was just the...waves.'

'Okay.'

'Okaaaaaaay,' I said in a voice that made it sound like I was copying him.

He raised an eyebrow at me and I laughed, one short bark of laughter that, if I was close to landing a fish, would have scared it away.

‘So what if we catch a shark?’ I asked. *Great question, Iz.*

‘We won’t.’

‘Oh.’

‘Did you ever see *Jaws* and the bit where the shark tipped the whole boat up and ate the skipper?’

‘Yes I did.’

‘Me, too.’ Of course you have. *Why else would you have mentioned it, Iz? Also, why all the shark chat? That is not going to help the mood.* Actually, the thought had really freaked me out. I glanced over my shoulder, the sea ominously dark behind me, a huge expanse of small waves. Could you even see a fin if it was there?

‘So, just to check,’ I coughed, ‘there are no sharks of note in these waters.’ *‘Of note’ aka Could Tip Over the Boat and Halve a Man.*

‘Well, there are but we won’t be seeing them.’

‘Duh, da, duh, Da, duh, da...’ *WHY ARE YOU DOING THE THEME MUSIC, Isobel? PULL IT TOGETHER.*

I trailed off and Andrew stared pointedly out at his line. No more shark chat.

‘So,’ I said in a sing-song voice.

‘Ssh,’ Andrew said, gesturing with his hand for me to turn the volume down.

‘Oh, sorry,’ I whispered.

‘The fish,’ he indicated.

‘Gotcha,’ I said, and then winked at him. *Winking? What are you, Iz, a fifty-five-year-old amateur magician? No one winks.*

The silence dragged on and there was nothing on my line and I was getting a bit bo-r-ed.

'Andrew,' I whispered, holding up two fingers. 'Charades?'

He shook his head.

'Okay, probably right, I rock at charades,' I whispered, going back to staring.

This obviously was enough of a competition for Andrew to show some interest and he waved me on so I panicked, thought of something fish-related and proceeded to mime the excruciating two-word film, *Free Willy*, much to my horror, and his. *COULD THIS BOAT TRIP BE GOING WORSE FOR YOU, DOOFUS?* What had come over me? When the hell had I decided charades would work? Christ.

Andrew had cheered up after catching two fish in an hour. He hauled them up, thrashing around on the end of his line, and I tried not to be squeamish about things as he removed the hook, smashed their heads on the side and put them in the bucket he had brought along.

I gave him a thumbs-up after the second catch and went back to staring at my line that had not been nibbled on by anything. I was so bored by now I was half-hoping a Great White might start circling simply to distract me. My last thoughts had included: what nail varnish was I going to wear later? Why had I never seen a bat in my life? Had people really fancied Bates from *Downton Abbey* or had they been lying? And which nineties band would reunite next? So many thoughts, so many lofty thoughts.

'So what do you do for a living?' Andrew asked me in a half-whisper when perhaps it had been clear I was drifting off. I realised this might be the first thing he had asked about me. *Getting per-so-nal* I thought, then realising I still hadn't replied.

'Oh, TV,' I said loudly and then really quietly as he put the finger up to his lips again. 'Well, I was trying to be a presenter but recently I have been doing other jobs, too.'

'I know someone who was trying to be on TV,' Andrew said.

'Really?' I whispered.

'Yeah. He didn't make it.'

'Oh.'

'So what do you do for a real job?'

My heart sank at the question. A real job. What did I do?

'Stuff,' I mumbled. 'Mostly promotional work and sales, so I am employed to represent brands and, oh, it's pretty dull,' I said, feeling hopeless.

Andrew nodded. 'So the fish might not come if we are being this noisy,' he said, doing the zip thing on his lips and then adding, 'So ssshh' because he clearly thought I was shit at mime.

'Okay,' I said, putting my finger up too and feeling a momentary sense of relief that the conversation was ended.

Should I feel relieved the conversation had faded off? Why weren't we connecting on a deeper level? Was it me? What happened to that friendship we used to have all those years ago?

These thoughts consumed me throughout the day and I felt a little knot in my chest release as we dragged the boat back into shore. Maybe, a little voice piped up, maybe I didn't need to try harder, didn't need to find a way for it to work?

The sun, weaker now that a lot of the midday rage had passed, shimmered over the horizon. Walking back across the beach, hands swinging by my side, one momentarily brushed against Andrew. I thought of saying something then, of turning to him and asking him straight there, on the sand, whether he felt anything between us. Was I just clinging to an old memory? Opening my mouth to say something I stopped, squinting at a figure with a backpack on the terrace of the cafe.

'Dex?' I ground to an abrupt halt, taking in Dex standing there, his stubbled hair dark in the daylight, his backpack brand new, creases still on the sides, clutching it to him like a stuffed toy.

'Dex! What the hell!' I started jogging towards him, one hand on my hat as I ran. 'You left American soil!'

Dex looked up and grinned at me, jumping down off the stairs of the terrace to come over. Dex who only got a passport to be served alcohol in bars. And now, here he was, looking utterly bewildered, taking in his surroundings, sweating in his jeans and black shirt which made him look like a nightclub bouncer.

Hugging him tightly, feeling like a bit of home had arrived, I grinned at him, punching an arm. 'I can't believe you're here.'

'Is Mel?' he said, looking behind me as if I might be shielding her from view. He pushed his hair back with a hand.

'Yes, well not with us, with Du—'A momentary panic made me stumble across his name. 'Friend, our friend.'

Oh no – where *was* Mel? She'd told me earlier she was going to find Duncan. Hopefully she hadn't found Duncan and now was just reading quietly, the Bible or some thing, nearby.

'She'll be along soon,' I said, quickly turning around. 'Dex meet Andrew. Andrew, Dex.'

'Ah,' said Dex, his face lighting, eyebrows lifted. 'You're Andrew, eh.'

'Yes,' said Andrew slowly, confusion crossing his face.

Oh my god, what was Dex about to say? How much had Mel told him? How much had I told him? He couldn't ruin this.

'Andrew is a friend, weirdly, that I knew when I was younger,' I said, my eyes concentrating on him in a way that said, 'NOTE THE TONE, DEX'.

'Yeah I know,' he chuckled. 'I know you guys go way back,' he added. Not picking up on it then.

'And you know that because,' I paused, turning to Andrew, 'because I used to tell him all about my school and all the people in it, everyone, teachers, pupils, the caretakers, well, Dex calls them janitors, and well Dex has a GREAT memory for small things, don't you, Dex?' I asked, not stopping to let him intervene. 'So weird that we often say, "Gosh, Dex, how do you remember that ha ha?"' I had definitely started to perspire during my speech and was casting about for something else to say when I spotted Mel at the other end of the beach. 'Mel!' I slumped in relief.

Mel was walking slowly back towards us, laughing up into the face of Duncan, oiled bare chest on display.

Dex had turned, pushed his hair back once more, eyes sparking with energy. 'Where?'

Wanting to stop him seeing her, I faltered. Could I point somewhere else? Oh god, Mel, don't touch his arm and STOP SMILING like you're an extra in a Peter Andre video.

Too late, Dex had spotted them.

'Who's that?' he asked quietly.

'My mate Duncan,' chipped in Andrew.

'Yes, Andrew's mate,' I said, trying to quietly send Dex a subliminal message that Duncan was not a threat, was gay or a eunuch! *Think eunuch, Iz. Eunuch.* I attempted to send him this message telepathically.

'He's like Ken,' I explained. 'You know the Barbie doll guy,' I went on, hoping Dex would think eunuch.

'What, smooth?'

'Yes, smooth,' I said, wondering why Dex still looked put out. 'And we wonder about him, you know,' I whispered, trying to turn my body away from Andrew.

'What do you wonder about him?' asked Andrew, narrowing his eyes in question.

'Oh.' *ARGGHH,* I couldn't do this, I couldn't endanger our afternoon. 'Just, we wondered what kind of guy he is, he's a closed book.' I shrugged, realising I had just made him sound more mysterious and exotic.

'Well I think he's pretty bloody easy to read,' Dex muttered.

At that moment Mel spotted us and started waving, her teeth pearly white in her newly tanned flesh, water droplets on her torso and arms from a swim then, when she spotted Dex, she stopped dead still on the sand. Duncan walked a few paces on still talking and then turned to see her standing there, jaw dropped, planted in the sand.

'Well, let's go and say hello,' I said, striding towards Mel. 'Mel,' I called in my mum's super-posh, high-pitched voice. 'Melissa.'

Mel walked past me, eyes on Dex, and we all sort of

melted into the background looking at things: the ocean, the sand, the...

'Ooh, Andrew, Duncan, look – an ant! It's carrying another ant on its back,' I said, pointing at the ground.

'Where?' asked Andrew, crinkling his eyes and examining the ground.

'Oh they were just there,' I said, pointing vaguely, one eye on Mel and Dex, not wanting to interrupt but also sort of wanting to witness the big reunion. I couldn't believe he had travelled so many miles – and he hates travelling – to see Mel. It was gorgeous, like a beautiful romantic movie and I felt a pang in my gut that I couldn't imagine anyone doing something like that for me. *Hey be happy for her, Iz.* And I was, it was lovely.

They were talking in low voices and gesturing. The hug was a long time coming, and then I heard Mel's voice raised, her hands gesticulating at Duncan. Oh no. And Dex looked mad, his chin jutted out, pouty bottom lip

'I didn't ask you to come!' Mel screamed at Dex.

It seemed the whole beach fell silent. Andrew froze, looking off at the reef, I stared at my toenails, coughed quietly.

'All this way and you're draped over another man...'

Soooo this was not going well. It seemed the romantic reunion was not really happening. I needed to fix this, it was ridiculous. They loved each other. Mel had been thinking about him the whole time, putting up with Duncan's posturing but never serious. Only, before I could step in, someone else did.

Duncan walked across. 'Hey, mate,' he said in a voice that did not suggest he was, in fact, Dex's mate.

'Duncan, don't,' I said.

'No, Duncan,' said Mel, one hand up to her left. 'Leave it.'

'I don't like to see you upset,' he said.

'Seriously, who is this guy?' said Dex, throwing his hands up in the air.

'A friend,' Mel stressed. 'And this isn't about him.'

'Look, I'm tired, I need a shower, I need a drink.' Dex rubbed his face. He did look tired: pale face, red-rimmed eyes.

Mel stood, arms crossed, breathing out heavily. 'Okay, okay.'

'Hey, Mel,' I said, forcibly dragging her off to the side leaving Dex eyeing up Duncan, Duncan crossing his arms in the way that he thought made his muscles look bigger. *Oh man.*

'Go.' I smiled at her. 'It's Dex. I'll give you guys some time, you know, stay out of the room a bit.'

'But I...' She looked pale.

'Hey, he's here,' I said, trying to bring it home to her.

She nodded. 'Thanks, babe,' she said, drawing me in for a hug.

'It's a lovely thing to do,' I reminded her in her ear.

'I know, I got a shock and...'

'Don't.' I cut her off, laughing at her cross expression. 'Go play nice.'

I watched them leave, Mel leaving space between them, not talking, and I bit my lip. Would they be okay? Mel could be so volatile when she was backed into a corner. And Dex had done this wonderful thing.

'Right,' said Duncan, an arm snaking over my shoulders. 'Drink?'

Andrew started walking away. 'Definitely.'

'Iz?'

'Oh I don't know,' I said, not wanting to go to a bar and laugh along as Duncan put Peter Andre's 'Beautiful Girl' on the karaoke machine to spend the next five minutes with his shirt off running a hand over his stomach. I was worried about Mel. I couldn't go back to my room yet, though, I needed to give them time.

'I think I'm just going to read my book,' I said, pointing to a lounger down the beach.

'Sexy.' Duncan nodded. 'Do you need me to come and read the sex scenes out to you?'

'Er, I'm okay,' I said, backing away.

'Do you need me to act out any of the rude bits?'

'It's *Pride and Prejudice*,' I explained. 'So there aren't many rude bits in it.'

'That is a tragedy,' Duncan said solemnly.

'Is that the one with Hugh Grant in?' asked Andrew.

'Um...No.'

'Oh.'

I thought briefly of my old fantasy, the well-read Andrew reading passages to me from old classics as he gave me a foot massage on the swing set. He wasn't that man. Not that it should matter I thought hurriedly.

I stood on the sand as they both stayed where they were. 'Okay then,' I said, patting my bag, 'best get on.'

Turning away, I wondered whether I should have gone with them. I wasn't going to read my book, I wasn't sure I had my Kindle. Maybe I felt a bit disloyal about Duncan and Mel. Maybe seeing Dex had reminded me about LA and why I was out here. Had I really got anywhere? Andrew had seemed keen today, last night, so why was I pulling away? Why did I feel relieved to have got rid of them?

I lay down on the lounger, pushing the straps of my bikini down, and rootled around in my bag for my book. Bingo. Darcy and Lizzie, you can take my mind off things.

Half an hour and some considerable amount of dribble later, I was dreaming of darkness. I was wading through a stagnant river, dead leaves collecting on the surface, reeds wrapping themselves around my ankles as I moved slowly across. It was getting deeper and I was trying to reach the little turtle in the middle but I was afraid, my pulse thumping through my body, my head twitching at every sound but I had to reach it and the water was getting higher and...

Chapter 38

I opened my eyes in shadow and panicked briefly as my dream seemed to be coming true. There was a man above me, holding something. I WILL DIE FOR SURE my head said.

'Gah,' I say, holding up my Kindle as if I was about to throw it.

'No, don't strike me with your Kindle, I might never walk again,' laughed Zeb looming over me.

'What the hell? Why are you standing over me like Death? Who does that?' I asked, lurching into a sitting position and hoiking my straps back up before I flashed nipple. Again.

'I'm not standing over you like Death. Anyway, Death stands behind you with a scythe. Like this,' he said, walking behind the lounger and holding up an imaginary scythe, his face in a Death-like grimace.

'Very reassuring,' I said.

Zeb flopped on to the lounger next door, one leg bent and one dangling over the edge, his arms crossed behind his head. 'I was mooching and wanted to see how long I could stand over you before you woke up and freaked out.'

'What a comforting thought.'

'Three minutes,' he said, closing his eyes. 'You were talking in your sleep, too, something about reeds and turtle yolk. It was weird.'

'Well, I like to keep you amused.'

Zeb turned to me. 'So where's your new partner-in-crime? Mel?' he asked noting my blank face.

I felt strangely snappy as I replied, 'She's with her boyfriend.' I stressed the last word, wondering why I felt the need to point it out so badly.

'Boyfriend,' he repeated. Did he look disappointed? His eyes still had the same energy, his lashes thick and dark.

'He turned up suddenly, from LA,' I said.

'Sounds good.'

'So I can't go back yet; she's with him and he's just appeared off a plane. It's kind of awesome, really. Well she might brain him or send him back but...'

'Why?'

'She's cross with him: he proposed to her and...'

'What a SHIT,' Zeb interrupted. 'I know girls hate it when we do that.' Zeb smacked an open hand on his lounger making me jump.

I laughed. 'Well, yes, I suppose it doesn't sound bad, but she...Her parents were in love and now they just yell at each other and throw stuff.'

'What stuff?'

'Whatever comes to hand. Mostly words.'

'Hmm, but don't we know that sticks and stones hurt but

names will never actually hurt.'

How did he always manage to make everything lighter? I was balled up worrying about her, but he was right to laugh about it; it wasn't something I could do anything about and Mel would be okay.

'So you're free now,' Zeb asked, cutting across my thoughts.

'Free, aside from this very important sun-worshipping.'

'Vital.' He nodded solemnly. 'Well, why don't we film another clip for the site? People went nuts for the cave piece and it would be great to add more.'

My interest was piqued. 'What do you mean "nuts"? As in crazy comments?'

'No, just loads of traffic; it was shared a lot. It was the most-popular post this month, actually,' he said, looking at me with a wide smile.

I felt a warm glow in my stomach. My video was popular, people liked it. 'That's great.'

'So, up for doing another one now?'

I panicked a little as I realised he was serious. His camera bag was half-submerged in the sand, he was physically attached to the thing.

'Oh I don't know, my hair is all gross and sand-filled and...'

'Come on, Iz, you look perfect, all sun-kissed and natural,' he said, making me feel hot all over.

Laughing, thrown by the comment, I found myself agreeing. 'Okay, okay.' I sat up. 'Where shall we set up and what do you want it about?'

'The beach itself, Juara, what's on offer. Whatever you like, Iz.'

I sat and thought for a bit, the same familiar excitement opening up inside me as I had new ideas about the kinds of things we could mention: the sky-dive, the snorkelling, the waterfall in the jungle... Zeb pulled out his camera and, without really thinking first, I asked him if I could take a look.

There was a momentary pause and then Zeb handed the camera over. 'You press the triangle to chart back through.'

I nodded, thrilled to be seeing this side of him, the photos he was always taking. As I pressed the button I drew in my breath. 'These photos are brilliant,' I said, scrolling back through the shots of the pier, the dense charcoal-coloured cloud sitting like it was interposed on the pale-blue sky below. There were pictures of the cafe owner, mid-laugh, a hand clutching his side; Ahmad in the middle of a trick, the focus on his face touching and real. Zeb captured the mood of the beach perfectly, had taken wide shots of the turquoise sea, the jungle backdrop and, of course, the monkeys. There were pictures of me in the cave, one I couldn't believe was me. A profile. I was looking at something beyond, lost in thought, and the light traced around my face which was in darkness. It was stunning.

I hadn't got any more words and handed the camera back silently, not sure how to tell him.

'Right!' He clapped, perhaps feeling the mood had changed. 'Let's set up.'

We spent some moments choosing a good spot and I rehearsed in my mind what I would say. Raking a hand self-consciously through my hair, I took a sip of water and walked in front of the camera, waiting for Zeb to give me the signal to begin. And then we were off and this time we did two takes before both of us were happy with the clip. I had been presenting to camera and I simply told Zeb about the island: the beauty, the assorted animals, the monkeys...His hair shook as he chuckled at one part, a hand covering his mouth so his laughter couldn't be heard. It filled me with a confidence I hadn't felt in years and when we finished I felt elated, breathless with the buzz of doing a job well done.

'We need to do more of these,' Zeb mused aloud and I found myself nodding keenly.

He sat back down on a lounger to put the camera away and I joined him, perched on the edge, looking down at my thigh only inches from his. I felt the urge to move closer.

He finished packing up. 'Have you eaten?' he asked zipping up the bag and stretching out his legs. He wiggled his toes into the sand. For some reason I found myself blushing as I stared at his feet.

'Um, no, but well...'

'Want to join me? I was going up to the cafe at the end there; they do this epic Egg Foo Yong which I've become obsessed with. If it were a woman I would be with this egg thing it's so good.'

His jocular tone brought me back from somewhere and I laughed at him. 'Well that is certainly a lovely mental image and now I am desperate to meet this egg thing and check out whether she is worthy of your love.'

'Thank you, it's important, I need to introduce her to my friends, check she's the real deal.'

I felt my chest lighten as he said the word 'friends'.

'I'm honoured you would consult me on such an important matter.'

'It is important. It could just be a passing fad thing. Like the month where I only ate Jammie Dodgers and then realised I was living a half life.'

'We've all been there,' I said, reaching out to pat him on the leg.

He looked down and the air seemed to fill with heat and the sound of an insect. I snatched my hand away.

The restaurant was tucked away behind a row of huts. Enormous flowers in fuchsia crawled and twisted up and round the thin columns that stood between tables. The makeshift place had wooden tables and jam jars filled with orange and white daisies. A couple of tables were taken and people were having conversations in low voices. Tea lights were ready to be lit when the sun went down.

We'd been in the restaurant for all of three seconds when the waiter, dressed in a red football shirt, came running over to slap Zeb on the back like he had known him for ever. 'They do it!' he announced in a loud voice so that the people at the next table looked over at us curiously.

I frowned in confusion but Zeb was laughing. He nodded. 'Amazing, the Chelsea goalkeeper must have been dodging them for a bet.'

'No, no, they have pure skill.'

'Look, we've been over this.' Zeb waggled a finger at the waiter who whisked off to fetch menus. 'Die hard Man U fan,' Zeb whispered, a hand on the small of my back as he steered me over to a table in the corner. 'I literally have no idea what I'm saying but it's easier to go along with it,' he whispered.

The waiter returned, holding two menus. 'We are going to Champions League!'

'You let yourself believe that,' Zeb said, shaking his head as the waiter walked off once more.

I leaned across the table. 'Seriously, what is going on?'

'You basically say cynical stuff about his team and he gets passionate and gives us money off our bill. Try it!'

The waiter bounced over again with a small notepad in his hands. 'We keep playing like this, we win the title.'

Zeb pursed his lips and looked at me, a minuscule nod.

'Hmm I'm not...so sure,' I said, adding a big frown afterwards for good measure.

'You like football, too?'

'Yes.'

'What team do you support?'

'Oh, I...' I thought back to the earlier conversation. 'CHELSEA!' I practically shouted in his face.

The waiter's eyes opened wide. 'Oh no, no, no, lady, you have it all wrong.'

This was going well; he was smiling at me with all his teeth. Both rows. He had a gold filling. This was easy.

'Yes we are very good.' I nodded eagerly.

'We just showed you who was boss.'

'You did?' I looked at Zeb, panic creeping into my voice. 'Oh you DID, but we will rise again like a football Phoenix from the ashes of defeat and...'

Zeb was doing the international hand signal for 'wrap it up'.

'And...And we will get you,' I said in actually quite a menacing voice.

Zeb was making cutting motions on his neck now.

'Get you,' I whispered as the waiter backed away from us, our drinks order forgotten.

Zeb put his head in his hands. 'Well, there goes our ten per cent, oh sociopath.'

'What did I do wrong?' I wailed.

'So many things that it is safer to just move on and not mull it over.'

The waiter returned and Zeb banned me from speaking to him on any subject, managing to get him back on side discussing some rubbish refereeing. He was so successful my lemonade arrived almost a second after I ordered it. The ice clinked against the edge of the glass as I sipped at it, the smell of grilled fish and flowers clashing in the evening air. We ordered the Egg Foo Yong and it was as fantastic as Zeb had promised: a light folded omelette filled with rice and meats and vegetables. It melted on my tongue and Zeb laughed as I shut my eyes and made 'nomming' noises after the first mouthful.

I put down my fork and wiped the corner of my mouth with a napkin. 'You are absolutely allowed to have a crush on this egg dish, it is incredible. If it were keen, I would ask it to move in with me.'

'Too slow, it would already be living with me. It's totally happy there.'

'Okay, fine, I will move in with you both and we can all be together.' I blushed as Zeb responded with, 'You're very welcome.'

I became aware of my pulse, my fingers and thumbs suddenly feeling foreign to me as I went to pick up the fork.

Zeb was telling me a story about Ahmad and his attempt to perform a magic trick with lighted sticks that had basically ended up almst burning his hands, but my laugh came slowly. I had been focused on his full mouth, hearing the words, but my reaction was impeded by random thoughts about his lips. *Oh man, Isobel, get a grip on yourself.*

My phone buzzed in my pocket and when Zeb went to the loo I checked it for messages. Mel asked whether Dex and her could join us for drinks somewhere.

As Zeb returned, so tall in this cosy space, his dark hair almost black in the light, I asked him. For a brief moment I hoped he would say no. There was something so magical about this place and I didn't want to share it.

'Of course,' Zeb said, following it up with another easy smile.

I texted her back and, half an hour later, Mel and Dex arrived, both beaming. Dex had changed into a light-blue shirt and jeans and Mel was wearing yellow crop trousers and a white cotton top. Her red hair winked from the fairy lights that had been switched on a few moments before.

Once the introductions had been done and we were settled at the table with drinks, it was clear that Mel and Dex were very much back on form. I loved them in this mood; gentle mocking, a brief squeeze of a leg or arm. There was such a tangible spark between them. They didn't have to change who they were around each other. They didn't have to strain for conversation or put on a false face. A thought flickered briefly as I looked over at Zeb. Then I raised my glass to them both.

'Here's to Dex coming out from LA,' I toasted.

'Yes,' Mel grinned, giving him a kiss on the cheek.

Conversation flowed easily and even on lemonade I felt giggly and punch drunk at times. Dex and Zeb were talking cameras and famous photographers. I hadn't known Dex was such an enthusiast and Zeb was leaning over the table, his voice passionate as he talked. 'The first photo must have been amazing, people seeing this image emerge like a miracle. I would pay a lot of money to go back there and be in that moment.'

'When was all that happening?' asked Mel, who had always had this random interest in historical facts. Well, facts generally.

'Start of the nineteenth century,' Zeb replied.

'Cool, although it wouldn't be my first choice.'

'Where would you go back to if you could time travel?' Zeb asked, his blue eyes darker in this light.

Mel thought for a second, glass to her lips. 'Further back,' she said eventually. 'Like the first time man ever made fire. That would have been a freaky night.'

'Iz?' Zeb asked, shifting his body towards me.

'Hogwarts,' I said without a pause.

'Er, we said the past not a fake world.'

'Ruin the game, Mr Fun Police, if you can go back to the medieval period and see the camera guy.'

'Er, more like the nineteenth century and his full name was Mr Niépce, thank you very much,'

'Well, whatever, your majesty. If you can do that, I want to go back to Hogwarts when Harry turned up.'

'But you know Harry and Hogwarts aren't real. In the actual real world. You do know this. Isobel.'

'Yes,' I said (quite slowly as, if I'm being honest with myself, I do secretly believe that if I hope enough somewhere Hogwarts does exist and one day I WILL receive my letter telling me I am a witch and I can go there and my patronus would be a squirrel). Note to self: do not admit to the time that I tried running at that wall in Kings Cross. That was a sprained ankle I could have avoided.

Zeb was laughing into his beer.

'How about you, Dex?' I said, sniffily turning away from Zeb.

'I'd go back and tell Hitler he was a jerk and no one likes him now.'

Mel wrapped an arm around his shoulders and squeezed. 'That'd show him,' she said. 'Okay, hello, I'd like to change mine. I would go back to the day before a day I knew all the lottery numbers and then dump you lot and go and live the dream on a yacht and be friends with celebrities like Madonna and Gwynnie. FYI I would totally know her well enough to call her that, and Madonna would be 'M Dog' and we would be like the Cool Girl Triumvirate and do yoga and stuff and make some kind of new gluten-free smoothie that makes you lose weight when you drink it.'

'What are you saying about our friendship?' I wailed in mock-horror. 'I could be like M Dog. I could wear my bra wrong and work on my abs. I would totally do that for you,' I said.

'Okay, fine.' She sighed. 'I won't go back and win the lottery and become friends with celebrities.'

'Yay,' Dex and I cheered.

'Why are you cheering, Dex?'

‘I don’t think I’d get a look in if Mel was hanging out with them.’

‘You totally would,’ said Mel, stirring her drink. She pointed her straw at him. ‘As long as you were a backing dancer – all celebrities seem to fall for the backing dancer. Or the bodyguard.’

‘Actually, I think that was just Whitney Houston,’ I pointed out.

‘What the hell is going on?’ asked Zeb to nobody.

The evening veered from one conversation to another and I hadn’t laughed this hard in weeks. I felt light-headed and full of declicious food, surrounded by friends and good thoughts. I had long since abandoned the lemonades and had drunk a delicious bottle of white wine. Everything felt woozy and brilliant. As the night wore on, Mel had started to look at Dex with INTENT and the tea lights had long since died. Mel and Dex left and Zeb and I stayed on for a few more minutes. I didn’t really want the night to end but I couldn’t be sure what Zeb was thinking. I wasn’t able to read his expression. He suggested we left and we got up. Thanking the waiter with a ‘Go Chelsea!’ Zeb steered me out by the shoulders before I made it any worse.

We wobbled up the narrow high street together, babbling and laughing. Ducking under a hanging basket, the trailing flowers tickled my face as we came to a stop outside my hotel. Feeling suddenly shy I looked towards the door. ‘This is me.’

‘Great,’ he said. He was standing so close. *WHEN DID HE GET SO CLOSE?* I felt all the breath leave my body as he seemed to lean in towards me. My brain was whizzing with thoughts such as *HE IS LEANING* and *IS THIS WHAT*

I WANT? and *IS THIS ACTUALLY MY HOTEL?* and *DOES MY BREATH SMELL OF FISH?* and *I LIKE HIS FACE.* My brain gets really shouty when it speeds up. He was still leaning and I started to close my eyes, felt a warmth spread through my stomach, reached a hand up.

'IZZZZZZZ!' A shout jolted me backwards.

'ISOBEL.'

'Yes,' I said, snapping to attention and looking into the semi-darkness behind Zeb. I couldn't see his face. Was he disappointed? Had he been leaning in to kiss me goodnight? Was I imagining things? Was I drunk? (Yes, but really, was I drunk and not realising he was just leaning because he was pulling a petal from my hair – those hanging baskets are basically a hazard – or was he not leaning but I was doing drunk leaning?)

'Iz, where are you, that is not our hotel,' came the call from the first-floor window of a hotel three doors back. Mel was dangling out of it in, I think, just an electric-blue bra.

'Awkward,' I laughed, looking back at Zeb.

Zeb tucked me into a quick embrace and I felt my body relax into his – the warmth of his chest underneath his thin shirt, his arms encircling me. He squeezed me and released me so that I felt all the breath I had been holding rush out in one go.

Turning back to the hotel, I said goodnight, wondering what I was feeling and what had just happened.

'Wait, Iz.' Zeb stopped me, his hand reaching out for mine.

I turned back, seeing him there, a new expression on his face. My insides turn to goo.

'Meet me tomorrow, I want to surprise you,' he said in a rush. 'Ten o'clock here, okay?'

I nodded wordlessly; I would have agreed to anything.

Turning back around, I walked quickly back to the hotel, pushing open the door and racing up the stairs wanting to tell Mel, wanting to run and jump on her bed and whoop.

Pushing open the bedroom door, Mel was standing in her dress, a small bag in her hand. She looked up. 'Hey,' she said grinning at me, an eyebrow raised in a question.

I couldn't help but grin. 'Hey.'

'As much as I desperately want to find out what is going on with you, missy, Dex has got a single room so I'm sneaking out to see him there to have all the sex, so talk to me more in the morning okay, babe.'

I let the sex and the babe thing go and let her kiss me on the cheek. 'Definitely, I'm glad for you guys,' I said as we hugged. 'About the togetherness not the sex bit,' I said into her hair as an afterthought.

'Me too.' Even in the semi-darkness I could see her eyes sparkling with it.

She padded out of the room and I changed and cleaned my teeth, my foamy mouth smiling back at me as I brushed. Turning off the lights I got into bed, my mind still running over the evening. As I lay looking up at the murky grey of the ceiling, I squeezed the bunched-up duvet in my hand and grinned to myself.

Chapter 39

Where are you? A

We're at the bar if you wanted to join :) A

Dunccan said yOuu h8ot an I aghree weree r uu/ :) Aa

We7"s a pi99cp a

Really enjoyed last night. Will be picking you up for the surprise later this morning... Z x

Waking to the buzz of a text, I lay, head resting on the pillow, one eye open, grasping with an arm for the phone I thought might be on the bedside table. Feeling my way round a Kindle, a now-empty plastic glass, coins and the lamp, I emerged with it in my hand, lifting it in front of the one open eye and reading. Frowning in confusion as I scrolled through them, I couldn't help smiling slowly as I read the last one. Surprise! Who doesn't love a surprise? (Exception: those with a serious heart condition.)

An hour later and I was pulling on a cotton dress, the green straps making my freckled shoulders look even browner. Drying my hair quickly and throwing on some blusher and mascara, I felt bolder; chin up, shoulders back, I was excited about the day ahead. Grabbing a bag, I left the room, noting the satisfying slap of my flip-flops as I made my way down the stairs, scooting past a mop, the smell of disinfectant in the air.

Emerging into the day, scorching and bright, I plunged my hand into my bag for my sunglasses, wincing as I grappled with them.

'Isobel.'

Andrew was outside the hotel door, a pamphlet in one hand, a foot up on the hotel wall behind him. He removed it and stepped towards me.

'Oh!' I started, the sight of him throwing me into a spin. His sandy hair and pale skin was in stark contrast to the man I had been expecting. I readjusted my thoughts, scrabbling for why he was here.

'I've been waiting for you,' he said in a jumble. 'I wanted to see you today.'

'Oh.' I could feel my eyes widen as he looked at me, pink in his cheeks as he waited for a response.

'Today, as in today, today.'

'Er...yes.' He played with the button on his shirt distractedly, like he was tweaking a shirt nipple.

Trying not to be distracted by it, I went to explain: 'I sort of have plans and well, I wasn't...'

Andrew touched my forearm. 'Iz, I wanted to talk, I'm going back to England in a couple of days and, well, you see, I thought maybe...look, come out on the boat and...'

He was going back to England. I blinked at this news. Andrew Parker was leaving.

'Home,' I interrupted.

'Well, yes, I have to get back, start lesson planning for the new term, you know, but I wanted to see if, well why don't we...' He stumbled over his words, waving the pamphlet round as he did so. It was on conservation. There was a turtle caught in a net, one sad eye looking through the space between. It seemed to be saying, 'Help me.' I kept staring at it as Andrew kept talking about the new term, leaving, going to the beach. I had come all this way, I had found him. All those moments in LA when I had wondered how my life had spun out of control, all those memories of us as children and he would leave me and it would be over. I would be back to the start with nothing to show for it.

Andrew finished and was clearly waiting for me to respond. He was leaving. I had to see him if he was leaving. I would have to tell Zeb. I thought of Zeb's roll of laughter last night, me clutching my stomach as hiccoughy tears filled my eyes. I wanted to see him, wanted to see his surprise.

'Andrew, look, I'm sorry,' I said quickly. 'I sort of promised someone.'

Andrew deflated in front of me, one hand combing through his hair.

'I could catch up with you later and maybe...'

'But we want you there. I want you there,' he said, his voice getting higher. Oh god, how long had I waited for this moment? He wanted me there. He was asking me. *What was I doing?* I felt my body tear into two and as I was wringing my hands like a clichéd heroine in a movie, Zeb appeared behind Andrew, in khaki shorts and a loose cotton shirt, a huge smile on his face, his camera slung over his shoulder. He lifted his sunglasses up as he moved towards me and opened his mouth to say something, and then closed it again, his face guarded as he took in Andrew.

'Isobel.'

'Hi,' I said, feeling so much emotion in those two letters.

'Hey.' He nodded to Andrew.

Andrew ignored him, focusing his eyes on me.

I stared at the pamphlet. Christ. I *was* that turtle.

'Andrew was just telling me he was leaving soon,' I said, feeling hopeless, my stomach swirling.

'I wanted to see her today,' Andrew said, not looking at Zeb, eyes still trained on me.

I smiled weakly, my cheeks straining with the effort.

Zeb didn't say anything and I filled the gap. 'I said I couldn't because of…' I indicated him.

Andrew turned to him. 'If it could wait, mate.'

'Iz,' Zeb said, looking at me, 'it's fine, you do what you need to do.'

I wrung my hands again. What I needed to do? *Was that the same as what I wanted to do?* If I was being honest, what I wanted right now was to be that girl over there with a shopping bag. Her up-coming decisions looked easier:

skimmed or semi-skimmed, with bits or smooth. Could I be her, please?

Zeb was there, waiting, and Andrew was staring at me again.

'Make a decision, Iz,' Zeb said quietly.

My brain was screaming a hundred different things, my palms felt sweaty. 'Well if he's leaving, I...but...' Images from last night piled through my self-conscious again like a hazy, warm memory.

Zeb nodded once. 'I get it,' he said, hitching the camera bag up on his shoulder. 'You two have a great day.' He smiled, raking a hand through his hair. He nodded at me, mouth half-attempting a smile.

I watched him walk back the way he came, his trainers leaving sandy marks in the track, his hair curling at the back. I took a step in his direction, wanting to run alongside him, to join him.

Andrew was grinning widely. 'Great,' he said. 'Now you're free, where do you want to go?'

Dear diary,

I still miss Andrew all the time. I went to the pier on my own today and looked at the claw machine with the soft toys underneath and I remembered the best day when the machine had got stuck and Andrew and I had played and played and he won the rabbit holding a heart on my bed that said 'Best Friends' for me.

Sometimes I want to run away and search for him, but I know Mum and Dad would be sad if I left as when we watched 'Annie' together, Mum kept hugging me when Annie ran away and kissed me on the head lots. Maybe he will come back and I won't need to run away and find him. If I concentrate really hard I think I can send him messages to get him to come back. It used to work when we thought of a number out of ten. He used to guess right all the time.

I'll keep thinking of him over and over and maybe if I keep doing that – POOF! – he will appear.

I x

Chapter 40

We walked into the jungle and I tried to re-trace our steps and find the waterfall again. I didn't know why I had thought of that place immediately but as we moved through the humid forest, swatting insects that hummed in front of our faces, I wondered if it had been such a good idea. Andrew seemed to be approaching the day with all the energy of a Geography teacher running a field trip and we had to stop four times to talk about the different variety of plants.

I didn't really know what was wrong with me; I should be approaching the trip in a more positive way. I had got what I wanted, after all, and knew I was being churlish, pouting every time Andrew wanted to show me another deciduous tree.

Andrew was here, the man I had travelled across the globe to find, was offering to spend the day with me and I knew I should be lighter. I recognised this mood, used to be like this when Stewie talked to me about flight paths and air traffic control. I hated myself when I did that. I gave myself an internal pep talk, a lot of quiet back-slapping, and to show it had worked went overkill when he pointed out a plant that could turn into actual soap. 'WOAHHHHHH.' He took a step backwards as I rubbed it over my palms and stared at him with wide eyes. 'IT'S LIKE ACTUAL MAGIC.'

After a few false starts, ending in walls of bracken and some vicious-looking spiky bushes, we found the little copse, the ground speckled with shadows, the waterfall tumbling over the rocks and into the pool below. It was as glorious as I remembered and, as I crunched over the dried mud and weeds, my damp skin craved the chill of the pool, only the odd leaf disrupting its surface.

'Waterfalls are formed when a river is young so this one would have been made hundreds, maybe thousands, of years ago.'

'Gosh!'

I went to remove my top and shorts, feeling strangely embarrassed all of a sudden, as if on automatic. Andrew gave me a tight smile as he did the same and an awkward silence descended. Like we were nineteenth-century newly weds on the first night, slowly undressing for each other, snatching glances as we stepped out of our clothes. We kicked off our shoes, hollow laughs.

Stepping onto a flat rock, slippery, the algae clinging to its edges, I gingerly moved across to plunge in. Andrew was behind me, swearing as he stubbed a toe on something.

'You alright?' I asked over my shoulder, wondering whether this had been such a good idea.

'Yes.'

'Okey doke, Batman, ha, ha.' *Really, Iz – Batman?*

I stepped into the water, gasping as the cold surged through my body, legs practically numb and skin covered in goosebumps. Wading out to the waterfall, glad to be moving, my legs pumping in a breaststroke, warming my body, I thought back to the last time I had been here. It seemed so long ago really, stumbling into Zeb naked as a naked thing, bristling as he'd teased me. Turning to say something to Andrew, to drag myself back to the present, I frowned as I saw him on the flat rocks beyond, one toe poised over the water, his arms crossed over this chest.

'All okay?'

'Yes.'

'Honestly,' I said, swimming back towards him. 'It's pretty cold but amazing once you get in.'

It *was* amazing. I had never felt so clean. I felt my whole body was being cleansed from the inside out with fresh, pure water.

'I was wondering,' Andrew said, foot back out on the side, 'about lizards, whether they come here.' He peered into the dark-green water as if searching for them and I felt my heart drum a little faster. I thought back to the enormous monitor lizard I had seen – he had been a sizable animal – and wondered.

'I don't like them.'

'Well, I think they'd be more scared of us than we are of them,' I said with a confidence I didn't quite feel. Lifting my leg sharply as I imagined something brushing against it, my feeling of calm relaxation seemed fragile. Andrew had managed to find a rock to stand on and his ankles were now submerged.

'Maybe I'll just paddle,' he said, smiling at me and lowering one foot, eyes wide, before snatching it back. 'Or sit on the side.' He scooted over and sat on a rock, leaving wet feet marks, then he looked at me treading water in the pool, his chin in his hands.

Feeling like a nana after about thirty seconds, I swam to the edge and lifted myself out, plucking the bikini bottoms back into line and hoping he wasn't able to make out any cellulite in the dappled light. Wrapping myself in my towel and putting my flip-flops back on, I shook out my hair and smiled at him.

'Well that was lovely,' I said in my most-hearty voice. 'Ready to go back?' I asked, hoping that perhaps Dex and Mel might be around and we could spend some time with them. Not that it wasn't nice seeing Andrew alone like this but maybe they would make things easier. Then things would flow more easily and I wouldn't have this slightly knotted feeling in my stomach.

'Okay,' he said, standing up and walking across to me.

Pulling on my clothes, I could feel his presence inches away from me as I knotted the tie on my skirt and readjusted my bra strap.

'Right,' I said in my hearty best English voice. 'Let's go what-ho. Ha, ha!' *What was wrong with me?*

We left the copse and made our way back to the narrow track, snaking down past trees and bushes, the odd rustle above us and the constant chatter of insects all around us. As the path narrowed out, we walked together, the sun beating a path through the canopy of trees, the air still close and muggy. I took a sip of water and focused on what Andrew was saying. Something about fresh water supplies; apparently they were falling at an alarming rate.

'We should be worried,' he said solemnly to me and I nodded my agreement.

'Hmm,' I added to show Real Concern.

My arms swung loosely at my sides as the path flattened out and we could see the hint of blue sea beyond, a couple of colourful rooftops. We were back at Juara beach and I felt a lifting in my chest. Oh god, I had to say something, I realised with a sinking heart, this was just hopeless. I could feel the same irritation sweeping over me when I couldn't force the feelings. This would be like Stewie all over again and it wouldn't be his fault; we just weren't compatible. I looked at Andrew's profile, his straight nose, the wave in his hair – and started to speak. 'Andrew, do you think maybe, well we are different people now aren't we, from our childhoods I mean...' I was babbling, I knew I was babbling, but this was just awkward. *How would I phrase the next part? Could I just say something about how he must have realised it too, that we didn't have an enormous amount in common and...*

Something brushed my hand. Andrew's hand. I jerked a fraction and then left my arm frozen there, wondering if it had been a mistake or not. He brushed it again and then suddenly we were holding hands, interlocking fingers, not quite matching so that a couple were just poking out. I didn't want to readjust it though, was holding my breath at the same time. Holding hands was progress, major progress. This was intent. Andrew definitely liked me. Our hands were slippery with water and sweat from the walk, but they were glued together now, the grip firm. *Wow, this is strange, not what I had expected. Had I read this situation completely wrong?*

My head felt full. The memories from our childhood, those safe feelings conjured up by talking about the past, our life in England, all swept into my consciousness. I felt a slow smile spread across my face, my cheeks lifting and I looked up at him through my lashes feeling like that child again, uncertain and tentative. I couldn't really believe this was really happening. I had come all this way and now I was making my dream a reality. My fantasy man in the cottage with roses, the relaxing English idyll that could be mine. I mean, we didn't have a lot in common but we could find things. And, anyway, those kind of details would work themselves out. *Wouldn't they?*

We got to the dirt track that headed back to the hotel and wavered.

'Beach?' he suggested.

'Good idea.'

He turned to me and I paused before looking up at him. So close I could make out the individual hairs of blond stubble, see a crack in his bottom lip, his lashes lighter towards the ends. Leaning down, he kissed me gently on the mouth. My body froze and initially I stiffened, felt an awkward clash on my gums and then tried to relax into it. He pulled away pretty quickly, a hand on his neck, a blush starting at his cheeks.

'Sorr...' I started.

He moved in again and my eyes remained open in surprise. In the distance I could make out a familiar blur, someone turning and walking away. I frowned and went to close my eyes, concentrate on the kiss. I was K.I.S.S.I.N.G Andrew Parker up a tree I sang to myself and then giggled once. *Oh no. Don't giggle at him, Iz.* Too late, he had pulled away again.

'Sorry,' I repeated. 'Just unexpected,' I said.

'I like you, Isobel,' he said, one arm around my shoulder.

'Me too,' I said, nodding energetically. Was I nodding more than I should? Had I imagined kissing someone else?

We walked on in silence and made our way down to the beach where, further along the sand, Duncan could be seen playing Frisbee with Liz. I say playing, Duncan appeared to be mostly firing the Frisbee at Liz who spent much of the time scooping it off the sand. Duncan turned, spotted us and rolled his eyes in exasperation. I gave them a half-wave and Andrew ignored them both. Turning his back, he moved in the opposite direction and I hurried to catch him up.

'Shall we join them?' I asked, sort of hoping the answer might be yes. *Wow, when had I wanted to spend time with Liz?*

'No, they're better off alone,' he said, flicking out his towel in an angry snap and carefully brushing sand off its corners.

I flapped out my towel and cringed as tiny grains of sand trickled over the area he had just cleared. He was clearly trying not to look cross, but his back shoulder muscles were all tense and his mouth was fixed in a line. I padded around, trying desperately hard not to disrupt the sand further, gently lowering myself on to my towel, dragging my bag slowly towards me and rootling around for my iPod.

We spent most of the day reading or listening to music. There was one quite cute moment where I had offered

Andrew one of my headphones and we had bent our heads together to listen to 'Happy' but then I had kicked sand with my tapping toes by accident and Andrew had to rear up and tidy again so the moment hadn't lasted. Still, that had been sweet. We had looked like central characters in a rom-com for like three minutes. We hadn't talked much the rest of the time and when Duncan had come over to say hi, Andrew had sort of growled his responses so I figured something was up. Deciding to act like the girlfriend, I broached the subject when he had left.

'So what's that about?' I asked, clearing my throat.

'What?' Andrew played it dumb.

'You two,' I motioned down the beach with a hand, 'are you not talking?'

''s fine,' Andrew grunted, clearly not in the mood to share.

'You can tell me,' I said in my most gentle voice, reaching a hand across to place over his. I slightly misjudged it and I ended up holding on to his forearm which would have to do.

'It's nothing, I'm just not in the mood to hang out with other people today,' he said, glancing down the beach where Liz was staring back at us, a Frisbee hanging by her side.

'Oh right,' I said, thinking he wanted to spend time with me. *Cuuuuutttteeeee.* This had all happened so quickly and I lay back down listening to the beats thump through my head, feeling the sun warm my body, my heels resting on the hot sand. I was here, in paradise, with Andrew Parker who wanted to just spend some alone time with me. This is what I'd wanted, I reminded myself. I glanced sideways at him. He was staring, unseeing, straight ahead at the ocean, his mouth turned down.

Sitting in the shade of the cafe at lunch, I watched the tide draw in, washing rhythmically over the same sand, the darkened patch ebbing backwards as the water rolled out again, then the same process all over again like the sea gently breathing in and out, in and out. Looking at the motion settled me and the whole world seemed calmer for it. Zeb and I could do a piece on it, something about the sea, the way it makes you feel. Then I realised that Zeb might not want to. I felt my stomach tighten at the thought that somewhere out there he might be cross with me. I wondered what his surprise might have been.

I hadn't seen Mel or Dex all day but was pleased if that meant they were spending some quality time together. I couldn't imagine a more perfect place for two people really in love, the places they could explore. I thought of the waterfalls, caves, the underwater world I had visited in these past weeks and grinned to myself. Andrew was chewing on the last of the baguette we had shared for lunch and grinned back, red onion marmalade stuck in his teeth. I indicated it with a finger and he picked at it before rubbing fruitlessly over his teeth with a napkin. It made me giggle and he excused himself and went to the loo.

Feeling guilty for laughing, I sucked on the last of my strawberry and banana smoothie, hearing the gurgle of air in the straw and then the silence that followed as I waited for him to come back. This was going well, wasn't it? I mean, we were bound to not have loads to say as we were still getting to know each other. And it felt nice, him sitting across the way from me, eating companionably. I mean, we had shared a baguette which boded well. I was sure there was a phrase about people who share food having successful marriages or something. I hopped up when I made out Mel walking past on the track.

'Mel,' I called, shading my eyes with one hand as I emerged into the sunlight.

'Hey.' She grinned, punching me good-naturedly on the top of the arm. 'You're here,' she said.

'Er yes,' I said rubbing at the spot. 'No need to slap me round the face to double-check.'

'I missed you.' She grinned.

'Hardly.' I laughed, recognising the rosy glow in her cheeks, the glint in her eye. 'I take it you and Dex are back on form?'

She grinned even more widely, her white teeth flashing. 'Hell yes, I had forgotten how brilliant he was in bed too, we've been at it all morning. I can barely walk straight.'

I clapped both hands over my ears in mock-protest. 'Mel,' I whined. Then I noticed something – a spark, a momentary glint. I lowered both hands slowly, eyes trained on the spot. Mel shifted on to one foot, a shy, uncertain smile now waiting for my reaction.

'What,' I said, holding up her left arm, 'is THAT?' I peered forward and took in the beautiful ring. A diamond seemed to be suspended in a ring of silver. It was stunning. 'It's gorgeous,' I breathed out. 'Does this mean...?'

Mel bit her lip and then nodded once. 'We talked and talked and well then he did that thing I love with his tong—'

'Melissa Conboy!' I shouted.

'Ha, ha, he didn't, Iz, he didn't. It was amazing, actually, he walked me down to the beach this morning. I was sooo annoyed as it was like the middle of the night and he had made me sit on the sand and as the sun came up I saw he had lined up all these pebbles that said "Just Marry Me" and then he got down on one knee with this whole speech planned about my mum and my fears and the fact that he never really wanted anything to change and I just found myself saying "Yes, YES,"' she repeated laughing as I squeezed her tightly.

'Yay, yay, oh WOW!' I said, holding her at arm's length. 'That is brilliant. You two are completely perfect and it will be fabulous, I know it, I know it.'

'Yes, so do I,' she said, the happiness bursting out of her every pore.

'I'm glad, I'm glad, I'm so GLAD.'

Mel laughed and hugged me again then, drawing back, she looked strangely serious all of a sudden. 'And where have you been?' she asked.

'With Andrew.'

'Oh.'

The air felt thick with something I couldn't put my finger on. 'What?' I asked.

Mel avoided my eye. 'I thought. It's nothing really.'

'Mel,' I whined, knowing when she said it was nothing it was always, ALWAYS something.

'Well I bumped into Zeb earlier. What happened with you guys?'

'What did he say?' I bristled.

'Not a lot.' She sighed. 'Did you guys fight?'

'No. Nothing happened,' I said, crossing my arms over my chest. 'Why? What did he say?'

'Not much. Well, he made a comment about you and...' She jerked her head over towards the cafe. 'So,' she dropped her voice to a whisper, 'is it on?'

I scraped the floor with a toe. 'Yeah I think so, he seems different, keen.' I looked up at Mel needing reassurance, a big grin. I thought I detected a momentary flash of something else but then she took my hands and squeezed them. 'Well if it's what you want,' she said, excited for me. 'That's great.'

I nodded quickly as she said it. 'Great,' I repeated. It *was* great, wasn't it?

'Zeb said he was heading back,' Mel added in a rush. 'Said goodbye to me.'

Jerking my head as I heard the words, I felt a sharp sting in my chest. *He had said goodbye, to Mel and not me. He was going*. My brain was clouding with images and questions again and I was slow to respond.

'Leaving? He didn't say.'

'I think he came to find you earlier but you were er...busy.'

I knew for certain Zeb had been the figure I had seen in the distance. He had seen the kiss. He knew I really was with Andrew. I held a hand up to twiddle with my necklace, rubbing the pendant back and forward like a worry bead.

'Oh,' I muttered, feeling a gloom descend over the day. *Why was I feeling this now?* I knew I had made the decision this morning and, anyway, maybe the feelings I'd felt weren't reciprocated, I might have read too much into things. And Andrew was here, offering what I had come all this way to find. I had to give it a chance, had to believe in it.

I swallowed slowly, plastering a smile back on my face. 'Well hopefully I'll see him before he goes.'

'Yeah, I liked him,' Mel said, pursing her lips as if she was about to say more.

'Look, I better get back, Andrew will think I've run off.' I laughed, the noise sounding hollow. 'We'll catch up later today?'

Mel nodded. 'Definitely.'

'Now, go be with your fiancé,' I grinned.

'Oh I am so not using that word.' She shivered.

'Okay, babe!'

Laughing, I turned back to the cafe and pushed through the door, my eyes readjusting to the shady interior, two silhouetted figures standing opposite each other with their hands on their hips. It was Andrew and Liz. I sidled over, feeling my forehead crease as I took in Liz's expression. She looked like someone had stolen her Sunrise Muffin.

'Hi,' I said, waving both hands as if to emphasise the point.

She didn't look at me but continued to glare at Andrew. If looks could kill he should be clutching his stomach right about now and keeling over.

Andrew was staring back, his face set, a steely look in his eye. I hadn't seen him like that, so fired up. I stood next to him and he put his arm around my shoulder. It still felt a little foreign, but I tried to relax into it. It seemed to have broken the spell as Liz looked at the arm, back at him and then turned quickly and left, wiping her face as she walked back on to the beach.

'Was she okay?' I asked. I mean, Liz and I were never going to be best friends but she looked upset.

Andrew didn't reply.

'Has anything happened between you guys?' Andrew wasn't looking at me, seeming to be sneaking a peek in the direction Liz had left. 'Andrew,' I said gently, reaching for his arm. 'It's okay, if something's happened you can tell me.'

He looked down at my arm as if it were something he had never seen before. 'It's nothing,' he said after a pause.

It was clearly something.

I took a breath. 'Well if you need to tal—'

'She's all over Duncan,' he said, an unpleasant sneer to his voice I'd never heard before.

'I'm sure not,' I said, surprised. Liz had never shown an interest in Duncan. I realised, with a flash of guilt, she had only ever had eyes for Andrew.

Did Andrew like Liz? Was he only here with me to make her jealous?

'Hey,' I continued. 'What happened between you two?'

'I really don't want to talk about it,' he said, his mouth still in a thin line.

What was going on?

'So!' I clapped my hands, realising I had better change the subject. 'What shall we get up to this afternoon? Snorkelling? I know a great place,' I babbled, determined to break this strained silence.

He seemed to jerk out of his reverie for a moment. 'Snorkelling.'

Thank goodness, I thought, glad for a second to have an excuse to leave this atmosphere. *Oh that couldn't be good.*

'Great,' I said, 'I'll get my things.'

Things stayed the same for much of the afternoon. We had stopped the boat in a deserted bay around the corner from

Juara. Andrew seemed to be in the same mood, answering questions and throwing me smiles but not really present. I began to wonder whether I had read all the signals wrong, had misunderstood him this morning, but he kept repeating that he wanted to be there when I checked.

'So, seriously, what was that with Liz earlier?' I said in the middle of a never-ending conversation about sea algae.

'What?' Andrew looked at me sharply, brown eyes piercing.

'Well I wondered if anything had happened. I thought she looked cross.'

Andrew grunted something in response, mumbling into his chest.

I took a gulp. 'I thought maybe Liz liked you, you know, that's why she was getting upset?' I suggested quietly, the realisation creeping over me more and more. All those times they had been whispering, walking together, eyes catching.

He didn't respond, looked out to the sea not meeting my eye.

'I obviously picked up on something that wasn't there,' I said, forcing myself to let out a light laugh.

Again he didn't respond. Then, after a moment, he shook his head. 'She likes Duncan,' he said in a quiet voice.

'How do you know?' I asked, realising I was getting somewhere.

It should hurt more than this. Andrew liking Liz should hurt me more. And if it doesn't then...I let that thought be swept away as Andrew continued.

'I saw them together laughing and she says, well it doesn't

matter, it's obvious...' He tailed off, perhaps embarrassed that he was sharing so much.

'I don't think it is,' I said slowly, realising that what I was about to say was going against everything I had rushed out here to achieve. 'Look,' I said, turning to him. 'This,' I said pointing to him and to me and having a horrendous Randy-related flashback as I realised it sounded like I was about to dump him.

Andrew obviously realised it, too. 'Don't, Isobel.'

'No, I think we both know I need to say this,' I continued, swallowing quickly. 'We were great friends in the past, lovely, lovely friends,' I said, my voice softening as I remembered our shared childhood, the boy I had so loved. 'But we are different people now and we don't have a great deal in common.' I laughed looking round at the boat.

'But I was thinking about England, about when we go back,' Andrew said.

We I thought. *He said 'we'. We were never going to be a 'We'.*

'Who do you really want to go back to England with? It's not me Andrew, is it? I can tell you like her, and it's okay, she likes you.'

I let that thought settle, watching his face lift a fraction. He did like her. 'Do you really think?' he asked and in that moment I felt we were finally connecting in the way we used to. We were finally swapping each other's secrets. I took his hand. 'I really do, and you are perfect for each other. Truly.' And as I said it, I knew with certainty it was true. They were suited to each other.

Andrew's face split into a smile and he looked at me, the boy with the wave in his hair pulling me in for a hug. 'Thanks,

Isobel,' he said and I felt we could be back in Southsea, our skinny legs dangling over the side of the pier.

'My pleasure,' I said next to his ear.

'What about you?' Andrew asked, as he revved up the engine to move on.

'What do you mean?' I asked, knowing perfectly well what he meant. To avoid talking about it I laughed at him. 'Anyway, before I think of someone else, I should probably ask you to take back your curse.'

Andrew's eyebrows joined together. 'What curse?'

I looked at him, aghast. 'I can't believe you don't remember that. You cursed me. Just after we got married in the playground. And then you married Jenny.'

He chuckled. 'Oh my god, I remember those weddings. Wow, we were weird kids.' He snuck a look at me. 'Er about Jenny...she meant nothing.'

'I know,' I said solemnly. 'I forgive you, BUT a curse is a curse.'

'Well,' he said, squaring his shoulders and holding out a hand to place on the top of my head. 'I take it back. I absolutely take it back and hope you find the perfect someone.'

'Thanks,' I said my voice smaller suddenly, my chest expanding with a feeling of foreboding. I knew who my perfect someone was, was it too late?

'And that someone might be...Duncan?' Andrew hinted with a smile at the same time as another face filled up my whole head, stopped my breathing. *Was it too late?*

I shook an answer. 'No, god no.' A laugh, a click of a camera, a pair of blue eyes. I realised with growing panic that I might have lost them.

'Do you mind if we go back?' I asked suddenly. 'I think I need to see someone.'

'Of course,' Andrew said, turning the boat around and heading back round the coast.

I sat back, listening to the engine turning over, the bounce of the waves, the spray from the sides as we skirted the island.

'Hey...' Andrew said a few minutes later, squinting as he stared at the shore. 'Is that Melissa?'

I looked and sure enough it was Mel, waving with both hands, big waves which at the moment in my mind seemed the universal sign for: THERE IS A SHARK BEHIND YOUR BOAT. I whipped my head first one way and the next but the turquoise-blue water seemed empty of any fins and yet Mel was still waving. Panic seized me as Dex joined her, both beckoning us. *Had something horrible happened?* I thought of Mum at home, Moregran. *Had someone called*?

I splashed breathless into the shallows and waded across to them. Mel was up to her knees and looking at me, her face confirming my worst fears. Something had happened.

'What is it?' I gabbled, scared now.

'It's Zeb,' she said. 'Ahmad took him to Tekek, there's a clinic there but he said he was bad...'

Cold seeped into my chest despite the sun beating down at me relentlessly. 'What do you mean "bad"?'

'I don't know exactly, I couldn't understand...he said he was grey, not breathing. He looked scared, Iz, he seemed scared.'

I felt my knees wobble. 'I have to see if he's okay,' I said, running onto the sand and not waiting for anything, just needing to get back to the hotel and get to Tekek.

Andrew and Mel were calling me as I stumbled across the sand, my ankle twisting as I moved quickly over the uneven beach, sporadic weeds bursting through as I neared the track back to the hotel. Rushing past Reception and straight up the stairs, I back-tracked as I noticed the cards in the hallway. Phone numbers– people who might be able to get me there.

I dialled a couple, drumming my fingers on the wall in frustration as they just rung on and on. Mel appeared in the hotel doorway, hovering uncertainly at my shoulder as I looked at her with wide eyes, the mobile held up to my face. Everything felt speeded up and when I finally got through to someone on the end, it was all I could do but gabble urgently down the phone, the hotel name, the clinic in Tekek. I think he sensed the panic and a rusting 4x4 was screeching to a stop outside the hotel within ten minutes.

I bundled myself into the car, wet, sandy hair scraped back into a ponytail, a T-shirt flung on over some shorts. Mel gave me a quick kiss and it was only really then that I remembered Andrew.

'Tell him I'll be in touch and tell him to go for it.'

Mel frowned.

'He'll understand,' I said. 'Please tell him.'

'I will, of course I will,' she said, hugging me again and then slamming the door.

Mel's pale face, stark against her bright-red hair, grew smaller as we veered down the track and then disappeared from view as we bumped into the jungle and off to Tekek and the doctor's clinic. I was squeezing my knuckles tightly, mouthing a prayer to nobody, hoping that nothing serious had happened and that Mel had been wrong and he was alright. The driver met my gaze in the mirror a few times but the combination of my pallid face and short responses soon put a stop to too much conversation. My head was just too full to concentrate and all I could hear was Tekek, Tekek as we careered and jarred through the track of tree roots, the road growing wider and smoother as we neared the main village, a large dirty sign – a red cross on a white background – confirming that we had arrived.

Thanking the driver who seemed to have halved the cost, I leaped out of the vehicle and ran towards the clinic, pushing open the main double doors, feeling the weight of them, suckered to the sides. Breathlessly I approached the reception desk, littered with peeling notices of people coughing into tissues, vicious-looking needles and more.

'Please,' I said, thankful no one else was there waiting. 'I need to see Zeb, Zebedee, he came here earlier, he—'

The short nurse, who was wearing round glasses, held up a hand authoritatively. I screeched to a halt.

'He come in. We get him to Mersing, mainland hospital, very good.'

Hospital.

The rest of her words seemed to slow and blur in front of me as I realised Mel had been right. Something serious had happened.

'What happened? What's wrong with him?' I asked, sucking in my breath and biting on my lip. Her answer seemed to drag out of her.

'He need doctor. Emergency, emergency,' she said which just made my heart pound more.

‘How do I get to him?’ I asked, feeling fretful tears spark the back of my eyes.

‘Ferry leave, later ferry.’

‘I’m sorry?’ I said, confused.

‘You,’ she pointed. ‘Get later ferry. Mersing.’

‘Right, right,’ I said, wishing I owned a helicopter.

I knew where the ferries left from and I backed out of the clinic, turning into the road, the full heat of the day wrapping itself around me, suffocating me as I walked, half-jogged to the jetty.

The Mersing ferry was going to be another hour and I had never felt time lag this slowly before, dozens of images of Zeb running through my mind. Zeb, energetic, bursting with positivity, I couldn’t imagine him grey, hurt. I felt an ache in my body, clutched my stomach, concerned I was about to be sick. I tried to push the images away, not focus on it but all I could see was his face.

I called Mel. ‘I’m going to Mersing,’ I said.

‘That’s the mainland, Iz.’

‘I know, I just, I’m going,’ I said firmly. ‘I’ll call you when I know more.’ I heard Dex in the background; he sounded worried. They both did and I didn’t want to stay on the line with them any more; I wanted to stay focused. I needed to get there.

‘I’ll be okay,’ I reassured them.

Nodding and hanging up, I breathed in and out deeply, trying to calm myself. *It might just be a precaution, they might send lots of people to Mersing*.

The ferry trip itself was dreadful. I felt nauseous from the moment I sat below deck, in an unmoving plastic seat, a faded life raft on a peg to my right, a sign bolted into the wall below a smeared porthole telling me what to do in case of an emergency. *It has already happened*, I thought. I didn't know what I might find. I knew I had to go there, he would be alone and, at this thought, the fact that he had been injured with no one there to go with him made my eyes sting. I balled up my fists and flexed my fingers, repeating the action, fiddling with the hem of my vest top.

God, what had I been thinking? Wasting all this time in paradise running around trying to make things work with a man I had lost all connection to while a man who got me, really understood me and, better than that, seemed to like me for me, had been there all the time.

The ferry ride seemed to go on forever. *COULD YOU BE SLOWER, FERRY?* It was as if we were crossing an ocean rather than a thin strip of sea: it seemed the mainland would never come. And then from the window I could make out the island, bleeding into view, slowly taking shape, the rise and fall of the land, then the tiny squares of houses as we gained distance, a thin strip of yellow beach, dots of people and then the covered jetty, hearing the sound of the idling engine as the ferry was steered carefully past idle boats in the water, seaweed and fishing nets hanging loosely from hooks by the jetty. I had raced up to the top deck, desperate to be the first off and into Mersing.

Thanking the crew, who had pointed me in the direction of a taxi that could take me to the main hospital, I paid hastily. Running down the jetty, past people rolling suit-cases, holding sunhats, enormous smiles on their faces like nothing had happened today, like nothing was wrong.

Sitting in the air-conditioned cool of the taxi, the fabric

patched and worn, covered in part by a faded patterned throw, I strained my neck to catch the first glimpse of the hospital, saw the red cross in the distance, an agonising wait at a traffic light nearby. An ambulance stood motionless outside glass double doors as people moved in and out of them, unhurried, as I tapped out a rhythm in my lap. The nerves were really mounting now. *What would I find? What was wrong with him?* The taxi driver gave me the occasional encouraging smile in the driving mirror but I found my face frozen in response, drained of the recent tan, my eyes startled. I turned away, focusing only on the entrance and praying to someone, anyone, to help him.

Rushing in across the polished parquet floor of the hospital, I waited in line, balancing my weight on one foot then another as the queue for reception worked its way through. A large white board behind the reception desk had names, dates and phrases written on to it in columns. I tried to make out anything familiar but soon gave up. It was a hopeless jumble of felt-pen markings and I might have been reading hieroglyphs. Doctors and nurses moved past in corridors off to the right and left, serious faces, a trolley of towels being pushed, another helping a little boy on crutches. *Where was he? Was he here?* For a brief moment I felt a genuine terror freeze my insides. *Had he made it? Had he survived the journey?*

Starting to panic and fret, I found myself jabbering at the young nurse behind the counter. He had an open face and was trying to keep up with me, his head tilted sympathetically to one side as his eyes creased. I didn't know where to begin and had simply repeated his name

Zeb and Tioman over and over again, hearing my voice as if it were a stranger's in a strangled tone I didn't recognise. *I had to calm down*, I thought, taking a breath and trying to compose myself. 'A photographer, Zeb...'

His eyes seemed to spark at the last and when I said photographer he repeated, 'English photographer, you are?'

'Wife,' I blurted, needing that to have the desired effect. How could I see him otherwise? They might refuse. He was here. He was here and this man knew who I was talking about. 'Is he okay? Can I see him? What happened?' I fired the questions back at him but the man seemed to not understand more.

'Photographer. Wife,' he said, standing up and moving round the desk. 'I show you.'

And he left his post to take me, muttering endless thanks at him down the corridor and into another ward, the signs translated into English but my mind too slow and fuzzy to really take anything in.

'He have head,' the nurse said, craning round and tapping himself on his own head. 'Head.'

'I know,' I said, not keeping up. That was good, wasn't it? Heads were pretty vital.

'He have head,' he tapped again and poked his tongue out a bit, rolled his eyes.

'Head,' I said, tapping my own now. 'A head injury?' I guessed, heart drumming as I quickened my pace. *Oh god, had he hurt his head?* The worst thoughts crashed through my consciousness and I found myself stopping, still in the middle of the corridor.

The nurse had run on ahcad and now did a double-take over his shoulder, no doubt noticing I was missing. He moved back towards me slowly. 'It's okay.' His smile was gentle and uncertain. He nodded once at me and beckoned me to follow with a jerk of his head. 'It's okay,' he repeated and I kept those words on a loop as I fell back into step with him. *It was okay, it would be okay, he was okay.*

The nurse pushed open a door and we entered a ward, a couple of fans moving overhead, some beds in a uniform line, bone-white, waiting for occupants. A window at the far end, a shiny cream curtain pulled around it, shielding anything else from view. On the other side of the room an old man stooped over a soup bowl, ladling it into his mouth, and a woman slept on her side, a window at the far end throwing sunlight over the foot of the bed, highlighting the thin pink blanket she had clearly brought from home.

The curtain seemed to loom ahead now, the nurse moving across to it to draw it back. I didn't know whether I was yet ready to see what lay beyond it, had dashed across here with no other thought than Zeb. I needed to know he was alright, but if he wasn't I wanted a few more moments of that, wasn't sure what I would find, what I would feel. The air seemed to seize up in my chest as the nurse drew the curtain back slowly, a lump in the bed where someone's legs were then, further up, a chest, a man, and then him, Zeb, lying, an eye opening at the disturbance.

'Iz.' He made a move to sit up and then, realising he couldn't make it the whole way stopped, a faint panting as he rested back on the pillow.

'Hey,' I said, coming towards him and trying to smile at him. The nurse melted away and I was too slow in my thanks, turning to mutter it as he left the ward.

He looked at me then, head sunk into the pillow. 'How did you get in here?' he croaked, his voice scratchy, lower than normal.

I shrugged. 'I told them I was your wife.' I blushed, feeling strangely embarrassed at the omission.

'Well, there goes my chances with the nurses,' he said, weakly attempting to raise an eyebrow as a nurse with a bottom as wide as she was tall pushed a trolley into the room, heading over to the man with the soup.

I was too worried to react and stared at the large roll of bandage wrapped around his head, hair sprouting out of it at the top as if it were a thick gym headband.

'Not my greatest look,' he said, noting my gaze.

'What happened?' I asked, concerned that he wasn't able to focus on anything for more than a second or two, his eyes closing involuntarily. 'Zeb,' I said, feeling panic rise up in my chest, my whole body clenching.

His eyes flickered and he was back. 'Fell,' he explained. 'I'd climbed up on some rocks, wanted a photo of...I don't remember...'

'Shhh, don't try,' I hushed, stepping forward, biting on my lip.

His brown skin was tinged with a greyish light, perhaps from the stark light of the room, the bumpy cream walls which needed a lick of paint, the chart at the foot of the bed, utterly indecipherable.

'What have you done?'

'Stiches.' He indicated his head with a finger, a pathetic attempt to point. 'I'm fine,' he insisted, sounding anything but, his voice sinking again, eyelids drooping shut.

'Zeb,' I whispered tentatively.

He opened his eyes slowly, taking me in, a lazy smile growing which made me want to cry. 'They're keeping me in because they think I have concussion.'

'Do you?'

'I'm not sure. I can't decide whether I can't read signs because I'm concussed or because they're in Malaysian.'

'Zeb,' I said, a gurgle of choked laughter rising in my throat. *If he could joke surely it couldn't be that serious?* My eyes were pulled as if on a thread back to the bloodied T-shirt on the chair beside him. The blood had streaked and matted on the material. I gulped, reaching out a hand automatically and placing it over his. His fingers curled over mine and he gave me a weak smile, blinking slowly as he seemed to zone out again.

'Stay, Iz,' he whispered as his head lolled a little to one side. 'Stay.'

I squeezed his fingers in response, not wanting to let go of his hand, awkwardly dragging a stool over with one foot.

'I'll stay,' I said. His camera lay on the floor by the chair, the lens was cracked. 'I'll stay.'

Epilogue

One month later

'Hold it steady, dingus,' I screeched, my hair falling across my face as I tried to balance myself on a rock on Phi Phi Don, a gorgeous beach in Thailand.

Zeb emerged from behind the camera lens, his turquoise-blue eyes crinkled in amusement. He sighed. 'When did I land such a hot girlfriend?'

We were making the latest vlog for our travel website and somehow I had been persuaded to dress up as a mermaid. Hair falling in waves, a flower behind me ear, I readjusted myself and was ready to go. The last few entries had been a huge success and the site was starting to attract advertising. It paid for our flights and board. We could travel anywhere.

'Hey, go easy,' I said, seeing him clamber up a little higher. I was quick to worry about him now; it had only been a couple of weeks since he'd left hospital.

This clip was focusing on trying to find deserted spots. Often the day-trippers flocked to some parts but, after a few days in the village and armed with some local knowledge, Zeb and I had discovered some incredible places. The shallow waters were inviting, packed with marine life, the water clear, the sand pristine. I felt like I was moving around a movie set at times, it was so jaw-dropping.

Next week we were heading off to Bangkok to pick up all the bustle and madness of the nightlife there. Zeb had already told me something about ping-pong balls that I hadn't needed to know, a filthy glint in his eye, his hair mussed from sleep. From there, east for a couple of months to be back in LA for Mel and Dex's beach wedding. She'd sent me the photos of her dress last night, a stunning backless lace dress. She was grinning in the pictures. She looked completely fabulous.

'Oi, fishwoman,' Zeb said, walking towards me. 'Stop undressing me with your eyes, it's indecent.'

'I wasn't undressing you with my eyes, you 'nana.'

''nana?' he frowned, pursing his lips together.

''nana,' I repeated firmly, holding my breath as he moved in front of me, his tanned chest inches from my face. I peeked up at him. His look, tender and amused, instantly lit me up and a smile spread across my face.

He traced a line down my jaw with his finger and I shivered. Pulling me towards him for a kiss I felt, as I had done this past month, my whole body cave in, curved into his, feeling his arms secure and warm around me. His mouth was firm on mine, a smile growing as he grabbed my bottom.

'Get off my scales,' I squealed, pulling away in mock outrage.

'Okay, but let's get this done so that I can ravish you properly.'

I felt my insides fire up, a heat spread through my body. I couldn't believe he was mine. Grinning as he dived back behind the lens, his face was quickly lost and only his thick, dark hair was around the camera in view. I readjusted my outfit and waited for his signal.

The red light flashed and he gave me a countdown. Licking my lips, I turned towards the camera. 'We're here in Phi Phi Don and it's total heaven.'

Acknowledgements

How to Find Your (First) Husband was great fun to write and, as ever, I had plenty of help along the way.

First, thanks to Eddie and Bobby Charlton for our insane night out in Singapore with David Beckham – if I'd written him in no one would have believed it. To the lovely inhabitants of Tioman Island for their warmth and hospitality – it really was an incredible place to visit. To Kirsty Greenwood for her endless cheerleading and friendship. As an early, enthusiastic reader I am indebted to her. To the thieving one-armed monkey on Tioman Island for returning my glasses case – you little scamp!

Hugs and thanks to my lovely agent Clare Wallace who is fortunately nothing like Randy. To the glamorous and energetic team at Darley Anderson who have always been incredibly approachable, good humoured and supportive. Thank you in particular to Emma, Sheila and Mary for all that you do in the Rights department on my behalf.

To Louise Cullen at Corvus, my unflappable editor, who truly loves women's fiction and who champions my books so well. To the fantastic tour de force that is Alison Davies – I am always bowled over by your enthusiasm and love working with you. Thank you also to Sarah Pocklington for some fantastic ideas. To Fran and her work in the Digital Team, Lucy Howkins, the sales reps and the whole gang at Atlantic Books who work tirelessly behind-the-scenes. To Emma Rogers for another fabulous cover and to Nicky Lovick for her eagle-eyed edit.

To the many bloggers, readers, writers that have been a source of constant online, and real life, amusement. Thank you so much for reading, reviewing and shouting about my books. I am always blown away by the generosity of you all and your desire to spread bookish love.

To the Martin and Major families for the fantastic holidays in Polzeath – truly my favourite place to be. You have made those weeks such fun and I have loved every minute. Even that round of golf at Rosearrow. You know the one.

Above all to Ben – a cracking example of an excellent husband. I love you lots and can't imagine life without you.